Falling for
Casanova

by

Debra Druzy

Falling for Casanova

Cover Art by *Angela Anderson*

The Wild Rose Press, Inc.
PO Box 708
Adams Basin, NY 14410-0708
Visit us at www.thewildrosepress.com

Publishing History
First Champagne Rose Edition, 2017
Print ISBN 978-1-5092-1340-5
Digital ISBN 978-1-5092-1341-2

Published in the United States of America

"Wanna call home?"

"And say what? I spent the night with some guy I just met? No, thanks. It's bad enough I'm crawling home after sunup. I'd rather not ruin this moment by inviting my parents into the conversation."

The aroma of fresh coffee drifted down the hallway, along with the clamor of clanking pans.

"Someone's in the kitchen." Joy's eyes widened in horror. "You have a roommate?"

"Nope," Tristan said, amused at the grown woman's sudden state of panic.

"Maid?"

He shook his head. "My buddy Nick. He's here to pick me up for work. And he cooks." Fried bacon and eggs with a side of burnt toast was Nick's usual wake-up call.

"I gotta get outta here." Joy scrambled off the bed and into his over-sized gray sweat suit. "Thanks for everything, but I need to go home." She slipped out of the bedroom and down the hallway.

Tristan yanked on his robe and followed behind, catching her before she reached the front door. "I didn't put your clothes in the dryer yet."

"Mail 'em to me."

"You don't have to rush out."

"No. I do. I really, really do."

"Your mother would actually tie your dog to a tree? All night? In the rain?" He pressed her back against the wall, getting close enough to kiss, hoping some memory of last night was enough to make her stay.

Dedication

For Mom, who'd prefer I write children's books.
Thank you for reading my stories anyway.
And Oliver & Otis, my favorite fur-nephews.
Lorraine & Ray, this one's for you.

xoxo

Chapter One

Joy clenched the black ballpoint pen, her clammy hand trembling as she filled in the narrow blank spaces on the job application—the first of such forms in almost a decade. It was stupid to let the simple action of printing her name intimidate her, but it did, so she moved on to the next question, saving that bit of pertinent information for last.

The job-hunt didn't knot her nerves as much as the embarrassing grapevine chitchat sure to follow once the neighborhood found out she was living in Scenic View *again*, with her parents no less, after she'd made a clamor about getting out of this one-traffic light town as soon as she graduated high school.

Now look at me, on a barstool in Mr. Lucky's pub of all places. Where everyone knew her by her maiden name. The only reason she'd kept her ex-husband's last name was for the sake of their two young sons, figuring she could always change it later.

Later. She snorted at the worthless word. That uncertain pushpin in life's perpetual calendar. A distant time when the things she hadn't done, but should've, wound up in a procrastinated pile of forgotten stuff she'd never do. When was *later* anyway? Whenever she'd scribble her signature, she swore to change her name sooner rather than later, alleviating the agonizing memory of being Mrs. Victor Weeks forevermore.

Imagine if Victor knew she answered a Help Wanted sign in a pub. The mother of his children slinging beer mugs and hot wings in a too-tight tank top like the women he was notorious for hooking up with during liquid lunch staff meetings, according to the rampant rumors. He'd laugh out loud until he burst a blood vessel, if only she were so lucky.

Screw Victor Weeks. He was the louse that put her in this predicament by destroying the illusion of the happy family-life she'd struggled to create.

The moment their divorce was official, two excruciating years ago, things changed for the worse—at least for Joy.

For Victor, life seemed better than ever after stirring the shit-pot. Who would've expected the philanderer to settle down again? Certainly not Joy. But history has an amusing way of repeating itself. The jerk had the audacity to move his pregnant fiancée-slash-secretary into the contemporary McMansion Joy had singlehandedly decorated with a meticulous touch, prettier than a Beautiful Homes magazine cover, which meant it was time for Joy to evacuate the studio apartment she'd created in the maid's quarters, where she wallowed-slash-played live-in nanny to her own children.

Child support would cover some of the necessities, but how the hell did he except her to get by on the puny alimony support? What a clever devil he was, having her sign a pre-nuptial agreement after getting her whacked out of her wits on tequila shots the eve of their elopement, once the doctor confirmed the miscarriage the week prior. She should've called the whole thing off, but the overload of irrational emotions had her forging ahead despite the omen.

Lost in the memory of her private hell, Joy carved a vicious hole in the job application to get the ink flowing. Determined to pull herself out of this pitfall, she took a deep breath in four counts, held on tight for seven, then released it on eight. Her former cardio-kickboxing instructor had called her a resilient fighter. That's just what she needed to be if she were going to get her life back in order. It was time to tap into the reserve of inner strength her ex-husband kept tamped down for too long.

Forget Victor the Dick-tator. He's not worth the tears, not that she had any left.

She shook the pen hard then printed her name. *Joy.* If only she could do it like *Prince, Bono, Madonna,* or *Shakira*—be mononymous. But she was no rock star. Just plain old Joy, doing her best to make ends meet. With a reluctant hand, she scribbled *Weeks* so it was illegible. And after a wavering heartbeat, she tacked on hyphen-*Barbieri.*

"There." With her chin low, she pushed the completed paperwork across the lacquered counter separating her and her prospective employer, Curt "Cal" Calderone, Scenic View High School's legendary super-stud whose bad-boy reputation trickled down the grades to Joy's graduating class.

She felt him staring her way from the corner of his eye. No doubt he'd recognize her but probably hadn't placed her face yet. Then again the last time he would have seen her she'd been fifty pounds heavier and wore her then-jet-black hair in an asymmetrical pixie-cut during her *Punk-Chic* period.

"You haven't done much waitressing, huh?" Cal

hunched over, leaning his elbows on the bar to study the sparse information on the page.

"Just a little." It wasn't a lie; however, she'd bet her bottom dollar waiting tables at Yummy-Cone's Ice Cream Palace over a decade ago wasn't the experience he had in mind.

"I'm looking for a girl to fill in on Mondays for now. Noon 'til nine. Unless it's jammin', then I may need you to stay 'til closing. Seven bucks an hour off the books. Plus whatever tips you hustle up, you keep."

"That's fine." She hid her face behind a long wave of sun-bleached hair. "I just need something part-time." With any luck, the weeknight crowd tipped well enough to supplement Victor's irregular payments so she could afford a decent roof over her head. It wasn't worth getting her hopes up by counting dollar signs just yet when she needed to land the job first. She crossed her fingers as Cal perused the form.

"Hmmm." He made the thoughtful sound as his eyes bounced from her face, to the paper, back to her face. "No. Friggin'. Way. I thought it was you. Joy Barbieri. How the hell've you been? Your mom said you're living in Florida, married to some rich dude. What on God's green earth brings you back to Long Island?" His booming voice carried across the hollow space, turning the heads of the lunchtime crowd in her direction.

"I'm, umm, relocating," was all she could say while praying the ambient glow of the pendant lighting hid her flaming-hot cheeks.

"Is that so?" Cal folded the page into quarters and stuck it in his back pocket. "Can you start tomorrow?"

Cha-ching. Already guesstimating her first day's

4

pay, she tried not to sound over-ambitious. "St. Paddy's Day?"

"It'll be hectic as hell. We're gonna need the extra help. Think you can handle it?" Cal tilted his head in deliberation.

How hard could it be? If she could dish out three square meals a day to her two high-maintenance kids, she could tackle this task. "Sure."

"Hang on just a sec, darlin'." Cal put up his index finger. Jutting his chin toward the chilled breeze and sunlight filtering in through the swinging door, he said, "Well, hello there, *Casanova.* Early, aren't ya? Where's your partner in crime?"

Casanova? Joy resisted the urge to crank her neck a hundred-eighty degrees just to get a load of this so-called *Casanova. What grown man refers to another grown man as Casanova?* Unless the guy's a total player? Of all people, Cal would be the one to know another player in the infamous game.

"He's runnin' late," Casanova drawled in a working class New York accent. He slid onto the barstool beside Joy, bringing a wave of cool air with him.

She kept her head straight and expelled a contemptuous snort. *For the love of God, any guy who answers to the name Casanova must have an ego bigger than Jupiter.*

"I'll check out the blueprints over a beer. We can talk about 'em when Nicholas shows up," Casanova said in a rich, honey-thick baritone that rubbed Joy the right way in all the right places, putting a hairline crack of curiosity in her willpower.

She inhaled a potent whiff of his musky

testosterone-laden pheromones, enough to make her ovaries tingle and her perception change. Damn her starving sex drive kicking into gear at the worst time. It took all her self-discipline not to sneak a peek at the face belonging to *that* raw scent. *That* rugged sound.

Instead, she drummed the tip of the pen on the countertop, diverting her inquiring eyes toward the mirrored wall behind the bar, but Cal's wide body blocked her glimpse of this so-called *Casanova*.

"Wanna work the door tomorrow?" Cal asked him. "Check IDs. Keep the peace with the patrons. We could use a backup bouncer."

"No, thanks. Those days are over for me. I'll take swinging a hammer over swinging a nightstick any day."

"I know a fella wanting to do some remodeling. Should they call you or your partner?" Cal popped the cap off a beer and set the bottle on a coaster. "Sorry, darlin', d'ja want one?" he said to Joy, but she shook her head.

Casanova chuckled. "Nick and I ain't partners. It's his business. I'm working for him until I figure things out. But if the job is small enough, send it my way. I can handle it without wasting his time. Lemme give you my number." He plucked a clean white napkin from the stack. "Excuse me, miss. Can I borrow your pen?"

Joy froze but her heartbeat quickened. "Huh?"

"The thing you write with. In your hand." Casanova's breath rustled her hair as he leaned closer. "Mind if I use it?"

"Oh. Umm. Sure." She blinked hard to clear the confused haze before sliding the pen toward him.

His thick fingers brushed hers in passing, sending a

shock rippling through her system, and she yanked her hand away on impulse.

After jotting down the information, Casanova returned the pen with a guttural "Thank you" that made Joy's toes curl.

"You're welcome," she exhaled, taking it from his fist, careful to avoid touching him this time.

Cal pinned the napkin to the corkboard behind the cash register, out of Joy's view. "The blueprints are in my office. I'll be right back." He smacked the countertop on his way around. "Don't leave, Joy," he added, "I'm not finished with you yet."

With Cal out of the way, she had a clear shot of the mirror, and the reflection of the man beside her. She might have been out of the Scenic View circle for a while, but she'd recognize a familiar face. Especially a good-looking one. Good thing Casanova was busy texting on his cellphone to notice her staring.

While her libido did a backflip, her brain dissected the man's bits and pieces, searching for a flaw. The dense layer of facial hair didn't detract from his wow-factor at all. In fact, it excited Joy even more, although it could use a bit of a manicure. She'd always had a secret thing for manly men. Men who weren't afraid of getting dirty, sweaty, injured. Even with the lumberjack beard, Casanova was handsome as hell and totally unfamiliar—a winning combination. An interesting specimen who looked like a fine fixer-upper; the kind of man who cleaned up well.

Without making direct contact, there was no way to tell the exact color of his light eyes under the dim bulb, but they were narrow and hooded. Bedroom eyes, hidden by the fringe of dark mussed up waves that brushed the collar of his faded denim jacket.

On the surface, Casanova was the polar-opposite of the metro-sexual, refined waif of a man her ex-husband had morphed into once his parents dangled the car dealership in his face in exchange for growing up and ditching the grunge lifestyle. What did she ever see in Victor worth marrying? Joy couldn't recall. Right now she couldn't concentrate on anything other than this mountain of a man seated beside her. There was something intrinsically sexy about a burly man. Powerful. Virile. Fearless. This Casanova was the dictionary-definition of rugged.

Geez, he must be a beast in the bedroom.

Cal returned too soon for any further ogling, which was a good thing for her pounding heart. He handed a cylinder to *Casanova*. Then to Joy, he said, "I'll see you at noon tomorrow." He gave her a business card that matched the Mr. Lucky's Pub shamrock logo on his black T-shirt, along with a flimsy mint-green tank top. "Wear that. And call me if you're running late. Or just call me." He winked. "Whenever."

Whatever, Joy thought, ignoring Cal's overt pass as she slid off the barstool and into her long black coat.

After stealing a glance at Casanova's left hand, relieved his ring finger was void of a gold band, she tried to snag his attention with some meaningful eye contact, but the guy was already engrossed in the blueprints stretched out on the bar.

Oh, well. The last thing she needed in her life right now was to fall for the first eligible *Casanova* to cross her path. At least she could walk out of Mr. Lucky's having accomplished the number one thing on her To-Do list: *find a job.*

Now all she had to do was *find a place to live* and she could cross off the top two items.

Shacking up with her parents in the short-term proved to be a massive mistake. Joy wasn't in town for forty-eight hours yet and already dreaded the road head. Sleeping on their living room couch wasn't what she expected. If she'd had the nerve to warn her folks she was planning a permanent vacation on Long Island, rather than just surprise them at the front door, maybe they wouldn't have assigned their spare room to her cousin Bruno, who'd taken over the brunt of the family barbershop since her father's heart attack a few months ago.

Joy scoured the community bulletin board at the firehouse for local rentals, desperate for anything promising. Some place suitable for her, two rambunctious boys, and a dog the size of a large squirrel.

Most ads were for things she didn't need or couldn't afford. Adopt kittens. Estate sale. Beach house for sale. Car for sale. Motorcycle for sale. Boat for sale. Lost dog. Lost earrings. Clown for hire.

Then on a slip of loose-leaf paper, she spied a handwritten ad for an attic loft apartment for rent. One bedroom. Living room/kitchen combo. Electric and cable included. Nine-hundred bucks a month. As close to perfect as she could find in a pinch, it was worth a shot.

On the walk back to her car parallel parked along Main Street, Joy squinted in the window of the Violet's Valise lingerie store. She wasn't as interested in the slinky ensembles as much as the Help Wanted sign. Just in case her new career waitressing didn't pan out, she ought to have a fallback.

"Welcome to Violet's," said a woman with silver streaked hair, folding panties onto a display table. "Can I help you?" By her crooked look, Joy calculated the woman's thoughts, trying to place the long-lost familiar face.

"Hi, Marie. Remember me?"

"Oh, my goodness. Joy Barbieri. I haven't seen you in ages." Marie dropped the merchandise to give a hug. "I'm so glad your dad is doing well. Is that why you're visiting?"

It was a better excuse than admitting divorce, failing at life, and running away from her grown-up home, so she went along with it. "Uh, yeah. Since Dad's heart attack Mom's been worried he'll over-exert himself. My cousin and I are helping her keep an eye on him."

"Oh, that Bruno. He's an artist with scissors." Marie fluffed her cropped hair. "Where are your sons?"

"Still in Florida with my, um, their dad. They're coming up at the end of May, after school lets out for the summer."

"How do they manage without their mother?" Marie sounded shocked.

"They're fine." Joy swallowed a downhearted sigh. As much as she missed her little boys, odds were they were loving life now that *Mean Mommy* was too far away to rule the roost. No doubt Victor and Felicity were serving cake for breakfast, candy for lunch, and ice cream for dinner. Allowing the boys to stay up past midnight on school days. Stuff that didn't happen on her watch.

While browsing the frilly things, Joy dared to ask,

"I was wondering about the Help Wanted sign."

"I just need an extra gal on Tuesdays and Thursdays for the spring and summer. It's my busy season," Marie explained. "Why? Are you interested?"

"I'll be sticking around town for a while, so I could use some part-time work."

"Would you be available to start next week?"

"Sure. Do I have to fill out an application?" Joy dreaded the necessary evil.

"No," Marie whispered with a wink. "Between you and me and the mannequins, it's off the books. Ten dollars an hour."

Relieved, Joy wrote down her cellphone number on a purple Post-It. Then, poised to leave, she backtracked. "Umm, Marie. Do you know anyone else looking for part-time work, *off* the books?"

"My sister needs someone to cover the store a few days a week."

"Lorraine still owns *Everyday's Christmas*?" It was good to know some things never change.

"I'll give her your number."

"I'd appreciate it."

With her outlook improving, Joy cruised the coastal road toward the Honey Beach condominium complex, then squeezed her car between two motorcycles in the crowded parking plaza. If her folks hadn't downsized from their small Cape to this retirement community, she and the boys could've moved into in the basement, giving this single mom plenty of time to get her act together.

Joy rang the bell since her parents had given the spare key to Bruno.

Her mother opened the door, releasing the aroma of

Sunday dinner: fried chicken cutlets and homemade tomato sauce. "Jeez, Joy. You have to do something about this monster."

No, hello. No, how was your day. Just Sophia's melodramatic sharp tongue complaining about the latest tragedy.

Uh-oh. "What'd he do?" Joy dropped her pocketbook on the hardwood floor to scoop up Rex, her three-year-old mischief-making fur-baby.

"What didn't he do? He peed on my laundry basket full of clean sheets. I dropped a bobby pin, and before I could pick it up, he snatched it and ran away. I had to stick my whole hand in his mouth to find it before he swallowed it."

"Sorry, Ma."

"That's not the worst of it." Sophia closed her eyes and rubbed her temples. "He destroyed your father's slippers."

Joy cringed, knowing their worth. "I'll get him new ones."

"They were his favorite pair." Sophia blasted an exasperated breath through her nostrils. "He's had them for years. Do you know how many I've bought and returned because he didn't like them as much as that ratty, old pair? On top of his heart condition, then finding out his daughter is divorced two years after the fact, and his business slowing down—the man has had enough to deal with. Now I have to tell him his slippers are in the trash. I can't handle all this aggravation, Joy. I just can't." She waved her hands in the air. It was no secret the influx of uninvited visitors invading the stringent woman's sanctuary left her flustered.

"Bad boy." Joy scolded the Shih Tzu with a kiss on

the head. "Don't be naughty, or we'll be sleeping in the street."

"Just put him in the kennel?" Bruno paraded down the hallway, dressed in towels—one as a skirt, another draped over his shoulders framing his freshly shaven chest, and a terrycloth turban.

"Why don't you put on a bathrobe?" Joy glared at the occupant of the bedroom that ought to be hers.

"Why don't you worry about finding yourself a place to live and stop gallivanting around town, expecting me to babysit your gremlin," Sophia snapped at her daughter, then bent to swipe Bruno's wet footprints with a dishrag without a complaint.

"It's gonna be hard as hell to find an affordable apartment that allows pets, you know." Her cousin plopped on the lumpy couch where Joy rested her head for the past two sleepless nights and crossed his thick, hair-free legs like a Juliette Prowse L'eggs commercial. "It's easier to score a hunky homeowner instead."

"For you, maybe." Joy snorted. "I'm doing fine on my own." *Or at least I will be, once I get out of this crazy house.*

"My mother always said there's a lid for every pot." Sophia wobbled around the counter separating the living room and kitchen to probe the pan of sizzling cutlets in spattering oil. Then sipped a wooden spoonful of tomato sauce before adding a dash of the missing ingredient.

Joy frowned at the long-lost quote. "I never heard Grandma say that."

"Well, I sure did." Bruno leaned over to snatch a nail file from the pencil cup Sophia kept next to her crossword puzzle books on the end table. "And it's totally true. Like I tell the single ladies at the salon: There's someone for everyone. You just have to know where to look."

The last thing Joy needed was another guy to wreck her life. Speaking of finding a man, she derailed the conversation to a safer subject. "Where's Daddy?"

After wiping her hands on a new dish towel, Sophia selected a nail file and joined Bruno on the couch. "Playing dominoes on the boardwalk."

"It's kinda cold, isn't it?" After living in Florida for so long, anything under seventy-five felt like sub-degree temperatures. Today the thermometer reached a brisk fifty-five degrees with the sun shining, but it felt closer to freezing with the wind rolling off the Long Island Sound adding an extra bite to the damp air.

"Oh, please…" Sophia rolled her eyes. "Since his heart attack, nothing stops your father from getting out of the house. If it's not dominoes, then he's at the OTB, or the Knights of Columbus, or bowling. Where've you been all morning anyway?"

"Job hunting."

"*Aaand*?" Bruno probed as if he were an integral part of this conversation.

"And none of your business."

"Well, you could be helping us at the shop," Sophia added.

Joy shook her head. Living under the same roof was painful enough. Working together would be sheer torture. She wasn't *that* desperate yet.

"Rex needs to go for a walk." Joy wrestled the pooch into the sweater he hated and the new harness she forced him to wear since leaving the big backyard in Florida.

"If you see your father, tell him *gravy* will be ready in an hour. Are you eating with us?"

"You don't have to wait for me."

"Don't give me that nonsense about not eating meat, Joy. You grew up eating meat. A person can't live without eating meat." Sophia paused her rant, inhaled, then added in a calmer tone, "We're having macaroni too. And salad. I'll leave out the pepperoni. Just make sure you're home by three."

Home? This condo wasn't home.

The house in Florida never felt like home.

The one place Joy ever considered *home* was a zombie house, condemned by the town, or at least it was during her last trip to Scenic View for Thanksgiving. She'd cruised through the old neighborhood hoping to jostle some warm memories once she came clean to her parents about the divorce, after suffering through the third-degree of them wanting to know why Victor didn't make the traditional holiday trek. The little house had been in worse shape than it was the previous trip, with generic gray boards covering the windows and doors. It was upsetting to witness, almost as disappointing as her divorce.

Joy hadn't the heart to drive by again since arriving on Friday, but with the good fortune of finding two potential jobs, and possibly a third, she mustered up the courage to set out on foot, using Rex as the scapegoat to do a little inconspicuous trespassing on Hollyhock Hill.

Chapter Two

Beneath the awning of Mr. Lucky's Pub, Tristan Casanova shivered despite the added layer of long johns under his jeans. Without sunshine, the afternoon felt colder than the predicted fifty-five degrees. Had he paid attention to the weather report, he would have hopped in his buddy's truck rather than ride his Harley into town.

Good thing the St. Paddy's parade down Main Street finished in the nick of time. As soon as the Scenic View High School marching band's music faded, the gray sky opened and the wind whipped the rain sideways, sending everyone running for cover.

Instead of following the crowd toward the firehouse for corned beef, cabbage, and non-alcoholic family-friendly fun, Tristan grabbed the door handle to the bar, seeking some adult beverages.

"Where you goin'?" Nick caught Tristan's elbow. "Aren't you comin' with us?" His other hand wrapped around his new bride's shoulder. Between Nick's big frame and Lily's flaming red hair, they looked like King Kong and Little Orphan Annie.

"Nah." Tristan waved away the invitation.

"Let him go, Nick," Lily said. "He'd rather have fun with the big boys."

"What're you talkin' about? We always have fun together." Nick frowned, torn between his woman and best friend.

"I'll catch up with you two later." Tristan scratched the itch under his beard. As much as he wanted his buddy's company, Nick was a recovering alcoholic and his wife wanted to keep it that way. Plus they were in the honeymoon phase, while Tristan was still wrapping his mind around the healing stage of his recent divorce from the woman he could never make happy.

"Well, don't get too hung over. I'm picking you up for work tomorrow. Early." Nick pulled off his leather jacket to cover Lily's head before the lovebirds raced down the sidewalk.

Tristan watched them splash through puddles while he huddled against the brick wall to light a cigarette with a few other committed smokers. He tucked the Zippo back into his jacket pocket as he took a long drag, flicked away the ash, then studied the hypnotic glow of the cherry-red tip. He'd always been able to quit whenever the thought crossed his mind, but it had been harder than usual since the divorce. He took another drag and held it, savoring the moment in case it was his last, before exhaling with a slow, methodical hum.

Seeing Nick happily remarried after so many years of being a devout divorcee gave Tristan a glimmer of hope that love could be found the second time around. It wasn't a need-to-have, but it sure would be nice to have someone willing to fill the empty space in his bed. Someday.

His best friend wasn't the only one lucky in newfound love, Tristan's ex-wife Stacy had a new boy-toy. The one good thing to come out of that hellish union was their daughter Nicole. Damn, he loved his little Niblet like crazy. Could hardly wait for his turn to see her.

Finding a good woman who didn't mind a man with a kid wasn't going to be easy. But nothing that's worth having ever comes easy. And tasting like an ashtray wouldn't do anything to help his cause, so he snuffed out the butt in the sand bucket beside the door before going inside.

The sort of woman he needed to find in the immediate future was a qualified housekeeper who could do double duty as a reliable backup childcare provider. Putting Nicole in daycare was one thing, however finding a nanny to handle the everyday chores, fix healthy meals, and not screw up the laundry would simplify his complicated life. He wanted his daughter's transition to be a seamless switch after living with her mother for six months straight, to moving into his place for the other half of the year. Things would change when the toddler was old enough for public school, but this was the arrangement Stacy suggested so he had to be ready before June rolled around.

The kicker to making this grand plan work included Tristan coasting along on terminal leave from the police force, using time he'd accrued during nineteen years on the job. Hanging with Nick until the end of the summer lessened the stress of his collapsing life, but once the dust settled from the whirlwind divorce, he'd return to Star Harbor and go back to work, putting off retirement for a few more years. Wouldn't that be a unique way to piss off Stacy, knowing she was banking on collecting half his pension as part of the divorce agreement.

Or he could grow old in Scenic View and let Stacy

win.

Nothing was set in stone.

For now he was content swinging a hammer for Nick's multifaceted property development business.

After completing the first project of renovating a Cape Cod cottage, Nick let Tristan move into it, rent-free; a clever ploy to entice Tristan to stay. As cozy as the place was, there was no sense getting attached to anything around here, despite Nick's best efforts. Nicole already had a routine at her familiar daycare center in Star Harbor. Scenic View was just a pretty little pit stop on the winding road of life, to collect his thoughts, regroup, refocus.

Then again, at least here Tristan had his best friend's moral support. As fortunate as he was to have Nick in his life, it was tough not to be envious of the guy. Besides finding a good woman, the man became the sole beneficiary of a million-dollar windfall from some long-lost relative, while Tristan watched his lifetime of hard work slip through his fingers and into his ex-wife's pocketbook. *How is that fair?*

Mr. Lucky's loud crowd was just the sort of mind eraser he needed to escape his troubles.

Tristan slid onto the last empty stool at the end of the bar and laid a hundred-dollar bill on the glossy wood to catch the bartender's eye. He'd need a quick buzz before opening the envelope from the attorney.

"Jack and Coke, please. Two." He gestured with his fingers, making certain his order was clear over the Irish guitar ballad vibrating from an amplifier across the room. The thickening mob already stood two-deep at the bar, so once his first round arrived he pushed the money forward and said, "Keep 'em comin'."

After tossing down the first cocktail, he milked the other.

By the fifth drink, his scalp began to tingle. Still it was too soon to tell if he was high enough to read the letter burning a hole in the breast pocket of his denim jacket.

Maybe the news wouldn't be as bad as he suspected. *Yeah, right.*

Maybe if he got lucky he'd catch a glimpse of the woman he saw here yesterday—tall and elegant, with an angelic profile, multi-tonal streaks of blonde hair and dark roots, reminiscent of a sunflower. Kind of made him sorry he didn't accept Cal's offer to work just to get to know her better.

Geez... Who'm I kiddin'. He hadn't hit on a girl in so long, not since dating Stacy, he'd forgotten how.

When Tristan caught sight of the glorious vision in a tight green Mr. Lucky's Pub tank top, his heart sped up, pumping all the blood to his crotch—*it's her.* His eyes honed in on the waitress' cleavage as he squinted to read the nametag pinned on her chest. *JOY.*

Joy. A pretty name for a pretty girl. A perfect name for a sunflower.

Between the booze and her boobs, Tristan felt pretty damn good, he didn't want to risk making a fool of himself by talking to her. Instead, he watched her dart from table to table with a confused smile. She disappeared behind the swinging door to the kitchen and emerged with a steaming aluminum tray, carrying it toward the buffet station along the back wall.

"Hot stuff coming through," she shouted to bodies in her path.

Hot stuff is right. Tristan slammed the cocktail and

chewed an ice chip that got sucked up in the flow. With a fascinating face and curves that didn't quit, Joy was hot stuff for sure.

Then she dropped it…

The guitarist stopped mid-song to announce, "Let's hear it for Joy and her slippery fingers," which made everyone in the joint applaud and laugh while she buried her face in the oven mitts.

Cal rushed to the scene with two bar-backs to pick up the mess. "Just have a seat, darlin'." He nudged her onto the vacated barstool beside Tristan. "Don't worry. You're not the first one to dump a full tray of Buffalo wings. And you won't be the last. Let's hope it's the only tray today. It's my fault for starting you too soon. We'll try again tomorrow."

"Sorry, Cal." She grabbed a napkin to dab her eyes and swipe her nose.

"Don't be. Lemme go check on the cleanup. Relax and have a drink. You can watch how things move and groove around here. This guy'll keep you company. Joy Barbieri meet Tristan Casanova."

Joy twisted her lips in a doubtful grin and flashed her lashes between Cal and Tristan. "Your name's really *Casanova*?"

"Don't let it fool ya. Technically, it means *new house* in Italian. Which makes sense I guess being I'm a carpenter. I assure you I'm no playboy." Tristan wanted to smack himself in the forehead for letting the alcohol do the talking.

Joy nodded, seeming to take it all in. "Good to know."

"Keep an eye on her, will ya, Casanova." Cal patted Tristan on the back before stepping away.

No need to ask twice. Tristan hadn't been able to take his eyes off her.

Yesterday's wavy hairdo was straightened and pulled off her oval face into a sleek ponytail at the nape of her slender neck, showing off thin silver hoop earrings as big as bracelets. Her sun-kissed shoulders tempted to be touched but he kept his hands to himself. Lean biceps looked like she worked out. Made him want to crush the pack of smokes in his pocket and do some push-ups. Anxious manicured fingers shredded the napkin to smithereens on the bar.

"Just call me Tristan." Scratching his furry chin, recalling the standard come-ons that never worked in his experience, he decided to play the safe route of being a decent person and slid one of his stockpiled cocktails toward her. "Here—the bartenders are busy so it might be a while—have one of my Jack and Cokes. And don't worry, I didn't spike it or anything. Not that you would think I did. I've been a cop for so long I figure everyone has a mind as suspicious as mine," he rambled low over the wailing guitar solo and doubted she heard a word, but didn't bother repeating the unnecessary warning.

Her weak smile reached her sparkling sea-green eyes then grew a little wider. He could swear she was blushing or maybe still flushed from the embarrassment of dropping the tray. Either way Tristan could've stared at her all day.

She leaned closer to say, "Thanks," over the din.

Her feather-light voice tickled his eardrum then spread through his system until it reached his groin, making him moan in glorious agony. "My pleasure," he said between clenched teeth.

Joy lifted the glass to sip from the narrow stirrer-straw and winced.

"Too strong?" Tristan gulped a mouthful, immune to the potent flavor.

She shook her head, scenting the stale air with strawberries and sunshine from her wagging ponytail. "I prefer my drinks strong. Like my men."

Tristan might've fallen off the stool if one boot wasn't planted on the floor. Either she was coming on to him or trying to be funny. Without a clever comeback, he chugged his cocktail instead. "Cal looks like a pretty strong guy."

"Cal?" She cocked a skeptical eyebrow. "What's he have to do with this conversation?"

"He's your boyfriend, right?" Playing dumb came easy when a pretty woman got him this hard, he could hardly sit right.

"Where'd you hear that crazy rumor?"

Relieved to be wrong for a change, he shrugged. "I didn't. I made it up."

"If you're gonna lie about me, at least give me a happy ending with a single guy."

"I just figured. I mean, I knew Cal had a girlfriend. I thought you must be her by the way he talks to you and all."

"The only reason he treats me like anything other than a piece of ass is because he knows my folks forever."

Good to know. Tristan nodded, taking it all in. *Damn good to know.*

The bartender delivered two more drinks and Tristan pushed another one toward Joy. Feeling a little bolder with some help from his friend *Jack*, he slid his stool closer, confirming the delicious fragrance was all hers. *Yep, sun-ripened strawberries, all right.* His stomach growled, and he quieted it quick by tearing a piece off the loaf of soda bread in the basket on the bar and stuffing it in his mouth. "Wanna piece?"

"Eeuuw. Are those raisins in there?" Joy wrinkled her nose at the dark clumps in the offering. "No, thanks."

"How about a bite from the buffet?"

"There's nothing up there I can eat. I'm an ovo-lacto-pescetarian."

Tristan strained to hear over the crowd singing I'm looking over a four-leaf clover in unison. "What's an octo Presbyterian?"

"No. I said ovo. Lacto. Pescetarian. Like a vegetarian, except I eat fish, eggs, milk, and honey."

"Wow. I never met one before."

"Really? I'm surprised." She swirled the straw in her glass. "It's not so rare. And it's not as strict as vegan law."

"Still, it's gotta take a lot of discipline."

"Yeah. It does. I can't ignore the smell of bacon. Makes me crazy. Like a shark sniffing blood."

"Bacon makes me crazy too." Tristan sighed, wishing for a plate of it, with eggs over easy. Hash browns would also be good right about now. Corned beef and cabbage wasn't going to cut it. And Buffalo wings were too messy to eat in front of the girl he wanted to impress. "You from around here?" It was the best segue he could think of without a game plan.

"Mmm, you can say that. I've been living in Florida since I was eighteen." She tapped her fingernails rhythmically on the bar.

"Staying in town long?"

"I think so. Most likely. If things work out." She gazed at him sideways. "You're new to Scenic View, aren't you?"

"How can you tell?"

"For starters, you're not hanging with the village idiots." She jutted her chin in the direction of the fools doing a drunken Irish jig on the dance floor.

"I've been here since the middle of January."

Joy picked up her glass and clinked it against his. "Well, lotsa luck o' the Irish to you."

"To you as well."

Since arriving to this close-knit harbor-side town, Tristan hadn't clicked with anyone other than Nick, who didn't count since they were already best buddies. He never expected to meet someone special, in a dive bar of all places, but that's what Joy was. His gut told him she was different—unless it was just the hunger pangs talking, but he didn't think so—with her easy conversation and the way her bright eyes focused on him as if he were the only person in the whole room. The last thing he wanted to do was something irreparably stupid in her presence. So he played the game conservatively and let her call the shots.

The bartender brought another round, and Tristan pushed them both in Joy's direction while he switched to seltzer with lime.

When the guitarist whistled the first few notes of the next tune, she squealed, "Oh my gawd, this is my jam," in a Long Island accent as thick as Nick's wife's. Maybe it had something to do with the alcohol that caused her to hop off the stool and drag Tristan to the dance floor for the acoustic version of "Moves like

Jagger"—moves Tristan did not have, but he didn't resist.

While he swayed with his thumbs hanging from his belt loops, Joy spun in circles, waved her arms in the air, wiggled her bottom clad in black fitted yoga pants, looking hotter than any MTV video-girl he'd seen in the last two decades.

Everyone was watching her, but her gaze was locked on him as she mouthed the words, "*Look into my eyes and I'll own you...*"

And that's what happened.

Tristan's heart flipped. In that moment he knew Joy was no ordinary girl. He'd been buzzed by booze and broads before but it never felt like this. Frantic yet fantastic. Helpless but in total control. Like free falling off the razor's edge in a sweet dream; he didn't want to wake up.

On the other hand, he didn't want to hit rock-bottom. He'd been there, done that with Stacy, and wasn't doing it again no matter how tempting Joy might be. Even if he got a second shot at true love, could he trust the odds of finding it here and now in Mr. Lucky's?

Am I nuts? I must be. To consider falling for a woman he just met.

Why couldn't he enjoy the moment? He damn well deserved to have a good time like every other hard-working, red-blooded American man, and stop talking himself out of things that hadn't even happened. *Yet.*

Watching her dance moves did something strange to him that made him choke his conscience, stifling the incessant wise voice. His feet stepped further apart as he rocked side to side until he was spinning her in his arms. He could do this forever…

After an hour on the dance floor and a few more high-octane cocktails, Joy gasped, "Let's get outta here."

"Don't you wanna tell Cal you're leaving?"

"Nuh-uh. I'm gonna be sick." She dashed toward the backdoor, pinballing off the bodies in the way of her Irish exit.

Tristan trailed her to the parking lot where the wet blast of damp air was an instant buzz-kill.

To keep her out of view, he guided her toward a dark corner beside the dumpster to power-puke in semi-private. Holding her ponytail from falling in her face was the least he could do considering those were his drinks that got her this hammered.

"Let it out." He rubbed figure-eights on her back hoping to soothe the agonizing upheavals. "Don't worry. No one's watching," he lied as a dozen people stumbled out the same door, snickering and pointing at Joy retching. When she stopped upchucking, he said, "I think I oughta take you home now."

She stopped short under the lamppost. "No—I don't want my folks to see me like this."

"Wanna come back to my place then?" Tristan lit up a much-needed cigarette, took a couple of drags while she contemplated an answer, then snuffed out the cherry-tip between his thumb and forefinger, and stuck the butt in his jacket pocket to dispose in a trashcan later.

"I dunno," she slurred, swiping the spittle from her lips with her bare forearm. Her eyes were wet slits, leaking streaks of muddy mascara down her cheeks, and her golden complexion faded to a faint shade of ivory. Despite her wilted condition, she was still pretty.

"Come on. Just for a little while. You can clean up. Lie down until you feel better. Then go home after you sober up. I promise nothing'll happen." The last detail he added to ease his own mind as much as hers.

Holding her head between her hands, she said, "Yeah. I guess. Okay. If you really don't mind."

"Not at all. Thing is, I got here on my motorcycle. We'll have to take your car if you're okay with me driving. Otherwise I'll call a cab."

Joy's head bobbed in an awkward headshake. "It's parked on Main Street. But my stuff's in there." She pointed to the bar.

"Let's grab it." Tristan tugged her arm to follow.

"I don't wanna go back inside. Can't you get it? It's in Cal's office."

"I'm not leaving you out here alone."

"I'll be fine, really."

"You sure?" He propped her against the brick wall beside the back door, and she slumped to the concrete. "Even better. Don't move."

"Where'm I goin' like this?" Joy hugged her shins with her forehead resting against her knees.

Tristan poked his face in the doorway, flagged the first familiar fellow, and said, "Get Cal. Quick."

Cal emerged. "S'up, Casanova? Where's Joy?"

Tristan pointed to the limp body on the ground. "She's bombed. I'm gonna drive her home. Mind grabbing her stuff from your office?"

"Well, that didn't take long, darlin'." Cal stepped out to examined Joy's inert body. "One night in the bar and you're riding the hot mess express." He chuckled. "I wouldn't let you go off with just anyone. Tristan's a good guy. I'd trust him with my own sister."

"Don't tell my folks, okay?" Joy mumbled.

"I ain't saying a word. Last thing I need is a tongue-lashing from Sophia." Cal returned in a jiff and handed the long wool coat and heavy handbag to Tristan with a wink. "Get home safe, ya crazy kids."

Under the bright lamppost, Tristan dug through Joy's bag searching for the keys and found everything but... An open wallet containing nothing but her Florida driver's license, two bucks, and a few business cards. Hairbrush. Pens. Cellphone. Breath mints. Pint-sized bottle of spring water. Packet of tissues. Bottle of aspirin. Bag of unsalted sunflower seeds. Compact umbrella. Expensive-looking leather gloves. Dog biscuits. Cellphone charger. Pepper spray. And other random junk. "Ready for a zombie apocalypse, I see," he murmured, stowing the urge to smile as she wasn't in the mindset for jokes.

"Here..." He shook a few mints into her palm. "This'll get rid of the foul taste." At the bottom of it all, under a little spiral notebook and a bunch of loose receipts, he found the single keyless fob.

With his helping hand, she stumbled around the building and down the sidewalk.

"There it is." She pointed across the street where dozens of cars lined the curb.

When he pressed the alarm button to figure out which vehicle it could be, the headlights on a gleaming white Jag with a black ragtop flashed. "Nice wheels."

Before getting in the passenger seat, Joy puked again, most of it landing down the front of her coat. "Oops. My bad."

"Oh, man." Tristan winced. "Better take that off."

He slid the garment from her shoulders with care, then folded it with the inside out to keep the mess contained, and stuffed it in the trunk where he found a reusable grocery store sack suitable for a barf bag. "If you get sick again, do it in here."

Before slamming the passenger door, he draped his denim jacket over her like a blanket, then slipped into the butter-soft leather of the driver's seat and adjusted the rearview mirror. With a push of the Start button, the engine revved to life and the dashboard glowed like an airplane cockpit.

Geez, what a luxurious ride—he could get used to this.

An uneasy sigh escaped him as the annoying voice inside his head resurfaced with its moral two-cents. *Bringing a sexy drunk woman to your home isn't a good idea.* Something a respectable father would never do while his daughter lived with him. But Nicole wasn't here yet, so doing it just this once wouldn't hurt anybody, would it?

He tugged the whiskers under his chin, contemplating the worst-case scenario, which might be the best if he got lucky.

Then his vivid imagination fast-forwarded eighteen years, at the possibility of some random guy driving his drunken baby girl home from a bar. *Hell no.* He rubbed the heels of his hands into his eye sockets to erase the awful vision.

The responsible thing would be to drive Joy to her own house, let her deal with the parental repercussions, and he'd call a cab from there. "Are you positive you wouldn't rather me drive you to your place?"

Joy gave him a blank stare. "Why? Ya changed

your mind? 'Cause I'll go back in the bar. Cal has a couch in his office."

"Nope. I didn't change my mind. Just making sure you didn't change yours." Tristan strangled the steering wheel as he pulled away from the curb, hoping he didn't wreck her fancy car on the short ride home.

There was no reason to get jittery by this woman, who had fallen asleep with her head limp against her chest like a deflating blowup doll. Before he did change his mind and relinquish her to Cal's care, he turned off Main Street, following the winding road toward his renovated rental on Hollyhock Hill.

Chapter Three

"Come on, sunshine. We're almost there. Just a half-mile more." Tristan patted Joy's knee, coaxing her to hang on, like he was afraid she'd toss another round of cookies, but her gut was hollow.

His roving hand wasn't doing anything to help straighten her wandering thoughts as it inched up and down her thigh—not in a sexual way. At least it didn't seem that way to Joy.

"How'ya doing? You okay? Talk to me." He alternated between staring out the dark windshield and glancing at her.

She mustered enough strength to whisper, "I'm fine." With hope, the reek of vomit was only noticeable to her spinning head.

He removed his palm from her leg, switching hands on the steering wheel to hit the button that rolled down the front windows. "Better?"

The blast of cool wet wind was the perfect quick fix. "I think so."

"I hate to wreck this beautiful leather interior, but it'll be a whole helluva lot easier to sop up the rain than, you know, barf. Blame it on me for giving you all those cocktails."

"No. It's my own fault. I shoulda gone home after I dropped the tray. But seeing everyone have a good time, I wanted to have fun too. Have a few drinks.

Dance. Hook up with some hot guy. You know?" The words tumbled out as if they were coming from someone else's lips. "When I say *hook up* I don't mean just knocking boots. A bootie call. Getting laid. Or whatever the kids call it these days." Joy flicked her blurry eyes in his direction, anticipating the worst reaction. "I just wanted to meet someone decent—"

"Sorry to ruin your night." A strained smile carved his profile aglow in the headlights from an oncoming vehicle.

"If you let me finish, I was gonna say meet someone decent…like you." Her vision may be cloudy but she'd already seen enough to be attracted to this stranger's physical assets. Blue eyes. Straight nose. High forehead. Chestnut-brown wavy hair with a shimmer of gold that matched the rugged whiskers framing kissable lips. *What woman could resist this hunk's all-American good looks and effortless charm?* Certainly not Joy. Never in a gazillion years did this divorcee expect to make an instantaneous mental connection with any man, never mind the first one to come along. Could her mother and Bruno have been right? Could this pot finally have found her lid? More like flipped her lid to think he'd want anything to do with a woman with so much baggage.

Tristan's lack of a response had her wishing she'd kept her stupid mouth shut.

"Did I say something wrong?" She could always blame it on the booze if she did.

He cleared his throat. "Uhh, no. Not at all."

After a few turns, he pulled into the driveway of a single story Cape Cod cottage that looked like the others on the block, except his had the most extreme exterior makeover. She'd noticed this place on her walk with Rex but didn't pay much attention to it as she focused her thought-power on how to acquire her old boarded up shack.

"Here we are." Tristan killed the engine. "Home, sweet, home."

Home? Joy gagged at the sight of the house next door, with its missing shingles and crooked red shutters. Under the dim streetlights, it looked less like a forlorn shanty and more like the long-lost memory where she'd spent the best years of her childhood. The moment he opened the passenger door she leaped out and dry heaved on the grass, spitting up nothing but bile.

"You oughta lay down before you fall down." He guided her up three porch steps and set her on the wicker chair while he unlocked the front door.

After a few mind-clearing blinks, she mustered the nerve to say, "I don't remember this place looking so pretty."

"It used to be a mess like that one." He jutted his chin toward Joy's old house.

A *mess* was an understatement. *More like a dump.*

"My buddy bought a bunch of foreclosures so we can fix 'em up and sell 'em. Actually, I'm in charge of fixing 'em. He handles sales."

Tristan held the door and nudged her in first when a Yorkie greeted them, yapping as it skidded across the glossy hardwood floor. It jumped up on Joy's leg, barely reaching her knee. The fleeting thought of leaving Rex in her parents' care longer than necessary filled her with guilt, but she pushed the ache aside. Even though she's not in the market for a man, she was enjoying Tristan's company, a little too much. *I may never have another opportunity to meet a guy as nice as this one. My lid. Finally.*

"Get down, Cookie." With greased lightning reflexes, he snatched the pup before it slipped outside. "I hope this wild thing didn't scare you. She only attacks if she wants to meet you, otherwise she'd be hiding under my bed."

"It's okay. I love dogs."

A slow sated smile curled his lips, reaching those heavenly eyes, as if Joy passed some unspoken initiation. "That's good to know, 'cause not everybody does." He adjusted the wall switch, dimming the track lighting that illuminated the entryway into the living room. "Bathroom's the first door on the right."

With his hand on the small of her back, he guided her in the right direction then switched on the blinding light inside. Sparkling silver and slick black decor assaulted her pupils, forcing her to squint. *Wow. He must have some maid.*

"I'll get you something to change into." He disappeared down the dark end of the hallway, taking the fur-baby with him.

Joy shut the door. A glimpse in the mirror over the sink made her cringe. Runny mascara created dark rings under her deep-set eyes. She dragged her middle fingers under the bottom lashes to wipe away the makeup but made it worse.

Tristan returned with a pile of clothes and a bottle of spring water, setting it on the granite counter before pulling a few towels from the linen closet.

"How about some aspirin?" He plucked a little tube from the medicine cabinet and dropped two pills in her palm. "Think you can handle a shower?"

Joy wobbled as she swallowed the medication with a swig of water.

"We better make it a bath. Just to be safe."

"I can wash up in the sink."

"Trust me, you'll feel a million times better in here." He bent to turn the spigot, and Joy's jaw dropped at the sight of his perfect tush in well-worn blue jeans. When he glanced over his shoulder and caught her staring, his sensational smile bloomed. "Why dont'cha have a seat while it fills."

He pointed to the bamboo bench, and she collapsed onto it.

Steam clouded the room, making it difficult to breathe until he opened the window. From a plastic jug, he poured in a thick stream of pink bubble bath solution. The concentrated cotton candy scent made her sick again but the urge to puke passed once the smell faded with the cool breeze.

"You take a lot of bubble baths, huh?"

He turned off the water with a chuckle. "It's for Niblet—I mean, my daughter Nicole, not me." From a drawer under the sink, he pulled out a new toothbrush and a small tube of toothpaste.

Joy caught the informational tidbit but lacked the conversational skills to ask for details during her momentary lapse of reason.

"Shut the door, but don't lock it. I wanna make sure you don't drown." He backed out with a wink. "Take your time. Shout if you need anything."

Alone at last, Joy peeled off her puke-crusted yoga pants and tank top. Kicked off her panties and socks. Then unclasped her push-up bra. To avoid contaminating his beautiful bathroom, she balled up the polluted items and stuck them in the corner beside the little stainless steel trashcan.

Slipping into the hot water was an unexpected pleasure. Her ex-husband had insisted they install a Jacuzzi tub even though Joy believed it was a frivolous expense when a standard bathtub-shower combo would do the same job. Because Victor thought he could afford it didn't mean they needed every modern convenience money could buy. She wasn't the sort of girl to indulge in a bath anyway, not with two little boys on the move.

God, she missed her kids.

It stabbed her heart to know they didn't feel the same. She'd been gone five days and Victor hadn't called once to put the boys on the phone. Joy didn't dare call them. Not after he'd said *don't call us, we'll call you.* That was his way of driving the knife deeper.

Plus his new pregnant fiancée was moving her stuff in this weekend. Joy didn't need to embarrass herself with an emotionally charged dialogue with the boys who would no doubt repeat what she said to their father, if they bothered to pick up the phone at all.

It was a good thing she was still numb from the whiskey to feel anything beyond a quick squirt of tears that got lost in the bathwater.

She splashed her face to calm her nerves then settled back for a deep soak that soothed more than any massage showerhead ever could. A quick slosh around her bits and pieces with a sudsy washcloth and she was ready to get out but opted for a few more quiet moments, using the luxury of Tristan's gracious hospitality to contemplate her current living arrangements.

Behind heavy eyelids she envisioned the day her two rambunctious boys moved in with her, praying it would be a dream rather than the nightmare she anticipated. The pressure to find a suitable place to live was stressful. Her sons needed space. A playroom. And preferably a backyard like they're accustomed to with Victor. No way would a single-bedroom attic apartment cut it.

The roaring wind rustled the trees outside the open window, luring her from the tranquil drip-dropping of the water faucet, inviting her to sneak a peek.

There *it* was—the dilapidated house next door. Near, yet so far out of reach, she was crazy to get attached to the idea of having it. But it was the perfect place to raise her boys, if she could find a way.

Crisp air sent a shockwave of goosebumps over her wet skin so she sank beneath the water for warmth.

I need that house. But how would she get it? She could never afford to buy it if it were on the market. Even renting it would be out of her price range. Perhaps if she made the case to Victor he'd help with the finances. She hated to beg but was willing to do it for the boys' sake.

"How'ya making out in there?" Tristan knocked and the door opened an inch. "Just making sure you're alive."

"I'm fine." Joy slid deeper to avoid his eyes over the edge.

"You can run more hot water if you want."

"That's okay. I'm getting out now."

When the door clicked shut, she struggled to her feet. Dried with the plush black towel. And dressed in a pair of cozy men's marble gray sweat pants and matching pull-over sweatshirt. Despite her height, the length was huge on her. Nothing like Victor's mini-man clothes. He used to complain how tall she was in heels so she'd gotten into the habit of wearing flats everywhere they went. Tonight she felt like a petite flower, dancing with Tristan as he towered over her five-eight frame. A total turn-on she never experienced.

Barefoot, with wet hair wrapped in a towel, she stepped out of the bathroom expecting Tristan to be waiting on the couch but discovered Cookie snoozing there instead. So she tiptoed in search of him.

A pale stone fireplace separated the living room and dining room. Warm ivory trim accented rich mahogany walls. Dark wood blinds hung in place of curtains. Everything was sooo…masculine. No frills. And more importantly, no sign of a woman's touch— beyond being totally spotless—as far as Joy could see. Well-versed in every home-design magazine offered in the racks at the supermarket checkout, she decided his place was *modern rustic*.

"In here." His words echoed off the blank walls.

She followed his voice, finding him in the dim kitchen with his head in the stainless steel refrigerator. Even bent over in baggy sweatpants, he looked as good from the backside as he did from the front.

Tristan pulled out an armful of items and set them on the slick black counter that matched the bathroom decor. "Have a seat."

Joy slid onto a barstool. Watched him wash and dry apples then slice them into thin wedges, arranging them on a white marble platter. He diced cheese and sprinkled them next to a fan of crackers. Ran some red grapes under the waterspout and patted them dry with a paper towel. "This is quite the bachelor pad."

Without turning his head from the task, he flicked his eyes at her. "Ya like it?"

"I do. It's cozy yet cool."

"That's the look I was going for." He pushed the dish closer so she could pluck a plump grape off the vine.

"You did all this yourself?"

"Yep. It was a disaster. We had to gut it before it was livable."

"Looks like it could be in a decorating magazine."

His smiling eyes lit up his whole face. "You're sweet, ya know that?"

Joy's cheeks burned from his compliment and she lost her voice. She was having a hard time keeping her wits with this particular breed of *Casanova*. Whatever his good-guy game was, she was falling for it, helpless, willing, and without a net.

Maybe it was the booze in her blood boosting her confidence but she was feeling flirty for the first time in ages. Batting her lashes, she tossed the tail end of the towel over her shoulder as coy as a hair-flip.

He twisted the cap off two bottles of spring water and poured them into tall glasses with ice before sitting at the counter across from her. "Feelin' any better?"

Still not a hundred percent sober but not nearly as drunk as she was two hours ago, she nodded as a new kind of eruption began in her belly that had nothing to do with too much alcohol. "I don't usually indulge in anything more than a few glasses of merlot."

"So, you were puttin' me on when you said you like your men like your drinks?"

Recalling the overt remark, she crushed her eyelids

and bit her bottom lip. "Yeah, kinda. I only said that so you'd think I was fun."

"Fun?" He laughed. "Ralphing in the parking lot is hardly what I'd consider a good time."

"Sorry." She could've shriveled up and died.

"It's not a bad thing. It happens to the best of us. I just figured a big girl like you could handle your liquor."

Big girl? Joy cringed. Although she was tall, she hadn't considered herself *big* in years, not since she lost the baby weight.

"Wait. That came out wrong." Tristan must have read the horror in her face because he added, "I meant to say big girl as in you're an adult. You work in a bar after all. I'm actually relieved you're not a big drinker." With the plate in one hand and their glasses in the other, he led Joy to the living room where he set everything on the coffee table before shooing the pup off the couch. "Take a hike, Cookie. Go to bed."

Joy concealed a yawn; bed sounded like a good idea. At least his cushions were firm. She might actually get a good night's rest for a change. "I'm surprised I'm still awake." Joy pulled the towel off her head, letting it drape around her neck, then finger-combed the tangles from her long waves.

"Me, too. For a moment I thought I'd be running you to the ER for alcohol poisoning. You must have gotten it out of your system. Keep drinking water. And put a little food in your stomach."

With the frosty glass clasped between her hands, Joy shivered as she sipped and rubbed her bare toes to create some friction for warmth.

"Are ya cold?" Tristan snatched one end of the

damp towel from her shoulders, pulling her closer until it slid off, then balled it up and tossed it on the floor.

Anticipating the curiosity of his kiss, Joy braced for his lips to brush against hers, torn between relieved and disappointed when it didn't happen. "A little chilly. I haven't adjusted to the climate in New York yet. One day it's fifty degrees, the next it's thirty."

He spread a chenille blanket over her lap and she tucked her ankles underneath then tugged the hem up to her chin, catching a whiff of lavender fabric softener. "That's March for ya. Comes in like a lion like they say." Using a little remote control, he turned on the fireplace. "Gas. So much easier than wood, although definitely not the same. How's that? Better?"

The heat wave reached her cheeks.

"Perfect." It was impossible to conceal a sated smile and control her loose lips, unhinged by her fuzzy head. If she didn't know better she'd swear he was seducing her between the bubble bath, the tasty nibbles, and the hypnotic fire. If only he'd kiss her to put her theory to rest. "All we need is a little Marvin Gaye, and this would be the best first date ever." The joke came out awkward and she wished she could take back the words.

His friendly smile narrowed to a thoughtful tense line. As sweet as this Casanova might seem, a definite glimmer of mischief shone in those dazzling eyes. "Is that so?"

"I didn't mean *this* is a date. I know it's not a date. I, um…This is…You are, uhhh, a really nice guy. I'm not used to a man being so good to me."

He lifted a brow. "What kind of man are you used to? If you don't mind me asking."

Oh, here we go. On instinct, her thumb rubbed the naked ring finger on her left hand; she'd sold the plain gold band in a Florida pawnshop for pocket money to get to Long Island. Not wanting to ruin the good vibration with negative energy, she decided not to mention her ex-husband. Instead she shrugged, stalling long enough to mentally rummage through her excessive baggage, debating what to say without revealing too much.

"I just mean I'm not used to guys being handy with a kitchen knife. Or a hammer." Her eyes swept the room, glimpsing Tristan's massive frame as he sat beside her, close enough to feel the heat of his thigh against hers, but not so close he would sense her waning willpower. "How long did it take you to do all this?"

"Two months. I wanted everything to be toddler-ready before Niblet comes to stay with me."

Joy was tempted to talk about her own offspring but bit her tongue instead.

"Her room's not done yet. I figured I'd let her pick out the paint." He reached to grab a framed postcard-sized photograph from the end table on his side of the couch and handed it to Joy.

"She's adorable." Big denim blue eyes matched her daddy's, with white-blonde hair Joy figured must come from the mother. "She'll be here soon, huh?"

He nodded, putting the picture back in its place. "Not soon enough. She's coming down from Star Harbor to spend the summer with me. This place is just a temporary fix for me to recuperate from my divorce. I'm on leave from the police force for a few months—I can either ride it out and retire early, or pull the paperwork and go back to work in September." With a grunt, Tristan got up and picked through the pockets of his denim jacket on the coat tree. He returned with a folded envelope, smacking it against his palm. "This is the news I've been waiting for. I meant to open it sooner but I've been dreading it. Mind if I read it now?"

"Go ahead," Joy whispered, adding a silent prayer that this kindhearted man got what he wished for.

He ran his index finger under the flap and sighed before sliding out the paper. Scanning the words, he shook his head and hummed a few times. Then let out cheeks full of air before dropping it on the coffee table.

"Everything okay?"

He half-shrugged, half-nodded. "Nothing I didn't know before. I was hoping things changed. Nicole's still coming in June." He smiled. "But my ex-wife gets her all winter so I won't see my kid for Christmas unless I'm in Star Harbor to drop by." Listening to the blow-by-blow of his devastating divorce and child custody details seemed to level the playing field.

"How old is she?"

"Just turned three in January."

"She's still young. You could always get away with doing Christmas in July."

Tristan squinted one eye, scrunching half his handsome face. "Say what?"

"Just celebrate Christmas in July instead of December. Would she really know the difference?"

"You're still drunk, aren't you?"

Joy gave him a playful backhanded slap to the biceps, realizing it was the size of a firm russet potato. "You can totally pull it off. All you have to do is decorate and wrap some gifts."

"You really think it would work?" He bit a wedge of apple.

She shrugged and plucked a grape from the vine. "If spending Christmas with her is important to you, I think it's worth giving it a try. Don't you?"

"Maybe. I guess."

After hearing his daddy-dilemma, Joy was compelled to share her own mommy-misfortune. Thankfully she thought twice before opening her mouth, but before she could clam up completely a skeleton bone tumbled out of the closet. "My ex-husband—"

Tristan's body snapped to attention. "What about him?"

"He told our boys there's no Santa."

"'Cause of religious reasons?"

"Nope. Just because he thought it would build their character not believing in lies."

"Seriously?" He frowned.

Joy nodded, guilty for her part in ruining the holiday. "And for whatever reason, I went along with it." She shook her head in disbelief that she agreed to the selfish scheme. "I let it happen. They're only seven and five. They've never celebrated a real traditional Christmas like I had growing up. A few times, when I realized what a mistake it was, I tried telling them about Santa Claus. But their father had done such a number on them, brainwashing them at such a young age, their whole childhood is shot. Not just because of Santa. But the whole idea of magic. That anything is possible." She could've laughed at the revelation, almost forgetting all about it herself.

"No Easter bunny either?"

45

"Nope."

"Tooth fairy?"

"None of that stuff. He thought it was a waste of time. Lies used to keep kids in line. I guess after being married to a man who didn't believe in magic and emotions and all that feel-good stuff, I started to believe maybe he was right."

Tristan simply stared, his jaw slack. "Geez—what kinda dad would do that? Your ex sounds like a real piece of work."

Glancing at the flickering flames, she feared the waterworks would come if she looked into his eyes. "Yeah...he is." Joy gulped the ice water as if it could drown her shame with the temporary effectiveness of booze.

"Lemme get you a refill." He padded to the kitchen and returned with another bottle of spring water. "Would you help me?"

Confused, Joy asked, "With what? Opening the bottle?"

Tristan gave her a puzzled glance. "No. With what you said about Christmas in July."

"I'm sure you can handle it. Just put up a tree. Hang stockings over the fireplace. Wrap some toys. If you don't mind the neighborhood thinking you're crazy, string some lights on the house."

"I'm so busy with work. Plus I'm not good with stuff like that."

"What are you talking about?" She waved her hand around the room. "Look at this place. You have a knack for decorating—you could be a woman."

"Really?" His wolfish smile revealed pearly, straight teeth. "A woman? How so?"

Joy leaned back. "Not a woman like you wear ladies' underwear or anything. Especially with a beard like that. I just mean, you know, you have a flair."

"A *flair*?" The corners of his outer lashes crinkled as he chuckled. "What the hell's a flair?"

She exhaled before turning as blue as his eyes. "A talent for decorating."

"I have other talents too." His voice dropped a sultry octave.

Her heart drummed while her pulse pounded in her ears. Nose-to-nose, the sweet apple on his warm breath had her toes curling. "I bet," she whispered, licking her lips.

"Wanna see?"

Here it comes. "Oh, yesss." She closed her eyes expecting a kiss, but instead he leaped off the couch. Her lids snapped open in time to see him snatch a photo album from the bookshelf before plopping back down beside her, thumbing through snapshots of houses in various stages of construction. "You built all these?"

He nodded. "What can I say? I also have a flair with tools."

Joy marveled at the structures as much as the brawny man in the images. Whether high on a ladder. Swinging a hammer. Heavy lifting. Reading blueprints. It was clear Tristan enjoyed his work. "You certainly do."

"But not so much with the finishing touches, unless it's a job for someone else. That's why I don't have any pictures on the walls. Or an area rug. Or any of that extra stuff." With each word his heavy breath was as unsteady as her own. He leaned closer, electric energy filling the gap between them. "This place could use a woman's touch. Especially if I'm gonna turn it into Santa's off-season workshop. Whaddaya say?" His finger stroked beneath her chin, tilting her face toward his.

You can barely help yourself, how can you help him? Swallowing the urge make a promise she might not be able to keep, she sighed instead. "I would if I could. But I can't." Even though she inched back to her end of the couch, his hands held her shoulders firmly in place while his hungry gaze roved from her eyes to her mouth.

Tristan's furry cheek brushed hers as he whispered in her ear. "Please."

His tender tone would have shattered her heart if it hadn't already been broken. And his beard was surprisingly soft; she imagined it trailing across every inch of her body. "I don't know," she gasped on the last bit of self-restraint.

Just do it. Maybe he really is your lid. The silly sentiment had her second guessing her reliable conscience. Although there was no denying it was in the back of her mind since the day she saw him, it made no sense to start something she wasn't prepared to finish. But there was no fighting fate, especially when Cupid's arrow aimed straight between her thighs.

Carnal nature had her mounting his lap like a stallion. Mouths crushed together. Tongues swirled in bliss. Hands all over groped for more.

Who knows who ignited this inferno, but God his kiss felt good. Just what the doctor ordered to cure Joy's crumpled confidence and resuscitate her flatlined libido. Helping him fake Christmas was the least she could do to repay him for confirming she was still a desirable hot-blooded woman.

So she muttered an indecipherable "Yes" to his relentless question and would deal with the repercussions later.

Chapter Four

After a moment in make-out heaven, they pulled apart, panting.

"Sorry." Tristan sat back, drying his lips with the side of his hand.

Joy blinked a few times, looking blissfully intoxicated which was a million times better than her earlier version of an inebriated mess. "For what?"

"The beard. I hope it didn't scratch."

Her legs tightened around his hips. "I didn't mind at all." She cupped his cheeks in both hands, stroked her thumbs along his whiskers. "Really."

"I wanted to kiss you since I saw you yesterday at Lucky's. I would've waited to take you on a real date but you have me so riled up I couldn't help it. Hope you're not mad."

"Not at all." Joy sighed. "Just shocked. And I mean that in a good way. The best way."

"Then it's okay if I kiss you again?"

A coy smile filled her face. "Absolutely."

Tristan made a silent vow to follow her lead and not wreck the full moon's mojo, or St. Patrick's lucky blessing, or whatever fantastic coincidence that brought this passionate minx to him. This time, as their lips touched, he kept his eyes open while hers fluttered shut. Then she locked her calves behind his back and began a slow grind against him. If it weren't for the sweatpants, he'd bury himself to the hilt inside her right now. His eyelids finally drifted lower as he hung on for his life.

The last time he had sex was with his now-ex-wife and that was too long ago to recall any details. If he had to guess, it was for some holiday—probably his birthday. Who knows? And right now he didn't care. Not anymore.

Joy was exactly what he needed. A feminine touch. Confirmation he still had what it takes to excite a woman.

The best part of it all was he'd already set his sights on this one. And now that he had her where he wanted her, he didn't want to screw it up.

"Do you, uh, wanna see my, um, bedroom?" he dared to ask, hoping his words didn't ruin the magical moment.

She bit her bottom lip and gazed up at him between a fan of lush lashes. "Yeah. Okay."

That's all Tristan needed to hear. With her legs still wrapped around his hips, he carried her down the hallway not bothering to turn on the light before letting her fall backward against the foam mattress where he dove into the warm welcoming spot between her thighs and slithered up her body for more kisses.

Rain beat against the window and thunder rolled in the distance. *Dammit.* He'd left his motorcycle in the parking lot behind the pub. If Joy were any other random woman, he'd ask for a raincheck and hop in his Camaro—if it were running right—to shoot downtown to rescue his Harley, but her deft hands worked their way down his torso, making Tristan forget all about it as a slight convulsion shot from his gut to his groin.

Cool fingers slipped under his sweatshirt until she

worked it up and over his head. Then soft palms explored the thatch of hair on his chest, gliding shoulder to shoulder, across his pecs, down his abs.

Tomorrow he'd renew his commitment to his old workout regime for sure. The equipment was in the basement; might as well make some use of it. In the meantime, he'd let her make use of him.

She reached between his thighs, cupping his most tender parts before curling her fingers around his erection. "Wow," she whispered. "This is all you?"

Tristan's cheeks got hot at her unique compliment. He should have put on underwear; that would have kept his junk from hanging loose. Her pulsating palm had him struggling to respond. "Whaddaya think?" He snickered as he kissed her, amused by her amazement. "I got a mouse in my pocket or something?"

She maneuvered her feet up to his hips, and using her toes inside the elastic waistband, she lowered his baggy pants with ease, down past his knees then kicked them to the floor.

"Boy, you're flexible."

"Yoga helps. Ever try it?"

"Never."

"I'll show you sometime." She squeezed her strong thighs around him, rocking to the side, urging him onto his back like a professional wrestler.

Tristan wasn't used to this sort of woman-handling and didn't mind it one bit. He let her have her way, rolling over, pulling her on top to straddle him.

"I hope you don't mind. It's been so long since I've been with a man. I know how I want it, if you don't mind giving it to me."

"Not at all," he mused, lying there.

Wide-eyed and mesmerized as a kid at Christmastime, he watched her in the bit of light filtering in from the far end of the hallway as she tugged the sweatshirt over her head exposing quite a feminine figure if he ever saw one.

Stacy never undressed for him. She always scurried away to do it in private. In a corner. Or her walk-in closet. Or the bathroom. Then burrowed beneath the blankets before they made love with the lights off.

Joy finger-combed her long damp hair, letting it cascade over twin globes the size of softballs, perfect enough to be silicone implants. But when she took his hands and guided them to her supple breasts, Tristan was thrilled to discover they were natural. His palms slid down delicate ribs that narrowed to a taut stomach. For a woman who produced two children, she was firm and fit.

"You have an incredible body." He trailed a finger down the vertical line that separated her abs. Dipped into her belly button before slipping into the waistband of his sweatpants that looked so good on her.

She lifted her bottom, letting him slide off the baggy pants. When he squeezed the cushion of her hips, she moaned in response and settled back with her ankles tucked beneath her. With both hands, she grasped his hard-on with firm fingers. "Are you *this* excited because of me?"

"All because of you," he mustered.

"Do you have a condom?"

Boy, Joy didn't waste time or words.

"Actually, no."

Her wry smile turned serious. "Does that mean you don't sleep around? Or you just don't use protection?"

"I haven't slept with anyone since my wife." He dreaded mentioning his ex in this moment but wanted his message to be clear. "She lost interest in sex after having the baby," he explained on impulse. "I should say she lost interest in sex with me."

"Tsk." Joy made the thoughtful sound with an empathetic headshake. "After my second son was born I worked so hard for this"—she swept a hand down her killer bod—"you have no idea."

Tristan tried not staring at it, focusing on her face instead. "I can imagine."

"We were lucky to stay married for so long with all our problems. Neither of us wanted more kids. Victor decided sex was *unnecessary*. He didn't want to use the condoms *I* bought. And he refused to get snipped. Even though I was on the pill, I didn't trust him to be clean, you know, because I knew he was sleeping around. So we just opted out of sex. With each other. He had flings. I had toys."

"His loss."

"Your gain. And it's your lucky day 'cause I happen to have a condom in my bag."

Joy jumped off the bed, darted down the hall, and returned in a flash with her oversized purse. "*Voila*." She pulled out a foil packet like a rabbit from a magic hat. "Ribbed for my pleasure." She unwrapped it and rolled it down Tristan's straining erection. Straddling his hips, she hovered over the agonizing tip.

He clenched his teeth and gripped the bedsheet. *Ohhh, man. Could this be happening? Maybe I'm dreaming. Could she still be too drunk to know what she's doing?* Too bad he didn't have a breathalyzer machine to check. Not that he had the wits to stop her.

When she impaled herself, her shriek echoed off his bare bedroom walls. Cookie came running. It wouldn't be a surprise if the neighbors started knocking.

"Oh, my God," she gasped as she collapsed onto him.

"Are you okay?" He hoped so because he'd hate to stop now.

After coming down from the initial shock of penetration, Joy lifted her head, whipping her hair over one shoulder, revealing a smile that beamed brighter than the sun. "This is gonna be fun." She sat back, lengthened her spine, then buried him deep inside her private paradise. Pumping up and down, she found her rhythm. Slow at first, quickening her pace to a steady trot. "Oh, yesss."

Tristan could have burst if he wasn't so determined to hang on until this lovely Lady Godiva finished the ride. When she turned up the velocity to a canter there was no way he would last much longer, so he gritted his teeth and squeezed his eyelids, invoking all his willpower to hold back. *One Mississippi. Two Mississippi. Three Mississippi.*

She pressed her hands behind her, using his thighs for leverage as she rode him at a full-gallop like a thoroughbred champion. This was the Triple Crown and she was crossing the finish line. Her head dropped back and she sang her climax to heaven giving Tristan the cue to let loose.

Still joined at the hip, Joy melted against him. "That was divine," she breathed against his ear. "I could do that again."

Tristan let out a pent-up sigh. Even if they did have

another condom, no way could he manage a second round so soon. He yanked the edges of the blanket around them like a burrito and hoped cradling her love-worn body was enough to satisfy her for now.

Breathing in sync, he realized she was out cold. *Sexed herself to sleep.*

Moonlight crept through the bedroom window, spilling on her pretty face as she rested upon his chest. He brushed her hair aside to get a better view at the sleeping beauty, wondering how he got so lucky. *I could get used to this.*

When he married straight-laced Stacy, it was supposed to be a forever deal. How could he have been so mistaken? He sure as hell didn't want to be that wrong again. But something about lying with Joy felt so right, he didn't want it to end.

Night turned to dawn. And by six a.m. the sky outside his bedroom window was a bright gray.

Joy stirred, elbowing him in the gut, and he groaned. Startled, she kicked off the blanket and shot to her knees with fists on guard. A wild-eyed version of the willing woman who crawled into his bed hours before. "What the hell?"

Tristan flinched. "What the hell *what*?"

"What the hell happened?"

He squinted, getting his bearing. "Are you serious?"

She scanned the room then down at Tristan's naked body. "Oh, my gosh." Her cheeks reddened as she figured out the answer to her own question. "I'm so sorry." She hid her face in her hands but he pulled them away.

"Sorry for what?"

"Sorry for…I'm not exactly sure, but I can guess. And it can't be good if we're both naked."

"Are you kidding? It's all good. Amazing, in fact."

"Where are my clothes?"

"In the washing machine. You threw up on yourself. Don't you remember anything?"

She shrugged, scratched her head, and rearranged her hair to shield her breasts. "I kind of remember. But I thought it was a dream or something."

"When you say dream, you don't mean nightmare, do you?"

"No. Not at all. When I say dream, I mean, holy cow I must be dreaming. This is too good to be true. That kind of dream."

Tristan concealed his smile, figuring it was best to sort out the situation before proclaiming the start of a beautiful relationship. "I drove you here in your car because you didn't want me to take you to your parents' house."

"Rex," Joy shouted and Tristan's heart sank.

Rex? "Look, I didn't know you were involved with someone." He rubbed his face, wishing he never hooked up with her. So much for doing a good deed. Now he'd have to dodge a boyfriend. "I thought we were both on the same level."

"Rex is my dog. He's probably missing me right now. Knowing my mother, she has him tied to a tree all night."

Tristan exhaled a world of relief. "Wanna call home?"

"And say what? I spent the night with some guy I just met? No, thanks. It's bad enough I'm crawling home after sunup. I'd rather not ruin this moment by inviting my parents into the conversation."

The aroma of fresh coffee drifted down the hallway, along with the clamor of clanking pans.

"Someone's in the kitchen." Joy's eyes widened in horror. "You have a roommate?"

"Nope," Tristan said, amused at the grown woman's sudden state of panic.

"Maid?"

He shook his head. "My buddy Nick. He's here to pick me up for work. And he cooks." Fried bacon and eggs with a side of burnt toast was Nick's usual wake-up call.

"I gotta get outta here." Joy scrambled off the bed and into his over-sized gray sweat suit. "Thanks for everything, but I need to go home." She slipped out of the bedroom and down the hallway.

Tristan yanked on his robe and followed behind, catching her before she reached the front door. "I didn't put your clothes in the dryer yet."

"Mail 'em to me."

"You don't have to rush out."

"No. I do. I really, really do."

"Your mother would actually tie your dog to a tree? All night? In the rain?" He pressed her back against the wall, getting close enough to kiss, hoping some memory of last night was enough to make her stay.

"Knowing her, she probably dropped him off at the pound. He already peed on her laundry basket and ate my father's slippers. I can't imagine what else he's done while I've been gone. That's why I need to find an apartment fast."

Tristan almost invited her to stay here but decided

against it once he glanced inside his daughter's empty bedroom. Nicole would be here soon. How would he explain a new woman's presence? A live-in nanny? That might would work to his benefit, but Joy might not like it.

"I know." She snapped her fingers. "I'll just tell her I found a place and that's why I didn't come home. I'll say I was testing it out overnight."

"You think she'll buy that story?"

Joy rolled her eyes. "I was divorced for almost two years before I told her the truth."

"How the hell'd ya get away with that?"

"She never visited us in Florida. And I only came to New York for Thanksgiving. I gave my ex everything he wanted in the divorce if he'd just play along."

"Why?"

Joy sighed with her arms across her chest. "If you must know, in the beginning, when I was in college, my mother warned me about getting involved with Victor. But I didn't listen. I guess I was afraid she'd rub it in about being right—as usual. I can't imagine what she's gonna say if she knows I spent the night with a stranger. God," she growled between clenched teeth, "what's wrong with me. Despite how this seems, I've never been a slut."

"I don't think you're a slut."

"Of course *you* don't. I gotta go. I need air. I need to get home." She lunged for the front door just as Nick stepped in her path, blocking the escape route with his massive frame. Joy slammed into his broad chest and he straightened her by the shoulders.

"Who's a slut?" Nick's wide smile and curious

eyes aimed straight for Tristan.

"No one. Never mind." Tristan waved the insulting word away. "I shoulda called to tell you I'm gonna be late for work today. Say hello to Joy."

"Whoa." Nick glanced her head to toe. "Nice catch, T." Then he squinted, studying her face. "Hey, I've seen you. Your picture is hanging in Bob's barber shop."

The color in Joy's cheeks faded from flaming red to ghostly white. "I'm his daughter."

"Small world." Tristan gestured toward the door, hoping Nick took the hint to leave but the man didn't stop talking.

"Then you know Lily." Nick held up his left hand, wiggling his ring finger. "She's my wife. Do you need an alibi or something? Tell your mom you spent the night at our place—albeit we're living in a camper until the house is rebuilt. But your parent's love Lily." He pulled out a cellphone from the back pocket of his jeans. "Lemme call her right now."

"No." Joy's eyes widened. "Don't mention it to anyone. Especially Lily. I'll be the one to tell her."

"Ya sure? I'll bet they'd buy it. Not that I want to support your lyin' habit. But I'd hate to see you get burned over a one-night stand with my buddy."

Tristan restrained the urge to punch his best friend in the mouth for uttering such thoughtless words. "She's not a one-night stand, guy." He put an assuring hand on Joy's shoulder, but she shot wild, incredulous eyes at him like he was the one who said the wrong thing.

"Whatever, *guy*. I'm just saying you two don't have to come out of the closet yet. In fact, stay in as long as you want. Breakfast is on the stove. I gotta do an estimate. I'll meet up with ya later," he said to Tristan. "That your Jag?" he asked Joy before walking out the door.

"Yes."

"You didn't drive here drunk, I hope." Since joining AA, Nick was on the lookout for prospective members.

"I drove." Tristan answered fast on Joy's behalf, praying she didn't dart out the door.

Nick smiled and nodded his approval, shooting Tristan with wide-eyes that spoke volumes. *Pretty girl. Fancy car. What's she doing with you?* No doubt his friend will expect all the dirty details. "Wait. You left your Harley downtown all night?" He shook his head in disbelief. "He must be in love with ya or something if he chose you over his motorcycle."

Tristan instantly regretted giving his friend a spare key.

Before Nick left, he said, "Let me know if you need a ride later to pick it up."

"Joy'll take me to get it. Right?"

"Uhhh…" The sound she squeaked out was barely audible. "Huh?"

Tristan winced at the horror plastered on her face. "Look, don't mind him. He didn't mean *love*. But the truth is I do like you. And I hope this isn't a one-night stand. I didn't mean for us to hook up so suddenly, but since we did I'd like to do it again sometime. Soon."

Joy shook her head. "I thought I could handle a fling, but look at me. I'm almost thirty years old and still scared my parents will ground me. I have an ex-husband who hates me. And two boys who don't even miss me. You don't want to get involved with a mess like me."

"Let me decide who I want to get involved with." Tristan tugged Joy's hand, pulling her away from the screen door, and she didn't resist. "It's still early and you have an alibi. At least have a cup of coffee. You eat eggs, right? I know you don't eat bacon. I'll toss it out if it bothers you."

"You know what? Screw it. I'm in the mood for meat."

Chapter Five

Joy hadn't consumed bacon since her last nervous breakdown.

It was an unforgettable binge for the records, spurred by the divorce papers Victor had shoved at her that sweltering August morning. On her twenty-sixth birthday no less. She'd chucked the pages over the banister of their three-story Spanish-style mansion then ran out the door in pajamas.

It was no surprise. She'd seen it coming head-on but refused to swerve. The man was a notorious stinking cheater. She didn't want to be in the loveless marriage anymore than he wanted her around, so it was inevitable their happily-ever-after came to a bitter halt, despite Joy's high hope to sustain it a few years longer until the boys were out of elementary school. She'd figured Victor would roll with the punches like she'd been doing, going through the motions until the time was right to pull the plug on the miserable union. After all, she'd put up with the farce of a relationship this long without uttering a snide word about Victor's piece of ass on the side.

To ease the pain that fateful day, she'd driven around Panama Beach aimlessly for hours, circling *Chuck's Pizza-On-The-Run* a dozen times before breaking down and pulling up to the drive-thru window. She ordered a large pie with the works and devoured it in the front seat of her previous Jag, dripping oil and tomato sauce all over the creamy leather interior. Then washed it down with grape soda straight from the two-liter bottle.

To top off the worst day ever, she'd slept in her car in the Taco Tuesday parking lot because she refused to go home to Victor. A knock on the driver's side window scared the bejeezus out of her. Waking up to the stern face of a hunky police officer was paralyzing enough, but not as bad as his presumption she was drunk behind the wheel, giving her a breathalyzer test for assurance. One glance at his silver handcuffs ignited her overactive imagination, being hauled to jail without anyone to call to bail her out. Joy bawled like a baby in the officer's arms, who was kind enough to listen to her personal tragedy and let her go with a warning. Still shaking, afraid to drive, she inched up to the drive-thru window like a regular customer rather than a lowlife loiterer and ordered a few breakfast burritos and a strawberry milk shake.

That twenty-four hour feeding frenzy had ended in a power-puke worse that last night's alcoholic binge.

This morning the bacon overrode that bad memory with the right combination of crispy-chewy smoky-saltiness. "This is perfection," Joy said between bites. Although she'd regret it later, she savored another piece.

"That's Nick for ya."

"Wait. Your daughter's name is Nicole and your business partner's name is Nick? That's a cute coincidence."

"Not really." Tristan smiled. "First of all, Nick and I are not business partners. The business is his. I work for him, for now. He's Nicole's godfather, so she's named after him. We've been best buddies since we were eight. The reason I came to Scenic View was 'cause he convinced me it was a good idea. Get some distance and time away from Stacy and the divorce drama. It's far enough from Star Harbor yet I'm still in New York State. Before he relocated here, he lived in my basement apartment, so he and Nicole are close. If she's gonna live with me, having good old Uncle Nick around might help her adjust. Make things feel normal. Help me care for her. As you can see he's already taking care of me as my personal chef, waking me up for work with a hungry-man's special. He loves to cook. I'm lucky I can make a sandwich."

"I can cook. Veggies. Fish. Salads."

"Salads don't really count as cooking."

"Have you ever had diced salad? There may not be any cooking involved but the prep work is pretty labor-intensive. Not to mention the battle scars from the mandolin."

"Maybe you'll show me how to make it. I don't wanna feed Nicole three square-meals of chicken nuggets and mac 'n cheese."

Every time Tristan mentioned his daughter, his blue eyes lit up as bright as the morning sky shining through the wide window where her crooked old house next door loomed like a hideous eyesore. It was a shame the intermittent owners neglected it. Joy wondered if there was a way to salvage it without having to knock it down first.

"Everything okay? Earth to Joy."

Joy blinked then flicked her eyes away from the glass. "Yeah. Fine. I could use a refill." She wiggled her empty mug.

He grabbed the pot and filled it to the brim. "You like this strong, too, huh?"

"Hmm?"

"Last night you said you like your alcohol strong. And today you're drinking your coffee black. I was just making an observation."

"Oh, yeah." She smiled, amazed he remembered what she'd forgotten. *What else did I say?* It was hard not to imagine the absolute worst spewing from her drunken lips. But considering he refused to abandon her, it couldn't have been so bad.

"Do you wanna shower before heading home?"

She shook her head. If she got back into his tub, she doubted she'd ever want to leave. It was bad enough she didn't want to climb off the kitchen barstool. Like the dilapidated house next door, Tristan's place was the perfect size for her and the boys. If only she could figure out a way to claim her old home.

When the air raid siren went off in the foyer, Joy sprang from the seat, scrambling to find her over-sized pocketbook and the cellphone inside. "Victor's calling."

Tristan followed. "Are you sure you want to talk to him now? Maybe you oughta call him back later."

"He never calls. It's probably important. Maybe the boys want to talk to me." She fumbled with the buttons. "Hello."

"Where the hell are you? I called your parents' house, and they said you've been out all night." Victor's nasal, high-pitched-for-a-man's voice shrilled over the line so loud, Tristan's eyes snapped open. Joy held the phone away from her head before her ex-husband blew her eardrum.

"Put it on speaker phone," Tristan whispered, tugging Joy back to the kitchen.

She set it on the counter between them. "Everything's fine, Vick. What's going on?"

"Everything is *not* fine. Your mother's freaking out. She doesn't know where you are."

"I spent the night at a *friend's*." Joy smacked her forehead, caught between a lie and a hard place.

"Well, she laid into me. Blaming me for everything. I knew you should have told them we'd gotten divorced two years ago. I don't want to be dealing with this nonsense now. I'm in the middle of planning a wedding with my very pregnant, very stressed fiancée. I don't need the added drama. And neither does Felicity." Just like Victor to care about his needs first. How he feels. How the turn of events affected his mental state.

Joy sucked back tears. Not because she felt bad for herself but because of her ex's humiliating harsh words in front of her new *friend*.

Tristan slid off the stool and came to her side, putting his hands on her shoulders. "What's wrong with this guy?" he whispered against her ear.

His hot breath sent a ripple down her spine, straight to her core, making her want to climb into his arms for protection and maybe another glorious ride between her thighs.

"Look, Joy, I know we decided the boys would live with you once their summer vacation starts. But Felicity and I were tossing around the idea of them spending half a year with us, and the other half with you—"

"What are you talking about?" Joy shrieked, breathless. "The judge already gave me primary custody."

"I know. But it's not fair I just get them on holidays."

If it weren't for Tristan's hands holding her in place, she would have slipped off the seat into a blubbering puddle on the floor. Stunned into silence, she didn't even know what to say if she could find her voice.

"I knew you might not like the scenario, which is why I got a new lawyer to help figure this out. But after it sinks in, I'm sure you'll agree. The only home they've ever known is here, with me. Why ruin that for them? I can give them a better life. Even with the child support, you'll never afford to give them what they have now…" Victor rambled on.

Tristan flipped an envelope to the blank side and jotted words with a black marker then held it up for Joy to read. *Tell him you'll think about it. Call him tomorrow. Hang up now.*

She whipped her ponytail with a violent headshake and mouthed *No.*

"Just do it," Tristan whispered.

Releasing a shaky breath, she clenched her teeth and said, "I'll call you tomorrow, Victor." She hung up without a goodbye, without talking to her precious babies that hated her so much they'd rather live with Victor and some other woman than their own mother.

Tristan took her cellphone, pressed a few buttons, and shut down the device before setting it on the counter. "I added my phone number to your contacts. When you're about to freak out and call Victor, dial me instead. As much as he might want to keep the boys, I'm sure deep down he knows they need you more. Let him stew for a while. It'll give you time to think."

Joy held her breath for so long she could have fainted. When she let it out, she ripped into Tristan. "You don't know Victor at all. He's right about everything. I can't afford to give the kids what they have now. My in-laws own everything. The car dealership. Our house. Our life. Victor just collects a salary because they know he can't be trusted with money. Or women. I signed a stupid pre-nup without even reading it because I was too drunk to know what it was."

"Seriously?"

She nodded, hoping she didn't look as ignorant as she felt. "Unfortunately." *God, what's this nice guy gonna think of me now?* "I was too excited about getting married, I didn't care at the time because I thought we'd be together forever. Who thinks about divorce on the night before their wedding? Even if I can find a way to afford giving my boys the life they're used to, I don't want to force them to live with me if they don't want to. I don't need them hating me more than they already do." Joy sobbed.

Tristan rubbed her back, stroked her hair, kissed her temple, and as much as she wanted to shrug off his affection, she secretly loved this gentle man's touch. "How could they hate you? They're just kids. They don't know what they want. You shouldn't take it personal. I bet Victor will change his tune sooner than you think. You've been away for what—less than a week? He's been the primary care giver for five minutes. Things are bound to fall apart on his end. Give it a little time. Meanwhile plan your strategy for when he gives up rather than wasting your energy on an emotional meltdown now. Don't let him know how you really feel. Don't give him the power."

"This is so hard, Tristan. I feel like I should fight for them. But they don't even want me." Something inside her snapped. She'd thought her heart was broken before but now it was shattered beyond repair. Weeping in his arms, tears flowed for the children she loved with every fiber of her being. Children that no longer wanted her in their lives. "My boys don't miss me. They haven't even called me. They…" She could barely get the words out. "They h-hate me."

"Shhh. They can't possibly hate you. How could anyone not love you is beyond me. God, I just met you and I think you're incredible. And after last night." He stopped rambling long enough to take a breath. "Nick's right. I could totally see myself falling—"

"Don't." Joy pulled away, swiping her face dry with her sleeves. "Don't, okay. Just don't."

"Don't what?"

"Don't say *it*." Salt stung her eyes as hot streams burned her cheeks. "I can't bear to hear the word. It's meaningless. Victor said he loved me. That he'd love me forever. And he didn't." As much as she despised the word, she'd give everything to hear her sons say it to her once more. "It's just another four-letter word."

"I didn't mean to upset you, Joy." Tristan stood, stunned like he was the wounded one.

How could he think this one-night stand was something more than what it was?

Joy needed to make things clear. She couldn't handle a new man while still dealing with the old one. Maybe in another time. Another place. Another dimension.

But not here. Not now. Not like this. Not while her heart was still an open wound, damaged so deep she doubted she'd recover in this lifetime.

No, she couldn't get involved with Tristan beyond this moment. Besides, he had just as many unresolved problems. Starting a relationship under these unstable conditions wasn't fair to either of them. And then there were children to think about.

"I need to get going. You need that ride, don't you? Let's go." She grabbed her car key and bag.

Tripping over the threshold, she scurried for the Jag.

Tristan jogged ahead to open the driver's door for her before folding his big body into the passenger seat.

She took the familiar turns at forty miles per hour even though twenty-five was the limit on these winding back roads.

"Easy, cowgirl," Tristan said more than once with his hands on the dashboard for support.

She zoomed through the parking lot behind Mr. Lucky's and pulled alongside the lonely motorcycle, dewy from the overnight down pour.

"Hey." Tristan took her hand and squeezed. "Don't worry. Things'll work out."

Joy nodded, unconvinced.

With one foot out the door, he said, "I want to see you again. Call me, okay?"

She sighed, holding back a fresh wave of tears. "Sure, okay. I'll call you. Later." She forced the painful words without giving him the consideration of making eye contact.

"Is that a promise?" he asked, with a hopeful tinge to his honeyed voice.

She wanted to say yes but knew it was a lie. So she half-shrugged, half-nodded then sped off as soon as he slammed the door.

When she got to her parents' she rang the bell because they still hadn't cut another spare key for her.

Her mother swung the door wide, glaring. Then, without a word, returned to the living room to have her coffee with *Kathie Lee and Hoda* on TV.

Rex scurried across the carpet, scratching Joy's shin until she scooped him up.

"Hey, boy," she whispered in the dog's furry ear. "It's nice to know someone missed me."

"*Sooo.* Where the hell have you been all night?" Sophia shouted during the commercial break, rattling the walls.

"Quiet, Ma. You'll wake the neighbors. I met up with old friends after work," Joy lied.

"You didn't shack up with that Curt Calderone from the bar?"

"Geez. Of course I didn't shack up with Cal." She turned her face toward the wall and cringed. "I stayed at Lily's." Hopefully her mother wouldn't question the baggy sweat suit because Joy was prepared to roll right into another whopper, giving the credit to Lily's big bear-sized husband.

"Oh." Sophia calmed down. "Well, still, you should have called. Every minute is like an hour. I was up all night waiting for you to come home."

"You could have called my cellphone if you were so worried." She put down the dog and headed for the kitchen for something to wash down the bitter taste of the anxiety pill she'd popped before walking in the front door in anticipation of this showdown.

"I don't have your *new* number," her mother huffed.

"Yes, you do. I wrote it down. It's hanging right here on the refrigerator." Joy snatched the paper from under the magnet and waved it.

"Who can read your chicken scratch? You should've been a doctor with such terrible handwriting. Then you wouldn't have to take a job waitressing in a bar."

"Bruno has my number. You could've asked him."

"Your cousin was on a date last night. I didn't want to bother him."

"Well, you knew I was working late. You didn't have to wait up for me."

"Who can sleep with your husband calling all night long? Apparently he doesn't have your new cellphone number either."

"Yes, he does. I hung it on his refrigerator too before I left. I wouldn't have had to get a new cellphone number if he didn't cut off my service. And he's not my husband anymore, so stop calling him that. Call him Victor. Or my ex. But don't call him my husband. He was barely worthy of the title while we were married. He sure as hell doesn't deserve it now."

"*Excuuuse* me. The father of my grandchildren."

"Are you this hostile toward him? Or do you save it all for me?"

"I wouldn't be hostile at all if you would've told me the truth when it happened. I would've had two years to get over your marriage falling apart. What kind of daughter gets divorced and doesn't tell her own parents?"

The kind that doesn't want to deal with this

aggravation—then or now. "It's not your problem to get over. It's mine. And you're making it harder than it needs to be. I could have stayed in Florida and gotten less abuse from Victor."

"You should've stayed in Florida to be with your children."

"I thought you'd be happy if I moved back to Long Island so you and Daddy could be closer to the boys."

"Well, where are they?" Sophia asked wild-eyed. "In Florida. With their father. Without their mother. That's where. How could you think that would make me happy? If you were so concerned about being a good mother, as much as you are with catching up with old friends, you wouldn't have left your boys behind. And you would've been here to take Victor's call."

"The boys'll be traumatized enough by the move. I didn't want to ruin the end of their school year by taking them out before summer vacation started. Besides I need time to set myself up first before they get here. The three of us can't live on the couch. Maybe we could've squeezed into the spare bedroom, but you already gave that to Bruno."

"You're sure setting yourself up all right. For failure," Sophia mumbled but Joy heard it anyway. "And the only reason Bruno has the spare room is because he got here first. He's been a godsend, helping your father with the business since the heart attack."

"I know, I know. I won't be on the couch forever. Just until I find a place of my own."

"You think that'll solve your problems? Having a place of your own? How are you going to juggle working and raising the boys?"

"I'll figure it out."

"Sure you will." Sophia rolled her eyes in doubt.

The last thing Joy needed was her mother's tongue lashing but it seemed that's all the woman ever had to offer. Without the strength for combat, she took the harsh words like bullets to the soul, determined more than ever to survive this mess for her boys' sake.

"Look at you. You're a disaster. Your eyes are bloodshot. You haven't even asked why your *ex-husband* called. Don't you care?"

"I know why, Mother. We spoke."

"And?"

"And nothing. He wants to keep the boys. Full-time. Forever."

"What did you say?"

Joy paused, thinking she should have taken two pills instead of one. "I said I'd think about it."

"You can't be serious," Sophia shrieked.

The volume of the heated debate woke Bruno. He shuffled from his bedroom wrapped in a quilt and plopped onto the couch. "He called again a couple of hours ago when I walked in this morning. I gave him your number."

"Those are your children. They need a mother."

"Victor thinks their future stepmother is more suitable for the job than me."

"That's ridiculous. Wait until your father finds out. He'll hit the roof."

"Why upset Daddy? It's not gonna happen. I'm not letting him keep my kids forever. I'm just playing my cards right. I'm sure once Felicity gets a long-term dose of my tiny terrors, she'll be quick to pack them up. Especially if she's got one on the way."

"Who's Felicity?" Bruno asked, stretching out

horizontally in Joy's assigned spot.

"Victor's fiancée," Sophia snarled.

"By the way, your father walked *your* dog. Yesterday afternoon. Last night. And this morning when he went to put in his daily numbers. We aren't a free dog-sitting service, you know. If you want to stay with us until you find an apartment, that's one thing. But if you're going to be out all day and night, maybe you should put it in a kennel."

"It's a *he*. And his name is Rex. Geez, Ma. You act like I wanna be here invading your space. Like I wanted this whole mess. You don't have to be such a"—Joy held her breath, then belted out—"such a bitch." There, she said it. And now that she did, she didn't know what to do between her mother and cousin staring at her with laser eyes and slack jaws. Thank God her father wasn't here to witness this.

Sophia gasped. "How dare you speak to me like that?" She charged down the hallway then slammed the bedroom door.

Bruno shook his head in solemn disappointment. "Congratulations."

"For what?"

"For proving you're the bigger she-devil. You better apologize if you know what's good for you."

"Yeah, well…" Joy knew he was right but wasn't in the frame of mind for conversation, or apologizes, or anything. She wanted to run away.

Is it still considered running away at twenty-nine years old?

She backed out slow, with her purse on her shoulder and the pooch in her arms. Once the front door clicked shut, she sprinted to her car.

Chapter Six

"What am I gonna do now?"

In the condominium parking lot, Rex wagged his tail in the front seat of the Jag anxious to go for a ride. But Joy sat there with her chin resting on the steering wheel as she prayed for answers.

Even with the anxiety pills Sophia managed to get on her daughter's last fragile nerve, causing Joy to burn the only reliable bridge in her life.

Well, maybe not the only bridge, but close enough.

Losing her cool was pointless. In order to survive as a single-mother, she'd need to get her act together fast.

She ran down the to-dos in her head.

One: find a place to live. Preferably with ample space for two rambunctious little boys that also allows pets.

Two: find a real full-time job instead of a bunch of part-time gigs. After last night, Cal wouldn't want her back anyway, so there goes all the prospective tips she was banking on. Maybe she could finagle some extra hours at Violet's and the Christmas Shoppe.

Three: trade in the Jag for something roomy and sensible.

Four. She sighed. It took all her willpower to ignore the stabbing pain in her chest and the overwhelming desire to add *call Tristan* to the list.

Falling for Casanova was the worst thing she could do right now.

Thank God Scenic View didn't have a drive-thru pizzeria. It was bad enough she broke down and ate bacon today. The last thing her waistline and cholesterol level needed was another emotional food fest.

Scrolling through the contacts in the cellphone for her local go-to gal-pal, Joy found Tristan first under C. Lord knows she wanted to call him but it made more sense to erase the number and remove all temptation. Her finger hovered over his name, torn between Dial and Delete, but rather than make a hasty decision, she skipped over it.

Instead she dialed Lily Lane, who was more of a surrogate-sister than a conspiring girlfriend. A pang of guilt stabbed her heart for only calling in the past to check on the folks without having to talk directly with them. The last time she'd spoken to Lily was in February to say she couldn't make it to the wedding. Joy didn't dare mention her plan to return to Scenic View, just like she never mentioned the years of marital problems, not wanting the sensitive information to leak to her parents.

Lily answered on the first ring and Joy sucked in an uneasy breath. "Hi, Lil. Mind if I swing by?" Less than ten minutes later she pulled into the driveway, shocked at the remnants of the burned down bungalow.

Wearing a pink bathrobe and a tangle of flaming red hair, Lily waved from the luxury camper in the yard. "Come on in. Check out my castle on wheels."

"My parents told me about the fire, but I had no idea…" Joy sat at the compact table in the motor home with Rex nestled between her feet, feeling guilty for not reaching out to Lily sooner.

"A total loss. But not really." Lily made a fresh pot of coffee. "I got Nick." She wiggled her ring finger sparkling with diamonds. "We're living here until we figure out what to do with the house."

Joy blurted out the devastating details of her topsy-turvy life while Lily refilled their mugs, nodding and listening.

"We've only got the one bedroom but the couch converts to a bed if you need a place to stay. I know your folks can be a bit much to handle sometimes."

"Thanks for the offer but I'll be all right. That is, if my mother lets me through the door." Joy mustered the nerve to ask for a favor. "I was wondering…do you think Nick might have an affordable place I can rent?"

"I don't know much about his business but I'll talk to him for you."

"Thanks." Joy sipped her black coffee. "I'm glad things worked out for you, Lil. You deserve it after all you've been through." Of all the kids growing up in the neighborhood, Lily had the roughest ride, living with her alcoholic mother after losing her dad in a fire.

"The bungalow would have needed to be leveled anyway if I were to fix it up. Nick's handy, so I don't have to worry about anything but picking out the colors."

"He seems like a nice guy."

Lily cocked a suspicious eyebrow. "And how would you know?"

Joy's face got hot. She should have kept her mouth shut. It was bad enough the grapevine would soon be burning up with tales of her drunken exhibition with

Tristan on Mr. Lucky's dance floor, plus whatever rumors sprouted from their public display of inebriated affection. It didn't make sense to attempt denying it, but she could down play everything. "I, uhh, met him. This morning."

With a slanted knowing look, Lily asked, "You met *my* Nick? May I ask where?"

"Well…" Although there was no reason to get tongue-tied and twisted in front of Lily, Joy paused, wanting to ensure her story got out straight and without any misunderstanding. "At his friend's place."

"Ah-ha." Lily smiled bright. "Nick told me Tristan has a houseguest this morning. I didn't believe him, but he wasn't lyin'. You little vixen."

Joy cringed. "I asked him not to tell you."

"Don't worry. I won't tell your folks about your sexy sleepover party."

"Good. Because I already told my mother I spent it here."

"Next time your lie includes me you might wanna tell me first. But I can understand how you might've lost your mind for moment. Tristan's a *real* cutie."

Joy refrained from gushing about the guy that rocked her socks off. "I suppose."

"You *suppose*?" Lily pursed her lips in doubt. "Are you blind? Or playing dumb? I'm surprised no one scooped him up already. Well, he does have a kid, which might be a deal breaker for some women. But, hey, you have two. Can't get any more compatible than that. The guy's a keeper in my book. A total package for a single-mom like you. Brains. Looks. Body. Personality."

Joy kept her cool and shrugged as if her tryst with

Tristan meant nothing. "Maybe. If I was into that sort of thing?"

"And you're not? What else do you need?"

"I dunno. Never mind. Let's forget it."

"Are you sure we're talking about the same guy? 'Cause Nick said Tristan's nuts about you. You know what they say. First comes love. Then comes second-marriage."

"Whoa." Joy halted the conversation with her palms. "It's definitely *not* love." The four-letter word usually gave her a stomach cramp, but in the same sentence as Tristan it made her heart flutter like a schoolgirl with a puppy-love crush. "It's anything *but* love. That's just absurd."

"Then what is it? A one-nighter?"

Joy shrugged. "Let's just say it was a first-and-only. Just like my one night working at Mr. Lucky's. I'm sure Cal doesn't want me back. Honestly, waitressing isn't for me anyway. I don't know what made me think I could handle it. I was desperate and it was the first Help Wanted sign I saw." She paused for a breath and rubbed her forehead. "And then there's Tristan. The first decent guy to hit on me in so long. I can't believe I went home with him." Burying her face in her hands wasn't enough to hide her humiliation. "God, what was I thinking?"

"Joy Barbieri, you were never the Girl-Gone-Wild one-night stand type. What's come over you?"

Despite being drunk as a skunk, she knew exactly what she was doing last night and the fragmented memories had Joy wincing. Without admitting it, she unintentionally premeditated the whole thing the moment she stashed the condoms in her bag, just in case something suddenly came up. Instead of going home after Cal told her to end the night, she'd stuck around for Casanova's company. Sucked down cocktails like water. Gyrated like there was no tomorrow. Power puked in the rain. Did it in the dark with a guy she just met. All the stuff she should've done before two C-sections and stretch marks she'd squeezed into a few hours. To top it off, she ate bacon. She'd have to double-up on her roughage to work that poison out of her system before it undid all the years of hard work getting her body into this shape.

Joy sipped her coffee for the strength required to compress her whole life into a bad excuse for a night of poor judgment. "Well, after ten years of marriage and a torturous divorce, I figured it was time to *dabble* in other things. I settled down way too young. I missed out on all the fun. And last night I was so drunk my guilty conscience was off-duty."

"So what now?" Lily leaned closer as if she didn't want to miss a single syllable. "You're gonna play catch-up and sleep around with every guy in town?"

"Definitely not. And technically Tristan's from out-of-town. The more I think about it, the more I realize how dumb I was. I never should have gone home with him. Now I've gotta go into hiding until he goes back to wherever he came from."

"This is a small town. You're gonna run into each other sooner or later."

"Let's hope it's later." Joy crossed her fingers. "After he forgets about me."

"What if he decides to stay in Scenic View? You can't hide forever. But I can cut your hair so he doesn't recognize you."

The thought of Tristan as a permanent fixture in this tightknit community gave Joy a strange tickle in her tummy, somewhere between thrilled and terrified. "You think it'll work? Maybe color it too. I could use a makeover."

"Come on, Joy." Lily smacked her palm on the tabletop. "You can't be serious. You're not interested in him, really? Honest to God, not one iota?"

Playing coy, Joy studied the ends of her sun-streaked waves, curling a strand around her finger as if contemplating a new 'do when she was really blushing inside out. All this talk had her hot between the thighs, reeling back to the hazy moment of straddling Tristan on his king-sized bed. She crossed and uncrossed her legs, nudging Rex with her toe with the hopes of stirring the pooch so he'd beg to go outside where she could get some fresh air. But all she managed to stir were the memories she'd made with a man she couldn't forget.

"I dunno, Lil." She sighed. "I hate to admit I am a little interested. But what can I offer other than joyride once in a blue moon? My boys'll be here soon. I can't think of dating while getting them settled."

"I bet Tristan wouldn't turn down an occasional bootie call."

"What guy would?"

"I'm just saying he could probably use a fun spring fling after all he's gone through this winter with his messy divorce."

Her curiosity piqued, Joy asked the burning question without hesitation. "What do you mean *messy*?"

"From what I heard, it was as bad as yours but

super-quick. Her uncle's a family court judge—
something or other—and managed to push their case to
the top of the heap. They both wanted out. Tristan gave
her everything just to keep it clean for their daughter's
sake. Pension, alimony, child support, oh my…"

The fact that he paid without a problem
reconfirmed Joy's first impression that he was a good
man. "Good for her," she said halfheartedly, wishing
she had it so easy.

"Good for him too, 'cause at least he has options.
Even though Nick's heart is set on Tristan staying, I
kinda think he'll go back to Star Harbor once the dust
clears from his divorce. I mean, if he really wanted to
retire early he'd just do it, right? Why bother to buy
time with this terminal leave-until-he-figured-things-out
nonsense? Either way, doesn't mean the four of us can't
double date." Lily smiled, hopeful. "And if things get
serious between you two, he's only an hour ferry-ride
across the Long Island Sound."

Joy shook her head. Her old friend didn't seem to
see the bigger, long-term picture. "I'm not into a long-
distance relationship or getting involved with a guy
who has no intention of sticking around."

"You don't know what you want, which is why
he's exactly the kinda guy you need right now. Nothing
serious. Just fun. Why don't you give the friends-with-
benefits route a try? It's really just a modern version of
being in love for people with high libidos and fear of
commitment."

"Nah." Joy wrinkled her nose at the concept of
casual sex as if last night's sexcapade fell under a
classier category. "I don't think I'm cut out for that.
Besides, I don't want to use the guy for great sex."

"It was great, huh?" Lily waggled perfectly arched brows.

"Did I say great? I mean, you know, any sex is good sex."

"You didn't say good—you said great."

"Whatever I said, what I mean is I just can't have sex without the relationship to go with it. I thought I could, but I'm not that type. I'll just buy a *massager* from Violet's."

"Your mother'll get a kick outta finding that under your pillow."

"Since I'm living on the couch I'll have to hide it in my car." *In the glove compartment, where my anxiety pills are stashed, unfortunately, out of reach in this moment of dire need.*

"I suggest you get one quick. Especially if you're attracted to each other. Otherwise you'll have a helluva time telling him no. Anything you do say, can and will be used against your libido."

"You really don't think I can stick to my guns? I have willpower like you won't believe. When I set my mind to something, no means no and nothing else. No way. No how." In there had to be a double, triple, or quadruple negative, and Joy only hoped it didn't equate to a yes, because Lily was right, turning Tristan away wasn't going to be an easy task.

"Yeah, right. That's what I said when I met Nick. I was gung-ho against dating a firefighter—you know, 'cause of what happened with my folks—but he was relentless. In no time at all that man turned my mild side wild." Lily's cheeks started flaring to a candy apple red.

"I'm glad you have an amazing sex life, Lil. I

really am." Envy crept up out of nowhere and Joy couldn't avoid the cynical twinge in her tone.

"You can have one too."

"Not really. Not while my ex still terrorizes me, never mind when the boys come to town. It wouldn't be fair to drag Tristan into the mix. I think we'd both benefit from forgetting everything that happened between us."

"You could always throw on a wig and pretend to be someone else. This way you can get your jollies without getting jammed up with the complications of a relationship. Turn things up a notch. Add a dash of sexy sauce to the recipe."

"Does Nick know you're crazy?"

"He makes me this way. Did I tell you how he seduced me dressed up as Santa Claus?"

"Save that story for the next time I'm drunk because my brain can't deal with the image right now. Thanks for the talk. And the coffee." Joy stood and hugged Lily before picking up Rex.

"Come by whenever you want, okay? But I gotta warn you, Tristan might be here." Lily followed Joy out of the camper and down the driveway.

"I don't think I can handle another dose of that man. Sloshed. Sober. As myself. Or dressed as anyone else."

Joy got in the car, set Rex on the passenger seat, then started the engine as she slammed the door and rolled down the driver's window.

"Trust me, Lil, I wish I could be someone else sometimes so I wouldn't have to live my life in its current state of crapola. I simply don't have the mindset or the time for any extra-curricular activities. Plus, now that I think about it, I'm not into guys with beards," she lied, before putting the car in reverse and taking off down the road.

Chapter Seven

"Hey, whatever happened to Joy Barbieri?" Cal asked while shooting seltzer into a glass for Nick and popping the cap off a beer bottle for Tristan. "It's been two weeks and she hasn't been back."

"You askin' me? Or him?" Nick jutted his chin at Tristan sitting on the barstool beside him.

Tristan pretended to ignore the conversation. Joy was a sore subject for him and Nick knew it.

"She worked St. Pat's and that's it. I still owe her for the day." Cal wiped wineglasses dry then slid them upside down in the overhead rack. "I'd ask her folks, but it's been my experience that I'm safer keepin' away from Sophia whenever possible."

Listening, minding his business, Tristan knocked back the beer then swiped his lips with a fist and scratched the side of his furry face. He hadn't seen Joy. Hadn't heard from her either although he'd heard plenty about her chat with Nick's wife after their one and only night together. A night he'd thought meant as much to her as it did to him. Man, was he wrong.

"I'll pass the good word to Lily that you're lookin' for Joy. Those two girls have been thick as thieves since she moved home. Know what I mean?" Nick cocked his head at Tristan as if waiting for a reaction.

Despite Nick's latest attempt to goad Tristan into admitting it pained him that Joy never called, he sat like a statue and said nothing except, "Can I get another beer here?" He pushed the empty bottle toward Cal.

Although kissing-and-telling was never his thing, confessing to his best buddy about getting lucky with Joy had been unavoidable during the long workday, like two boys in the schoolyard. He'd kept the dirtiest details to himself but couldn't stop gushing about the good parts. Mostly about how Joy'd made him feel things he hadn't felt in forever, after all the hell he'd gone through with Stacy. For a minute, he'd almost believed he found someone to fill the void.

He'd expected Joy to call that night, if not the next day. But a day turned into two, which turned into two weeks without any contact. Her silence solidifying their one-night stand status.

But why? Tristan had no clue and was tired of beating himself up over it, wondering what he did so wrong for her to avoid him.

"How about you, guy?" Nick shoved the leg of Tristan's barstool, jolting him from his sinking thoughts. "Have you heard from Joy lately?"

"Nope." Tristan snorted in disgust. "I definitely have not." He returned his attention to the beer bottle, making a project of peeling off the label in one neat piece, wishing he could light up a cigarette in here. "A girl like that's outta my league anyway."

"Don't let the fancy wheel's fool ya. She's pretty much broke from what Lily says. Not that I wanna be spreading rumors but apparently her ex-husband doesn't have a pot to piss in. His parents control all the money. And they were real shrewd, having the dude slip Joy a pre-nup the night before their wedding after getting her drunk. So, compared to that jerk, you're a real swell fella. Maybe she's just playing hard to get?"

Nick's story jibed with everything Joy'd said so Tristan gave her extra credit for honesty, but it still didn't make him feel better. "Maybe she's not interested. Let's just leave it at that. Okay?"

"I dunno how any red-blooded American girl could avoid falling for Tristan Casanova, with those sparkling blue eyes, that great head of hair, and the temperament of a lazy lapdog," Nick teased. "Hell, if I were female I'd dig ya."

"Looks like those ladies sure as hell spotted you." Cal nodded toward the pretty patrons parading through the door.

"Whatever, guys," Tristan murmured, unamused.

"What I heard from Lily was that Joy didn't dig guys with facial fur. Maybe it's time you shave the chick-repellent?"

"Maybe you should mind your business and worry about yourself." Tristan massaged his manicured beard with a protective palm. "It's my face and I like it." Joy had said she liked it too. *Liar.*

"Well, winter's over, Grizzly Adams junior," Nick gibed.

Tristan responded with a playful jab to Nick's kidney that make the larger man grunt.

Nick returned the favor with equal force, socking Tristan in the biceps. "Time to shed, or molt, or whatever the hell animals do in the spring."

"Mate." Cal smirked.

"You must've done something really wrong to turn her off if she hasn't called. I'll have Lily find out what her deal is." Nick reached in the breast pocket of his flannel shirt for his cellphone but Tristan grabbed his sleeve.

"Don't. Just forget about it." He released Nick and regained his cool.

"Ya sure? It drove me crazy when Lily and I weren't talkin'. The constant wonderin' why she was so resistant. Not knowin' what I could do to change her mind. Askin' myself what I did wrong. But, like I always say, when it's right, it's right. Just gotta have patience."

Tristan knew what he did wrong—he shouldn't have taken Joy to bed. Shouldn't have touched her. Just let her sleep on the couch and left it at that. But she excited him beyond reason, and it had been so long since he'd been close to a woman, he couldn't help himself.

Now he regretted ruining a good first impression by taking things too far too fast.

Or maybe the round of casual sex spared him another full-fledged broken heart, nipping the inevitable in the bud sooner rather than later.

It didn't matter now anyway. He had bigger things to worry about than a woman who wasn't interested.

"I'm over it already. Besides, now's not a good time. I've gotta focus my energy on being a father. I need to find a dependable sitter, or a nanny, or day-care. Someone qualified to watch Nicole while I'm working for you. Someone affordable while alimony drains me dry."

"I already told you, I'll pay your bills as long as you agree to be my partner. We'll split the business fifty-fifty and then you'd have plenty of cash. Hell, Stacy's gonna take half your damn pension after taking every other penny ya got. And what if you go back on the job and something happens to you? What's Nicole gonna do without you? Stick with me and you'll have more than enough cash to build a new house rather than live in one of my renovated rentals. You could be making three times your cop salary, if not more. And you won't have to work nights and holidays. Seems like a no-brainer to me, but then again, look who I'm talking to." Nick chuckled.

"I dunno." Tristan shook the bottle by the neck, sloshing last bit of backwash. "My terminal leave ends in August, so I've got 'til then to decide whether I retire or not. This pit stop in Scenic View was supposed to be a temporary fix to get on track after the divorce. I was never planning on staying. Going back to Star Harbor will make it easy for me to see my kid on the occasion when it's not my turn to have her."

"Oh, quit it already, will ya?" Nick kicked the leg of Tristan's stool. "I can't stand the next five months living in suspense. Just make up your mind and take my offer."

"I heard the town's got a constable position open," Cal suggested. "Can't ya transfer?"

Tristan shook his head. "Doesn't work that way in real life. Only in the movies."

"Come on, T." Nick gripped the edge of the bar. "My uncle left me with an enormous responsibility. I need you here with me. There's no one I trust more than you—no offense, Cal."

"None taken." Cal refilled the bowl of nuts. "I'm not a handyman. I've got skills in different things." He winked at a trio of twenty-something gals in business suits coming in for a liquid lunch.

"Whaddaya complaining for?" Tristan snorted,

wishing for woes like Nick. "The old man also left you a ton of cash."

"Yeah, well, with the cash came a ton of work, like the contract for the town's marina expansion. I've gotta put someone in front of that project. Someone I can depend on. You've always been good at the smart stuff like math, money, and organizing. I'm better at swinging a hammer than punching a calculator."

"What you do best is fighting fires. You were a captain. Don't you miss it? Even for a minute?" Tristan wondered how Nick managed to change his whole life so fast and still recognize himself in the mirror each morning.

"Being a volunteer is good enough for me these days. Honestly, I don't miss Star Harbor as much as I'd expected. Meeting Lily was the silver lining around that dark cloud hanging over me. She even stuck by me after your psycho sister tracked me down and tried getting back together."

Tristan always regretted setting up Nick and Claudine, but at least his buddy made it out alive. Hopefully Claudine's husband-number-three can manage to keep her bipolar disorder under control going forward.

"I'm just saying it would make my life a lot easier if you'd work with me, not just for me."

No matter how much time passed, or how many new creases etched Nick's face, Tristan only saw his childhood companion in those dark eyes.

"So whaddaya say? Don't do it for me. Do it for Nicole. She'll reap the benefits. Who knows, maybe our kids'll take over for us one day." Nick's cell rang as if on cue. "Excuse me, fellas. My lady's looking for me."

After a whispered conversation, he announced, "Speaking of kids, I gotta run. Tristan, mind walking home? Otherwise I'll drop you off now."

"Go on. Don't worry about me."

"Good. 'Cause I'm on the clock." Nick checked his wristwatch. "Lily's biological clock." He smirked with a wink before darting for the door. Unlike other guys who stressed when their ovulating wives call for sex-on-demand like it was some kind of inconvenient project, Nick seemed to enjoy every *emergency* house call from his woman. Then again, it was no secret the man was anxious to start a family.

Tristan had the family. Albeit a dysfunctional, fragmented version of the happily-ever-after he'd thought he was signing up for at the time, yet a family nonetheless. Had he foreseen his life upside down he would have never married Stacy. But then again, if he never stuck it out with her they wouldn't have Nicole. The vicious hamster wheel of regret was torture.

He needed to get off the wheel. Off the barstool. Off Long Island. Go back to Star Harbor to be with Nicole and begin a new life in peace. However the thought of being near his ex-wife, knowing it would reignite a battle he wasn't in the mindset to fight, kept him firmly in place.

Cal swapped Tristan's empty beer for a fresh one like a mind reader.

Besides having Nick to pal around with, the good thing about living in Scenic View was people being busy with their own baggage and business to stick their nose in his.

Especially Joy. The woman must be the busiest of them all. She never called like she'd promised;

meanwhile Tristan hadn't stopped thinking about her. He figured he'd have run into her by now, unless she was purposely avoiding him. Maybe their one night of passion didn't leave the lasting impression on her as it did on him.

The flashback had him craving a cigarette so after paying for the beers he stepped outside and lit up.

The first day of April felt like early summer and was even warmer in the sun, so Tristan tugged off the denim jacket and slung it over his shoulder. Joy's sweet fragrance had rubbed onto the collar that night but was long gone now. It was crazy how he missed her and he hardly knew her. Sure, he could've weaseled his way into her life through Nick and Lily, but why bother if the woman had no interest in him.

He stopped in front of Bob's barbershop, now called Bellas & Fellas Day Spa according to the banner hanging in the window. Peeking through the plate glass, he hoped for a glimpse of Joy but only saw his hairy reflection.

Maybe what Nick said was true—maybe she didn't like the beard.

Maybe he ought to find a way to get his mind off this woman. Something positive to fill the gap between sleep and work. Anything…as if it were that simple. He sucked on the cigarette then expelled a thick cloud of smoke, replaying the dirty details of St. Patty's Day. The jingle bell on the barbershop door hurled a vague memory clinging to the fringe of his mind to the forefront.

What did they talk about that night? Christmas. In July. For Nicole. Decorating. He'd asked Joy for help. And she said something…

"Oh, yeah." He jammed the butt in a sand barrel on the sidewalk as he picked up the pace.

She had a part-time job working in the Christmas shop in town.

Still unfamiliar with the nooks and crannies of this place, Tristan hoofed toward Town Hall to study the cartoon map framed in Plexiglas. He found the spot marked *You Are Here* and connected the dots to *Everyday's Christmas Shoppe* on Scenic Circle, off Main Street.

Ten minutes later he was assaulted by the overwhelming scent of pine and peppermint as he entered the portal to the North Pole.

"Ho. Ho. Ho." The life-sized animated Santa Claus wearing bunny ears startled Tristan.

"Ho, ho, ho, yourself," he mumbled as his heart rate stabilized.

It was impossible to see through the artificial forest so he forged into the maze of greenery, following the faux snow trail toward the vacant service counter at the back of the store. *Someone's gotta be here if the front door's unlocked.*

Before he tapped the little silver bell beside the cash register, Joy emerged, wiping her palms on her jeans. "Sorry. I was tossing the trash out back. Can I hel—" She choked when she recognized him.

Unsure how this reunion would pan out, Tristan remained positive as he fought to control his anxious smile. "Hello, Joy."

"*Hell.*" She cussed under her breath then cleared her throat. Wide eyes sparkled under the strings of twinkle lights dangling from the ceiling but her bright smile seemed forced. "Hello, Tristan."

He ignored the tension in her tone and amped up the sweetness in his. "How've you been?"

"Fine. Just fine. Everything's fine." With her back board-stiff and eyes avoiding his, Joy didn't seem as fine as she claimed.

"I never heard from you. I thought you might've gone back to Florida," he lied.

"Nope. I'm still around. But I'm not working at Mr. Lucky's anymore." She tossed her hair over her shoulder, drowning out the seasonal scents with an intoxicating wave of sweet strawberries.

He gripped the counter, curbing the urge to stick his face in her silky web and breathe her in as he'd done that one night. "Yeah. I heard."

"How'd you know where to find me? Or are you doing some early Christmas decorating?"

"I remembered what you'd said about working here part-time."

Joy shuffled some papers on a clipboard without taking her eyes off him. "What can I do for you?"

"For starters, you can tell me why you never called." He didn't intend to harp on the sore subject, but it was on his mind, and he couldn't stop the words from rolling off his tongue.

"Look…" She sighed. "You seem like a nice guy. I don't want to hurt you. But I'm not ready for a relationship."

"Me?" Tristan snorted at her ridiculous hypothetical situation. "Get hurt? By you? That'll never happen, however I appreciate your concern. And nobody said anything about a *relationship*." He nearly gagged on the word, which convinced him he wasn't as ready as he thought.

Crimson crept into her cheeks. "Well, I-I just figured, after that night…"

"I gotta be honest with you, I like you. But I got a lot going on, between work and my kid coming to town. Still, I'd definitely like some adult company with you, although I'm not ready to get soul-to-soul with anyone just yet. I thought we could, ya know, be friends."

"Friends, huh?" A devilish gleam flickered in Joy's eyes. "*Just* friends? Or the kind with benefits?"

A pang in his pants took him by surprise. He wasn't about to say it, but since she had, he wouldn't refuse. "I was gonna leave it at friends for now. But if you wanna work benefits into the picture, I'd never say no."

Joy put her fists on the curve of her hips, lowered her chin, and glared at him with laser eyes. "I bet."

"Look, if you wanna be friends *without* the benefits, we can do that too. I just figured since we're both divorced with kids, we have at least that much in common."

She sighed, shaking her head in doubt, but something in her softening posture and the dangerous grin curling her lips as she rolled her eyes to heaven whispered *sure, what the hell, why not, what've I got to lose*. "I don't know, Tristan…"

He took her hand—warmer, softer, smaller than his—and a shock sizzled up his arm, bounced around his torso, before settling in his groin. Friends. Benefits. Whatever. As long as she didn't say no.

"Come over to my place tonight. Bring your guard dog. If you're not comfortable then we'll forget we ever had this conversation. Whaddaya say?"

A smirk twitched on her lips. "Humph," she

expelled in deliberation. He must have piqued her curiosity in a positive way since she didn't blurt out no. Narrowing her eyes, she half-nodded, half-shook her head, then mumbled, "Maybe."

Chapter Eight

Joy scraped the dinner plates into the trashcan so her mother could rinse them before loading the dishwasher.

"Watch what you're doing," Sophia scolded at the bits of corn and crumbs missing the wide mouth of the pail.

Distracted by the earlier conversation with Tristan, Joy blinked until his image faded.

"I'm going to Bingo Night at the firehouse."

"That sounds fun," Joy said halfheartedly, wondering what to wear tonight.

"Why don't you come? It starts at seven. Then I don't have to bother your father for a ride." Her mother didn't like to drive during the daytime, never mind at night.

"I have plans."

Sophia's face twisted in disbelief. "What kind of plans?"

Although Joy hadn't officially accepted Tristan's tempting invitation, still convincing herself it wasn't some crude April Fool's ploy, she spent the rest of the afternoon inventing believable escape routes with enough potential for getting out of the house, however none of those stories bubbled to the surface now that she needed one. Going to Lily's popped in her head, but knowing Sophia, the woman might want to stop by for a visit. Being honest would never work because anything remotely resembling a date would send her mother into interrogation-mode, especially with Victor stirring the shit pot long-distance.

"I, um…I'm going to look at an apartment." The fat lie came out of nowhere, but since it could be true for working people with no daytime hours to house hunt Joy rolled with it without flinching.

"That's great." It was no secret her mother was anxious for the houseguests to leave so she could get back to a normal life. "A garden apartment?"

"No. A basement apartment."

Her mother lifted an impartial shoulder. "I'll tag along. I'd love to check it out with you. Then we can go to bing—"

"No, Ma," Joy snapped, then sweetened her tone to avoid suspicion, "I mean…it's okay. This is something I need to do alone. Not that I don't want your opinion. But this is a decision I should make without anyone else's input. I'm the one who has to live there."

"What if the landlord is some kinda weirdo? A pervert or something?" Sophia shook her head as she dried her hands on the dishtowel. "I don't think it's safe for you to go alone to a stranger's house."

Heat climbed up Joy's neck. "Don't worry. Rex is coming with me."

"You're bringing the dog, but not me? Unbelievable." She threw the dishrag in the sink then stomped out of the kitchen.

"Ma," Joy shouted, but Sophia didn't stop until she reached the end of the hallway and disappeared behind the bedroom door. Passive-aggressive is what the therapist called this behavior; Victor did the same toxic thing.

Terrific. On top of shameless lying to her mother, Joy hurt the woman's feelings, again, making things worse. Where were her anxiety pills when she needed them? In her car, out of reach to do any good now. Her folks must have something in the medicine cabinet to nip the blooming stress-headache in the bud. An aspirin and a hot shower would have to suffice.

She figured it would be hard moving back in with her parents. But not this hard. Every move she made, they were right there, giving the third degree, minding her business. It would be nice to be honest with them— on everything. But their tendency to overreact and blow up at any misunderstanding set Joy in avoidance mode similar to the way she operated when she was married.

It was time to let go of the traumas of her past and let her mind wander toward the potentials of the future. Or at least the prospect of tonight.

Not including her one-night fluke with Tristan, which couldn't be counted since she was too bombed to make a rationale decision, Joy hadn't been out with a man in forever; she'd forgotten what it was like. If she were seriously considering seeing him again, she ought to play hard to get while being hard for him to resist.

Friend with benefits would never work for her no matter what sort of modern love Lily might try pushing.

Besides, Tristan barely qualified as an acquaintance.

And she was too softhearted for casual sex. Got attached too easily. Required something more than just sleeping with a friend to satisfy her libido. Sex was as much mental as it was physical, for her anyway. Once she allowed a man into her mind, there would be no way to stop her heart from wanting more.

By the time Joy tiptoed out of the bathroom, her mother's purse was missing from its usual spot on the chair beside the front door.

Bruno emerged from the kitchen with a bowl of ice cream and plopped on the couch, startling her. "What'd you do to upset Aunt Sophia this time?"

"Nothing," she squeaked in self-defense and tucked the corner of the towel tighter under her armpit.

"Something must've happened," he said, with a shrew cock to his brow.

"I don't wanna play bingo tonight," Joy snapped. "That's all."

"You sure? Because she was pretty upset when she left."

Ignoring his interrogation, Joy dug out a brush from her pocketbook and dragged it through her dripping locks with a rough hand.

"Wet hair is weaker than dry hair. It'll break and you'll wind up with split ends."

Joy rolled her eyes at his unsolicited advice, wishing she had a bedroom with walls. After a moment of deliberate silence, she exhaled. "I'm going to check out an apartment. What's the big deal?"

"Hmmm." Doubt laced his breath. After all the years being a hair dresser, spending so much time with the opposite sex made Bruno a difficult man to fool. "Really?"

"Of course, really." Getting caught in the lie made her stomach cramp. Hopefully she didn't sound as guilt-ridden as she felt.

"If that's all you're doing, why'd couldn't Aunt Sophia go? What's the big deal?"

"Some things I need to do on my own," she huffed with a haughty chin tilt.

"Did you think, maybe, your mother wants to spend a little time with you?" Her astute cousin always had his aunt's back.

Just because they let Bruno have the spare room, on top of giving him full reign of the barbershop to turn it into a chic little male/female boutique salon he renamed Bellas & Fellas, he somehow thought he knew more about her folks than she did. Maybe he did.

Struggling to withstand his mental squeezing without cracking under pressure, Joy gave a careless shrug. Distracted with the anticipation of seeing Tristan, she checked the contents of her oversized duffle bag that contained every basic necessity she owned.

"Are you just looking at the place or moving in?"

"Ya never know." Getting caught in a web of lies was climbing high on her laundry list of worries; she just wanted to get the hell out of here before she said too much.

Bruno shot to his feet and put his face in Joy's, snatching her full attention. "You live out of that bag. Everything you fled Florida with is in there. So, cut the crap, okay? You might be able to fool your folks, but you can't fool me." He scrutinized her with laser vision. "What's really going on?"

She bowed her head like a remorseful child.

"We all have secrets, Joy. Lord knows I hear enough of them from the ladies at the salon. I'm like a vault so you have nothing to worry about."

What a relief it would be to share this classified information with someone. She wavered, considering coming clean, but clammed up instead. "Quit bugging me. Geez."

"Let me remind you, it's April first, so anything you say can be retracted with an April Fool's *gotcha* and we can forget all about it." Bruno waved his hands like a magician, making any incriminating words disappear.

"Okay, fine. I met someone. April Fool's. Gotcha."

"Lemme guess...some stud from cyber-world sent a snapshot of his junk and got you all hot and bothered? Trust me when I say lots of divorced women go through dry spells. That's an über-hot topic at the salon. I hope you have enough sense to avoid hooking up with any freaks you meet online, interested in nothing more than a booty-call."

Cringing at the concept, she spat, "You're disgusting."

"Don't blame me. Blame the new world of dating. It used to be *I'll strip for you if you strip for me* in the flesh. Nowadays, it's *message me a photo of your privates and I'll message you mine.*"

"If you must know, we met in person. In a bar actually."

"That's original," he snorted. "And you're not telling your parents about this top-secret lover because..."

"He's not my lover. And you know why I don't tell them things—I don't want the lectures. I'm looking at thirty in a few months, for chrissake. Thirty and divorced." Joy slumped, cupping her face in her hands, rubbing the tension from her forehead. "I oughta be allowed to date if I want, except my mother wants me to focus all my energy on being a mom."

"A mom? To who, your dog?" He jutted his powerful chin toward Rex dozing in the corner and snickered, then apologized. "I didn't mean anything by that remark. But the kids don't even live with you yet. If anything, now's the time to get your ya-yas out, before they're here to ruin any chance of fun—not that kids aren't terrific, if you're into that sort of stuff. Never mind—you know what I mean. So, is this guy legit or what?"

"Legit?" She squinted, confused. "What's that supposed to mean?"

"You know…Is he into you? Or is he just looking for a warm body in his bed?"

Joy would have snapped back something snarky, but she wasn't a hundred percent sure what Tristan really wanted from her, considering he wasn't dead-set on staying in Scenic View once the summer ended. If nothing else, at least he'd make for a nice transitional relationship. "I…I think he likes me. That's what I'm hoping to find out. I mean, he invited me over for—"

Bruno stuck up his palm. "I don't need details, cuz. No names. No places. No info. As far as I'm concerned, I know nothing. I see nothing. I hear nothing. I just want peace in this house between you and your mother. Aunt Sophia loves you. You know she's a control freak. Just let her freak flag fly, it doesn't mean you have to salute it. The woman only wants the best for you and your kids. So do us all a favor, don't go starting a relationship with someone who has nothing to offer because you'll never hear the end of it. And do yourself a favor and don't fall in love with the first guy to come along."

****

Cruising under the speed limit to Tristan's, Joy followed the last glimpse of the fading fireball as it sank behind the tall oaks just starting to bud. She knew the way to his house on Hollyhock Hill better than she knew the pangs of her own racing heart.

What if this is a bad idea? An April Fool's prank? She couldn't stand being set up for a letdown. Not again. Not after everything she'd been through—was still going through—with Victor. She was finally standing on her own two feet.

Sort of.

Sure, she was sleeping on her folks' couch. And waitressing at Mr. Lucky's proved to be a bust. But she was making a few bucks off the books working at Violet's Valise. Plus, if things play out her way for once, the part-time slot at Everyday's Christmas would be a full-time position by the fall.

Up and down the steep hills, Joy alternated between a lead foot on the gas and riding the brake, weighing the pros and cons of seeing Tristan again. No matter what reason she conjured for turning around, her high hopes returned to the fact that he sought her out and invited her here.

To avoid any reports of her whereabouts traveling through the grapevine to her parents, she steered clear of the firehouse and took the long way in case anyone paid attention to the new sporty set of wheels that always seemed to turn heads in a town filled with heavy-duty pickup trucks, SUVs, reliable minivans, and economy sedans.

Parked in Tristan's driveway, Joy collected her wits, debating if she should back out and take Rex to the pet shop instead. The pup did well while the car was moving, but now that they stopped he scratched at the door to get out.

"Let's get it over with," she convinced her reflection in the mirrored visor, doing her best to ignore the remnants of her childhood home next door.

Toting in the bulky overnight bag was a bit presumptuous. *What am I thinking, packing for a sleepover?* So she left it in the car and just brought Rex.

"I wasn't sure if you'd make it." Tristan stepped outside the screen door with an ear-to-ear grin.

Inching up the driveway, Joy almost blurted out she wasn't sure either but bit her bottom lip instead, preventing her weak smile from spreading as wide as his. Dumbstruck by the notable difference in Tristan's appearance, she stopped and stared, wondering if he was the same man—

It wasn't just the navy blue tie and cornflower blue collared shirt combination, with dark-washed jeans, polished harness boots, topped with a fitted black leather jacket, making him look like he stepped out of a metro-sexual biker boy fashion magazine, that had her frothing.

Nor was it his glossy, slicked-back hair.

It was his clean-shaven jaw, which looked even better without the manly fur.

Joy snapped back to reality when her dog tugged on the leash in order to reach the ornamental Japanese maple tree and lifted his hind leg. "No, Rex. No. Bad boy. Sorry…"

"Don't worry about it." Tristan's chuckle sounded half-amused, half-nervous. "It's fine. Really."

"I'll douse it with some water so he doesn't kill—"

"Forget about it." Tristan ambled down the porch

steps and nudged her toward the front door. "Aren't you cold?" His breath formed a cloud with the unseasonably crisp temperature.

Not anymore, Joy mused as his slight touch ignited every nerve along her spine, spreading to the rest of the body.

"Get inside before you catch a cold or something."

She followed him up the three steps, and he opened the door, letting her go through first. Memories of their night together flashed like a wild and crazy silent movie in her head. Just when she thought she didn't recall much, she remembered...everything. The bathtub. The kitchen. The couch. The bed. The kiss. The sex.

Once she stepped over the threshold, he crushed her in a hug so tight even his jacket squeaked. "I'm glad you came."

One whiff of his fresh earth and tanned leather scent and she knew—she was glad she came too.

Joy pulled away only to keep her curious eyes on him, unable to believe the tremendous transformation. "Wow. You look...great. Really, really great." She could have said a dozen other adjectives—handsome, gorgeous, sexy, doable—but it was best to keep it simple to avoid saying something stupid.

"And you... You're..." He shook his head as if searching for the right words and just exhaled a smitten sigh instead.

Suddenly self-conscious at his grazing gaze scanning her from head to toe, her cheeks flared with heat. She hadn't known what the night would entail, so she slipped into something simple—her favorite faded skinny jeans, topped with an ivory cap-sleeved blouse with tiny pearl buttons down the front, under a flowy cranberry sweater, and silver ballerina flats that felt more like comfortable slippers.

His bright eyes locked on hers. "Captivating…"

It'd been so long since an attractive man complimented her with such sincerity, she couldn't respond beyond whispering a husky, "Thank you," in return. "Don't take this the wrong way, but I can't help noticing how you look so…" She narrowed her eyes, unable to tear them away from his sculpted cheeks and strong chin now that she could see them without the blur of facial hair. "*Different.*"

He rubbed the bare skin as if he missed an important piece of his true identity. "It was time for a change."

"I hope you didn't do it for me." Joy's lips moved faster than her brain. *Of course he didn't…why would he?* "I mean…I kinda liked the beard. A lot."

"You did?" His brows lifted in surprise. "I knew I shouldn't've listened to 'em," he mumbled.

"Them—who?"

"My buddies. They've been harping on me for weeks to get rid of it. So I went to your family's shop after I saw you and had your pop take it off."

There was no reason to ask how he knew her relatives—small town, one barbershop, loose-lips Lily, and the velocity of the grapevine.

"I guess I could get used to you without it," she said mindlessly, before she could stop the words from falling out. Stroking his smooth cheek was tempting, but luckily she had enough sense to keep her hands safely to herself. As much as she wanted to jump his bones on the spot, what she needed was his friendship. Sex would have to wait until she got past the awkward stage of seeing him again after avoiding him.

In order to break the spell, she shoved her pet between them. "Say hello to Rex." The pup went to town licking Tristan's cheeks and Joy felt an irrational pang of jealousy.

From the dim hallway, Tristan's Yorkie inched closer, reluctant to meet the new furry houseguest in her master's arms.

"Come on, Cookie. Don't be shy. You remember Joy, don't ya?" He scooped her up in one big hand, held her close to his chest as he nuzzled his nose against the top of her head.

Joy's heart melted at his tenderness toward the animals.

"Meet your new"—he glanced at Joy to fill in the blank, then suggested—"playmate?"

Half-shrugging, half-nodding, she said, "Friend is a good place to start."

He turned Cookie around and let Rex smell her tail end. Then did the same with Rex, letting Cookie enjoy a whiff. "There. Best buddies for life now that we got the preliminary greetings out of the way." And just like that, Rex followed his new companion to the kitchen, little nails tapping the hardwood floor.

"You're like the Dog Whisperer."

"Nah. That's an old trick—getting to sniff without having to submit levels the playing field. They should get along fine for a while unless they fight over food, but I put out an extra bowl for Rex."

Joy followed Tristan to the kitchen and set her oversized pocketbook on a stool before noticing the two rubber placemats side-by-side against the wall—one pink with polka dots, the other blue with stripes. On each were two bowls—water in one, kibble in the other. Her heart flipped. Victor never acknowledged Rex, never mind treat the dog like part of the family, even before they filed for divorce.

"That's very thoughtful, Tristan." She swallowed a lump of gratitude before any sentimental tears escaped. "I don't know what to say."

On the counter was another setting for two—a cheese and fruit platter, small white dishes, and stemmed glasses, reminiscent of their first *technically-not-a-date* date.

"I didn't know if you wanted to stay in. Or go out." Tristan ran a hand through his hair, damp with moisture as if he showered moments before she arrived. "Actually, I wasn't sure if you'd even show. I thought your definite-maybe was just an April Fool's joke."

Joy bit her lip, leaving out her similar concern over the silly holiday threat. "I wasn't sure either. I mean…I wanted to see you. But I don't know how this'll work. Friends with benefits."

"Ya know what, just forget about that." Tristan waved his palm as if erasing the past. "I don't know what I was thinkin'. The guys at the bar filled my head with crap about why you didn't call me and how chicks don't dig dudes with beards. Then I saw you—saw how you looked at me—and I didn't know what to say. I didn't want to say *nothing* and let the opportunity to see you again pass without at least trying."

"You consider it an *opportunity* to see me." Joy's smile bloomed. His words were like a bandage on her broken heart, a warm blanket to her soul that had been cold and lonely since her love life hit the skids. She couldn't remember the last time anyone made her feel so special.

"Of course. What else would you call it?" he asked with an innocence that left Joy no room to doubt his words.

Still, she shrugged as her logical head and reckless heart waged a silent struggle over her weakening willpower.

Tristan narrowed his eyes in scrutiny. "You don't think I'm serious, do you?"

Again she shrugged, afraid if she opened her lips she might lunge at him, seeking the kiss she craved.

"I'm not a player, Joy." He edged closer.

"I-I…uhh…never said you were." She tripped over her words, taking a step back, nearly tumbling over the dogs.

He caught her wrist so she couldn't get away. "I wouldn't lead you to believe I was interested in you if I wasn't. Trust me—I know just how much divorce sucks. When everything was said and done, I swore I'd never get involved with another woman ever again—"

Joy tugged her hand to get away, but Tristan held on tight. Sure, she could break free with a swift knee to his groin, but she wasn't in danger, and, to be honest, she wanted to believe him, needed to believe him. There was no way a man could make her feel so good if his intentions were truly bad. The real issue had nothing to do with Tristan's good intentions but everything to do with Joy's readiness to fall in love again.

"Not unless she was worth it." He pressed his lips to her forehead. "And you, sunshine, are worth your weight in antimatter."

"Huh?" She lifted her chin at his odd evaluation.

"Did you know antimatter is the most expensive

thing on earth? It's more valuable than LSD and diamonds 'cause it's so hard to find." He released his grip on her as he fumbled with his words. "I saw something about it on the Science Channel." His hands squeezed the backrest of a wrought iron barstool as if trying to bend the coiled metal. "Oh, never mind."

"That's interesting. And flattering. No one's ever compared me to antimatter, or LSD, or diamonds before."

"That was dumb to say. I shoulda just compared you to diamonds."

"Well…" Joy smiled, capturing his fingers before he reshaped the backrest. "The fact that you think I'm in the ranks of diamonds is pretty incredible." She put his hands on her hips and curled her arms around his waist.

Kissing her neck, he breathed against her ear, "*You're* incredible."

Behind the zipper of his jeans, a familiar firmness pressed against Joy's belly. "And you're…" *Rock hard.* "You're…" She inhaled his pheromonal aroma, getting love-drunk off his potent scent. The well of desire she'd thought dried up during her marriage started to trickle between her thighs, and she hadn't even sipped the wine yet so she couldn't blame her wantonness on the booze. Aroused beyond self-control, instinct and intrigue had her rubbing against him in response. "You're a thoughtful host," she purred for a lack of anything clever to say. "Either that, or you're trying really hard to make me and Rex feel welcome."

"Rex is always welcome in my home. So are you. You know that, don't you?" He tugged her ponytail, tilting her head to view her eyes.

When Tristan licked his bow-shaped lips, Joy couldn't resist planting a soft, closed kiss on them, and pulled back to check his reaction.

"Hey, now..." His mischievous smirk reached those starry blue eyes, more heavenly than the dusky sky. "You sure are a go-getter, aren't cha, sunshine?"

Driven by her overloaded libido, she batted her lashes. "I guess what they say is true."

"What's that?"

"When a girl sees what she wants, she can't help herself." The bold words were a surprise to her ears. Without a second thought, she wrapped her arms around his neck and pulled him down, sucking his kiss, his breath, his energy, until they folded onto the hardwood floor.

Tristan cradled her neck in the crook of his elbow. Matched her kiss and took it further, swirling his tongue against hers. Nibbled her lips. Her chin. The tender spot at her throat. "Ya still living with your folks?" he murmured.

"Unfortunately," she gasped, helpless under his spell.

"Stay with me," he whispered between gentle pecks along her neck. "You need a place. And I got a spare room. Plus I'd enjoy the pleasure of good company. It's a win-win all around."

Yes. Joy silenced her sex drive before shooting off her mouth and shook her head no. "That's not such a good idea." She refused to lift her lids, stuck between the bliss of his kiss and the fear he'd see the truth in her lying eyes.

"Really?" He put his nose to hers so there was no way to avoid eye contact.

"Um…" Unprepared for his startling invitation, she had no plausible fib to fall back on. "No."

"Then stay." His gaze mirrored the tenderness of his plea.

"I can't. It's not right."

"Says who?"

Joy shrugged.

"Just stay until you find a place. I'll see what Nick has for rent. I shoulda thought of it sooner. I woulda, if you called me."

"I didn't mean to blow you off, Tristan, really. I just didn't know if getting involved with you was the right thing—"

He cut her off with a soft kiss before she had time to close her eyes, and he kept his open too, watching her watch him. His tongue made love to her mouth. Deep, warm, connected. A sensual, soul-binding kiss that melted her inside out. Nothing was more intoxicating than a good, knee-weakening kiss from the right man—thank God she was already lying on the floor.

"Does this feel wrong to you?"

Before she could answer, Tristan had her sweater off and the blouse unbuttoned with a single hand. With the other hand supporting her, he managed to unclasp her bra. Lust filled his eyes, scanning her face to her bare breasts, and his fingers followed the invisible line from her throat to her belly button.

Joy's chest heaved, anticipating his next move.

When he lowered his head to drop a torturing trail of kisses from one straining nipple to the other, she gasped in delight. Her words were MIA, otherwise she'd scream: *Finally. Yes. Please. More.*

Instead, she hung on for the ride as he eased her back against the cool wood floor. He popped the button of her jeans and it ricocheted off the wall with a *plink* before bouncing away. She raised her hips as he slipped them down, along with her panties, self-control, and inhibitions.

Still fully dressed, Tristan positioned himself between her knees, aiming face-first toward the top of her thighs.

"What're you doing?" Joy pushed him off but his weight was too much to budge.

"Whaddaya think?" He chuckled as he peeled off his leather jacket and tucked it under her head, then dove down and kissed her *there* just as he'd done above the waist. A master of the art, he combined all the sensual tricks of the trade—suckling, nibbling, gnawing, working her into a tizzy with his magical mouth.

Finally she surrendered and her blurry eyes fluttered shut.

But the beautiful bliss didn't last long once her cellphone rang a recognizable tone from her purse. "Tsk. It's my mother."

Tristan lifted his head, mouth glistening as he smiled from between her knees. "You really want me to stop so you can answer it?"

"Nooo," she heaved. "I don't want you to stop. Ever."

The intruding sound ceased, but Joy couldn't get it out of her head, even with Tristan's tongue lapping her into a frenzy. There must be an emergency if her mother stopped playing bingo to make a phone call.

"Wait—" She grabbed fistfuls of his hair and

tugged hard enough to separate his head from her crotch. "I gotta know what she wants. My dad had a heart attack a few months ago so when she calls I can't help but think the worst."

"Gotcha." He rolled off easily, swiping his lips with his sleeve.

She sprung to her feet, grabbed her bag off the stool, and dug deep to the bottom. If her mother learned to text, Joy wouldn't have to wait for the whole voicemail to play. She listened to the message with one eager eye on Tristan as he slipped off the tie and coiled it neatly around his fist. *"I had a headache so I left bingo early. On your way home, pick up half-and-half for your father's coffee in the morning."*

While he unbuttoned the collar of his shirt, his eyes widened with concerned curiosity. "Everything okay?"

Joy nodded as her mother yammered in her ear. *"How'd it go with the apartment? You still there or are you done yet? What time'll you be home? What're you doing that you can't answer the phone? Call me when you get this message. Love you. Be careful."*

"Everything's fine. I need to pick up coffee creamer on my way home tonight."

"Hmmm. That sounds like a clever insurance policy so you won't pull another all-nighter." He headed in her direction, shrugging out the shirt like a slow strip tease.

God, how can he think of getting sexy while talking about her mother? But instead of taking off his undershirt too, he slipped his shirt around Joy's shoulders.

"Wanna take a quick ride to the store now and drop it off so your folks can rest easy? Get your little errand out of the way so we have the rest of the night to play." He waggled his eyebrows.

"Not really." She buttoned it from the top down, then cuffed the long sleeves.

"Come on…" He picked her clothes off the floor, put the flimsy blouse, sweater, and underwear on the counter, and handed her the pants. "You're seriously not planning on spending the night here?"

"What kinda question is that? Of course I didn't come here with the intention of sleeping over. I just figured we'd spend *some* time together, not the whole night."

"Oh. Okay." Tristan nodded, but the pained look on his face made Joy think he wasn't okay.

"Look, Tristan. I like you. I really do. Friends-with-benefits isn't for me. I was married for ten years to the second guy I ever kissed. Dating was never my area of expertise. When I met you, and we did what we did, I don't know what I was thinking to do such a risky thing with a man I didn't even know."

"So, what're you saying?" His fading smile flat-lined. "You regret being with me?"

"Not at all. I just didn't plan on anything other than living in that moment. After Victor and I split up, I used to say crazy things to make myself feel better, about how I wasn't gonna invest my time committing to anyone."

"Are you tryin' to make me feel better? Or worse?" Tristan retreated behind the counter, putting the granite slab between them. He might as well be a million mental miles away and Joy wasn't sure she could reel him back.

"Let me finish. I talked a big game about how I

was gonna go out with a bunch of different guys, like trying on new shoes."

"I don't wanna keep a girl from an extensive shoe collection. I mean, you can never have enough shoes—right?"

"Stop, Tristan. I said all those things before I met you. Then I did what I did with you. And no, it wasn't a mistake. Not at all. You made me realize I don't wanna try on a lot of shoes. I'm happy with one pair."

"I doubt any girl would be happy with one pair of shoes." A quick smirk appeared but he stiffened his lips, killing the potential smile. Still, she took it as a hopeful sign.

"I realized I'm not a one-night stand kinda girl." With each word Joy inched around the bar, leaving him no place to go unless he hopped over the countertop. "I like the idea of being with one man. I like the idea of knowing what comes next. I like security. And I like you. But I don't wanna put that kind of pressure on you. You've got your own issues. Your own ex-wife and ex-life." Close enough to touch him, she kept her hands to herself because she wasn't sure if he wanted her after unleashing her honesty. "This thing between us, I don't know what you call it, but I want it. I do. I'm just…I'm not sure if now's the right time for us."

"Aww, sunshine." Tristan shook his head as if looking at the most pitiful puppy in the window. "Come 'ere." He pulled her head to his chest. "You think too much. Anyone ever tell you that?"

Swaying together, Joy tried shaking her head yes, but he held it so firm all she could do was listen to his heart beating as rapid as her own. *Maybe it's time for an anxiety pill or two. Or just a glass of wine. No. No alcohol.* That was how she wound up in his bed the first night.

"How 'bout this? I've got some milk in the fridge. We can drop it off—"

"Half-and-half," she clarified.

"Okay. We'll stop at the mini-mart for half-and-half, drop it off to your folks, then we'll come back here to finish our date with ice cream sundaes and a movie on cable."

"That sounds like a great idea...except I didn't tell my folks I was going out with you tonight. I lied and said I was looking at an apartment."

"Is being with me a problem for them?"

"No. Not at all. You're perfect. Me being with anyone is a problem in their minds 'cause I should be setting up a nest for my boys, not hooking up with the best catch in town."

"You think I'm a catch?"

She rolled her eyes and chuckled. "Duh." *Does he not really know his own worth?* "Let's just say, to a pescetarian, you'd be the motherlode of catches. I don't give my folks too much information about my personal life because my ex talks to my mother and the last thing I need is him knowing my business."

"Gotcha." Tristan's firm nod was a good indicator that he understood completely, from one divorcee to another. "We'll pick up where we left off another night."

After finishing the cheese, fruit, crackers, and only a few sips of wine since she planned on driving, they walked their dogs around the block twice before he escorted her to the Jag once she kissed her pooch on the head and left him snuggling with Cookie in the living room.

"You sure you don't want the shirt back?" Joy hoped not because the woven fabric arousing her bare breasts was the perfect keepsake.

"Wear it to sleep and dream of me."

"I'll dream of you anyway, without the shirt," Joy teased in a husky drawl.

"Oooh, that's kinda freaky-deaky, sleepin' topless on your parent's couch, thinking of me. I don't know how I feel about that. I'm not the kinky kinda guy."

"Tsk." She gave him a playful back hand to the belly. "I didn't mean it like that, you perv."

"The offer still stands, ya know." His voice dropped an octave and a seriousness slipped into his tone. He tilted his head and locked eyes with her. "My spare room with a full-sized bed versus your parents' couch. Think it over, seriously."

"I will."

"Meanwhile, don't worry about Rex, he'll be fine."

Remorse seeped into her smile, killing her good mood. "I don't feel right leaving him here. You're sure it's no problem he stays with you and Cookie? I'd put him in a kennel until I find a place but I don't have the heart, and I can't stomach hearing my mother complain about him."

"It's fine, Joy. And if nothing else, it's a little assurance you'll be back." He winked.

"I'll swing by to spend time with him whenever I can. Plus, on payday, I'll give you money toward his kibble and treats."

"How's tomorrow?"

"I don't get paid 'til Friday."

"I mean, come over tomorrow. After work. We'll

finish what we started before our night got derailed." The bright streetlight outlined Tristan's features with an ethereal glow, and Joy cupped his smooth cheek, absorbing his warmth, ensuring he was real and not some figment of her wishful thinking.

A heart-aching sigh escaped her lips, and it took all her effort to deflect the urge to linger a little longer for no reason except to stare at his magnificent face. It had taken all her adult life to find the right man, yet she hadn't found the courage to do what she wanted most, which was to stay.

Like a carousel of guilt, visions of her parents, her boys, and her ex replayed in her head. "I really oughta go."

When he leaned in for a kiss, it was like touching lips with an angel. Could he be the answer to her prayers? *Maybe. Hopefully.* A strange stirring in her soul said he was everything she needed in a companion and more. A mediocre night's sleep on the lumpy couch should help her see things clearly.

Tristan opened the driver's door, obstructing her path as if he didn't want to let her go.

Joy skirted his big body to slide behind the wheel. He shut her door as she started the engine, and she rolled down the glass for a final farewell.

"Drive safe." He reached through the open window to squeeze her hand. "Call me when you get home."

Backing out of the driveway, she said, "I will."

Debra Druzy

Chapter Nine

While Tristan swept up the dog kibble scattered on the kitchen floor, he found the lost button to Joy's pants and dropped it in a shot glass on the counter for safekeeping. Luckily one of the pups hadn't discovered it first. Then he debated throwing her abandoned clothes in the washing machine but didn't want to destroy her stuff, so he put them in the spare room on the bed she could have claimed.

If she lived ten minutes away, plus another fifteen to stop at the mini-mart, it shouldn't have taken longer than thirty minutes to get home. But an hour crept by, so where was the phone call? Was it too early to worry? He had a flashback to the last time she'd left his place, promising to call and never did. But this time was different—he had her dog as collateral.

At least the pooches were comfy, sharing a blanket on the floor in the corner while Tristan paced, checking the signal on his cellphone every few seconds to make sure it worked.

Finally it rang in his hand and he fumbled with the button on the screen. "Joy?"

"Tristan." Her voice trembled as if torn between tears and trauma.

The reception was terrible and he worried he'd lose the call. "You okay?" He pressed the phone to his ear to hear her better.

"I-I'm fine."

"Where are you?" By the sound of the honking horns it was obvious she wasn't home.

"I was pulling out of the mini-mart and some guy ran the stop sign—"

"Don't move. I'll be right there."

He grabbed his jacket and keys as he sprinted out the front door. With his Camaro still in need of an engine part, he hopped on the Harley, strapped the helmet under his chin, and rumbled down the road.

When he spotted Joy's crumpled sports car on Main Street, his heart froze.

Then he remembered: *She's okay. She'd called. She's alive.* Although by the damage to the passenger side, anyone in the death seat would've wound up in her lap. The vehicle that T-boned her was a jacked up monster truck that looked like it could've swallowed the little Jag like a pill. If he had to guess, the driver was the extra-large dude smoking a cigarette, talking to the EMTs, while Joy sat alone, shivering under the bright streetlight, her angelic face as pale as her pearl white car.

When she saw Tristan, she leaped into his arms.

"Hey, sunshine." For her sake, he did his damnedest to appear calm even though his pounding heart was ready to burst. "You hurt?" On quick inspection, she was the perfect specimen of health until he spotted blood trickling from one corner of her mouth. Examining her skull with gentle fingertips, she winced once he discovered a lump above her left ear. "Geez. That's some knot you got. How do you feel?"

"Okay, I guess. I'm still alive. Just shaken up."

"Yo. Fellas," he hollered to the EMTs. "The lady's

bleedin' over here."

"I told them I'm fine. Can you believe the air bag didn't work?" She exhaled a humorless, nervous laugh. "What a hunk of junk. I wouldn't be surprised if Victor rigged it, hoping to get rid of me. I knew I should've traded it for a mini-van."

"You're not fine, Joy." He zoned in on the spot hidden by her thick hair; his thumb and forefinger circled the area.

Joy flinched from the smallest pressure. "Please, Tristan. It's just a bump."

"Just a bump?" Scrutinizing her vehicle, it was impossible to miss the shattered driver's side window. On the verge of losing his cool, he lifted her chin with an unintentional rough touch, checking her pupils. "You broke the glass. With your *head*. Do you have a concussion?"

"No."

"How do you know? Are you a doctor?"

She shook her head, as helpless and confused as she'd been on St. Patrick's Day, only it was worse to see her in such a state because she hadn't been drinking.

"Are you nauseous? Dizzy?"

"No. I just wanna go home." She sat on the curb, hugging herself, with Tristan's arm around her for extra security.

"Did you call your folks?"

"No. Just you," she said weakly, boosting his ego.

"What's the number? I'll let 'em know you're okay." He reached for the cell phone in his breast pocket.

"No." Before he could get it out, Joy slapped his

hand. "I've driven them crazy since I've been here. This'll just upset them even more. I'll tell 'em in person, when I get home."

While the tow truck carted away her mangled vehicle, the EMTs checked on Joy again at Tristan's insistence. Without going to the hospital for a CT scan, they couldn't confirm if she suffered a mild concussion, but she refused to get in the ambulance.

"Victor's gonna kill me," she repeated, more worried about the car than her health.

Tristan was tired of hearing her lousy ex-husband's name. "Accidents happen. Insurance'll cover it."

"He's not gonna be happy when he finds out it's totaled. That's a dealer car." Joy buried her face in her hands and sobbed. "I left my duffle bag in the backseat. It has all my—everything."

"Don't worry. Things can be replaced." Tristan glanced at the white clouds streaking the midnight sky and gave God a mental high-five for sparing this woman's precious life.

Her sobs were almost inaudible over the din from the thin traffic at this late hour, until she gasped for air, trying to steady her breath. He would've sat on the concrete slab with her until sunrise, counting cars speeding by until she was done, but she was exhausted, injured, and could use some TLC.

Finally he tugged her by the hand to help her up. "Come on."

She pulled away, whining, "I told you I don't wanna go to the hospital," as stubborn as his toddler.

"We're not. I promise." He put his only helmet on her pretty little head, careful of her injury. "We're going home."

"Let's just sit here a little longer. Please. I'm not ready to face my folks yet."

"I mean *my* place."

"Oh." A fragile half-smile cracked her childish frowny-face. "Okay, I guess."

Tristan straddled the Harley, started the engine, and put up the kickstand. "Ready?"

With a sigh, Joy slipped the long strap of her bulky purse over her head, across her body for safekeeping, then climbed behind him. She locked her arms around his waist as they rolled away.

When they arrived at his place, she was antsy, and Tristan realized getting her here was the easy part. Convincing her stay the night would take some sweet persuasion.

"Are you worried about your dad having to drink his coffee black in the morning?"

"I'll call my cousin, just to let someone know what happened. I'll ask if he can pick up the half-and-half." She plopped her purse on the coffee table, dug through to find her cellphone, and curled up on the couch.

"You sure?"

"Yeah. I already came clean to him about you, minus the specifics."

After apologizing to Bruno for waking him at midnight, she spilled the quick and dirty version of the collision. "If they ask where I am, just tell them I'm sleeping at a friend's. I'll tell them what happened when I get home," Joy whispered before hanging up.

However sleep was the last thing Tristan would let Joy do with a possible concussion. Instead he made a fresh pot of coffee and lured her to the kitchen with the cheese Danish he'd picked up at the bakery that afternoon, intended for dessert before their date was cut short.

"I can barely keep my eyes open, never mind eat." Joy yawned then dropped her head on the breakfast bar.

"That's just too bad, now isn't it." He filled two mugs and pushed one in front of Joy. He gulped from the steaming cup, equally as exhausted, yet determined to stay awake for her safety's sake.

"Why are you being so mean?"

"You didn't want to go to the hospital when you had the opportunity. I won't risk you not waking up by letting you sleep."

"What're you talking about? Nothing's wrong with me."

Frustrated by her defiance, he slapped the marble countertop on his way to the freezer for an ice pack. "If you fall asleep with a concussion you could slip into a coma."

"That's a myth, ya know." Joy grimaced at the cold pressure from a rock-solid package of peas.

"Whether it is or not, I'm not chancin' it."

"Well, I am." She smashed the bag on the counter, pushed the coffee aside. "I gotta lay down before I fall down." She slid off the stool and Tristan caught her elbow, keeping her in place.

"You cracked a window with your head. That's a traumatic injury. God forbid you really don't wake up—" He shook her for effect, careful not to add to the damage. "What am I gonna tell your parents? What about your kids?" If he didn't want to make love to her as much as he did, he could've throttled her for arguing with him for trying to do the right thing.

"My kids..." Joy rolled her eyes and snickered.

"Like they'd care."

"What's wrong with you? Don't say that."

"Well, it's true." She diverted her glassy green gaze toward the kitchen window.

With a firm grip under her chin, Tristan tilted Joy's face upward, giving her nowhere else to look but into his eyes. "They're young. They don't know any better." Especially if their father's the mean-spirited jerk she described.

She shrugged. "They *are* young, but that's when a kid needs their mother, right? If they don't need me now, they never will." A sprinkle of tears turned into full-blown waterworks.

When he softened his grip to get her a tissue, she bolted from his arm. He sprinted behind her to the living room where she dove facedown on the couch.

"Awww, Joy." He tried to hug her, hold her, console her, but she clung to the throw pillow, not budging, even after the sobs stopped. "I didn't mean to upset you." Finally he flipped her onto her back. "I'm not gonna let you fall asleep, so don't even try it."

"I'm exhausted. Please...let me rest my eyes." The harder he tried to keep her awake, the tighter she squeezed her eyelids together. She bucked and pushed, but still couldn't shake him off. "Damn you."

With no sensible way to end this losing battle, Tristan did the one thing he could think of with Joy pinned supine beneath him. *Time to break out the heavy artillery.* "Stay still, will ya." He snatched her slender wrists above her head with one hand while the other found the zipper of her jeans, already working itself down during the struggle without the button to hold the waistband together.

She stopped thrashing and her lids flew open to almost double their usual size. "What the hell're you doing?" she shrieked.

"Whatever it takes to keep you awake. Unless you don't want me to. Better speak now, sunshine, or forever hold your peace, 'cause anything you say, can and will be used against you."

A wicked smile curved her sealed lips.

"I'll take that as a yes." A quick dip with his fingertip proved she was as slick as a fresh lubed engine.

"Wait." Joy pointed to her purse on the coffee table. "Put one on if you wanna get it on."

He intended to dive down face first, but if she wanted the real deal he wouldn't argue. After kicking off his jeans, he found the strip of condoms, tore one off, ripped open the foil with his teeth, and rolled it on. Hang on, love..." He aligned himself between her thighs. "We're going for a ride." With one hand guiding him home, he slipped inside her like a key in a lock.

With a devilish grin, she giggled and gasped upon each syllable between plunges. "What. Are. You. Gonna. Do...bang me until sunrise to keep me awake?" She squeezed her legs around his hips, synching her rhythm to his.

"Seems I'm gonna have to. Myth or not, you won't take my advice, so you leave me no choice." Equally breathless, he grunted each word, having a helluva time splitting his attention between grinding and gabbing. "Now shut up, will ya. Just enjoy it."

Joy shut up all right, so quiet he wasn't sure if he killed her or if she fell asleep despite his best efforts.

Worried, he paused, and stroked the fringe of hair

off her forehead to get a closer look. "You *are* enjoying it, aren't you?"

She flashed those mesmerizing eyes that mirrored his own lust-laden hunger. "Just kiss me already," she said, breathless, then curled her arms around his neck, pulling him down.

When her cellphone rang again, she ignored it. They both did, caught in a tangle of limbs.

Tristan's volcanic release left him listless, and Joy seemed spent as well but he refused to take her to bed.

Instead he opened the windows wide to cool things off and turned up the volume on the TV, making it impossible to sleep. As an extra precaution, he set the alarm clock on his cellphone for fifteen-minute intervals.

When the dogs nipped at his hand dangling off the couch, he realized he'd fallen asleep with Joy snuggling against his chest, shivering naked under a thin blanket.

"Wake up." He shook her, gentle at first, then nudged her harder when she didn't respond right away. "Joy."

"What's wrong?" she mumbled, rubbing her eyes.

"We slept, that's what." He pressed a button on the cellphone to see why the alarm didn't go off and discovered the battery had died.

"And I survived. See, I could've gone to sleep after all."

Patting her head gingerly with his fingertips, he found the knot. "At least the bump's gone down."

"Good. Then we can skip a trip to the doctor today." The blanket around her shoulders wasn't big enough to cover her lower body, so she skimmed past Tristan to get another one from the pile in the corner.

His vision zoomed in on her curvaceous hips that rivaled the girls in the glossy magazines. And to think, this gorgeous goddess wanted him—a divorced dad. Just when he'd gotten used to the idea of never finding The One to fill all his empty spaces, along came Joy, a perfect fit in every way. The yin to his yang. The woman plucked a chord deep in his soul, like discovering a new favorite song. Things may be developing sooner than he ever would've expected, and faster than he'd allow in usual circumstances, but this affection connection transcended any ordinary physical attraction, although there was no denying her super sex appeal didn't hurt the situation.

After a quick, collaborative shower, Tristan decided he never wanted to wash his own back ever again. He supplied her with a fresh set of his clothes—another pair of cozy sweats, an over-sized T-shirt, and let her wear his leather jacket, while he wore the denim one. From the garage, he dug out a spare helmet.

"Ya ready to go?" He clipped the strap under her chin.

"Nope."

"Come on. They're just parents. And you're an adult. You gotta see 'em sometime. I bet they're worried about you." He planted a quick kiss on her sweet lips, then slammed her face shield down before she slipped onto the seat behind him.

It was a short distance to the condominium complex however Tristan extended the trip by stopping at the mini-mart for a pint of half-and-half and taking a slow cruise along the coastal route before pulling into the parking lot.

Joy jumped off the back and yanked off the helmet,

smoothing her windblown ponytail. "I should've taken an anxiety pill but I left them in the glove compartment."

"Don't worry. You don't need a pill. You're a tough cookie. You'll be fine. I'll wait right here." Tristan pointed to his place, planted on the motorcycle seat.

"Oh, no. No way. Now that I'm already in a world of trouble, you're coming with me."

"I don't know about that." He clung to the helmet pressed against his gut. "Maybe you oughta diffuse the situation before I meet your family."

"Don't be such a baby."

"Me? You're the baby, afraid of your parents."

Joy stared into Tristan's eyes as she curled her finger, beckoning him like she'd done on the dance floor St. Patrick's night, and she owned him once again. Like a charmed snake, he followed her down the sidewalk and up the staircase along the outside of the building.

"If you woulda just told your mother you were spending the night with me you wouldn't've wrecked your car, driving around town at midnight."

"Touché."

Tristan grabbed her on the landing, pulling her against him. "I like a girl that can almost admit when I'm right." He kissed her with confidence. "You're a strong, independent woman. They're just parents, same as you. You're allowed to have friends. It doesn't make you a bad mother. You just happen to be in the middle of a sad situation. And unfortunately you have an ex who isn't making it easy."

"Why couldn't I have had an ex as good as you?"

He looked at her cockeyed. "Sunshine, if you married me you wouldn't have to worry about having an ex." She hugged him hard and didn't let go until he pried her off and prodded her along. "Let's get this over with. Just be cool."

Joy unclasped her fist to ring the bell with a reluctant finger, then sucked in a breath while she waited.

Mrs. Barbieri opened the door with a contemptuous scowl, glaring at her daughter, then Tristan, as she wiped her hands on a dishtowel before snatching the little cardboard container from Joy's fingers. "Well...look who decided to come home."

Mr. Barbieri slammed the newspaper on the kitchen table, sending a small stack of lottery tickets fluttering to the floor. "Where the hell've you been?"

Joy summed up the situation without much detail: leaving Tristan's house last night. Stopping at the mini-mart. Wrecking the Jaguar. "I'm okay."

"Why didn't you call us?" her father boomed.

"I spoke to Bruno..."

"He didn't tell us," her mother snapped.

"I'm sorry—"

"You're sorry," Mrs. Barbieri huffed, rolling her eyes. "You're not happy unless you're ruining everyone else's day, making us miserable. Waiting. Worrying. Every minute is—"

"Like an hour—I know, Ma."

"Let me guess where you spent the night." Mrs. Barbieri's laser vision scanned Tristan from head to toe. "Humph..."

"I went home with Tristan after the accident."

"Nooo kidding." Joy's mother sneered.

The sight of Mr. Barbieri's deadpan face made Tristan regret not taking the man's daughter straight home last night. *Niblet.*

"You," Mr. Barbieri spat, eyes narrow, nostrils flaring. "You were in my shop yesterday, weren't you?" He rubbed his clean-shaven cheeks, making the mental connection. "With the beard?"

Tristan ran a hand down the day-old stubble, recalling the barber who took good care with a straightedge razor. If Mr. Barbieri knew then what he knows now, no doubt this over-protective father would have slit this customer's throat, and rightly so. "Sir…" He put up his palms. "I don't mean to be speak out of turn, but—"

"Then *shaddup*," Mr. Barbieri roared.

"Daddy," Joy squealed.

"Don't daddy me. You stay in my house, and then you don't have the decency to say where you're going and when you'll be back. You don't think we worry about you?"

"I'm almost thirty—when are you going to stop treating me like a child?"

"Never," her mother shouted, red-faced. "You'll always be our child."

Tristan interrupted on impulse. "I agree with your mother."

Joy shot him a dirty look.

"Look, Mr. and Mrs. Barbieri, I have a little girl of my own, so I would react the exact same way as you. I apologize for my part in this. But my only intention was to take care of your daughter."

"Take care of her?" The old man's voice cracked as his eyes darted from Tristan to Joy. "You're back in

Scenic View for five minutes—how long do you know this clown?"

"Take it easy, Bob, please. Calm down. Your heart—remember." Mrs. Barbieri rubbed her husband's back until his panting slowed.

"I met Tristan at"—Joy stalled—"at Mr. Lucky's. On St. Patrick's Day."

"The *other* night you didn't come home." Mrs. Barbieri nodded slow, connecting the dots. "Isn't that right?"

To ease the tension of this cross-examination, Tristan blurted out a less scandalous subject. "I know of a few houses available in town—"

"A house?" Mrs. Barbieri glared in her daughter's direction. "Seriously Joy, how on earth do you plan to pay for it on a part-time salary?"

"I don't mean a house to *buy*. I'm talking about a rental," Tristan explained. "There's one I'm fixing up right now. With a yard. Perfect for two kids and a dog."

"Where is the dog anyway?" Her mother's eyes roved the floor.

"I put Rex in a kennel until I get squared away," Joy lied. "Why must you criticize every aspect of my life, Mother? I can afford to rent a house. Lord knows, there's no way me and the boys can live here. Can't you just be glad I have a friend who wants to help me?"

"You mean a *boyfriend*," her mother chided.

"Boyfriend?" Mr. Barbieri sneered. "What about your husband?"

"Ex-husband," Joy said through clenched teeth.

"So, that's it? You're not even going to try working things out?"

"Daddy, I told you already—he's with someone

else. She's having his baby. Besides, even if that wasn't the case, I don't love Victor. I haven't been in love with him in years. I'm sorry it took me so long to tell you about the divorce, but I didn't want to upset you. I know how mad you were when you found out I married him in the first place. I didn't want to let you down again."

"You can't seem to help yourself, can you?" her father mumbled before turning his back, ending the conversation as he marched away.

"Daddy," Joy cried, but it was too late, Mr. Barbieri slammed a door at the end of the hall.

"When are you going to grow up, Joy? When are you going to stop disappointing your father?" Mrs. Barbieri followed her husband.

"I'm sorry," Joy whispered to an empty room. Then she turned toward Tristan, shaking her head as she said, "I'm sorry I made you come in with me." A fat tear rolled down her cheek and she swiped it with a swift fist. The pained expression tugging her pretty face was easy to read, torn between staying here to please her parents and wanting to run for the hills to save her life.

Before she made another hasty decision she'd regret, Tristan took her elbow, nudging her toward the door. "Come on, sunshine. Let's go home."

Chapter Ten

Once Tristan dropped off Joy at his place and set her up on the couch with a steaming cup of black tea, a fleece blanket, and the remote control, he ran out to do some unspecified errands despite her insisting he stay home to recuperate after all the drama. With Rex and Cookie nestled between Joy's knees, she flipped the TV channels, searching for something comical to erase the agonizing memory of the verbal lashing from her parents but it didn't work.

Thinking of work—good thing this was her scheduled day off, otherwise she'd have some explaining to do to Lorraine about why she hadn't shown up. That bit of relief eased her mind enough to gather her wits, fortify her frayed nerves, and figure out the future while she drifted in and out of a much-needed nap.

The rush of water rattling the downspout jolted Joy awake.

Heavy rain gushed against the living room windows, making it impossible to see anything between the blinds except the glowing dots of streetlights along Hollyhock Hill.

How many hours had passed without a phone call from Tristan? Her empty gut tightened into a nervous knot. No matter how careful the man might be, riding a motorcycle was daunting enough without inserting a downpour and darkness into the equation. New anxiety stripped away the last bit of her crumbling composure.

Then the springs of the screen door squeaked. *Finally.* Jangling keys probing the lock had the dogs leaping off the couch, barking out of synch.

Strange, there was no warning of rumbling tailpipes to announce Tristan's arrival. Joy froze—if it wasn't Tristan, then who could it be?

His friend Nick had a key. Maybe the man was coming to fix another meal.

Worst-case scenario would be his ex-wife, *Whatshername.* They shared a child after all, perhaps he entrusted the woman with a spare key. Joy and Victor had two children; still she was doubly sure she'd never give the jerk a key. Wouldn't Tristan have mentioned something about his ex having a key when he invited Joy to move in?

Just in case... She would've sprinted down the hallway to hide before the front door flung open but it was too late, so she threw the blanket over her head hoping to blend into the furniture.

"Joy?"

Tristan. She exhaled in relief then emerged from her cocoon, stretching and yawning for effect.

"Sorry to wake you." Empathic eyes searched hers. "Feelin' any better?"

"Much. Back's a little sore still."

He touched the bump on her head. "Swelling's gone down." Warm hands rubbed the aches along her spine with just the right amount of gentle pressure as he nudged her toward the front door. "Take a look outside. I got somethin' to show you." His chest puffed up with pride.

Joy spotted an object larger than a breadbox with wheels parked in the driveway.

"Whaddaya think?"

It was difficult to know what to think considering the details were blurred by rain.

"Can't take a motorcycle everywhere, can we?"

We? Joy's heart smiled but she fought to keep it off her face, not wanting to take this *we*-business too seriously, too soon.

"A pickup truck was my first choice, figuring I could take it to work when you're not using it. But a van makes better sense, ya know, for the kids. Nothing fancy. Good enough for toting tools and tots.

His face brightened with boyish delight as he flicked a wall switch wired to the floodlights over the garage, illuminating the night like sunshine. "*Ta-da.*" The shower tapered off to a drizzle, revealing the rain-slick custom paint job.

What the hell? A solid dark moss would've been perfect. Even metallic olive would have been nice. But garbage truck green? With thick white racing stripes down the hood and along the side, no less. Not quite the family vehicle she'd pictured carting the boys around in; it was more like a tailgater's wet dream. Lacking words to match Tristan's excitement, she pressed her nose to the glass door and bit her bottom lip in soundless shock.

Say something. Anything. From the corner of her eye, Joy stole a glimpse of him as his chest gradually deflated and she stifled the wisecracks. "Uhm…hmm…thank you." Hopefully she came across more grateful than her meager mumbling sounded.

"Ya don't like it, do you?" His face drooped like a

kid whose ice cream cone landed upside down in the sandbox. "I shoulda checked with you before buying it, huh?"

Thinking about flying over the radar around town in this minibus made Joy cringe and she stalled to answer. She forced a sweet smile then hid her lying eyes by putting her nose to the glass again. "I like it. I really do. Really…What's not to like? You're right, it's awesome." She slathered on the fib before tossing a glance over her shoulder in time to catch his smile returning in full force—*Thank God*, the last thing she wanted was to insult his judgment after he'd gone out of his way to do something so considerate. *The type of vehicle doesn't matter—it's the thought that counts.*

"I bought it from a New York Jets super-fan who's upgrading to a tricked-out camper." Tristan beamed as he spun the key ring on his finger. "Another guy wanted it but I got there first."

"Wow." She refrained from giggling at his innocent enthusiasm. "You got lucky, huh? Where's your Harley?"

"At the dude's house."

"You oughta get it before the rain starts coming down again."

"I asked Nick for a ride but he's busy. Are you up for givin' the Green Machine a quick spin? It's safer than a sports car."

Physically, she was well enough to drive, but psychologically, the thought made her uneasy. "I don't feel like driving right now."

"Don't let that accident wreck your confidence." He kissed her forehead. "The sooner you get behind the wheel the better off you'll be."

"Oh, fine." Joy sighed as she slipped on her sneakers and into the cardigan.

Once she climbed into the driver's seat, adjusted the mirrors, and eased out of the driveway onto the empty road, she realized he was right as usual. When the mist turned to crystals, melting like tears on the windshield, she flicked on the wipers without a fumble. Not much different than the Jag, only bigger. Waiting at the intersection for the green arrow, Joy glanced at Tristan's perfect profile in the stream of headlights from oncoming vehicles. *What a fine looking man. Why would a newly divorced man want to spend so much time with one woman when he could easily date someone different every night of the week?*

"Everything okay?" His eyes touched hers, and she snapped her head forward.

"Umm. Yeah. Of course." Her heart fluttered faster than the wiper blades. "You didn't have to do this, you know."

"Do what? Buy a practical vehicle? This isn't exactly practical, is it?"

Joy shrugged, forgetting what the Green Machine looked like on the outside from the comfort of the captain's seat. "Practical enough."

"More practical than the Harley, that's for sure. I can't even bring home a pizza. I probably shoulda got a sedan or an SUV, but this baby caught my eye and I couldn't refuse. I've been meaning to buy a family car since my ex kept the minivan," Tristan rambled.

Tempted to ask if his ex kept anything else—like the spare key to the front door—Joy refrained as she concentrated on the road. When they got to the house where his Harley stood under the carport, he gave her a smooch before hopping out and leading the way home through the freak flurry.

Their appetite kicked in before the pizzeria closed, so they phoned in a large cheese pie for delivery and ate it in the living room while watching the weatherman's report of the spring snow shower.

"So..." Tristan inhaled a third slice then licked tomato sauce off his fingers. "Like I was telling your parents, Nick's got a few rentals that might interest you."

His sudden switch of the gears, from precipitation to property, gave Joy conversational whiplash, and she gagged on a glob of mozzarella.

"You okay? Here—" He handed her a glass of water. "Take a sip."

When she regained her composure, she blurted the first thing to pop in her head. "How 'bout the house next door?"

"Yeah, he owns that one too. But it's a mess. It'll take a few months before it's ready. In the meantime, he's got a bungalow on the beach that we renovated. Not sure how you feel about living so close to the water with the kids and the dog."

Restraining her disappointment over never getting her hands on her childhood home, she swallowed a sigh. "Something with a fenced in yard would be better."

"That's what I thought. There's another house but it's only got two bedrooms. The boys can...can—" Tristan fought back a sneeze and lost. "Share."

"God bless you." Joy offered him tissue from the box on the end table. "If the price is right, I'd give them each a room."

"Where would you sleep? On the couch?" He slid her a disapproving glance. "He's got other property outside Scenic View if you don't mind living a few towns away."

Disheartened, she shrugged; tired of this conversation, exhausted from this whole crazy day.

"Or…" With his lips pressed tight, he inhaled through his nostrils and held it in quick contemplation. "How about you and the boys stay here. With me. The house looks small, but there's plenty room for all of us." His words fell out slow, as if he'd already given extensive thought to the delicate situation before releasing it to the universe. "Just until the right house comes along. Or forever." He smiled, hopeful.

A nervous giggle escaped her throat. "I don't want to cramp your style."

"I wouldn't've asked if I thought you would. So whaddaya say?"

"I—" She bit her tongue, stopping her scrupulous brain from spitting out some morally appropriate, polite refusal, while the sharp pain deterred her hasty heart from leaping over the edge of happily-ever-after singing *yes, yes, yes* in orgasmic enthusiasm.

"Before you say no, come on…" He tugged her by the wrist. "I never gave you the full tour, did I? See for yourself, then make an educated decision."

Joy skated in her socks as he pulled her across the hardwood, around the already familiar first floor. "You've seen my room," he said with a subtle grin, not making it sound as sleazy as he could've. "Next door's Nicole's room—I'm not done painting it yet." He flicked on the light across the hall, where Joy spotted the clothes she'd abandoned last night in his kitchen, neatly folded on a full-sized bed. "I don't want you to feel obligated to sleep in my bed." A smattering of red crept into his cheeks. "I mean…I wouldn't kick you out if you did." He flinched as he fumbled for the words as if he neglected to rehearse this part of the sweet speech. "That didn't come out quite right, did it?"

She shook her head, not because she agreed, but because she understood his adolescent awkwardness, feeling something similar.

"Then there's the…the"—*sneeze*—"basement." He opened a door to a downward staircase and flicked another wall switch.

"You okay?"

"Just allergies."

The open floor plan was nothing elaborate, with beige wall-to-wall Berber, pale paneling, and a drop ceiling with florescent lights. A treadmill and free weights occupied one corner diagonal from the washing machine and dryer squatting next to stacked laundry baskets and a tall rubber garbage pail doubling as a hamper to catch the dirty clothes from the chute upstairs.

"I bet your boys would love a *testosteroom* all to themselves."

"A testoster-what?" Joy cocked a curious brow.

"You know, a hangout all to themselves. My brothers and I had a No Girls Allowed zone to keep our little sister out of our stuff. It wouldn't take much to partition this space into two bedrooms and a den."

If her boys were a little older, they'd love the junior man-cave concept, however Joy doubted a five- and seven-year-old would stand one night.

"Put a big TV over there." Tristan pointed to an

empty wall, mapping his vision in the air, waving his hands like a magician. "Do they like video games?"

"Does your daughter like princesses?"

"I'll take that as a *hell, yeah*. We'll get a couple of gaming chairs. An Xbox or PlayStation, or better yet, both. It'll be like heaven."

Tristan's idea started materializing for Joy, and as much as she would have loved to say yes to everything, she couldn't.

To avoid any impulsive promises she'd wind up breaking, she hopped on the treadmill, put in the key and pushed the Start button. "I haven't worked out in weeks." That was the truth, and it was showing in snugger-than-usual clothes. "Do you use this stuff?" she huffed, adjusting the speed to a slow powerwalk in socks.

"I did in my old house. After I moved out, I was gonna put it all in storage, figuring I didn't know how long I'd be staying in Scenic View. Why bother to move it here to there, only to move it again, ya know?"

Joy nodded, panting, feeling the burn in her calves. After a minute, she dropped the speed, pulled out the key, and hopped off before hurting herself without sneakers.

"Nick talked me into setting it up. Said we'd get back into our old workout routine." Tristan snorted as if a private joke crossed his mind. "So far it's been collecting dust. But feel free to use it whenever you want. Maybe you'll motivate me to get back in shape."

"I like your shape."

Tristan smacked his stomach. "It used to be better. If you move in, we can exercise together." He took her hands, weaving his fingers with hers. "Whaddaya say?"

She averted his invitation by playing coy. "We don't have to live together to work out together."

"I know." In a fluid motion, Tristan pulled her against him and circled his arms around her waist, keeping her hands at the small of her back, giving her no alternative but to arch toward him. "But I want you here."

How could she debate the pros and cons of moving in with the pressure in his pants teasing her tummy? *This isn't the time to be making commitments and living arrangements.* "I would, but I don't know if that's a good idea."

"'Cause of what your folks'll say?"

Bingo. Her stomach clenched at the unwanted reminder. "I never thanked you for coming to my rescue last night, did I? And then putting you through my parents' wrath today."

"Being a cop for so long, I've witnessed more than enough domestic disputes. I felt bad they ganged up on you. I can understand overprotective parenting, but you're an adult. You're not cheating on your husband. You haven't abandoned your children. In fact, all I see is a good woman trying to make a place in the world for herself and her kids. What more do they expect from you?"

"They want me to live life by their rules. They never got over me eloping with Victor. I knew they wouldn't've approved of me getting married so young to someone they didn't even know. Then I got pregnant, and that made everything harder. When we divorced, I didn't tell my folks until after the fact, so in their minds I'm just a sneaky liar. They don't realize how hard it is to talk to them sometimes. I didn't have the guts to tell 'em the truth. What can I say? I'm just a chicken."

"No. You're not." Tristan's eyes locked on Joy's as he swayed her in his arms, still holding her hands hostage above her backside, not giving her any way to avoid the full force of his attention. "Sounds to me like you're a people pleaser. Worried what others think. What they're gonna say. How they're gonna react. No matter how tough you try to be, I can see it on your face…the hurt…the pain. You gotta do what makes you happy, sunshine. Life ain't worth living if you don't live the life you want. For yourself. And your kids."

Joy blinked; it was the only way to escape the brutal honesty of Tristan's words. Thank God a lump thickened in her throat, otherwise she might argue he was wrong, when in actuality the man was a gazillion percent right. Everything he said took her therapist months to conclude. How could he know her so well in such a short time? Was she really that transparent? "Maybe one day, after we've dated for a *respectable* length of time."

"Who determines what's respectable? Your parents? Just remember, sometimes *one day* never happens." His wise, fatherly tone made Joy doubt her uncertainties. "You deserve to spend your time with people who love you unconditionally, not people who want you to fulfill all their conditions."

Joy cringed at the word. "Don't…don't use that four-letter word. Pick any word other than *love*." She spat it out like fuzz on her tongue.

"Okay…I get it." He snickered, seeming unoffended. "It's too soon for definitives. Normally I would agree with you. The word just slipped out—not that the sincerity isn't there. I wouldn't have asked you to move in if I didn't feel something for you. Something more than wanting to have a good time."

"No…I'm sorry. I just have a hard time hearing *that* word directed at me."

Tristan released her wrists only to wrap his arms around her shoulders, pressing her head to his chest as he spoke against her hair. "If you don't think you and the boys'll be happy here then—no hard feelings—by all means, I'll help you find a more suitable place. It won't change how I feel about you. Although my gut tells me you already like it here, just as much as Rex."

"I do, but…" She curled her arms around his hips and hooked her thumbs in the belt loops of his jeans. "It's not that I don't agree with everything you said…"

"But, what, sunshine?" He lifted her chin, angling her face toward him so her eyes couldn't lie. "If I'm wrong, then tell me. If I'm right, then stay. Don't worry about what anyone says. Your folks. Your ex. I'm sure your boys'll get used it. If anyone asks why we're moving so fast, just tell 'em we're old friends from a previous life. Or don't say anything all. What does it matter as long as you're happy? Tell me the truth…" He dropped kisses across her temple. "Do I make you happy?"

Joy melted into the warmth of Tristan's embrace. His rapid heart pounded beneath his sweatshirt as quick as her own. He made her feel…everything. Above all, he made her feel safe. "Yes. You make me happy. Being here, with you, makes me happy."

"Then stay."

His tender tone soothed her aching soul. "You make it sound so easy."

"It is." He chuckled. "Just don't leave. Ever…" His

mouth teased hers.

"Ohhh, Tristan…" she gasped, under his spell.

"Less debating," he murmured, "More kissing. Maybe it'll convince you I know what I'm talkin' about."

Conjoined at the lips, still wrapped in each other's arms, Tristan inched forward, forcing Joy to walk backward until her calves touched the hard edge of something solid. He nudged her, and she tipped back; her cushioned tush made a soft landing on the staircase, and he dropped to his knees one step below.

Without breaking the kiss, they crawled up the staircase like an octopus in a frenzy. When they reached the first floor, he scooped her up and carried her to his room, where he dropped her on the bed with a bounce.

In the heat of the moment, Tristan was a record-breaking rodeo cowboy, peeling off the clothes she borrowed from him, never taking his mouth off her skin. It happened so fast, but it felt so right… She never wanted to leave. *Tristan's right about everything.* Soft swipes of his flat tongue had her grasping tufts of his silken hair, steering him toward her pearl of pleasure, not that he needed any assistance finding the sensitive spot. The multi-talented *Mr. Right* happened to be a master at the art of oral foreplay—something Joy lived without during her marriage. The strange and powerful magic of Tristan's eager mouth recharged the dying battery of her lonesome libido.

Thank God he was the one and only one-night stand on her sexual resume. What luck to have found him first. She needed this…needed him. Needed to feel important. Welcome. And that forbidden word…loved.

Wait—what happened to reclaiming her

independence? Falling for Tristan wasn't part of the original plan, but he truly was a Casanova—saying all the right words, making all the right moves, giving her all the right feelings. If only her heart and ego weren't damaged goods.

Why couldn't I have met him before Victor?

No—that's terrible. If I hadn't met Victor I wouldn't have my two beautiful boys...who want nothing to do with me. Joy moaned, desperate to shove aside the depressing thoughts as she strained to keep her attention on Tristan's lavish affection.

Maybe the boys'll like him. Maybe they'll want to be with me again, like they had when they were babies, if I found them a suitable stepfather.

Stepfather? Don't get ahead of yourself.

While his tongue swirled against her skin, her mind was a neurotic circus. Faces of her boys, her parents, her ex, his daughter flooded Joy's conscience, so she slammed the mental door, kicking the maddening mob out of her head. *Sayonara.* Leave her alone to concentrate on Tristan, his magnificent mouth, his nimble fingers which pressed all the right buttons, especially the one deep inside, making her scream for more.

*Sweet Lord...*she could get used to this undivided attention.

Joy gripped the blanket to ground herself while he drove her to the edge, one-handed. *Ride 'em, cowboy.* She squeezed her eyes, gritted her teeth. *Yes, yes, yes.* The overwhelming wave crashed Joy's consciousness, catapulting her into an endless lust-laden sea. Once she ceased writhing in pleasure-pain, she drifted with the blissful tide, floating on and on and on...forever.

Tristan parked his fully dressed frame beside her on the mattress, then smoothed away the strands of hair clinging to her cheek. "So?" He leaned over her, blocking her view of the spinning ceiling. "Did'ja like that?" His face beamed with satisfaction and a smug smile teased his lips.

Laying there recuperating, all she could do was breathe and blink as the haze cleared from her brain. *Like* it? She would have said she loved it, but after making a huge fuss over the little word, she gave a lazy nod instead. "Mmm hmm."

"Good to know. Think you can handle the real deal?" He wagged his brows.

Joy slid a weak hand down his torso until she reached the prize in his pants, sizing up the generous girth under the denim. "Is this rocket in your pocket ready for lift off?"

His confident expression melted into a heavy-lidded, drunken grin. "Ready when you are, sunshine." He rolled over, rummaged through the nightstand drawer, and pulled out a carton as big as a tissue box. "Economy size." Tristan held it up proudly, grinning as innocent as the devil in a halo. "They were on sale. I just spent all my cash on a new car, so I gotta budget what's left of my money." He winked. "Plus, with one new sibling on the way, I figured your boys have enough to handle. We don't want to steal Victor and his fiancée's thunder. They'll think we're just tryin' to show 'em up with an even cuter kid. Then your folks'll get all crazy, trying to control everything. Besides, we're young enough, we have plenty of time to make a baby."

Scratching her head, his train of thought added to

her dizziness. "You talk too much, ya know that?"

"And you get me horny too much." He adjusted the inseam of his jeans for proof.

Joy pressed a firm palm to his broad chest as if it were enough to hold back this big bear of a man. "You're sure this just isn't about sex?"

Tristan circled her wrist with one hand and wove his between hers. "It's about kissing you goodnight. And your hair spread across my chest in the morning. About washing each other's backs in the shower. It's everything. Sex is a bonus. The benefit of being your soulmate."

"Soulmate?" Joy almost choked.

"Of course. Dontcha believe in soulmates?"

She shrugged, downplaying her curiosity in his theory.

"Don't tell me your ex-husband ruined that for you too?" He shook his head in disbelief then balled his fist, mumbling, "First Santa, now soulmates. Geez, what I'd like to do to that guy."

Sure, Joy felt something out of the ordinary for Tristan, but did it qualify as soulmates? She didn't know. "What do you consider a soulmate?"

"A soulmate is…" His gaze searched the ceiling as if the answer hovered somewhere above and beyond, and his smile brightened. "That one person who's your perfect fit."

"Was Stacy yours?" Her chest tightened anticipating his response.

"I thought so, at one time. But we were different people way back when." Tristan leaned on the mountain of pillows against the headboard and pulled Joy into the crook of his arm. "How 'bout Victor?"

154

"No. Not at all." She gazed into his eyes, gauging his reaction, hoping anything she said wouldn't sound too stupid as she let the truth fly. "I was lonely. All my friends in college were engaged, planning graduation-weddings. Victor happened to be in the right place at the right time. It just seemed like the right thing to do."

"So he really wasn't your soulmate, huh?" A strange grin twitched on his lips that made her sit up, wanting to know why.

"Does that sound funny to you?"

"Of course not. I'm just glad he's not your soulmate, 'cause that leaves the position open for someone else. Like me."

"I'm not looking for a soulmate."

"That's too bad. You already found him."

"How can you be so sure?"

"I just know." He brought her palm to his heart. "In here." Then with his index finger, he traced a line from the tip of her nose, down her throat, stopping at her cleavage, stroking the space between her breasts. "All that feel-good magical stuff...it lives right in here. In your heart. Along with hope. Dreams. Wishes. Happiness. And that dreaded L-word you don't wanna hear." He glided his finger back up the trail and tilted her chin to see into her eyes. "Soulmates, too."

"It's pretty crowded in there."

"You'd be surprised how much can fit."

"Maybe." *Who am I kidding?* Tristan was right on all accounts, so why was she resisting? "I guess."

"No maybe. No guessing. Either you feel it or you don't. I know how I feel. And since you're here, laying on my bed, in my arms, in your birthday suit, you must feel it too."

It was too soon to assign words to her jumbled emotions. "I don't know what I feel. I just know I don't want to be anywhere else than here…with you."

Tristan unleashed a pent-up sigh of relief. "That's all I wanted to hear." He sprang off the bed and kicked off his pants, yanked the T-shirt over his head. Standing there, between Joy and the bedroom door, light spilled in from the hallway, setting his profile aglow, from his tousled hair to his jutting erection.

I do that to him. It was almost hard to believe… "Wow," she whispered at the glorious sight of his arousal.

Even on the best day of her marriage, she had to work Victor to his full length with her hands and mouth before his little soldier stood at attention. However Tristan's willing warrior seemed eager to see her.

When he dropped one knee on the mattress, putting that ginormous joystick within reach, Joy couldn't resist stroking him from root to tip, making him suck in a sharp breath through his clenched teeth.

He likes it.

She did, too. He was softer than a rose petal. Thick and hot between her fingers. She stroked him again, hoping for the same subtle approval. "Does that feel good?"

"Oh, yeah…I love your hands on my body." He groaned and pushed his pelvis toward her. "But—don't take this the wrong way, sunshine—my head is pounding."

"I know. I can feel it." She gave him a gentle squeeze, and it throbbed in her palm.

"I'm not talking 'bout that one. This headache's been coming on all day."

As he fell onto the bed, Joy rolled aside to give him her warm space. "We don't have to do this. Just say so, and I'll stop."

"That's it—I don't want you to stop."

"Wanna take two aspirins and wait a little bit? See if it goes away?"

"It's probably allergies kicking in. Keep doin' what you're doin'. You're taking my mind off the pain."

"If my hands make you feel better, maybe my mouth would be like medicine."

Wide-eyed, Tristan nodded. "Yes, please…"

Joy crawled between his legs, and with her fingers wrapped around the length, she angled him toward her lips as she lowered her face, taking him in her mouth.

"Awww, God. Yeah. That's it." He clenched her hair, easing the burden off her neck as she bobbed. "Let's play doctor more often."

The man was so easy to satisfy. Nothing at all like the exhausting effort to work her ex into an unusable pencil stub. She gave Tristan her all, anticipating his volcanic eruption, but he nudged her aside instead.

"Stop. I don't wanna finish like this. Dontcha—ah, ah, ah…" He fought a back a sneeze but lost. "Dontcha wanna come together?"

His glassy eyes and rosy nose were enough to make a swift diagnosis. "I'll take a rain check when you're feeling better."

"If you gimme a minute I'm sure I'll get my second wind." He sniffled.

"Don't worry about it. I'll tell you when I'm ready to collect." Joy shivered. It was too mild to put on the heat yet too chilly without the covers.

"Grab a T-shirt." He jutted his chin toward the tall

dresser of five drawers.

She started in the middle but it was filled to capacity with socks.

Tristan aimed his thumb toward the ceiling. "Up."

In the next drawer was a stash of boxer-briefs, so she slipped into a pair more comfy than a thong.

"T-t-top." He struggled with the word as a trio of sneezes jolted him upright, reaching for a tissue box on the nightstand.

"I think it's time to do laundry. You're running low." As she counted three undershirts left in the drawer, her fingers brushed something cool…hard…metallic? "I'll throw in a load of whi—" A glimmer caught her curious eye. *Handcuffs*—just like the ones they sell in Violet's Valise Sextra-Special Online Store. Pushing the shirts aside, she uncovered a pistol too. It was no secret the man was a cop on-leave, but she hadn't expected to find this *stuff*. Joy left the gun, untouched, and pulled out the cuffs. "Well, well, well…" Nodding, smiling, she turned to show him what she'd uncovered.

"Well, what?" He blew his nose like a trumpet. "Oh. No."

"Ooh, yeah…" She sauntered toward the bed, holding steel circles to her bare breasts like a bikini top. "Can we play with them one day? When you're feeling better?"

"No way." He buried his face in a fist full of fresh tissues as he caught another round of sneezes.

"Have you ever used them foolin' around?"

"Never."

"I find that hard to believe, Officer Casanova," she teased, working all her curves. "Bondage is the latest craze with all the play-date mothers ever since *that book* started circulating."

"I wouldn't know. Stacy didn't do play-dates. And she wasn't into sex games. W-w-why?" He sneezed. "Are you?" A devilish smile curled his lips.

Her ex might have been a great philanderer, but he'd been nothing more than a vanilla-lover to Joy. And with his bite-sized physique, being man-handled never crossed her mind. "I dunno. I never tried it before either. And I wouldn't've trusted Victor enough to lock me up."

His interest piqued, Tristan propped his back higher against the pillows. "You're saying you trust me enough?"

"Maybe. I mean...if we're really soulmates like you say then I have nothing to worry about. Do I?"

He scratched the back of his head as if contemplating the right answer. "Look, they aren't for sex games, sunshine. Do you know how many perps wore these cuffs? Get 'em away from your skin. Geez. They ought to be sterilized first." He snatched them from her hand.

"So you *would* be willing to use them on me?"

"You're serious." He arched a suspicious brow. "You really want me to put you in handcuffs?"

"Yep." She crawled between his legs, lowered her face to his crotch, and put her Jockey-clad tush high in the air, wiggling it for effect. "Then I want you to get behind me and—"

Tristan slipped out from under her and jumped to his feet. "Joy, I appreciate your untapped kinky side. We'll go to the store to get all the props you want. Cuffs. A vibrator. Nipple clips. Whatever you like. Just don't play with these." He put the handcuffs back in their place, deflating the erotic mood.

"Okay. Fine. I was just kidding anyway," Joy lied. She rolled off the bed to slip on the T-shirt when Tristan captured her wrists from behind.

"See. Not a very comfortable position, is it? Now imagine those heavy steel cuffs." His inescapable grasp mimicked the real deal as he induced a miniscule taste of pain that made her damp between the thighs.

Being handled by this he-man had her insides hot and tingly. A groan of wanton pleasure squeaked from her throat. "I am."

"This isn't too rough for you?" In a fluid motion, he spun her while maintaining his grip. Face to face, with fingers laced behind her back, the vulnerable position accentuated the arch of her spine, pressing the tips of her breasts against his chest. "You really want it like this?"

Her cheeks flamed with embarrassment and moisture clouded her vision of the outlandish fantasy she craved. "I do."

"Seriously, Joy. Are you messin' with me? 'Cause I don't wanna hurt you."

Tristan would never hurt her; she was certain of it. Inching up on her toes to reach his lips, he met her halfway in a potent kiss before he trailed down her neck to nibble one tender bud then the other. At the mercy of his mouth, she gasped, "Please."

"I'm pretty sure I can have my way with you without cuffs." He chuckled.

"True. But it's more than that."

"Can't I just tie you up with a rope?"

"You have any?" Her voice quivered with new

hope.

"Not within arms' reach. But I have a belt. How 'bout a tie? Will that work?"

"It's not about being tied up with a rope, or a belt, or a tie. I saw the cuffs and…and it turned me on, that's all. Let's just forget it." She wriggled away then pulled the T-shirt over her head.

"You sure?" Tristan sneezed and yawned in one awkward motion. He rubbed his face like giving his eye sockets a massage and plopped backward on the bed with a painful grunt.

"You really don't feel well, do you?" Joy pressed the back of her hand to his forehead. How could she have misread his body heat? "You have a fever."

"See what you do to me?" He grinned, but his glassy eyes were no joke.

"No, really—get some rest. No more foolin' around until you're better. I'll make you some tea." She wrapped the blanket around him like a big baby in a cocoon.

It seemed like ages since she tucked in her boys. She'd forgot how much she missed it. Missed them. Her babies would be all grown one day and the opportunity to make memories will be gone.

But they didn't want her; they told her so. They wanted their father. It didn't help dwelling on it, but how was she supposed to avoid it? Joy blinked back a tear before it could fall.

"I know you don't want to hear this"—Tristan's lips twitched at the corners as he grabbed her hand before she could escape, pulling her back into the moment—"'cause you think *love* is a dirty word. But I just gotta say it—I love you, Joy. I really do. Don't look so sad because I won't let you play with my handcuffs. I'll tie you up some other time if that's what you want. All day and night—like my little concubine—if that'll make you happy. My own little Princess Leia in a dog collar and a golden bikini. Tie you up. Tie you down. I just want you to be happy."

As silly and eccentric as his offer sounded, it soothed the sting of his refusal and the rejection from her boys. For a moment she forgot her tears, and let a smile slip from under her frown. "Promise?"

"Sure. I promise."

Chapter Eleven

The flu put Tristan out of commission like an anvil flattening Wyle E. Coyote. His illness-induced dreams were a mash-up of dark images and nonsensical words, churning without direction or meaning. Not exactly nightmares. More like Alice in Wonderland-ish fantasies. And in all of them, Joy was there, saving him from the pitfalls. He took the subconscious message as a very good sign.

"Well, whaddja think would happen if you never get vaccinated?" Joy chastised in a mild tone, following up with a soft kiss on the forehead, lingering long enough to test his temperature with her lips. While Tristan drifted in and out of a fatigued fog for more days than he could count, she'd been keeping him alive with fluids and meds like a regular Florence Nightingale.

"I don't like putting that crap in my body," he mumbled low but it was still loud enough to rattle his aching brain.

"That *crap* could've kept you from getting the full-blown flu. I bet you make sure your daughter gets vaccinated." No matter how hard his defense, she had a quick comeback. "Maybe next year you'll think twice."

Gritting his teeth and staying quiet was his passive-aggressive way of agreeing with the woman as she served another shot of liquid decongestant that tasted

Debra Druzy

worse than Jägermeister and two tablets to relieve the body pain and headache, before inserting the thermometer beneath his tongue.

Waiting for the mercury to rise, she tucked the blanket around him like a mummy. Opened the window an inch, letting in a sun-soaked breeze to freshen the stagnant germified air. Propped his cellphone on the nightstand beside a cup of steaming tea and new box of tissues.

When the time was right, she pulled out the thermometer and squinted to read the results. "No fever for a change. That's good. Don't forget to take another dose around one. I'll call to remind you."

"Where ya going so fast?" He grabbed the hem of her new seafoam green bathrobe, not letting her get away.

"Gotta get ready for work before I'm late…again. We're both lucky my boss likes me." Joy's sweet giggle had him feeling guilty for putting her through this rigmarole. He'd make it up somehow.

"Where today?"

"The Christmas Shoppe. I don't know how much longer I can juggle two jobs. Lorraine keeps giving me more hours, although I shouldn't complain because I need the cash. If she ever lets me go full-time I'll have to quit Violet's."

Tristan lost the thread of their conversation but enjoyed the sound of her melodious voice.

He'd slept in bliss most of the time since getting his ass kicked by the wicked virus but one thing he realized through his haze was Joy seemed a lot more relaxed now that she had the run of the house while he was laid up. All her tiptoeing around, orbiting his space,

164

doing her damnedest not to disturb the sick man's semi-coma for fear of cramping his style was lost in the stratosphere. Now she buzzed about like she owned the joint.

Tristan sank back against the re-fluffed pillows and watched her dress, like a strip tease in reverse, yet still just as exciting. "Is that new?" he asked knowingly since she'd moved in with nothing but her dog and purse. To replace the clothing lost in the car accident he'd offered her his credit card, but she refused to take it and he lacked the energy to press the issue.

"I picked up a few mix and match pieces. Nothing expensive. I'm on a tight budget, ya know. And as much as I love borrowing your clothes, I can't wear 'em to work." She pulled off price tags on pale blue capris and a floral short sleeve top. Spritzed the air with a bottle of vanilla fragrance and stepped into the mist. Pulled her golden hair into a high ponytail. "Call if you need anything. I'll try to get out early."

"Don't worry. I'll be fine." There wasn't much trouble to get into while sleeping.

One last peck on Tristan's scruffy head and Joy was out the door and he was out cold once again.

****

After days of only getting out of bed to answer nature's call, Tristan dropped his bare feet to the shag rug and pushed himself off the mattress. Feeling every bit of his thirty-nine years, and then some, his joints could use a little oil. Maybe coffee would do the trick. He hadn't had a cup o' joe since getting hit with the viral Mack truck.

Dragging the blanket, he shuffled down the hallway, shaking off this rigor mortise. At first it hurt to move, but once his muscles warmed up, he felt like his old self, only older. Creakier. Hairier.

His face itched, driving him nuts. The shaggy beast in the bathroom mirror looked vaguely familiar. This was how he'd started growing the first beard—avoiding the razor for a couple of weeks.

A shower would be great right now, but first he wanted to let Joy know he was ready to return to the land of the living.

Following the pounding sound floating from the open basement door, he found her running on the treadmill at a pace that would have him gasping.

What a sight for sore eyes in fitted black shorts and a tight turquoise tank top. On a scale of Jabba the Hutt to Jillian Michaels, Joy was hotter than Princess Leia in a gold bikini. Made him feel like a decrepit old man in the soup-stained undershirt and faded flannel pajama pants. To keep up with this fitness fanatic, he'd better get back into a routine, otherwise his only hope would be for her to abandoned her fear of getting fat and join him on the carnivorous side.

The best thing to come out of the flu was being too sick to sneak a cigarette. Joy, the fitness junky, didn't smoke, nor did she break his chops to stop, putting the onus on him, which somehow relieved the pressure to quit. Plus being off the job helped a lot, as much as being out of his ex-wife's line of fire. Without the old triggers, the craving to reach for the pack wasn't there.

"*It's* alive," Joy shouted. Brimming with sweat, she jumped off the machine before it stopped, yanked out the earbuds. "I was starting to worry." She snatched a small towel from the back of a folding chair and swiped her face, then grabbed the bottle of spring water. "How ya feelin'?" she gasped between greedy sips.

The woman radiated health and happiness, which was instant medicine for his soul. His eyes could never get their fill even if he were to stare at her for a gazillion years.

"Better. You have no idea." It was true. But Joy's special care made being sick not so bad. "You oughta be a health coach."

"I appreciate your vote of confidence but I'm not the type to motivate anyone to do anything."

"Just seeing you now's got me motivated."

Joy's gaze fell to Tristan's crotch and the obvious arousal tenting the loose fabric. "Is that so?"

"I'm not talking about that kinda motivation. But you do that too. Watching you run—you've guilted me to start working out again."

"Don't do it out of guilt, Tristan. Do it because you want to live a healthy life and be around to watch your daughter grow up."

"And that's not supposed to make me feel guilty?"

"Do it 'cause you want to." She bent over to reach the load of laundry inside the washing machine then squatted as she shoved it into the dryer; the sight making Tristan's erection flex like a miniature body builder. "Before you're doing it 'cause you have to."

"What's today?"

"Monday."

"I'll start hitting the weights tomorrow."

"Wait until next week when you're fully recuperated. In the meantime, do some stretching and light cardio."

"That's it?"

"Yeah." She swung the towel over one shoulder.

"Start out easy and work your way up."

Tristan wanted to start out easy all right, and work his way up her tight curves. He grabbed her sweaty body in a hug, resisted her lips since he didn't remember the last time he'd brushed his teeth, and buried his nose in the crook of her neck to inhale the potency of her raw musk.

"I need a shower." She pushed her palms against his chest. "Don't take this the wrong way, but you could use one too."

Unoffended, he let her slip away to gather her things. Before heading upstairs, he spotted unfamiliar cardboard boxes filling a once-empty corner. "What's all this? I wasn't serious about you moving down here." As far as he knew, she'd been occupying the spare room to escape his germs.

"That's…uhh…nothing. Really." With a nonchalant sidestep, she beat him to the boxes and secured the partially open flaps.

"Lemme see." He stooped behind her, his groin to her backside, his hands on her waist. "What kinda nothing?"

"It's a surprise."

"For who?"

"For you. And your daughter." Joy pressed the lid from popping up.

Tristan caught her wrists in one hand and opened the top with the other. Red. Green. Silver. Gold. Sparkle. Glitter. "Christmas decorations?"

Joy glanced over her shoulder, revealing a half-smile inching across her tight lips. "Remember when we were talking about your visitation dates? You were upset your ex gets your daughter for Christmas, and I said just do Christmas any time because she's too young to know the difference?"

"Yeah." The silly conversation was a foggy memory.

"I picked up some clearance items from work. No biggie."

"Awww, Joy..." Tristan's heart swelled. This girl was way too kind for her own good. Even if her idea was wacky, it was the sweet thought that mattered. He hugged her, thankful she didn't shrug him off this time despite their combined grungy state. "Thanks."

With her long ponytail draped in front of one shoulder, he brushed his lips against the exposed skin at the back of her neck, lavishing the baby-soft, salty-sweetness along her spine. When she moaned her approval, a magnificent vibration rattled him, from teeth to groin. If he weren't so gross he'd throw her over the weight bench, tear off those itty-bitty shorts, and take her on the spot.

"Wanna join me in the shower?" Tristan growled his lust in her ear as she rubbed her bottom against his crotch.

"Race ya." Joy slipped from his hands and was at the top of the staircase like a victorious Rocky Balboa before Tristan climbed the first step.

He lugged his body at a snail's pace, hanging on the banister for support. *When did I get so old? I really need to get in shape.*

When he reached the second step from the top, Joy pulled him the rest of the way. "I don't think you can handle sex yet. Maybe you oughta take a nice hot bath...alone. Then I'll give you a massage. We can order in some pizza."

"That sounds good to me." His last massage was by a sadistic Neanderthal chiropractor who'd nearly killed him, fixing the slipped disks in his neck.

While she filled the tub, Tristan collapsed on the couch. The woman was right about doing too much, too soon. *Damn flu.* If it weren't for her, who would have taken care of him? Sure, Nick would have come by to make sure he was alive but it wouldn't have been the same. Joy was good for him. She was good to him. Too good, if there were such a thing. He wanted to make her feel just as good, if not better. Once he got his strength back, he'd return the favor and then some.

After the back rub, they polished off the pizza in the living room while catching up on the evening news. One glance at Joy curled up on the couch with her head on the armrest and Tristan knew she was out cold.

Time to turn on the laptop to do a little online browsing. There's gotta be something special he could find for her. Jewelry was the obvious choice however he was stumped on what she'd like. She never wore more than a pair of big silver hoop earrings and had mentioned not liking to wear anything around her neck. What else could he get her? A bracelet? Flowers? Perfume? A fancy designer handbag? Maybe Nick's wife could provide some insider information.

While she snoozed, he dug a little deeper into his internet research. After scolding her for playing with his handcuffs, he'd promised to get another set for the bedroom.

Violet's Valise was the first website to pop up. Besides kinky toys, there were frilly things she would look great in, and would feel even better peeling off her. Although he could slip into the store when she wasn't scheduled to work, this online shopping was way more convenient than making the awkward trip. Just drop a few X-rated items into the virtual cart, and Violet will build a personalized gift basket and deliver it to his front door. *Perfecto.*

****

The day before Easter the basket arrived. Lucky for Tristan, he'd gotten home from work before Joy.

"Yo, bro…" Nick parked his pickup truck along the curb to let Tristan out. "Looks like *some-bunny* showed up early." He nodded toward the porch at the oversized package wrapped in purple cellophane, topped with a big bow. "Let's break it open and see if there's any chocolate inside."

"Mind your sweet tooth, buddy. It's not that kinda candy."

His friend lifted a curious brow. "What other kind is there?"

"Eye candy." Tristan winked.

"You dirty dog."

"Don't tell Lily. I don't want Joy finding out. It's a surprise."

Nick locked his lip and threw the invisible key out the driver's window before zipping away.

Tristan brought the hefty basket inside. Before stashing it away until tomorrow, he wanted to make sure everything he ordered was there, so he set it on the kitchen counter and peeled back the plastic wrapping with care. Lingerie. Red fuzzy handcuffs. Nipple clamps—for beginners. A variety of vibrators. Ben Wa balls. Anal beads. A feather on a stick. Flavored body paints.

And just in case the toy handcuffs didn't do it for

Joy, he slipped in two pairs—brand new, never been used in the line of duty—he'd picked up from the police supply store. Then he rewrapped the basket and buried it under a blanket on the floor of his closet when his cellphone rang his ex-wife's infamous tune—a soundbite from the Jaws soundtrack.

What the hell does she want? Stacy rarely called just to let Nicole talk to him; nine times out of ten he was the one to pick up the phone if he wanted to speak to Niblet. He took a deep breath and let out a sigh before answering in a bored monotone. "S'up Stacy?"

"Hey, Trissy," she sang like she'd never wrung his heart out and stuffed it in a meat grinder. "Guess what?"

He hated when she called him Trissy almost as much as he hated her mind-games, almost as much as he hated her.

*No...wait...*Stacy may be a super-bitch, but she was the mother of his child. And hate was a waste of emotion. For Niblet's sake, he'd suck it up and do his damnedest to tolerate this detestable woman. With vague interest, he forced himself to play along. "What?"

"You know the *schedule*?" She could only mean the single most important schedule that mattered to him—the visitation schedule—where she took all the big holidays, leaving him with June through November.

His stomach clenched. "What about it?"

"I need to make a switch."

Tristan perked up. "What kinda switch?"

"Would you mind taking Nicole a little sooner?"

"No. Not at all." His heart sped up. "Why? Everything all right?" He slathered on a thick layer of concern when his only care was getting time with Nicole.

"Yeah. Things are great. It's just...I need a favor."

Tristan waited in silence, expecting the worst.

"Ya see, I have this opportunity...a vacation, sorta. But it's not really for kids."

Listening to her stumble over the words was irritating but he hung on for the punch line. "Where ya going?"

"Europe."

He rolled his eyes. "You do know they let kids in Europe." The instant he said the words, he wanted to punch himself in the face for giving her any ideas.

"Yeah, well...Garret wants to go backpacking."

"*You're* gonna backpack—across Europe?" He snickered. "You wouldn't camp at the beach when we were together. But you'll backpack across Europe with your boyfriend?"

"Garret's a photojournalist so this'll be a working-vacation. I'm going as his assistant."

"Oh, I just thought he was a perpetual college student. What happened? He graduated from taking naked photos of my wife, to taking photos of Europe. Or is he gonna take naked photos of you *in* Europe?" Tristan spit from belly-laughing so hard. Sometimes he cracked himself up, especially at his ex-wife's expense. He'd reached the point where he found humor in his pain now that he was over her. Now that he had Joy.

"You're an ass, you know that?" Stacy squawked above his laughter. "Well? Will you do it or not?"

Tristan caught his breath. "Of course I will."

The call became muffled, as if Stacy put her palm over the mouthpiece to let out a squeal of delight. "He said yes," she shrieked to someone on her side—Garret, no doubt.

"When're you dropping her off?"

"Dunno yet. I just wanted to make sure she has a place to stay."

"I'll always have a place for my daughter," he snapped, in case Stacy had any doubt. "Bring her by whenever. Just give me a heads-up so I'm home."

Tristan hung up, disappointed he didn't speak to Nicole, yet relieved he'd see her sooner rather than later. Before he could wrap his mind around the sudden change in plans and what it would entail, Joy walked through the front door after a full day at the Christmas Shoppe.

"Hey, sunshine. Have a seat." He nodded toward the barstool as he pulled the cork on a bottle, then handed her a cool glass of white wine. They could both use a drink as he rehashed the conversation, bringing her up to speed.

Joy's thin smile stretched until her eyes were crescent moons. "I can't wait to meet her. Let's do something special. Like a welcome home party. We can invite Nick and Lily. Fill the place with balloons. Get a swing set for the yard. And…" Her ideas were thoughtful and wonderful, better than Tristan could hope for, but it was all too much, too soon.

"Slow down." He pumped the breaks with his palms. "I appreciate your enthusiasm but let's not overwhelm her. It won't be easy separating her from her mother. Let's get past the first night and see how things play out."

"Wait—" Horror flashed across Joy's face and her green eyes widened to twice their size. "You think

Stacy'll want to stay the night? Here?"

"Nah," Tristan said on impulse, until the weight of the question sank in. "At least, I don't think so. I mean, I hope not."

"Do you want me to be here? 'Cause I can find somewhere else to stay…" Her excitement dwindled as she trailed off.

"Let's not worry about it now." It made no sense to feed her anxiety before working out the details with Stacy. "Besides, she's got a boyfriend so I'm allowed to have a girlfriend. It's none of anyone's business anyway."

"If it makes the situation any better, wanna pretend I'm the babysitter? Help keep your private life private."

Tristan shook his head. "I don't want to lie about our relationship."

"I wouldn't mind, really. It would actually take the awkwardness out of meeting your ex."

"You wouldn't be offended?"

"Not at all. I hope you aren't offended when I introduce you to Victor as my boys' future baseball coach."

"Baseball coach, huh?" He smirked and nodded, picking up what she was putting down. "Okay. I get where this is going."

"I don't wanna lie about my life. But I don't mind doing it if it means protecting our privacy and shutting down the drama before anyone has a chance to start an argument over something that's none of their business."

Furrowing his brow, he followed her fiery train wreck of thoughts, wondering how far she'll spiral the what-ifs if he didn't stop her. "All hypothetical scenarios. You're wasting your energy worrying for nothing."

"I'm just planning ahead. Covering my ass. Your ass. All the bases. And any curve balls that might be thrown our way."

"May I suggest forgetting about it for now." He wrapped his arms around her neck and pressed a kiss to her forehead. "I know what'll do the trick. A pitcher of Cal's Mind Erasers down at Mr. Lucky's."

"And which of us do you suggest be the designated driver?" Joy gave him the slanted look he'd grown accustomed to whenever she doubted his game plan, which seemed to be pretty often.

"Maxi Taxi, who else?"

Chapter Twelve

After weeks of using Bruno as a messenger between her and her parents, Joy woke up early on Easter morning knowing where to find one of them. Ducking in the back of the church, she scanned the parishioners until she spotted her mother's poufy platinum hair.

Once the service ended and everyone filed out, she stepped in line behind her mother, tugging gingerly on the woman's elbow to get her attention like she'd done as a child.

Sophia whipped around, feisty fists clenched. "Get your meat hooks off m—Oh, God, Joy, you scared the hel—" She slapped her palm over her mouth, then made the sign of the cross and muttered a prayer for forgiveness. "What're you doing here?"

Joy had no fight left in her; she'd been wrung dry. When she wasn't tending to Tristan and his flu, she'd been plotting this reunion, praying it worked, knowing any success or failure would fall on her. She didn't return to Scenic View to be closer to her parents only to wind up avoiding them. With nothing left to lose, and the most apologetic smile she could summon, she put out her arms and hoped for the best. "Hi, Ma. Happy Easter."

As quick as her mother's expression brightened at the unexpected sight of her estranged daughter, the corners of her mouth fell fast as if every bad memory came rushing back. *What's wrong?* was written in the soft creases of her aging face.

"I know what you're thinking." Joy put up her palms. *See—nothing to hide.* "I'm fine. Everything's fine. I just…miss you. And Daddy. How's he doing?"

Sophia's left eyebrow lifted in doubt, weighing her daughter's words. "Your father's the same. Sleeps late on Sundays. Eats too much cheese despite what the doctor says. He worries more about you than his own health. We both do. And don't tell us not to—it's what we do best."

Standing in the presence of all that is Holy must've changed her mother's tune because before Joy had to plead for forgiveness as she was prepared to do, on more levels than she could fit in a single breath, Sophia grabbed her daughter's hand and squeezed, not letting go. "Did you eat? Let's go to the diner for eggs Benedict. My treat. Wait—you don't eat meat."

Even though Joy's appetite was already sated after devouring lemon Greek yogurt topped with blueberries at Tristan's, she didn't mention it. Instead she sighed a *thank you* to God and let her mother lead the way, two blocks down on Main Street. "It's okay, Ma. I'll have whatever you're having."

"So…" Over their second cup of coffee, Sophia tapped her pointy red nails on the Formica as she broached the sensitive subject Joy'd been expecting. "Are you going to invite me over to see your place?"

"Sure." Joy smiled. Poised and prepared, she'd already prepped Tristan on the possibility of giving her mother the grand tour of *her* place, omitting any facts about a male roommate.

"Is *this* your new car?" Sophia wrinkled her nose at the tailgate mobile parked in the lot behind the barbershop, drawing admiration from three college hunks jogging in a line.

Without letting her mother's distaste play on her nerves, Joy nodded. "Well, it's not brand new, but it's new to me. I think the boys'll love it. Plenty of room for them and their stuff. More practical than the Jaguar."

Sophia shrugged then climbed in. To keep small talk at a minimum, Joy took the shortcut with a lead foot.

When they pulled into Tristan's driveway, Sophia clucked her tongue and shook her head in disgust at the eyesore next door, where Nick's crew unloaded building material and tools from the silver pickup truck into the single-car garage. Tristan was over there, somewhere. This was his new job site for the next month or so, since he'd convinced Nick to let Joy rent the property once it was up to code.

As excited as she was to tell her mother about the arrangement, it was too soon to raise anyone's hopes, especially her own. Besides—after learning the hard way to never get her heart set on anything in this life—it was a good idea to keep Plan B in her back pocket, just in case...

"Tsk...what a sin." Sophia couldn't tear her attention away from the wreck, even as she followed Joy to the front door of Tristan's pretty little cottage. "It didn't look like that when your father and I owned it, that's for sure. Such a shame no one took care of it."

Before her mother got the nutty idea of going next door to check out the damage up close, Joy rushed inside where two fur-balls charged down the hallway, yipping in unison.

"Geez, Joy, you didn't get another dog, did you?"

"Cookie's not mine. I found her in the yard the other day." Premeditating the lie made the words fall out without flinching. "I called the phone number on her collar, but no one's gotten back to me. She's been keeping Rex company while I'm at work. Isn't she sweet?" Joy picked up two plush toys and flung them toward the master bedroom, enticing the pups to scram, knowing her mother would detour in the opposite direction of the animals.

"Hmmm…" Sophia's gaze bounced around the stark walls of the small living room with a flat smile that matched her unreadable tone, as enthused as a crime scene investigator. The floor plan was similar to the Barbieri's old home but brought up to date with an earthy palette, raised panel doors, hardwood floors, and a gas fireplace.

"Lily's husband got this as a foreclosure and fixed it up as a rental." While Joy hung her keys and cardigan on the hook by the door like she's lived here forever, Sophia inched toward the kitchen.

"Looks good." Her mother nodded. "It came furnished and everything?"

"Uhhh…yeah." While filling the kettle with cold tap water and setting it on the stovetop to boil, Joy ran through the sketchy story in her head before opening her mouth. "The…uh…previous tenants moved out-of-state." She shrugged, adding a dash of drama to the mystery. "I guess it was easier to buy new stuff than take it with them."

From across the side yard, the clamor resonated from the open windows. Deep voices shouted over the din of Lynyrd Skynyrd's dueling guitar solo, a whining circular saw, and vigorous hammers pounding out of sync. All good sounds indicating progress being made was music to Joy's ears.

With a regret-laden sigh, Sophia peeked between the kitchen curtains at the dilapidated Cape next door. "I'm sorry I let your father sell that house. But he wanted to downsize. Does Lily's husband own that too?"

"Yep." To avoid saying too much on the subject, Joy bit her tongue and kept busy setting teacups, saucers, spoons, and sugar on the breakfast bar, listening to her mother ramble.

"Is your new friend, *Whatshisname*, the handyman, fixing it up?" The way Sophia spat the words, Joy wasn't sure what bothered her mother more: that he was a carpenter? Or a man, in general?

"You mean Tristan? Uh-huh." She nodded, unaffected, folding paper napkins into perfect triangles.

"Did you ask if you can rent it when it's finished?" Sophia slid a sideways glance at Joy.

"No." Joy paused before pulling the screaming kettle off the heat, twisting her face at the *absurd* suggestion despite it already being in motion. "That house is going up for sale," she lied as she poured scalding water with a steady hand.

"You've got a job now. Maybe you could buy it?"

"Owning a house is a lot of work, Ma. Renting is more my speed. Plus I don't have that kind of cash. If I did, I'd probably look into buying Lorraine's Christmas Shoppe."

Sophia rolled her eyes. "Owning a business is more work than working for someone else—trust me when I tell you. Your father started out working at his uncle's shop before deciding to open his own. It did well for a long time. But you know, times change. Men go to spas and salons now like women. That's why Bruno's here—to help Bob's Barbershop get with the twenty-first century."

"Why doesn't Daddy just sell it and retire?"

"That's what I tell him." Sophia waved her hand, dismissing the thought. "But he says he's not ready yet. It was Bruno's idea to change the name to Bellas & Fellas to draw a new clientele."

"Bob's Barbershop is a landmark."

"I know it. You know it. Everyone in town knows it. But if your father wants to keep the business alive, he's gotta make changes. It's a gamble, but modernizing it and adding day-spa appeal should draw the Scenic View Inn guests and the wine-tasting tourists passing through town. That's why your father's been cranky lately—he's worked so hard for so long to put his name on something, and your cousin came along and convinced him to change it."

"Change isn't always a bad thing."

"I know." Sophia sighed and rested her chin on prayer-hands. "If it works out, it'll be more money for everyone. Then your father could quit his crazy obsession with hitting the lottery. Still, I think his feelings are hurt that his name is coming off the building."

"And, as if you don't have enough going on, I show up out of the blue, tell you I'm divorced, and ask to move in."

"Yeah, there's that element of surprise we weren't expecting."

"I should've told you when it was happening, but...I was afraid of disappointing you again."

"We love you, although we may not agree with all your choices. You're a mother—you've got to understand wanting the best for your children. Honestly, I never liked Victor. I only pretended to because you were already pregnant."

"You knew?"

"Are you kidding?" Sophia reached across the counter and squeezed Joy's hand. "Of course I knew. We saw you at graduation and I knew, but I didn't tell your father because he'd get upset. A mother always knows. But when there was no baby, I figured something must've gone wrong. You didn't say anything, so I didn't say anything."

"I lost that baby, but I still married him anyway. I lied about eloping. About being pregnant. About the divorce. I'm a liar. How do you stand me?"

"Sometimes we lie because we think we're protecting the ones we love from a painful truth they can't handle." The lines in her mother's face softened. "More often than not, we lie to protect our self because we can't handle the fallout. Mistakes hurt. Admitting you made a mistake hurts even more. If you never make a mistake, you'll never grow. No one is perfect. The key is to learn from the mistake and move on. Do better next time. That's all anyone can hope for."

Joy nodded, absorbing the wisdom. When was the last time she spoke to her mother like adults? Never.

"I admit..." Sophia sighed as she rolled a piece of the napkin between her fingers, turning it into a paper thread and tying it into a tiny knot. "My first reaction isn't always pretty, so I can understand why you might've *omitted* a few details."

Squelching the urge to cry at her mother's sincere words, Joy swallowed the lump in her throat with a gulp of sweet tea. "I'm such a disappointment to you and Daddy. I ruin every good thing I touch."

"That's not true. I've always been proud of you. You just lived so far away you couldn't see it. And my voice doesn't translate well over the telephone."

"I should have been honest with you." Tears erupted, hard and fast, in an emotional cocktail of shame and redemption, but Joy stifled them.

"Forget about it. That's in the past. I'm over it already." Sophia handed her daughter a clean napkin. "Maybe you did me a favor keeping your secrets to yourself. For years, I lived in bliss, figuring your life must be perfect since I hardly heard from you, never mind hear you complain. But now, knowing how much you suffered, I want to choke your ex-husband for ruining your life."

"He hurt me, but he didn't wreck my life. He gave me two beautiful babies. I wouldn't have them if it weren't for Victor. I just wish they loved me." Joy buried her face in the napkin; she'd need a roll of paper towels to blot this wet mess.

Sophia hopped down from the stool to console her daughter. "You're a good mother, Joy. Of course they love you. What's not to love? You learned from the best."

"I did, didn't I?" Joy halted her tears long enough to smile. She held her mother tight, like holding onto a memory she never wanted to forget, burning this moment into her brain—her mother loved her, her mother was proud of her.

"So…" Sophia wiggled free to pour another round of tea. "You really wanna buy Lorraine's store?"

"She says she wants to sell it one of these days, but I'm not sure how serious she is. We talked about it in passing, and she mentioned holding the loan and I'd just pay it off. I figure if I bought the business first it would help me afford a house down the line."

"Whatever makes you happy." Sophia scooped sugar into her teacup and stirred slow, in awkward silence. "By the way…" She tapped the spoon against the brim before setting it on the saucer. "I didn't really mind your friend…Christian."

"Tristan."

"Yeah, him. He seemed like a nice guy. And if he's friends with Lily's husband and helped you get this rental, he can't be that bad."

"Daddy didn't like him."

"Don't worry about your father. He worries about you more because you're his only daughter—your brothers can take care of themselves. A father and daughter have a special bond. I'm sure he'll warm up to Tristan once he's over the shock of your divorce."

Joy felt better having her mother on her side for a change, although her confidence still wavered. "Ma…" Her heartbeat stalled as she hesitated in making a split-second bad decision that had her mouth moving quicker than her gut instinct. "I wanna be honest with you. This is Tristan's house. I'm staying here, with him, until the house next door is ready."

"What?" Sophia's eyes widened. "You two are living together?" Instead of screeching an octave higher as usual, her tone dropped to a rational whisper. "You just met. You hardly know him."

"Yes. But…" Joy held her breath.

"Look…" Sophia put her palm up. "You're a grown woman. I'll give you the benefit of the doubt because I don't want you to feel like you can't tell me the truth about things like this. Just, please, don't tell your father. I'll fill him in when I think he can handle it."

"Thanks, Ma."

"He's really fixing up the house for you?" Intrigue in Sophia's voice gave Joy new hope.

She nodded. "Lily's husband bought it from the bank as an investment. He was planning to sell it but said I could rent it until I get my finances in order."

Sophia bit her fist as if she might cry. "I can't believe your getting our family's house back. Your father will…" She pulled a hanky from her sweater pocket and dabbed the tip of her nose. "Your father will be so happy. I know he regrets selling it as much as I do. We were always so happy in that house. Your boys will be happy there, too."

"I hope so."

****

When Joy returned to Tristan's place after dropping off her mother at home, the open garage door piqued her curiosity. Before she could step inside to sneak a peek, Tristan emerged, wearing goggles and gloves, carrying a long board.

"Hey, sunshine. Don't you look as pretty as an Easter egg. Stand back. Don't want ya to get dirty." He flicked a switch on the worktable that started the circular saw whirring and fed the wood to the blade at the pencil mark, sending sawdust flying. A short piece hit the driveway with a thud and he turned off the machine.

"Almost done?"

Tristan pulled up the goggles to his hair, wiped his face with a bandana from his back pocket. "With the job? Or for today?"

"Both." *There was no way the house could be done yet, could it?*

"Soon." He pulled off his gloves and wiped his palms on the thighs of his faded jeans. "Couple things to do before I quit for the day. Should be finished by the middle of May if nothing gets in the way."

"The guys left?"

"I sent them home after your mother left."

"Sooo... Can I...uh..." She nodded toward the garage door. "Have a little look-see?"

"Not yet." His broad body blocked her view of the dark interior, cluttered with mystery materials and unidentifiable tools. "How'd it go with your mom?"

When Joy warned him a week ago about her peace offering plot and the possibility of inviting her mother to see *her* new place, Tristan agreed to stay away, which worked out perfect since the crew didn't mind putting in a few hours on a holiday after Nick offered to pay them double time.

"Well..." Joy sighed. "She likes your house."

Tristan cringed. "You told her?" He rubbed a hand down his dirty face. "Why?"

"I felt bad lying."

His expression softened in sympathy as he nodded. "Did she flip out on you?"

"No. But she wants to keep my dad living in the land of perpetual bliss, so she told me not to mention we're living together."

"I can go along with that. But what if he shows up at the door?"

"Would you mind saying you're visiting? Sorry to ask you to lie for me in your own home."

"Look, I don't wanna do it, but I will if I have to 'cause I don't wanna upset your folks. And I don't wanna see you get sick over all this. I'll say and do whatever you want." He put up his palms, surrendering to the story.

"Thanks for being so cool." Joy tugged the front of his T-shirt, bringing him close enough to kiss—a little salty, but just as sweet as ever.

A drunken smile tilted one side of his tired face. "Why don't you go on home. There's a few things I wanna finish first. Then I'll wash up and we can go to the diner for an early dinner. There's wine chilling in the fridge." Before she walked away, Tristan called her back. "Hey. I hid your Easter present so your mother wouldn't find it."

Her stomach fluttered at the thrill of receiving a gift. She couldn't remember the last time she'd gotten one, besides on Christmas and her birthday from her family. Despite her tiny heels sinking in the soil, Joy raced home, giddier than a little girl on an egg hunt.

Tristan didn't give her a clue or a starting point, so she began in the kitchen, with the wine of course. After peeling off her shell pink jacket and draping it over the back of the stool, she warmed up her biceps, preparing to apply some muscle action with the cork screw. However when she looked in the refrigerator, the slim bottle was already open. "What a guy."

Glug-glug-glug. With a shaky hand, Joy filled an oversized goblet to the brim and gulped it on her way to the living room. Rex and Cookie trailed behind, picking up toys, dragging them along. "We're not playing now, pups. I'm looking for something."

He didn't say whether the gift was smaller than an egg or bigger than a basket. Still, with his uncluttered décor, it couldn't be too hard to find—could it? For all she knew it could be hiding in plain sight.

She reached between the couch cushions. Shook out the blankets. Flipped throw pillows. Checked the entryway closet. And pulled out the six chairs tucked against the dining room table. Yet found nothing out of the ordinary.

The quest was harder than she expected. Was she even close? Hot? Cold? Getting warmer?

Joy narrowed her eyes as she scanned the space. "If I were an Easter present, where would I be?" She went back to the kitchen, ditched the glass, and grabbed the bottle by the neck.

Ah-ha. "The Christmas decorations." Maybe he hid it downstairs in her hiding space, figuring she wouldn't think of the obvious, but she was wrong. She took a swig as she checked the cup holder on the treadmill. *Nothing.* Behind the free weights. *Nothing.* Inside the dryer. *Nothing.*

Back upstairs, she checked the four corners of Nicole's future bedroom. Still nothing.

Nothing in the bathrooms either.

She opened the walk-in closet in Tristan's room. Looked high. Low. Then lifted a blanket…and there it was. As big as a laundry basket, wrapped in the familiar purple cellophane from Violet's Valise. According to the card attached to the bow, he shopped online, which is handled by the warehouse rather than the local shop.

"That sneaky devil. He shouldn't have." But she was glad he did. Even with her employee discount, the prices were out of this frugal mom's budget. After draining the last drop from the bottle, she set the basket on the bed and ripped into it.

The first thing she spied were two sets of shiny silver handcuffs just like Tristan's real ones; definitely *not* part of VV's catalog. There was also a set of the chintzy fuzzy red cuffs, the play-kind men thought women wanted. She tested the toy's strength and the center link cracked like a pretzel.

"Junk." She flung them over her shoulder and the dogs snatched them. "No, no, no. Not for you." Cookie gave up hers easily while Rex bolted for the living room. Joy caught him and pried the splintered plastic from his fangs then nudged both pooches toward the hallway and shut the bedroom door.

Fishing around the purple paper grass, she dug out crystal earrings. *Aww, he bought me jewelry too?* When she held the dangling sparkles to her ears, she noticed the unusual clasps. *Oh, wait... Not earrings—but nipple clamps?* She might experiment with a little bondage, but no way would she consider putting her boobs in the itty-bitty titty vises. "Nice try, Casanova. I don't think so." However as the wine wove its way through her veins, Joy's willpower wavered. "Okay...maybe...if he asks nicely."

Sifting through layers of satin and lace, she pulled out the undergarments and measured them against her torso. Sheer nighties revealed more than they concealed. Crotchless panties and G-strings matched skimpy bras with cut-out cups. Beneath the clothing was a long-handled French tickler. An opalescent shell containing Ben-Wa balls. Honey-flavored body dust. And exotic massage oils.

As the full force of the booze kicked in, the room started to spin, yet it didn't stop her from fighting her way out of the pale slacks, thin blouse, practical bra, and nude thong, and into a black teddy. Somehow she got twisted inside the fabric, and her head poked through the armhole. *Dammit.* Like an escape artist, she maneuvered out of the nightie without ripping the seams. On the second attempt, she got it right then checked her reflection. After a double-take with her double-vision, she crawled onto the bed and leaned back on the pillows propped up against the wooden slats of the headboard. She tested a few sultry poses before getting comfortable with arms stretched wide and legs curled to one side like a pin-up girl. Now all she needed was Tristan to find her like this.

What's taking him so long? She sighed. Every minute felt like an hour. Holding the sex kitten position was harder than she calculated.

After nearly nodding off, a bright idea popped in her head—handcuffs; that ought to boost the fantasy to the next level. She pushed the arch of the metal circles until they clicked opened, then attached her left wrist to the headboard. *Sooo easy.*

All she had to do now was attach the second set of cuffs dangling from the headboard to her other wrist, only it was too awkward to operate singlehandedly.

Humph. Maybe I should start over?

Joy strained to grab the key on the bed, tugging the blanket to drag it closer, but instead sent it flying into the air. It bounced off the wall with a clink and landed in the abyss of the shag carpet. Even if she could see it, she couldn't reach it now.

Maybe if she rolled onto her stomach she could stretch her leg far enough to find it with her toes? But the more she fought against the handcuffs, the more she realized it was a bad idea.

There was nothing left to do but wait for Tristan to rescue her from herself.

****

Joy jolted at the sound of her snoring, unable to sit upright with one numb arm locked to the headboard. The bedroom was dark like the sky outside the window. Either Tristan wasn't home yet or he hadn't bothered to look for her.

Then the jangle of keys hit the entry table.

Thank God. Tempted to shout his name, she bit her lip instead. After the trouble getting into this predicament, she might as well finish what she started. She shoved the web of hair out of her sleepy eyes and stifled a giggle.

"Don't tell me you got *another* dog?" said an unfamiliar feminine voice.

Shit. Joy rolled away from the door, as far off the mattress as she could, which wasn't very with one arm attached to it. Gnawing off her hand at the wrist suddenly seemed more appealing than being caught like *this*. Heavy work boots aimed toward the kitchen, followed by a second set of sharp heels. *Who the hell could it be?*

"Never mind the dog. I asked you to call before coming—didn't I?" Tristan's voice vibrated through the wall.

"I left a message on your cellphone. It's not my fault you didn't get it."

"You shoulda waited 'til I called you back."

"I couldn't. We're leaving earlier than expected to catch the tulips blooming in Holland. Tell me again, how you were lucky enough to find a housekeeper who doubles as a nanny?"

"Through a friend," Tristan lied.

"Are you sleeping with her?" A toe tapped nonstop like Morse code.

"It's none of your business what I do. And who I do it with," he huffed.

"It *is* my business if you think I'm gonna let Nicole live here for six months while you bone the babysitter under the same roof. I'm her mother—I have a right to know who comes in and out of this house."

Stacy's here. Joy cringed, praying the footsteps would lead toward the front door.

"Have I ever asked you twenty questions about your life?" he said.

"No."

"Then stop busting chops about mine."

"Is *that* her jacket? She gets kinda dressed up for housecleaning, dontcha think?"

Joy wanted to die. She clenched the blanket in a fist and whipped it over her body like a burrito.

"Uhh, yeah…" Tristan hesitated. "That's hers. So, what? It's Easter—she went to church before coming. She must've forgotten it here."

"I can tell when you're lying. She's your girlfriend, and you just don't want me to know."

"You're backpacking across Europe with your man-child lover. Why do you care what I do?"

"I don't. I'm concerned about my daughter being around some random slut."

"Quit worrying. She's gonna be just fine with me. The place is perfectly safe as you can see. A regular home sweet home."

"I'd feel more comfortable if I had a look around."

"Let's start in the basement. I'm gonna convert it into a playroom."

"Nicole will love that." Stacy's footsteps faded as she followed Tristan, but they were back soon enough.

"First door on the right is bathroom," he said.

"Mind if I use it?"

"Knock yourself out."

When she was sure it was safe, Joy took a chance and whispered, "Tristan."

The bedroom door opened a crack and he poked his head inside. "Why are you hiding?" He flicked on the light switch.

Buried in the blanket, she waggled her wrist, jingling the shiny metal bracelet.

"You did that to yourself?" He smirked.

"I thought it would be fun." When the toilet flushed, she ducked under the covers.

"Don't move." Tristan shut the light and closed the door as another opened.

Trusting that he would protect her silly secret, Joy sighed and waited for this nightmare to end.

"This'll be Nicole's room," he said. "The spare room will be an office."

"And in here?" Fingernails tapped on the master bedroom's door.

"My room."

"Can I see?"

"Why?"

"I'm curious."

"Forget it."

"Just a peek."

"Fine." He sighed. "That's all you get."

The knob turned. Joy held her breath. Watching with one eye, she prayed the pillow blocking her hand didn't slip out of place.

Tristan braced his arm across the doorframe, filtering out the stream of light that spilled across the bed. "See. Just an average bedroom. No biggie."

"Turn on the light so I can have a better look."

"Nope." Tristan's biceps held her back. "There's nothing to see."

"From what I *can* see, looks like a tornado swept through it. Your housekeeper sucks."

The insult made Joy flinch, which caused the metal to pinch the soft part of her wrist. She exhaled a whimper that Tristan obscured with a sudden hacking cough.

"I didn't hire her to clean my room. You oughta get your nose outta here 'cause I just got over the flu so it's loaded with germs. You don't wanna get sick for your trip."

"You have a nice place—I'll give ya that."

"It's not mine. It's Nick's rental."

"So, you're working full-time for him now?"

"Until I figure things out."

"You were always good with your hands." Joy heard the innuendo loaded in Stacy's words; she wondered if Tristan noticed it too. "Don't you miss being a cop?"

"Eh. Sometimes."

"Are you happy?"

"What kind of question is that? Of course I'm

happy."

"I mean, are you happier without me?" Stacy inched closer to him.

The last thing Joy wanted was to witness his ex-wife making a pass at him as he lingered protectively in the open doorway but she couldn't look away.

Tristan blasted an audible breath through his nostrils. "Let's not talk about the past."

"Was it so bad when we were together?"

"You left me. Not just once. You left a few times."

"But I always came back. You're the one who filed for divorce."

"And you're the one who asked your uncle—the big, important judge—to push it to the top of the pile."

"I know. It's all my fault."

"And it's way too late."

"It doesn't have to be."

"Yes, it does. And it is. You're going to Europe. Backpacking. With *Whatshisface*."

Stacy sighed. "I just don't know if Garret is the one for me. I think, maybe…you've been the one all along. I was too blinded—by motherhood and fantasies of what a marriage would be like—to see straight. That's why I'm going with him—to see if we can last the trip without breaking up."

"This isn't the time or place for this conversation. And I'm definitely not the person you should be talking to."

"I'm so confused."

"Not my problem anymore. I'm sorry it has to be this way."

"Are you really sorry? Or are you just saying it to make me feel better?"

"Just saying it. And now I'm saying it's time for you to leave."

"I should have loved you right when I had the chance. Do you think we would've stayed together if I never left?"

"Who knows what might've happened. But it's too late now. I just want my daughter—"

"Our daughter." Stacy's voice dropped an octave. The sliver of light between their silhouettes narrowed as she pressed herself against him, pushing his back to the door, swinging it wide open they almost fell through. "Just kiss me, Tristan. Kiss me, this way I can be sure it's over. If I don't feel anything then I know I made the right choice. I don't know what I'm doing anymore. I have this sick feeling I made a huge mistake."

"Kissing me would be the biggest mistake you could ever make."

"You're kidding, right? I'm throwing myself at you." Stacy's voice cracked.

"I don't wanna boot you outta here, but I will if I have to."

"Let me guess, you're still pissed I got half your pension in the divorce?"

"Forget the pension—you won't see a penny until I retire, and trust me when I say I have every intention of staying on the job until I croak."

"You bastard." Stacy gasped as if shocked by his claim, no more surprised as Joy who had hoped there was a solid chance of him becoming a permanent resident of Scenic View.

"When you see your boyfriend, kiss him, and if it feels right then you know you made the right choice. If it doesn't, then that's your own fault. I'll walk you to the car." Tristan glanced over his shoulder then shut the bedroom door.

Chapter Thirteen

Tristan all but shoved Stacy into her car before rushing back to Joy in his bed under the folds of fabric. There was enough light spilling in from the hallway to spot the sideways bottle on the floor. "Hey, you didn't save me any wine?" he joked but she was too inert to respond with anything more than light snoring. "Joy? Can you hear me?" He felt bad waking her, but he couldn't leave her with one limp hand above her head while the other fist curled beneath her chin against the pillow—peaceful yet awkwardly uncomfortable.

She lifted an eyelid and pulled a web of hair from her mouth with the free hand. "How'd it go with your *wife*?" she spat.

"You mean my *ex*-wife?" Tristan corrected in a gentle tone, not wanting to stoke the fire of her understandable animosity. "She's gonna drop off Nicole tomorrow." His fingers drifted from the warmth of her cheek, down the cool satin nightie he'd picked out that looked better on her than the internet model. "I see you found your Easter basket. Why'd you cuff yourself to the bed?"

"Seemed like a good idea at the time. I gotta pee. Please unlock me."

"Where's the key?"

"Dunno. Somewhere 'round there." Joy pointed toward the carpet and drew a wide circle in the air.

"Boy, are you a lucky lady. Be right back." Tristan sprinted to the entryway table to grab his keyring and returned with his spare universal handcuff key. Holding her delicate wrist, he inserted the skinny key into the tiny hole and turned it until the bracelet opened then massaged the indentation.

"My hero." She rolled off the bed and zigzagged toward the bathroom. If this were a car stop, no doubt she'd blow high on the breathalyzer test.

The sight of her nearly nude body flitting across the floor made him swell in his undershorts. "My Lord…" Had he known what she was up to this afternoon he would have quit working hours ago.

At the whoosh of the toilet, followed by the splattering of sink water, he rushed beside the bathroom door and flattened his back to the wall, ready to catch a pretend perp.

Joy yanked open the door and paused. "Tristan? Where'd ya go? Please, God, I hope Stacy didn't come back," she muttered.

Tristan bit his bottom lip as he waited to pounce, fighting the urge to laugh at the ridiculous role-playing game. But she started it.

When she flicked off the bathroom light and stepped over the threshold, he snatched her elbow and rumbled in his official tone, "You're under arrest, miss."

Surprised and off kilter, Joy stammered, "What're you doing?"

"You have the right to remain silent." With a gentler than usual touch, he pulled her arms behind her back as he pushed her chest to the wall in a fluid motion. "Anything you say can and will be used against you…" As he rambled the entire Miranda warning, the clicks of steel rings around her wrists sealed the deal, and she was cuffed just like a crime scene.

"Whoa…" A nervous giggle squeaked past her lips. "You're kidding, right?"

"Of course, sunshine." His erection strained behind his zipper as he pressed against her scantily clad curves. "I'm not in the business of arresting anyone these days."

"But you're gonna go back to it." Joy glanced over her shoulder at him. "I heard you tell Stacy."

"I only said it to piss her off. I don't know what I'm doing yet."

Her stance relaxed a bit. "This feels a little too real. You must've been really good at your job."

"Isn't this what you wanted? For me to cuff you?"

"I thought we'd just use them in bed."

"Why? Are you really gonna try to get away from me?"

"No."

"Then let's play cops and robbers. That's more my speed." Flipping a mental switch, he slipped right into the bad-cop character without missing a beat. "Who's your pimp?" He gave a gentle shove, hoping she played along.

"My what?"

"Come on, *sista*. I've had my eye on you all week, working this corner."

"I'm, uh, what should I do?" she whispered.

Tristan grinned. "Just go with it."

"Oh, yeah, that's right. This is my corner. If I don't score tonight my pimp's not gonna be happy. Can you help me out?" She glanced over her shoulder, batting her lashes, with a pout that made the powdery soft plea convincing.

Tristan nearly shot the loaded weapon in his boxers. Sucking in a breath, he said, "You're not propositioning a police officer, are you?"

She hesitated. "Maybe. Why? Is that a bad thing?"

"Uh, yeah. It's a really bad thing." Tristan chuckled at her innocence and changed gears, back to cop-mode. "I'm hauling you in. You'll spend the night in a cell and see the judge in the morning to set your bail. Is there someone you wanna call to let them know where to find you?"

"Well, I guess I could call my folks, but that'll kill 'em. And my ex wouldn't even care." Joy's voice cracked with weak tears.

Okay. Game over. "Shh…Joy, shh. We're just playing." Tristan spun her to face him, consoling her with a hug, but she wasn't having it. The tears were real and they were coming hard and fast.

"There's nobody I can call. I don't like this game anymore." Her body trembled with despair.

"You can call me anytime. Always. You know that."

"No, I can't." She buried her face into his T-shirt. "You're the one arresting me." If her sobs weren't so heartbreaking the scenario would be comical. "I have no one."

"That's not true." Tristan gripped her shoulders, pushing her arms' length away to view her damp eyes. "You got me."

Her tears slowed, and she cocked her neck to the side in doubt. "You're just sayin' that because you made me cry."

"You're wrong." All he wanted was to make her happy, bring her joy, and love her like she needed to be loved. So he leaned down and murmured against her salty petal-soft lips, "I love you, Joy. Whether you wanna hear the word or not, I don't know a better way to say it. I'm in love with you."

She gasped, releasing another weepy wave.

"Please don't cry."

"Don't worry," she whispered against his kiss. "These are happy tears."

"Wait." He reached for the cuff. "Lemme get these off you."

"No. I trust you. Let's imagine the bed is the backseat of your police car."

While Joy's tongue explored his mouth with a hunger that matched his own, Tristan inched in reverse, taking her with him. When his legs bumped against the footboard, he spun Joy and put her down on the mattress face first, making sure her head turned sideways so she didn't suffocate.

"You started this, sunshine. I gotta end it." With a slow hand, he rubbed a small circle on her bottom raised high in the air. "I gotta be inside you, or I'm gonna explode. You sure you wouldn't rather do this with the cuffs off?"

"Leave 'em." Joy's fingers twitched at the small of her back until she laced them together. "Take me now. From behind. With the cuffs on," she snapped as eager as he was for this moment. "I wanna know what it's like to have you in total control of my body."

"Promise you'll let me know the moment you don't like it, and I'll take 'em off."

Joy nodded under the curtain of hair covering her

face.

Tristan brushed the strands away. "I wanna hear you say it."

"Yes. I promise."

As much as he wanted to get this party in his pants started, he was hesitant of her position, with her shoulders supporting the weight of her upper torso. "Lemme know if you're not comfortable."

"Shut up already." She urged with a giggle. "I mean…ohhh, officer, I'm so sorry for breakin' the law. Teach me a lesson I'll never forget."

Rigid to the point of pain, Tristan popped open the top button of his jeans, ripped down the zipper, and kicked them off, along with his boxer-briefs. *Free at last.* He dug out a condom from the nightstand drawer, tore the foil with his teeth, and rolled it down the tender tip. With a quick dip of his finger, he discovered her coveted slick spot was red-hot and ripe for the taking. As Joy's hips rocked like a slow heartbeat, guiding him in the right direction, he braced for the plunge.

"You're absolutely sure you want it like this?"

"More than anything," Joy moaned with delight. She sat back, getting reacquainted with his anxious arousal.

He nudged her against his lap hoping she'd impale herself before he lost control and skewered her. "I don't want to hurt you."

"Hurt me?" She glanced over her shoulder, giggling with an impish smile and hungry eyes. "I know you'd never hurt me. Make me feel good," her husky voice dropped an octave, "like you always do."

Her lust-laden words put him over the edge and without thinking twice he drove his swollen sword inside her, slaying the sexy beast.

Joy howled in pleasure-pain—a beautifully aching song he'd grown familiar to since making endless love night after night after glorious night, like it was his job and she was the boss he was eager to please.

Her whole body clenched, melting around his stiff shaft. It was heaven and hell all wrapped up in the back end of this beauty. He slipped out, then in, slow and easy, increasing his delivery to match her rhythm until he pounded her as rapid as his heartbeat.

"You make me crazy, you know that?" He tugged fistfuls of her hair like the reins on a filly.

"Good. 'Cause you make me crazy, so we're even." He heard the underlying smile in her voice. "You make me do things I never thought I'd do, Officer Casanova."

"And you make me do things that would make me lose my job." With his knees to the mattress, he rocked against her, into her, riding them both to heaven in the back of his imaginary patrol car.

"Harder. Faster." Joy belted out demands that Tristan was more than happy to oblige with his mind clouded and his libido doing a backflip. "Come for me, Tristan. Please. I can't take anymore. These cuffs hurt."

At her plea, he poured into her. "Yesss."

She went limp first and he rolled alongside her to avoid adding pressure to the restraints.

"You okay?" Tristan pushed the hair from her starry eyes.

Nose to nose, Joy's sweet breath mingled with his. "That was intense. I'd definitely try it again someday."

Once he freed her wrists, they scrambled beneath the covers. He cradled her head in the crook of his arm while her fingers caressed his torso.

"So…" She twirled his thicket of chest hair. "I'm the new housekeeping-nanny, huh?"

"I already told you, it's not that I want to hide our relationship. I just don't want her knowing my business, like you not wanting your dad to know we're living together. Same difference."

"You're right." Joy sighed. "It just felt so icky…hearing your conversation. And watching her try to kiss you."

"I'm sorry about that, sunshine." Before she made a bald spot, he halted her antsy fingers and wove their hands together.

"Was she hard for you to resist? I mean—I saw her. She's very pretty. Any guy would find her attractive."

"What?" Tristan squinted in disbelief, then recalled Joy mentioning her ex-husband's cheating tendencies, which would explain her silly insinuation. "I'm not Victor. I have no reason to want another woman but you."

She hesitated, and he read the thoughts behind her eyes as she blinked one, then the other, separate, together, as if calculating the weight of his words. "Want? Or need?"

"What's the difference?"

"Need is dependent. Want is extra. I need air. I want ice cream."

"You want ice cream?"

"Not right now. I'm just differentiating. You need a family car. You don't need a Harley—you want it."

"Actually, if you're gonna ride a bike, there's nothing like a Harley, so I kinda need it." He chuckled, hoping to lighten the mood.

"You don't get it." Joy shot from the sheets onto her feet. "You don't *need* me. You *want* me. Like some object of affection. That's what you just said."

"I'm not seeing the difference."

"Need is something you can't live without. Want is something you desire to possess. Like a mansion. Or a yacht."

"I don't want a mansion or a yacht. I *want* you."

"Exactly."

"I still don't get it." Tristan got up to stop her from pacing before she stormed out of the room. "I want *and* need you, does that make you feel better?"

"I dunno. You need me to watch your daughter when you're at work apparently, according to your conversation with your ex-*wife*."

"Technically I don't need you to watch her 'cause I'm gonna put her in preschool. But I want her to get to know you in case you ever do watch her for whatever reason I'm not around. But if you can't, I can ask Lily."

"See what you did there?" Fury flashed in her eyes.

"Nope. Not at all." Frustration had him gripping his hair at the root. "What'd I do now?"

"You replaced me so easily. Just like that." She snapped her fingers.

"What? All I said was I'd ask Lily if you're busy. Why would I want to put any more on your plate than you already have? I thought you'd be happy I'm not expecting you to be a babysitter. Whatever I told Stacy was to get her the hell outta my house."

"Ugh." Joy threw herself onto the bed.

"What's bothering you so I can understand?"

"I want you to want me." She sat up with praying

hands centered at her heaving breasts. "I need you to need me. Don't you get it?"

It took everything in his power not to throw her on her back and ravage her again. Instead he chuckled at her plea. "You sound like a Cheap Trick song. What do you want from me, Joy? Tell me, so I know. Do you want me to want you? Need you? Love you?" He threw in the last one, knowing she wouldn't say it herself.

"I want it all."

Unable to resist, he smirked and sang, "If you want my love, you got it."

"Now you sound like a Cheap Trick song."

"What can I say? We're a couple of cheap tricks. I don't want to complicate this amazing thing between us with a boatload of baggage. We've come too far to let a little misunderstanding sink the ship. My ex is a pain in my ass. I just want my kid. I'm sure when your ex shows up to deliver your boys it won't be all lollipops and roses."

"Victor has no reason to come here."

"How else are your kids getting here from Florida? He'd put them alone on a plane?"

Joy shrugged. "Knowing him, he'll send his fiancée."

"I can believe Vick is a dick, but he can't be that big of a tool bag."

"You'd be surprised."

Chapter Fourteen

Over the splish-splashing from the bathroom in the hall, Tristan's booming voice sang, "Joy?"

She popped her head in the doorway, catching a glimpse of the rugged man with his drenched T-shirt and plaid pajama pants, up to his elbows in thick white foam as he bathed his toddler, who doused herself nose to knees in maple syrup at breakfast. "What's up?"

"Look at me, Joy." Beneath a mound of suds piled high on her curly blonde head, Nicole screeched, "I'ma whip' cream monster."

Joy couldn't help but smile. "You sure are."

"Would you mind grabbing Niblet's princess towel? It's probably in the dryer."

"You got it, boss."

Three weeks of portraying the live-in nanny/housekeeper, Joy was used to keeping up appearances in front of the observant three-year old to avoid any issues should Stacy probe her chatty daughter for information regarding Tristan's private life, as she'd been guilty of doing to her boys regarding Victor's fiancée.

Living in a blissful bubble under one roof with Tristan and Nicole, this parallel universe was everything and nothing like she'd thought it would be. Although she was still an outsider looking in on the dynamic daddy-daughter duo, Tristan included Joy in

Debra Druzy

everything, making her feel like a true blue insider. Suddenly her life was filled with an unexpected plethora of positive emotions as their romance grew exponentially, combined with the instinct to nurture his sweet and sassy child. Nicole filled a void in Joy's soul that made her miss her children even more.

As a trio, they were a perfect fit of misfits, which bared zero resemblance to her former failed life in Florida with Victor and the boys. If she dwelled on that painful punch to the gut for too long, a black cloud of shame and regret eventually gathered overhead, showering her with irrepressible grief. In those dark moments, she'd jump on the treadmill, putting the broken-hearted pieces together with sweat rather than tears.

Joy couldn't remember the last time she bathed her kids; once they were potty-trained they preferred their father to handle the bonding task. Nor could she pinpoint when the boys' aversion started or how deep it ran, but it was there, in every cold kiss and apprehensive hug. Nothing was more painful than saying *I love you* and never hearing *I love you too* in return. What made it intolerably worse was Victor instigating the negative behavior with positive reinforcement. It wasn't fair to blame the boys for regurgitating what they were taught.

Downstairs, Joy pulled out the pink hooded towel, still warm from the dryer. What a good dad Nicole had—the man thought of everything. He even paused in his current project in order to complete the pristine princess bedroom he'd promised—building a raised bed that resembled a miniature castle.

As much as she needed him to finish her house

210

fast, how could she complain about him doing something good for his child? He'd done so much for Joy after knowing her such a short time, and he guaranteed it would be done before the boys arrived. However the more time she spent with him, the more she realized she'd miss living with him, but at least they'd be neighbors, and that was almost as good.

"One princess towel for one pretty princess." Before she could hand it to Tristan, Nicole hopped out of the tub and into Joy's arms. "Happy Mudder's Day, Joy. I can hug you now 'cause I'm clean."

Joy'd begged Tristan not to acknowledge the Hallmark holiday, however he did it anyway and subtly well with a "Like a Mother" card signed in Nicole's toddler scrawl that hit a tender spot, plus a bouquet of Montauk daisies. It was hard enough phoning Sophia this morning to wish her mother a wonderful day. Hearing the sentiment from the heart-shaped mouth of a babe would have brought Joy to tears had she not already swallowed two anxiety pills with her coffee.

Tristan winced at his child's words. "I'm sorry, Joy. We were talking about her mom. And the cards she made for Stacy. And you." A concerned tug at the corner of his mouth produced an innocent smile. "Naturally, you've been like a second mother to her. I hope you're all right with it."

A damp-eyed Joy squeezed Nicole's little body, unleashing all the love in the world for her boys onto this angel. "It's fine." She bit back tears. "I'm fine. Thank you, baby. You're such a good, good girl."

When Joy was sure her heart would burst, Nicole responded with a wet kiss on the cheek and the most miraculous words. "I *luf* you."

Joy gasped. It was useless to fight it—the emotional dam broke and she couldn't hold back the waterworks. "I-I love you too." She uttered the four-letter word as if she never denounced it.

"Okay you two silly monkeys…" Tristan pried his daughter from Joy's embrace. "Lemme get you dressed." He ushered the child across the hallway. "And you…are you really okay?"

Joy fidgeted with the ends of her bathrobe belt, tightening the knot at her waist. "Of course. I'm just…you know."

"Dry those tears. We're going out for the day." He brushed her cheeks with his fingertips before shutting the bathroom door.

After splashing cool water on her face and patting her skin with the towel, Joy regained her composure with the help of some cleansing breaths. Feeling sorry for herself was becoming her new pastime, and she needed to snap out of it. She would've hopped on the treadmill for a sprint before showering, but Tristan had some grand plan in mind that included her.

The more engrossed she became in Tristan and Nicole's circle of love, the more she craved the same with Mason and Owen. How many nights had she dialed nine digits of the Florida phone number, always hanging up before hitting the final button, afraid of the rejection she'd grown to expect? Too many to count.

At last, Mother's Day arrived, the single day of the year she shouldn't fret over a phone call. It ought to be a given the boys call their mother, albeit an awkward and obligatory call at that. Still, it was a call she shouldn't have to place in order to speak to her children. Yet here she was, waiting not-so-patiently with a hollow heart, willing her cellphone to ring. It's bad enough the holiday fell on a Sunday when there's no mail delivery. If her boys sent a card it must have gotten lost in the mail because, according to her mother, only one envelope arrived addressed to Grandma Sophia. Nothing for Joy. You'd think after all these years, aware Victor doesn't *do* holidays like a normal person, it wouldn't bother her anymore, but it did. Maybe it was the agony of being so far from her kids for this long.

Very well, then. Joy could play Victor's game. School lets out the end of May and that's when he'll ship the boys up to Long Island. They can't send a letter without a stamp. She'll be damned if she'd be the one to ensure any Father's Day cards get mailed this year. But plotting the revenge didn't make her feel any better.

"Whatcha thinking about?" Tristan peeked into the bathroom as Joy studied her hopeless reflection.

"Nothing." She shrugged, knowing she'd vent if he pressed hard enough.

"Might as well spill it, Joy. Mother's Day's on your mind, and I know you're hoping your boys call."

Her throat cramped as she stifled the painful sob. "They didn't even send me a card."

"It's still early in the day."

Joy rolled her eyes. "I'm hopeful, not delusional. There is no mail on Sundays."

"Maybe it got lost."

"Well, my mother got a card from them." Knowing her ex, he would've only sent it to spite Joy but she kept the presumption to herself.

Tristan stepped into the bathroom and shut the door before crushing Joy in a hug. "I know it's a tough thing for you to do, and this an even tougher thing for me to ask of you, but can you try not to think about it?"

Although Joy knew he meant well, she still didn't need to hear it right now. "Yeah. Okay." The chemical reaction of his pheromones, fingers, and friction made her skin tingle beneath her robe, and all she could do was push her palms to his chest, forcing inches between them. When that wasn't enough distance, she yanked open the door to flee the confined space. "This is me, not thinking about it."

Tristan followed her down the hallway, past Nicole parked on the living room couch, entranced by the Sleeping Beauty DVD for the umpteenth time, with Rex on one side and Cookie on the other.

"What can I do to take your mind off it?" His broken smile said he was willing to do anything.

Joy shrugged. *Let me crawl back in bed and wither away.* "I've got a ton of laundry to fold." She jogged downstairs to unload the clothes dryer. With a full basket, she hurried back upstairs, dumped it on the bed in the spare room—*her room*—and picked pieces out of the pile.

"This isn't gonna take all day, Joy." Tristan sorted through the mound to match a tiny pair socks and made them into a ball. "Dontcha wanna do something fun?"

"Fun?" Joy snapped child-sized jeans in the air, smoothing the wrinkles before folding them in half. "Like what? Fly a kite." After lashing her wicked tongue, she bit it, knowing Tristan was only being nice, while she was being a number one bitch. *No wonder Victor left. No wonder the boys hate me.*

"We can fly a kite if you want." His gentle tone only made Joy feel worse.

"I don't know, Tristan." She tossed a small white undershirt, unfolded on the pile. "I don't feel like fun today."

He picked up the undershirt, folded it, and put it in the basket. "Maybe you'll change your mind after I drop Nicole over at Nick and Lily's."

"Just because I'm cranky doesn't mean she can't spend the day with us. I'll snap out of my funk once I shower." *After I take another pill.*

"I gotta be honest with you..." He folded the remainder of his daughter's clothes at twice Joy's speed. "I thought having Nicole around would be too much for you to handle today."

"You didn't have to do that."

"I know. But think of it this way—it's a win-win. They're trying to make a baby so having Nicole around will be an amusing preview for them. Plus we can use some extra *us* time."

"*Us* time?" While Nicole spent mornings in half-day preschool, Joy and Tristan scheduled morning meetings in the shower, saving water by washing each other's back and other body parts. "We aren't lacking any *us* time that I'm aware of, are we?"

"I can never get enough us time." He dropped the last item on the stack in the basket then curled his arm around her waist and slid a knee between her thighs—a move so smooth, Joy almost forgot her sour state. "We don't have to do anything crazy. How about going to the nursery to pick up some plants?"

His offer was too accommodating to shoot down. And the monochromatic landscape could use a pop of color to break up the greenery. "Yeah. Okay." Joy melted against him, almost wishing she didn't make the belt knot so impossible to untie. "I can get into some sunshine and gardening."

****

After they dropped off Nicole at Nick and Lily's, Tristan spent the afternoon two steps behind Joy as she meandered aimlessly through the colorful aisles of the garden center. Coming here might not have been a great idea after all—surrounded by couples who dragged their children along for the ride—the sort of reminder Joy didn't need on this maternally emotional day. It was a struggle just to get her attention long enough to decide which color impatiens she preferred.

"Do you like the pink? How about the purple?" Tristan scanned the various flats. "Red are pretty, dontcha think? Mix some white ones in there? Whaddaya say?" *Not much, that's for certain.*

"Yeah. Sure. Fine. They're all nice." The faraway look in her eyes matched her distant tone. She didn't even acknowledge the magnificent spectacle of the season's first monarch butterflies flitting from flower to flower.

There was no way Tristan could fix the hole in Joy's heart but he sure as hell would try taking her mind off it, even for a little while. "If you're not into this, let's find something else to do."

"No, no. I'm all right. This is fun. I love flower shopping. It's just...isn't it too cold?" She shivered in her red zip-up sweatshirt. "My folks used to start planting on Memorial Day."

"Wanna take a drive out east for some wine tasting? It's a beautiful day for it and it'll warm you up." Why didn't he think of the childless activity sooner? "Better yet, wanna catch a ferry over to the

216

casino?"

"Thanks, but…" Joy leaned into him, her head on his chest. "I'm not in the mood. I just wanna go home."

When they got to the house, she plopped on the couch as Tristan popped open a bottle of white wine.

"Stop trying to get me drunk. You know I'm a sure thing." She pushed the glass away.

"Take it. It's medicinal." He put it in her hands. "It'll calm your nerves. I hate seeing you so upset." It was after three and her boys still hadn't called. Tristan wanted to wring Victor's neck. No matter how mad Stacy ever was with him, she never used their daughter as a weapon.

Joy swallowed three glasses easily while Tristan milked one. Miraculously he no longer craved a smoke to go with his alcohol, thanks to the flu, but mostly because of her positive influence. Everything about this heaven-sent woman made him want to be a better man. With her inspiration, he'd gotten back on track with his long-lost workout routine and was finally fitting better in his jeans and even needed to wear a belt again.

"Come on." He helped her off the couch and led her toward the bedroom. "I know how to fix that frown."

"Please…I'm not in the mood to be arrested right now. I'm starting to think I opened the wrong can of worms asking for handcuffs."

Since their first night with the sex prop, he'd *locked her up* for the most minor infraction. Fork left in the sink. Guilty. Leaving the cap off the toothpaste. Sorry officer, I'll never do it again. Forgetting to buy milk on the way home. A crime punishable with hot and heavy sex. Doing it doggy-style became his new favorite position, next to Joy on top. "Okay, no cuffs today."

With the smallest nudge, Joy fell backward on the bed. "Be gentle please." Her weak voice broke as she curled around a pillow. "I'm fragile today."

"Absolutely." Tristan pulled off her white canvas sneakers and tossed them in the corner. Then peeled down her painted on blue jeans. When she grabbed the hoodie's zipper tab at her neck, he caught her wrists and shook his head. "Nuh-uh. I got this. You play Sleeping Beauty."

"All right." She smiled and laid back. "And who are you gonna be?"

"The Beast, of course."

Joy giggled. "Wrong fairy tale."

"Consider this a mash-up."

He dragged down the zipper deliberately slow, the hiss of the metal teeth killing the quiet as he revealed her tight white tank-top that matched skimpy cotton panties. He sucked in a breath at the pin-up worthy woman on his bed, hotter than any schoolboy fantasy. His gaze roved up her fit frame, taking in the sensational sight before falling upon her exquisite face. "I want you so bad."

"You got me." Joy licked her lips and batted glossy green bedroom eyes. "Now what are you gonna do with me?"

He knew it was the wine talking, but he wouldn't complain. Playing along, playing dumb, he asked, "What do you want me to do?"

"I dunno. We can try something other than the cuffs for a change."

His erection twitched, and he swallowed a lump of

excitement. "Really?"

"Sure." She smirked. "What else was in the magic basket? Refresh my memory."

He rolled off the bed to check the top dresser drawer where they stashed the adult toys out of Nicole's reach. "Nipple clips?"

She wrinkled her nose. "Not today."

"Anal beads."

"Nah. I'm not really feelin' it." Joy shook her head and grabbed a pillow, tucking it protectively between her legs. "I'm an exit-only kinda girl."

"How about Ben-Wa balls?"

"If you put those in, where are you gonna put that?" She pointed to his denim-clad crotch.

"Ohh…" His gaze narrowed on her bow-shaped lips. "I know where I can put it."

"Is that so?" Joy gyrated her hips against the luckiest pillow in the world.

A little sixty-nine action might feel fine right now, however Tristan wanted Joy to forget her troubles, not through hard labor on her end but mind-blowing, memory-erasing sex to scrub the Mother's Day misery from her brain. Never mind her unappreciative offspring and their demented dad—she deserved nothing but pure, sweet love.

He pulled out a few purple satin scarves, the feather tickler, and a bottle of oil. "I wanna do something just for you right now." With his knee on the bed, he leaned over her.

"Mmm…" she hummed in delight, watching with curious wide eyes.

When he lifted the hem of her tank top, she sucked in a sharp breath, arching to let him pull it off, inch by glorious inch, giving him full view of ripe breasts begging for his mouth. Clenching his teeth, it took all his effort to restrain the animal instinct clawing for release. *Patience, man, patience.*

He took her slender wrist and wrapped the slippery fabric around twice before lacing one end through the slat at the edge of the headboard. Strutting to the other side of the king-sized bed, he showed off his new and improved biceps with a few flexes as he tugged the ends on the second scarf, like a body-building magician, then did the same procedure to her other wrist, tying her tight, spreading her arms like a T.

Then he crawled in the space between her long legs, ran his palms down the outside of her firm thighs, teasing behind her knees with his middle fingers, debating if he should tie them down as well. "You're not gonna hurt me with these dangerous weapons, are ya? I kinda need 'em to be free for what I've got planned."

Tristan cupped her heel in his hand and brought her narrow foot to his lips. He kissed the tip of her little toe, inching his way up the slope, then the arch and the ankle, while Joy's neglected foot rubbed between his thighs, creating friction that set him on fire.

When her big toe found the fold of his zipper, she husked, "Take 'em off."

"Soon, sunshine." He flattened her legs to the mattress, then whipped out a third scarf.

"Wait—what're you doing?"

"Having fun." Blocking her vision with the strip of satin, he crisscrossed it behind her head before tying the ends into a big bow over her eyes.

"I can't see."

"That's the point. Just feel. You've been stressing out since we met and I'm worried you might snap one of these days. Just lay back while I give you a ride that'll clear your mind right up. Get all those cobwebs out of the cogs. Give you something else to think about for a change."

"I wanna know what you're gonna do to me."

"Trust me."

"But…"

"But nothing." To keep her from spoiling the treat by talking, he untied the bow at her eyes, keeping the taut knot in place, then fed her the long ends of satin, just enough to keep her quiet. "No more words from you—got it? If you say *no* I'll hear it. Moan and groan all you want—in fact, I'm hoping for it."

Nodding, Joy's body wilted into the mattress.

"Good." Tristan got up, switched on the clock-radio, and turned up the volume loud enough so she couldn't hear the bottle tops opening, the cream squirting into his hand, and the slick friction as he warmed it between his palms.

****

What's this crazy man doing to me? Joy swallowed a scream, reminded by the mouthful of satin this was supposed to be a quiet, reflective time for her to enjoy, not interrogate Tristan on his intentions.

His goal was obvious—to rock her world, which did quite well. All the time. Every time.

She used to nibble her sons' adorable baby feet, but it was nothing compared to Tristan's delicious torture. Victor never nibbled her toes, ever. *Is this something other couples do?* She'd have to ask Lily. When his strong fingers pressed deep into her sole, penetrating the arch, she howled through the fabric.

Tristan stopped. "Are you okay?"

"Esss."

"Want me to keep going?"

"Ooo esss…"

"Okay." Joy could hear the smile in his voice.

In this frenzied moment, there was no room for thoughts of her boys, or Victor, or her parents, or anything at all. Not with Tristan's tongue gliding up the sensitive skin inside her left leg, while his wavy hair tickled the right one.

Joy spread her limbs, giving him more space to work his magic as he nuzzled the top of her thighs, panting his hot breath against the flimsy material before snagging the waistband between his teeth and tugging off her panties.

He wrapped her legs around his neck as he leaned over to lap up the liquid heat leaking below her hips, lavishing the intimate place with the same languid treatment he'd given to the rest of her body, paying special attention to the swollen nub craving his friction.

Ohhh. She moaned her approval, encouraging him to dive deeper while she rode the wave of ecstasy but it was impossible to hear anything over the little clock-radio pumping out sultry sounds: a haunting organ, heavy drums, a whining lead guitar, and thumping bass. When the singer belted out, "In A Gadda Da Vida, honey…" Joy felt the rough timbre in her knees. Just as she got into the trippy melody, Tristan's tender touch halted and he got off the bed.

Joy lifted her head, wishing she could see through the blindfold. "Uhddaya doin'?"

"Don't you wanna hear something a little more…I

dunno…modern?"

"No." Joy shook her head savagely. "*Weave* it."

"You like that song?"

"Yeah…o' course. It's a *cwassic*. Just *weave* da song and keep doin' what ya doin'."

"Bossy lady." Tristan put back the psychedelic tune. "I like a girl who knows what she wants." He kissed her nether lips like he kissed her mouth, making her grind against his five o'clock shadow. When he snuck in a finger, then two, Joy would have hit the ceiling if not for the restraints.

Damn, his big idea, tying me down. If only she could reach his head, she'd shove his face even closer to her core, as if it were possible. The vibration from his hungry humming ripped through her body like a shock of pleasure. All she could do was writhe and buck like a captured animal.

Then he stopped.

Joy didn't need to see to figure things out.

The quick unzip and rustle of his jeans said it all. The nightstand drawer slid open, then slammed shut, meaning one thing: party time.

With her useless arms unable to brace her for what was coming, Joy dug her heels into the mattress and pushed back against the pillow. Tristan's knee urged her thighs wider as he fit his hips against hers. Like a compass needle, the tip of his arousal found her pleasure point-of-no-return and slid inside *slo-o-ow*.

"Yesss," he hissed against her ear. "Feels sooo good…"

The instrumental ended, and the singer's thick voice kicked in again, "In A Gadda Da Vida, honey…" as Tristan plunged inside, making her scream despite the scarf. He pulled out, then pushed in with equal force and speed, working her into a lather while his lips found her breast.

As the song came to a bittersweet end, Joy released the most delicious explosion in the history of climaxes. Tristan was right yet again, effectively driving out every aching thought from her head and filling the black void with shooting stars and ribbons of rainbows until peace washed over her. The perfect happy ending to a not-so-perfect day.

Chapter Fifteen

Tristan's cell phone vibrated on the nightstand and he reached for it. With squinty eyes, he struggled to decipher the text message on the glowing screen. *Maybe it's time for reading glasses.*

—*going 2 work?*—Nick wrote.

With Joy cradled in his other arm, he typed back one-handed with his thumb.

—*maybe later*—

—*no prob. i'll bring niblet home b4 dinner. have fun ;P*—

Thank God he had a friend like Nick. No doubt his daughter was in good hands.

Thinking of good hands…Joy's limp body stirred to life. Her warm palm cupped between his thighs and caressed his sleeping dragon, rousing the beast. The sudden sensation of her delicate, deliberate touch had his body humming.

"How ya feeling?" He curled her closer against his side.

"Pretty good." Even with sleep still fresh on her face she was stunning. "How 'bout yourself?"

"I guess you can say I'm feeling pretty lucky."

Joy propped up on her elbow and smiled down, licking her lips. "How 'bout I return the favor from last night? If you want."

Tristan bit back a smile. "Oh, sunshine, I want."

"I was hoping you would." She threw the blanket over her head and wiggled between his knees, giving him the sweetest morning wakeup call a man could ask for.

Polishing his morning wood with her lovely little mouth felt like heaven and he had a hell of a time holding back from exploding too soon. Joy had a knack for knowing the right amount of suction, as her head bobbed to the rhythm of her stroking hand like a fine-tuned machine.

Unable to stand much more, Tristan covered his face with a pillow and bit hard on the softness to keep from bursting. He wanted to save it so they could finish together. After another minute of terrific torture, he reached down to pull her off, flipped her on her back and straddled her. "It's that time again."

"Ooh yesss…" she hissed.

Firmly in place with his erection in hand, ready to go for it…Joy's cellphone rang.

Dammit. Tristan recognized the intrusive air raid siren that belonged to her good-for-nothing ex-husband, calling to mess with her head. Now the guy was messing with his moment and his orgasm.

Joy's eyes widened. "I gotta take it. It could be my boys."

Knowing how much it meant to her, he rolled off the bed to grab the cell from the dresser. "Sure you don't wanna call him back later?"

"Please, Tristan."

Unable to resist her plea, he pressed the speakerphone button as he handed it to her.

"Hello?" Her eyes locked on Tristan for moral support.

He squeezed her shoulder and whispered, "Be cool."

"Joy?" Victor sounded surprised, as if hoping for her voicemail instead.

"The boys want to wish you a belated Happy Mother's Day—"

"They do?"

"Yeah, but they just left for school, so I'll have them call you later, after baseball practice. I just wanted to give you a heads up."

Joy shook her head, gnashed her teeth, then with a feistiness Tristan had never witnessed, she exploded. "Why the *hell* couldn't you have my boys call me yesterday?"

"I totally forgot. We were busy. What's the big deal?" Victor's unsympathetic verbal slap made Tristan want to lunge through the phone.

"You were sooo busy?" Joy spat in disbelief. "On Mother's Day? Really? Doing what?"

"We spent the day with Felicity's family. On their boat. It's more like a yacht," Victor rambled as Joy's eyes rolled up into her head so far Tristan got scared that she might be possessed. "No reason to get all pissy, Joy. I said they'll call you later."

"Why didn't they send me a card at least?"

"You're mad over a stupid card? God, you're such a baby. Why don't you grow up—"

Tristan grabbed the phone.

"Don't, Tristan, please," Joy squealed and buried her face in her hands.

"Listen, dude—" Fuming, he unleashed his bad cop. "What the hell is your problem?"

"Who is this?" Victor's voice cracked.

"Never mind who I am. You're the father of Joy's children. It's your responsibility to make sure they call their mother on Mother's Day and to send the woman a card when they're on your watch. You're the one that ought to grow up and stop teaching your boys to be disrespectful jerks like yourself."

Victor snickered. "Joy, tell your *girlfriend* to get off the phone."

The unexpected insult smacked Tristan's ego like a metal folding chair in the face at a professional wrestling match, egging on his inner warrior. "Girlfriend?" He snorted, accepting the challenge. "I'll get off the phone after you apologize to Joy for being such a loser."

"Joy, I apologize you're such a loser," Victor mocked with a guttural laugh. "And your friend's a loser too. I hope I get to meet your loser-friend when I drop off the boys in a few weeks."

"Yeah, you'll meet me all right. I'll be waiting for you. You can count on that." Tristan squeezed in the last words when her cellphone beeped, indicating Victor hung up first.

While he pounded his fist into his palm, ready to rumble, Joy shook her head with wide shell-shocked eyes. "Why…why did you get involved? I could've handled him without you butting in."

"I'm sorry. But I can't believe what a prick he is."

"I told you he was…but you had to open your mouth, didn't you? I just want my boys. No controversy. No conversation."

"Someone needs to put that piece of garbage in his place. He can't treat you like this." Enraged, he shoved his way into his clothes: jeans, T-shirt, socks. It was time to get to work, building her house a-sap, if that's what it took to ease her worried mind.

"That's the way he is. Now I have to fix this."

"Fix what?" He rammed the belt through the loops, taking out his stress on the thick leather strap.

"Fix everything. I know…" Joy snapped her fingers. "I'll just tell him you're a friend from work."

"What does it matter?" He slapped a baseball cap over his shaggy bed-head. "He brags about his relationship to you."

"I'm not like him."

Tristan paused halfway through the sleeves of his worn flannel work shirt. "Are you ashamed of being with me or something?" He spewed the jealous words before he could stop them, without considering that surprise visit from his ex-wife when he claimed Joy was the housekeeper-nanny rather than admitting she was his woman. But that was more for Joy's sake, protecting her from Stacy's interrogation than anything else.

"Seriously?" Joy gave him the evil eye, as if reading his mind. "You, of all people, are going *there*?"

"Your mother already knows about us. So what's the problem? You're still concerned your father's gonna find out we're living together? I'm working on your house as fast as I can." That was a big fat lie; Tristan delayed the project to keep her under his roof, at least until her boys arrived, because he loved having her around, even next door was too far away.

"This mess has nothing to do with any of that."

"Then why don't you want Victor to know you have a boyfriend?"

"Because…" Joy squeezed the corners of her eyes

at the bridge of her nose between her thumb and index finger. "If things don't work out between us, I don't want him to know another one of my relationships failed."

Tristan squinted, trying to comprehend this unforeseeable future that had her so worried. "What are you talking about?"

"The less Victor knows about my love life, the better I feel. Just like you not wanting Stacy to know your business."

Touché. "Okay. But, Joy, you don't really think we'd *fail*, do you? I mean, I don't think that that all, on any level. In fact, I think the opposite."

"You say that now because things are so new but who knows what'll happen down the line? What if you don't get along with my boys? Imagine having to deal with pint-sized Victors, times two."

Tristan did, and his whole body clenched. If Joy's kids were anything like their father, he'd have a hard time keeping his temper under control. From all he'd heard, her boys made *Damien* seem like an angel. He hadn't even met them but already diagnosed them with a dire need of a swift kick in the ass and a lesson on how to treat women, especially the woman who gave them life. Maybe they'd be fine once they settled into Scenic View, being around their mother and maternal grandparents, and under Tristan's watchful eye.

"Look, I'm not in love with your boys—" The words tumbled out without him thinking but they were true.

"My point exactly. If they don't like you, and you don't like them, where does that leave us? I can't send them back to be with their father just so I can be with you."

"Joy, don't get crazy. Let's see what happens when we come to that bridge."

Fat drops rolled down her cheeks and onto the pillow in her lap. "I'm afraid I already know what'll happen." She curled up on her side, pulling the covers over her head.

Her agonizing tears shredded his heart. "Please don't get upset over something that hasn't happened." Tristan sat on the edge of the bed to rub her back but she moved an inch away to escape his fingers. He took the hint and stood. "I'm not going anywhere, sunshine," he whispered, doubtful she heard him over her sobs, "I just wish you'd believe me."

****

Joy wished it were so easy. Believing Tristan was one thing, but knowing how difficult her boys could be was another.

Tristan's daughter was so easy to love. A sweet little girl, with a typical three-year-old's temper tantrum tendency, but beyond that she was a breeze compared to the boys. Being around Nicole brought on the itch to have another baby. *No. Wait. Don't even think about it.*

Right now she had to get through today, and the next, and the next. One day at a time was all she could handle.

Mason and Owen would be arriving soon and their nest still wasn't ready.

Across the yard, the heavy hammering indicated something was happening. With hope, this secret project was near completion. The exterior seemed done, with mocha shingles and crisp white trim, however she still hadn't seen the interior but Tristan promised she'd be pleased. He was doing his best. Doing it for her. For her family.

There was no doubt in Joy's mind Tristan loved her. No doubt he'd stick around even if her boys were their usual tough-to-love selves. He didn't come across as a quitter when the going got rough. But how long would it last before he grew weary of adjusting the attitudes of another man's brood? Especially around his impressionable child.

Maybe being in the new surroundings, without their father, would spark a positive change.

Joy only prayed these weeks apart were worth it. Enough to remedy the major issues, like the disrespectful backtalk, public meltdowns, and treating her like a doormat.

After a quick cry in the shower, she gave herself a pep talk in the bathroom mirror, then slapped on some make-up and tugged her *Everyday's Christmas* T-shirt over her head.

Second to making love to Tristan, working was the best medicine for de-stressing. Not only was she reeling from the usual menu of tension—her ex, her boys, her parents—today she had to figure out how to undo the damage she caused with Tristan, hurting his feelings.

She cruised downtown in the Green Machine, windows open, radio cranked to some unfamiliar pop song with a cool beat and undecipherable lyrics.

In the lot behind the shop, parked in *Mrs. Claus'* spot was Lorraine's red convertible. With a careful maneuver of the steering wheel, Joy fit the wide ride into one of the designated spaces for *Santa's Helper*—except some punk reversed the *N* and *T* in black marker.

Joy stepped through the open backdoor where Lorraine sat on an upside down milk crate, sorting through delivery boxes. "Sorry, I'm late."

"Late?" Lorraine glanced from the pages on the clipboard to her diamond-studded wristwatch. "I wasn't expecting you at all."

"Really? Why?"

Lorraine shrugged. "Maybe I misunderstood. I thought you'd asked for the day off. Last week you mentioned having to do something the day after Mother's Day. I figured you were going somewhere for a long weekend. Maybe down to see your boys. Never mind." She waved the words away. "I don't know if I'm coming or going anymore."

Joy cringed, remembering how she'd anticipated the worst Mother's Day and the likelihood of drinking herself into oblivion, which would require the day after to nurse the hangover. "Oh, yeah, well, I had a change of plans."

Lorraine flashed big blue eyes at Joy, opened her mouth to speak, then closed it quick as if tempted to ask about yesterday but knew better based upon their prior conversations. She sighed. "You know, if I hold the mortgage on the *Christmas Shoppe*, and make you a partner, you'd collect a regular paycheck, with a raise, of course. Think you can live with that?"

"Yeah." Joy nodded slightly, refraining from being overly enthusiastic, afraid of getting her hopes up. "Of course."

"I'll be a silent partner. We can hire some off-season help while you run things. And during the busy season we can bring in two or three more people." Lorraine tapped her pencil on the legal pad. "If my numbers are right, this place'll be all yours in…ten years."

"That's all?" Joy feigned optimism with a hollow chuckle and a heavy heart. "Ten years?"

She diverted her attention toward the calendar pinned on the corkboard to avoid the boss seeing the defeat her frown couldn't hide, and sighed, struggling to accept the bad timing of fate's generous hand. Scoring this job was enough of a blessing. But being invited to buy into it was more than she'd ever dreamed.

Everything happens for a reason, right? Too bad the old adage did nothing to ease the disappointment.

Damn Victor for his part in this pitfall.

Divorce was a burden, not only for her head and heart, but her bank account as well. If only she could win in one area of her screwed up life for a change—to afford this prosperous business or purchase the dream house; she'd graciously accept either at this pathetic point and still work toward the other.

A vision of her childhood home on Hollyhock Hill flashed in her mind. Some of the best days of her life were spent under that roof; she was certain her boys could be happy there too. Even though she'd be renting it, that was almost as good as owning it.

In that blissful image, Tristan stood on the porch in worn jeans and a dingy T-shirt covered in sawdust, sweat, and splatted paint. Joy's heart swelled. Despite this morning's communication breakdown, she was sure she could trust every word he said about not seeing an end to their relationship, but rather just the opposite, because deep down, whenever she'd let herself think about it long enough, she couldn't deny feeling it too.

However, she refrained from speaking the truth for fear she might be wrong.

At the end of the day, Joy didn't need to be a business-owner or a homeowner in order to feel complete when she had Tristan on her side. The man was more than enough to keep her happy. She just had to work harder at not sabotaging a good thing.

"I can't read these tiny numbers." Lorraine handed the clipboard to Joy. "Mind taking over for me?"

"Sure." Joy flipped through the pages, seeing how much new inventory was left to sort.

"Just a reminder, I'm flying down to Florida tomorrow to keep an eye on my mother while my brother picks his daughter up from college."

"I didn't forget."

"With some luck I'll convince her it's time to move up into a nursing home—as much as she's dead set against it."

Joy dreaded the day she would have to do the same for her parents; she didn't even want to think about it.

"She's ninety. Her mind is going." Lorraine shrugged. "That's what happens. But the alternative to getting old is what—dying?"

A clammy chill of guilt crept along Joy's spine for feeling sorry for herself when life really wasn't as bad as it could be. Compared to most people, she was still kind of young-ish and in good health, which was worth more than…what did Tristan call it? Anti-matter. "Aww, Lorraine. I'm sorry."

"I was only planning to stay a few days but now Ray wants to tag along. He suggested we extend it into a *lover's* getaway at his condo on the beach." Lorraine giggled like a schoolgirl. "He's so romantic. How can a girl say no to that? We've been trying so hard to keep a low profile around town. It'll be nice to not worry about everyone minding our business."

"How long will you be gone?"

"Well…" Lorraine blushed. "He's semi-retired now that his son runs the liquor store so he's in no hurry to get back to Scenic View. Maybe two weeks? Surely not more than three or four. Do you mind running the show while I'm gone?"

"Not at all. Stay as long as you want. Don't worry about a thing." Joy said over the warm glow of the trumpet's timbre in Herb Alpert's Christmas Album, which Lorraine kept on repeat. "I've got it covered."

"I know you do, hon. And I appreciate it." Lorraine paused. "This thing between me and Ray is heating up like a wildfire, I'd hate to pick up and leave him when the going is good, you know?"

As her thoughts drifted to Tristan, Joy nodded. *I sure do.*

"He's such a sweet man. I got the funny feeling he wants to get serious. I'm not sure I'm ready for it though. I really like him. After my husband passed away six years ago, I figured I'd live the rest of my life alone. I never imagined dating again. I mean, after all these years of seeing Ray at the civic meetings who knew he'd be interested in me? He'd lost his wife two years ago so we had that trauma in common which is what started us talking, strictly as friends. Then last October after the meeting we went to Brawny's Farm for their Fall Festival. After some spiked cider, we went into the corn maze. Can you believe the son of a gun kissed me? I was shocked although it wasn't half-bad. I felt like a teenager. A week later he took me to the movies. After that we went for walks on the beach, ate ice cream at the pier, and just started spending all our free time together. At first I felt guilty, but my kids assured me their father wouldn't want me to be lonely, so I just went for it."

Joy's heart swelled as she listened to Lorraine and Ray's love story. It made her think there truly was hope with Tristan.

"Even though I'm not certain where it'll lead, I'm looking forward to finding out. I ain't getting any younger. Oh never mind me, I'm a ramblin' fool. I gotta hustle. How do I look?" Lorraine fluffed her white-blonde hair and wiggled her plump hips.

"Great. As always."

"Thanks, hon. I'm meeting my main man for lunch. Between you and me and the Christmas trees, I've been staying at his place for the past few weeks. I only go home to water the plants and pick up my mail. Don't mention any of this to my sister. She thinks we're still just friends. The last thing I need is for Marie to flap her yap to the biddies at bingo while I'm not around to defend myself."

"My lips are sealed." Joy twisted the imaginary key to her mouth then tossed it over her shoulder.

After a quick hug, Lorraine was halfway out the backdoor before she stopped short, snapping her fingers. "Would you mind watering my plants while I'm away?" She pulled a keyring from her purse.

"Of course."

She pressed the cool metal into Joy's palm. "I know you have a lot going on. If you ever need to escape, feel free to use my place. And as long as your dog doesn't mistake my new carpeting for the backyard, the little guy can stay too. I just figured I'd put it out there, in case, you never know. Oh, and when your boys show up, if you need to take off a few days to get them settled, just tape a note to the front door so the customers know when we're reopening."

"Thanks, Lorraine." The farewell hug lasted longer this time before the woman was out the door again.

With a newfound calm and a secret smile Joy sat on a stool at the counter, combing through inventory paperwork, with Lorraine's words reverberating in her head: *I'm not certain where it'll lead; I'm looking forward to finding out.* That's exactly how Joy felt about Tristan, only with a dash of fear of the unknown, multiplied by heavy baggage on both sides.

If only her damn ex-husband wasn't such a vindictive prick.

The memory of this morning's phone call drowned out the sleigh bell song playing over the speakers.

Now that Victor knew Joy had at least one friend willing to stand up for her, she could only imagine the wicked wheels turning in his balding head, weaving a way to sabotage her relationship. The sonofabitch got off on making her miserable. When they'd tried couples counseling during their first year of marriage, the therapist warned Joy she was in for some trouble after suggesting Victor had a Napoleon complex and narcissistic tendencies, to which he gave the therapist explicit directions straight to hell.

How could she ever live happily with Tristan while her ex was still an albatross around her neck?

Joy sighed, propped her elbows on the counter and cupped her cheeks as she figured out a solution. "I just need to keep Victor away from Tristan, that's all." For all she knew, the lazy louse would send the boys on an airplane with a hired sitter, just to avoid the trek himself—especially since Felicity was too far along to fly.

All her worrying was probably for nothing.

But then again she's never known Victor to back down from an argument. After the words exchanged on the phone this morning, it wouldn't be a surprise if her ex made the trip especially to pick a fight. However, if he didn't know where to find Tristan then he would've showed up for nothing.

Joy reached into her sweater pocket and squeezed Lorraine's house key like a lucky charm.

Chapter Sixteen

The warm breeze and crystal clear sky over the Scenic View Fire Department was ideal for the annual Memorial Day barbeque bash. Tristan claimed the first empty picnic table he found although he would have preferred a shady spot under one of the old oaks, but once the sun shifted in an hour or so they'd be out of the direct hit from the blazing sunshine.

Thinking of sunshine, Joy was in automatic mother-mode, slathering a second coat of sunblock on his daughter's porcelain skin. After she'd gotten past her Mother's Day meltdown, she managed to snap out of the self-deprecating funk, thank God. He only hoped this quick change of heart was true enough to endure the long hot summer once her boys were in the picture.

He would've avoided this shindig and spent the day putting the final touches on her place but he wanted to put in some quality time with Niblet—who skipped off, hand-in-hand with Joy's parents.

Her name alone was enough to fill his heart with…joy. How could he properly thank the woman who brightened his dreary life like a ray of sunshine? She'd been an accommodating asset at his side through the recent change in his family status to primary caregiver. Heaven-sent and all his, he counted his blessings every night, grateful the Good Lord above put her in his path. With the new love of his life and his daughter under one roof, things couldn't be more perfect.

"Taking the day off, huh?" Wearing an apron that read CHEF FOR THE DAY, Nick scraped charred burgers off the barbeque with a spatula and dropped them onto a platter of open buns.

"Boss's orders," Tristan joked with a wink.

"Good for you." Nick placed a sausage pinwheel on Tristan's paper plate beside a cheeseburger. "Making some memories with the *fam*. I'm glad to see you're back to some version of your old self."

"Hopefully a better version." Tristan smacked his abs with an empty hand.

"Definitely better." Nick nodded.

"Well, if you got free time, why don't you consider the constable position?" Chief Maresca chimed in, dropping limp hotdogs onto the flaming grid, wearing an apron that matched Nick's. "They're looking for someone to fill the spot."

"I'm still burning my time with the Star Harbor Police Department until my terminal leave is over at the end of August."

"And knowing this guy, he'll ask for his old job back on September first," Nick gibed as he stuck his elbow into Tristan's ribs. "Watch—he'll be living in Star Harbor like he never left."

"I don't think so, buddy." Tristan nudged Nick back.

"Why? 'Cause you finally found a reason to stay?" Nick slid his eyes in Joy's direction as she picked lettuce leaves from a big bowl with tongs.

"Yeah. I think I did." Tristan couldn't control his growing grin. "I mean, I know I did."

"Does she know it?" Nick flipped a slab of bloody beef on the grill, spitting juice into the air.

"She knows. But not about the ring I've got in mind. I'm saving it as a surprise after her kids get settled. I figure maybe the end of the summer."

"That's kinda quick, isn't it?" The chief painted red sauce on the ribs with a long-handled brush.

"When it's right, it's right—that's my motto." Nick lined up another set of raw burgers over the fire.

"If you're gonna be here for the long haul then you oughta apply for the job. I'll even put in a good word for you. Plus you don't really wanna be swinging a hammer for this guy the rest of your life, do ya?" the chief snarked with a smile.

Tristan smirked. Truth was he had no problem working for Nick, but oddly enough he almost missed being a cop. "Maybe. I'll think about it." He wandered away with a full plate, following Joy toward their picnic table.

Before he sat on the bench, he put down his food to wrap his arms around her waist, and kissed the back of her neck in a quick display of public affection.

"Tsk…" Joy giggled, shrugging him off, and he let her slip from his grip. "People are watching."

"Oooh, people…they're everywhere…watching us…" He played up his spooky voice, wigging his fingers for added effect. "You really think inquiring minds care about a cop-turned-carpenter and the Christmas Shoppe girl? Come on, sunshine, give me a little credit, okay? You know I'd never get all *PDA* on you if your folks were around to see. They're over there with Nicole, somewhere." He pointed toward the flock of silver-headed seniors entertaining their grandchildren

242

under a shady tree.

Joy narrowed her eyes and twisted her pretty lips, undoubtedly concocting a viable comeback. "How much longer before I can move in next door?" She slid onto the bench across from him.

Tristan shrugged, purposely neglecting to mention he'd received the Certificate of Occupancy last week. Technically she could move in anytime, but he wanted to do a few surprise final touches before the big reveal. "Soon." He downplayed the excitement of the situation.

"Can I at least see it?"

He bobbed his head, as if considering her request although he had no intention. She was getting harder and harder to put off. "I'd really love to show you, but I'm still waiting for the final inspection from the Building Division. You don't wanna risk any fines just for sneaking a peek, do you?"

"Really, Tristan, this is ridiculous. Just snap a few pictures with your cellphone so I can at least see the inside."

"Ridiculous? More like precautious." He fought hard not to crack a smile at his own fabrication. For lack of a decent comeback, he went with the safe strategy of picking a fight instead. "What's ridiculous is you, bringing your own burgers to a barbecue."

"Excuuuse me for contributing. If I didn't bring the veggie burgers, no one would have brought them."

"Because no one else eats 'em."

"Maybe if they tried it, they'd like it." By Joy's tone, he knew her words were aimed at him but he didn't mind; her persistence to try new things came with good intentions although there was no way he'd give up hamburgers.

Tristan rolled his eyes. "Oh, quit acting like you don't eat meat."

"I don't," she squeaked in defense, screwing up her lovely face with a furrowed brow.

He chuckled, amused at her attempted anger, getting a kick out of her feisty reaction as he prodded her along. "Come on. I saw you with my own eyes eating bacon in my kitchen."

"That was a slip."

"A slip?" He snorted in feigned disbelief. "Is that what you call it? It's not like you fell and a plate of bacon accidentally landed in your mouth."

With her arms folded across her chest, Joy shook her head, rattling her ponytail. "It is what it is, whatever you may think."

Tristan wolfed down his double cheeseburger doused with ketchup, layered with tomato, lettuce, and extra pickles, and considered getting up for another. "I think if you really don't eat meat, then you wouldn't've slipped—simple as that. But if you really *want* to eat meat, just do it, it won't make you a bad person. Anyway, you eat fish, and to some people that's considered meat."

Joy gave him the evil eye through thick lashes. "You know what I think? You just hijacked this conversation because you don't want to talk about the house," she rumbled low enough no one else but Tristan could hear. "Don't you understand? I *have* to be in there before the boys come. I need to get set up. I don't want Vic—" She clenched her lips and turned her head as if rewinding the words, reconstructing her thought. "I don't want my kids to show up and see I'm not ready for them when I've had plenty of time to get my act together, find a place to live, and create a space for them. I want to be settled. Order furniture. Set up their bedrooms. I need them to be comfortable on day-one, not give them a reason to complain, wishing they were living with their dad. The last thing I want is for them to live in limbo like I've been doing—"

The moment Sophia and Nicole came into focus, Joy clammed up.

Tristan jumped to his feet, ready to relieve Sophia, but the woman winked at him as if this fun-run wasn't finished, detouring toward a patch of dandelions at the bottom of the grassy hill. Whatever the reason for Sophia and Nicole's instant bond, he wasn't about to question it. Seeing his daughter's successful adjustment to this new life brought him peace of mind he never expected. Between Joy, Nick, Lily, and the Barbieri's as a support system, being a single father wasn't as traumatic as he'd anticipated, based on horror stories told by other divorced dads.

"Of all people to make a match—who'da thunk—your mom and my daughter would hit it off." Squinting in Nicole's direction, he wished he remembered his sunglasses, not so much to block the bright afternoon sunshine, but to hide happy tears welling up out of nowhere.

"Here ya go." Joy handed him a napkin across the table. "Sentimental stud," she teased with a tender smile. "Don't think I don't notice."

"Damn allergies," he mumbled, just in case anyone else caught him dabbing the dampness along his lower lashes. "I guess she's filling the void with Nicole until her real grandchildren get here."

"Nah. That's my mother. She's always been like

that. She can't stand me, but she has a soft spot for other people's kids."

Sophia and Nicole circled around again, aiming for the picnic table.

"That was an exciting adventure. I introduced Nicole to the ladies from bingo. And all Bob's domino buddies." Sophia plopped on the picnic bench beside Joy, snatched a napkin from the stack, then patted her forehead and upper lip. "Boy, am I pooped. That breeze feels good."

"Here—" Tristan snapped the seal off his bottle of chilled water and offered it to Sophia.

The wind caught the loose napkins, blowing them down the length of the table, and Joy hopped up to collect them before they got away. Then she lifted the little girl onto the bench and offered some food from her plate. "Wanna try a bite of my veggie burger, Niblet?"

"Nuh-uh." Nicole wrinkled her little button nose. "No tanks, Joy."

Sophia frowned. "Don't force the child to eat your fake meat."

"Tsk. It's not fake meat, Ma. Just vegetables." Joy lifted the top of the bun revealing a thin, beige patty, with a mosaic of red, yellow, orange, and green specks pressed into the sickly circle.

"Vegetables smashed together to look like a hamburger." Sophia waved her hand at Joy's fabricated food.

"I'm not forcing her. Just asking her to try it."

"You're trying to turn her into an *Episcopalian*, aren't you?" Sophia wagged her finger at her daughter. "It's not your job. That's his job." She pointed to

Tristan, then at Joy's plate. "Do you eat stuff like that?"

"Nope. I'm a *meatitarian*."

Sophia expelled a haughty huff through her nostrils. "Yeah, me, too."

"I'm a pescetarian, Ma," Joy corrected.

"Whatever, Joy." Sophia rolled her eyes. "You ate meat when you were a kid. In fact, you ate anything that wasn't nailed down. Did Joy mention, she wasn't always this svelte supermodel? In ninth grade, we enrolled her in Camp *Eatswithafork*." Sophia hiked a thumb at Joy.

"Uhh, no, Mother. I didn't mention that fabulous summer at fat camp. And it was called Camp East Fork. Thanks for bringing it up."

"What a waste of money sending you there. I have the only kid who gained weight. She didn't lose it until she went away to college. They say freshman put on fifteen pounds. Well, she lost fifty. Her father and I didn't even recognize her."

Tristan sat in stunned silence, waiting for the hormonal tide to shift between these two strong-willed, estrogen-laden ladies.

"Come on, Nicole." Sophia stood, smoothing her seersucker pants. "Let's get a hotdog. Then we'll have a snow cone, if it's all right with your daddy."

Tristan nodded his approval.

"'No cone? I never had one of dose? Dat like an ice cream cone or sumtin?" Nicole slipped her hand into Sophia's without question and they disappeared into the crowd.

"That was awkward." Tristan eyed Joy, trying to imagine fifty extra pounds on her trim frame. No doubt she would have been just as beautiful.

Joy didn't even seem embarrassed, as if she was used to this sort of public berating. Palms up, she shrugged. "That's my mother. Welcome to my world. Better get out while you can."

"Nah."

"Don't say I didn't warn you—your name might be next on her shit list."

"I think I can handle it."

"You know I'm not trying to force your daughter into being anything she isn't, don't you?" Joy said with a gentle defensiveness.

"Did you hear me complain? If she wants to eat veggie burgers, I'm all for it."

"Then why don't you taste it? Just to see what it's like. Maybe she'll be willing to try it if Daddy does it." Joy pushed her barely bitten burger toward him.

"Okay. I will. No biggie." A veggie burger was the very last thing Tristan wanted in his mouth, but for Joy's sake since she asked so sweet and to prove he was more open-minded than a three-year-old—he bit into it anyway. "Hmmm…Has an interesting flavor." It was gross, with the texture of a dry sponge. He wanted to spit it out but bounced it around his tongue instead, hoping to avoid terrorizing his taste buds until it slid down the pipe, unchewed. "But I don't want to make a meal of it. No offense."

Rivulets of fragrant smoke painted the air over the barbeque pit, beckoning Tristan for another link of crisp sausage, or ribs, or anything red-blooded to wash out the nasty taste.

Instead, he grabbed the closest edible thing—a fist full of pretzels from the plastic bowl in the center of the table, while Joy nibbled on her weird food, happy as a bunny in a carrot patch.

"Don't you miss eating meat? Forget bacon. I'm talking about a juicy, marinated filet mignon. Or roasted turkey with all the fixings on Thanksgiving. Or just a plain old hot dog." Tristan hoped his lighthearted, curious tone was enough to keep Joy from fretting over the house, which, undoubtedly, would be ready on time.

"Sometimes," she admitted with a reluctant half-smile. "But when I think of eating a calf or a little chick, my stomach cramps up."

"And you don't get the same physical reaction when you think of a cute fish-face?"

"Nope," Joy said straightaway.

"You don't feel a little bit sad for a salmon? Swimming upstream, going through hell and high-water to find its birthplace, just so it can spawn to make more salmon-babies for you to feast on." Tristan almost felt bad for the hardworking fish.

"I've told you this before, I draw the line at fur and feathers."

"Didn't you learn anything from watching Finding Nemo the other night? It was like a public service announcement—*fish are friends, not food*."

"Ha ha." Joy swallowed the last bite of her burger, licking her fingertips like she didn't want to waste a tasteless bit. "Food is fuel. I was an emotional eater for most of my life. It took me a while to break out of the habit. Now when I get upset, rather than pig out, I work out."

"No kidding." Tristan's gaze skimmed her sun-kissed cheeks, down the length of her graceful neck and satiny shoulders connected to toned arms—shapely but not shredded.

"I can see the fruits of your labor." Joy nodded toward his biceps, starting to get their healthy bulge back after a long stretch of neglect. "Working out is paying off."

Flattered she noticed, Tristan smiled, flexing without intent. "You've been a good inspiration." *In more ways than one.* "I even gave up cigarettes 'cause of you." And without the ugly withdrawal symptoms he'd experienced whenever he tried quitting in the past. This attempt, the timing must have been right. It also helped being with the right person, keeping him grounded and out of the high-stress zone. Plus their mattress Olympics occupied his attention; he forgot all about those cancer sticks. "You oughta be a personal trainer. A fitness motivator."

Joy shook her head. "I think I'm better off focusing my energy on *Everyday's Christmas.*"

"You really have your heart set on that store, huh?" Of course she did and he knew it, considering it made up a chunk of their post-sex pillow talk, daydreaming about her professional five-year plans and beyond. She was passionate about the shop and he had no doubt one day it would be her name on the sign where Lorraine's was now.

"I do. But I also have my heart set on the house…and you."

"You got me."

"For now." The confidence in her voice faded.

Tristan gave her a sideways stare. "I thought we were past that crazy talk?"

"We are." Joy twisted a napkin into a tight rope. "But still, I can't help but wonder how you and my boys will manage to get along."

He snatched her hands across the table and laced his fingers with hers. "Even if we don't, don't worry about it now. Give 'em time to get to know me first."

"Tristan…" Throwing her head back with a heavy sigh, she blinked a few times at the bright blue sky as if all the answers were up there somewhere.

"What's on your mind, sunshine?" Waiting for her words was torture but he downplayed his concern for her benefit.

When her gaze drifted back to his, a hint of suffering flickered in her tired eyes. Whatever was bothering her now must have been what kept her up last night, blaming the tossing and turning on an upset stomach. "If you, Mason, and Owen don't get along, you and I are going to have to rethink our entire relationship." She stole one hand away from him and, with her elbow propped on the table, rested her cheek against her palm.

"Seriously, I can't imagine them not liking me. Can you?"

Joy lifted a shoulder in doubt with a nervous smile tugging one corner of her lips. "No. Not really. But I don't want to jinx anything by assuming the best."

"So you'd rather presume the worst?"

"Yep." She nodded once.

Tristan narrowed his eyes, wishing he could read her thoughts in order to elevate her fears. "I bet you're investing all this unwarranted energy, stressing for nothing. But if worrying makes you feel better, don't stop because I'm asking you to."

"If Victor could poison their impressionable minds against *me*, their *own* mother, I can only imagine what he's filling their heads with about *mommy's friend* since having it out with you over the phone." Joy squeezed Tristan's fingers, hesitation straining the delicate lines of her face. "When the boys get here in a few days, I don't think introducing you right away is the best idea."

Joy's unexpected words threw Tristan off kilter. *Not introduce me?* How else would he employ his delicately planned damage control without meeting the boys? Disappointed, he released her hand and curled his fingers into tight fists, hiding his irritation by tapping his knuckles on the wooden tabletop to the music. "Are you kidding?"

She lowered her gaze, avoiding his, and shook her head.

"Then when?" His volume drew curious stares from people at the next table.

She rubbed her temples as if the conversation she started was too much to bear. "After they meet a few other people around town. Made some friends. This way when they meet you, you'll just blend into the mix."

"And in your grand plan do you have a specific date marked on the calendar for this calculated introduction?" Getting a straight answer from her was like talking to a perp. Now would be a good time for handcuffs, but rather than take her to the bedroom he was ready for the interrogation room.

"I was thinking…maybe toward the end of the summer, after they start school."

"Wait—what? You were *thinking*? How long has this been on your mind? And why on God's green earth would you bring it up now, here, in front of the entire town?" He whisper-shouted. "You'll let me keep your dog but you won't introduce me to your kids? What's up with that?"

"Tristan, shhh…" She shrank in her seat. "Everyone can hear you."

"I don't care about everyone right now. All I care about is your decision to *not* introduce me to your kids."

With a quick hand, Joy brushed a tear from her cheek as if she didn't want him to see. As if he wouldn't notice. "It's not a decision. Just the best tactic I can come up with to make the transition smoother."

"For them? Or for you?"

"For all of us."

"And how, *exactly*, is that gonna work anyway since we'll be next door neighbors?"

"I don't *exactly* know but I'm sure we'll figure it out. Besides you and I can benefit from a little personal space considering I'm technically an overnight guest who never left."

"Space? Don't even go there—that's a bad excuse for people scared of a good thing."

"I'm not scared of anything." But her wide glossy eyes and wavering tone revealed a different story.

"Coulda fooled me. You're scared of what your kids'll think. Of what your folks'll say. What your ex-husband'll do." He strangled the air in his fists. "And you know damn well you're more than a guest." His voice escalated so he slammed his mouth shut, giving him a moment to respond thoughtfully and adjust his volume. *Where the hell was all her gibberish coming from?* "What's really going on, Joy?"

"Calm down. Nothing's going on. I have one shot to make things work with my boys and I don't want to ruin it."

"Yeah, I get that. But what about us?"

"I'm not talking about staying away from each other forever. Just for a little while."

"And what about Nicole? You need some space from her too?"

"This has nothing to do with you and Nicole. I adore you both and you know it. But I can't afford to screw things up with my kids." Joy pressed her prayer hands to her profile and exhaled a long breath. "I don't know what else to do. And you don't even know if you're still gonna be in town once the end of August rolls around."

Clearly this domestic dilemma pained Joy as much as it killed him, so Tristian dialed down the intensity on his emotionally charged responses. He would've blurted out his intention to stay in Scenic View as a permanent fixture but he wanted to save that tidbit for a future surprise. Besides she'd probably presume he was saying it in the heat of the moment to undermine her grand plan.

"So…" He shrugged, making light of the whole situation—lighter than the hot air balloon everyone pointed at, drifting a quarter-mile above the firehouse. "This summer we'll just wave across the yard and next summer we'll plan some fun stuff—like beach trips, and barbeques, and baseball games."

"Thank you." Her weak words came out like a ragged whisper, as she swiped an escaped tear with her finger.

"Ya think you and I can find a way to spend time together without the kids?"

"I'm sure my mother won't mind watching them so we can go on a date."

"A date?" He chuckled. "That's a giant step backward, isn't it?"

"I need you to support me, not trash my idea. I'm doing the best I can."

"Nobody's trashing ideas. We haven't put in proper dating-time anyway. It'll be fun."

"You know the key Lorraine gave me, so I could water her plants while she was out of town?"

"Yeah."

"She said I could stay there until the house is done."

Tristan cringed. "You really wanna do that?" His heart said no, but her glassy green gaze said it was something she had to do.

"I think it's for the best. It'll just be for a few days since you said the house is almost done anyway."

"Starting tonight?"

Joy shook her head as if she really didn't want to go at all. "Tomorrow."

Looks like he'd be spending the week rushing through the finishing touches. With a conceding sigh, he said, "You oughta keep the van. You're gonna need it to get around town."

"You sure?"

"Yeah. Nick's got a pickup truck I can use."

"Another thing...Lorraine has new carpeting. Would it be all right if Rex stays with you?"

"Fine, Joy, fine." Nodding at her every word like a bobble-head doll, Tristan swallowed her small demands and forced a smile. This was harder than negotiating his divorce only because he was in love with Joy and didn't want to ruin a good thing over hurt feelings. "We'll do it your way."

But once the dust cleared, he wanted things back the way they were this morning, when he woke up beside her and everything in his life was perfect.

****

After the barbeque Joy dropped off Tristan and Nicole on Hollyhock Hill then cruised over to Lorraine's place to water the plants. She'd attended to them yesterday so they'd be fine for another day or two, but she could benefit from quiet time and a little space.

Her executive decision may have seemed harsh and selfish and made him feel bad but it was something she had to do to ensure things were as perfect as possible for her nuclear family's sake. It wasn't meant to be a tug of war between her lover and her children, but if it were the case, her boys would win every time, hands-down, no questions asked. What else was a mother to do? Sacrifice came with the territory and Tristan needed to understand. Period. The end. No room for discussion.

They say talking to plants helps them flourish but Lorraine's thriving greenery might be better off not hearing about Joy's bad day so she turned on the radio instead.

After lowering the window shades for the evening and switching on the small lamp in the corner, she sat on the couch, replaying the dialog from the day, wondering if she said the right things, and somehow nodded off.

When her cell played Tristan's happy ringtone, she jumped to her feet and grabbed the phone from her pocketbook.

"Hey sunshine. Coming home soon?" He sounded sad.

"I'm sorry." She stretched and yawned. "I fell

asleep. What time is it?"

"Almost ten." Tristan snorted a familiar fake laugh. "I thought maybe you decided to move in there tonight and forgot to say goodbye."

Another call beeped through and she glanced at the screen. It was Victor. "It's *him*. I'll call you right back."

"I love you." Tristan unleashed the four-letter-word that she no longer considered a crime, just as she cut over to the other call.

Joy's heart sank, wishing she didn't disconnect so fast. She would have said it too although she was still hesitant to say it first. It wasn't their habit to say I love yous since their actions always spoke louder but tonight he must have felt the need for long-distant reinforcement since she shook up everything that seemed to be going so well.

She collected her frayed nerves before saying, "Hello."

"God, you take forever to answer. What are you so busy doing?" Victor snapped as if she owed him an explanation.

Too mad at herself for ever upsetting the one she loved, Joy didn't have the energy to retaliate against the jerk she despised. She was still reeling from Tristan's *I love you* and the fact that he probably thought she didn't feel the same since she didn't return the words.

"You gotta pick up the boys at MacArthur Airport."

"What?" Joy's heart pounded, stunned. "When— now? You didn't tell me they were flying in today."

"Does it really matter? They're here. It's what you wanted, right?"

She stalled. "I would have appreciated a heads-up."

"Here's your heads-up—pick up your kids. They're exhausted."

Joy must've caught every red light along the route because it took forty minutes to get across town, onto the Long Island Expressway, and over to the airport. Then another twenty minutes to get into the parking lot, find a spot, and locate her children.

Too bad this reunion wouldn't be like the ones in the movies: racing through the terminal into a flying hug. Before approaching Victor, Joy turned on her cellphone's voice recorder app—something she should have done throughout the divorce—and tucked it into the breast pocket of her denim jacket to capture every word if he started trouble.

She peered around the pillar before making her presence known to her ex sandwiched between their two beautiful boys. Stepping up behind them, she knelt to their level in case she collapsed. "Hi, boys," she said soft and low, like approaching a pair of skittish pups. "I'm so happy to see you." Her fingers itched to hug them, but they just stared at her, confused, like she was some sort of dangerous stranger.

Victor turned with a scowl. "What the hell are you doing sneaking up on us like that?"

Neither boy seemed willing to be the first to inch forward to greet their mother. Victor didn't even suggest it. Joy didn't push it. She just sucked back her tears and pretended nothing bothered her. *Time, they just needed time*—it was the mantra she needed to keep sane. They all needed time to adjust to this new equilibrium.

Joy led them toward the exit where she parked as close as she could.

"What the hell is that?" Victor screwed up his face at the sight of the Green Machine. "Where's the Jaguar?"

"I-I thought you knew."

"Knew what?"

"It was totaled. I called the insurance company and filed a claim."

"Are you kidding me?"

"Why would I kid about that?"

"Totaled? Really?"

Joy nodded.

Victor let out a pent up sigh. "That's just great, Joy. You know how much that car was worth? My folks are gonna be flipping pissed. They warned me not to let you drive it while you were in Florida, never mind let you take it to New York. I was gonna drive it home. Now what am I gonna do?"

"Buy a plane ticket." Joy hoped.

Victor glared. "You know I hate flying. I only made this trip because of the car and them..." He hitched his thumb at the children like they were some terrible inconvenience. "I only had enough *tranqs* for the flight here."

"Have a few cocktails." Joy's gaze followed a plane taking off, wishing Victor was on it.

"That'll just make me have to get up to pee a dozen time."

Then wear a diaper, ya big baby, Joy almost spewed but she managed to restrain her tongue. "If you want to spend the night in the Scenic View Inn, I'll pay for it." She hoped he didn't really expect her to cover his expenses but she didn't want him staying with her.

Victor loaded the suitcases in the back of the van

as Joy strapped the boys into the backseat. While leaning over, she took an extra moment to inhale the powdery scent of their matching mop-tops. God, how she missed them. Then, out of nowhere, Victor bumped against her backside.

"How about your mother watches the boys and you spend the night with me?" He squeezed her hip. "For old time's sake."

Joy froze. *Like hell.* Her purse with the pepper spray was between the front seats, out of reach. *Damn.* "No, Victor," she said, firm, clear, and calm, as if disciplining the dog.

"Aww, don't get your hopes up. I'm just kidding." He released his grip. "Still can't take a joke, huh?" Victor opened the passenger door and climbed in. "I just wanted to see what you'd say."

What did he think she'd say? Joy wondered as she slid into driver's side, afraid to know.

"Let's get the boys settled in first, then I'll take a taxi to the hotel. Breaking the news that they're moving to this one-horse town traumatized them enough. I don't want to ruin their first night in their new home."

"I'm not officially in our final destination yet. It's still being…refurbished."

"Don't tell me you're squeezing in with your folks."

"No, I've got my own place." *Sort of.*

"Thank God. No offense, but I'm not in the mood to deal with your father."

Because you broke his little girl's heart.

Victor's phone rang some flowery tune. "Just be quiet, okay?" he warned before answering.

"No problem." The less Joy had to speak to this

castrated hellhound, the better off she'd be.

"Of course I'm not spending the night with *her*. Stop worrying," he said in a strangely sweet intimate whisper Joy didn't recognize. "I'm going to a hotel. But even if I did stay at her place, you know nothing would ever happen. Come on, Felicity, we've been through this. I thought you were over it. I know you're hormonal. But I told you already—I'm not even attracted to her."

Joy rolled her eyes, the feeling a million times mutual. The fact that Felicity was jealous of Victor and Joy being together was comical since the woman seemed quite confident when she snatched him away while he was still married. But being eight months pregnant must be getting the best of her.

The cellphone in Joy's jacket pocket rang Tristan's tune but she was driving and couldn't answer even if she wanted to, so she let the call go to voicemail. At the first red light, she changed the setting to Vibrate. No need to instigating any curiosity in her ex.

Cruising down the LIE, Joy intermittently glanced in the rearview mirror at her boys, asleep like two cherubs. As the reality of being with her little loves set in, a wave of warmth and calm washed over her, although she was undeniably more than a little scared what their reaction will be once Victor left. She gave herself a silent pep talk while ignoring her passenger rambling about his soon-to-be bride and their baby on the way. She had to make things work here with the boys because she couldn't stand the thought of moving back to Florida to be near them if they insisted on being with their father.

When they pulled into the narrow gravel driveway,

Victor snorted, "This is it? It's smaller than my shed."

"It's my friend's house."

"Don't tell me—the friend I spoke to on the phone?"

"A *different* friend. I'm housesitting while she's out of town." Joy cut the engine and got out, careful not to slam the van door and wake the children.

"How do I know Lorraine's not really a dude ready to pounce on me?"

"Does it look like a man lives here?" She unlocked the front door and stepped over the threshold, setting her pocketbook on the armchair beside the fireplace. To her delight Victor gagged on the unexpected odor of mothballs and disinfectant, which she was used to by now. Everything inside Lorraine's place was lacy, and doilies, and mismatched pastel floral-print, which must have put her ex at ease, although she wasn't thrilled being alone with the man that brought her the most misery. "The boys can stay in the bedroom."

"*Theee* bedroom?" Victor shook his head in disbelief.

"What did you expect? Lorraine's a single woman. This is a one-bedroom bungalow."

While Joy turned down the blanket on the full-size mattress, Victor carried in the sleeping boys one at a time and set them side-by-side before bringing in their bags. She slipped off their little sneakers, debated if she should remove their street clothes but decided to leave them dressed since they looked too peaceful to disturb, then tiptoed out of the bedroom and shut the door.

Victor dropped two suitcases beside the fireplace. "Where's that rat you used to have? At the pound?"

"*Rex* is staying with another friend until my place

is ready."

"Look who's suddenly Princess Popularity of Scenic *Skew*. You seem to have rekindled a lot of friendships in a short amount of time, huh? What about the *friend* I spoke to on the phone? Is he your boyfriend?"

Yes, Joy wanted to scream. Only a few hours had passed but she missed Tristan like crazy, wished he was here to support her, yet glad he wasn't so he didn't have to suffer through this nonsense with her ex. Instead she sighed, drained dry by the non-stop sequence of emotional events. "Does it really matter?"

"Yeah." Victor bobbed his head. "It kinda does. I want to know who's lurking around my boys."

"He's…" Tempted to admit she loved the man in question, Joy bit her tongue and blurted, "A guy from work. I think he's gay or something. I dunno. I never asked."

"You got a job?" He snickered. "Doing what?"

Joy didn't want to give in to his taunting interrogation, keeping the important secrets close to her heart, but she couldn't help it. "The Christmas Shoppe in town."

"Wow. You got new friends. A new job. A new house. And now you got the boys too." Victor paced the cramped living room, counting off Joy's assets with an odd glimmer in his beady eyes. "Had I known you'd be living the good life I never would've agreed to let you take the boys out of state." He chuckled malevolently. "I was so sure once you got here, you and your parents would be at each other's throats. I even bet Felicity you'd be back in Florida by July, making all this aggravation a waste of everyone's time." He circled

around, getting closer to her. "But look at you now."
She stepped back until her shoulder blades bumped
against the wall and the heat of his sour breath melted
her cheek. "You got it all, don't you? Including my
kids."

Joy swallowed a bitter lump of fear she hadn't felt
since before leaving Florida. *No, not fear...* She wasn't
afraid, physically, of this pipsqueak man-child. More
like repulsion mixed with the uncertainty of his
manipulative motive. Would he kiss her or clock her?
Either way, she could handle the situation. "I'll call a
taxi for you now."

"I was thinking, what if the boys wake up confused
and scared being in a strange new place?" Victor peeled
off his nylon jacket and plopped on the sofa, making
himself at home.

"We'll be fine."

"But they don't want you." He dealt the low-blow
in a subtle matter-of-fact tone that stung more than Joy
would ever admit. "They told me so."

She tightened her lips into a thin line and nodded.
"I'll manage."

"I know it hurts to hear but it's true. The boys want
their daddy." He shrugged as if he wasn't guilty of
brainwashing the children. "I even have an affidavit
from a reputable child psychologist saying this big
move is a bad idea. I was hoping I wouldn't have to use
it, but I'll be forced to give it to my lawyer if you aren't
nice to me."

"Nice to you? Seriously? The only reason the boys
have anything against me is because you poisoned their
innocent little minds. What did the psychologist say
about that?" A million potty-words popped in her head,

all of which would spark a fight she wasn't in the mood to finish.

"I did what I had to do to ensure I'm the favorite parent. All's fair in love and war, baby. You would have done the same thing if you could've."

"No, I wouldn't." Joy gritted her teeth. "Because I'm not a twisted troll like you."

"Troll?" Victor shot up, edging dangerously close. "You're beautiful when you're all pumped up, you know that?" He stroked her cheek with his knuckles. "Can't we stop fighting for one night and pretend we like each other for a change?"

"I'm more comfortable with the reality of us hating each other." Joy sidestepped to get away, hoping her phone was still recording this conversation, but Victor pinned her in the corner.

"Hate? I don't hate you, if that's what you think. Do I think marrying you was a huge mistake? Yeah, I'm not gonna lie. I should've cut you loose at the altar after the miscarriage, but you were so gung-ho to hold on to me, I figured, what the hell"—a malevolent smirk curled his lips—"she's good in bed and gives a decent blow job."

Raising her chin gave Joy an inch of height, enough to stare down her nose at the lowlife she once loved. "If anyone shoulda done the dumping, it was me."

"You would've been doing both of us a favor in the long run. But then again, if we never stuck it out as long as we did, Mason and Owen wouldn't be here today. I'm tired of this war. Let's just make peace and then we can be like all the other divorced parents, sharing custody, getting along like old friends."

Joy's fingers trembled with rage. She wished she could pretend, for the sake of sparing herself from whatever dopey ideas Victor had in mind, but she couldn't. "You're not my friend. I don't even like you. Actually I borderline despise you. If it weren't for the children, I wouldn't even speak to you."

"Come on, Joy. Stop being such a bitch. You used to be so sweet when you were fat. Maybe it was all the cookies in your bloodstream. Stop starving yourself to prove a point just 'cause you're mad at me."

"I've never starved myself."

"You quit eating meat. That's close enough."

"It had nothing to do with my feelings for you, and everything to do with making healthier choices. Why are you so ignorant?"

His dark eyes seemed fathomless, like black marbles in his shiny skull. "You always did play hard to get. From what I recall, it was kind of fun." He waggled his eyebrows.

"I only played hard to get with you, Victor."

"What's that supposed to mean? You give it away easy to other guys? Is that it?"

Joy shook her head, realizing Victor would never comprehend how repulsive he was to her after everything he put her through.

"Well, it doesn't really matter now, does it? We're divorced. Give it all away to anyone you want, I don't really care. And you can still play hard to get with me, but I'll still win," he sang, tauntingly, like this was some kind of playground game. "I always get what I want and you know it." Victor closed his eyes and puckered up as he leaned in for a kiss.

"No, you won't." Joy kneed him in the groin. She

could have gone for a harder hit but she didn't want his shriek to wake the boys. The last thing she needed was for Mason and Owen to side with Victor. *Mommy beat up Daddy.*

When Victor buckled in half, cupping his crotch, Joy darted to the bathroom and locked the door. Why the hell did she let this situation get so far out of control? What was she thinking? She snorted at her murky hindsight, knowing exactly what was on her mind—she wanted her children to see her as the quintessential good mom. The better parent. The peacekeeper. Once she had the kids in the van she should have burned rubber before their father climbed in the passenger seat. She had no good excuse for giving her ex the benefit of the doubt that he could be a decent person for once in his rotten life other than wanting this to be a smooth transition for the boys' sake, however it turned into a godawful judgment call as bad as marrying the guy in the first place.

She pulled the cellphone from her pocket, lucky to find the red battery icon with two percent left and the voice recorder app still collecting data, but that didn't mean both sides of the conversation were captured. If she were smarter, she would have spent some time playing with the functionality a few times to ensure it worked. Hopefully she had enough threatening dialog to use against Victor if need be.

But what if she didn't?

She ought to call the police, but what if they didn't see things her way? What if Victor looked like the poor victim he played so well? Joy didn't want to call her folks and drag them into this domestic dispute. And she wouldn't dare get Tristan involved. Seeing his name appear in the text message notification window made her heart flutter, but she didn't have time to read it.

Maybe she ought to listen to the recording? She pressed a button, stopping the numbers on the counter, then hit the black square to Save Recording. Her thumb hovered over the green triangular Playback button, but what if Victor heard it? No doubt he'd throw a tantrum and smash the device to smithereens. Then she'd be shit out of luck for sure.

Instead she tapped the red circle to start a new recording but the phone died. Now she couldn't call anyone.

"A door won't keep me out, Joy." Victor rapped on the other side. "I'll rip it right off the hinges."

Joy laughed at his exaggerated ability. Still she didn't want to take the chance of him trashing Lorraine's house, so she disengaged the lock but didn't come out.

Victor turned the knob, and the door swung open in eerie silence. "What's a nice girl like you doing in a place like this?" he teased, limping over the threshold.

Fury set her blood ablaze yet she refused to squirt an angry tear. Best to be done with this insane game and get on with the night. Knowing Victor, he wouldn't let up until he exhausted every opportunity to have his way with her. She just had to keep dodging him until he ran out of steam. Just like old times.

"Oh, come on." He puffed out his chest, looking more like one of his little boys than a grown man. "Please. I'll beg if you want."

"No, thanks. Really. I'm totally fine with abstinence."

"Why are you being so stubborn? It's not like we

never had sex before. Geez, Joy. You can't deny it was the best part of our relationship." Victor swayed her in his arms, working his way around until his hips pressed up against her from behind.

A bit of vomit burned a trail up her throat. Once they cleared the honeymoon stage, eons ago, sex with this crude creature had never been anything more than an obligatory effort on her part, but now wasn't the time to mention it.

"It's the least you can do since totaling the Jaguar without telling me." The familiar itty-bitty pencil stub in his pants poking her bottom was barely anything to be worried about.

"What about Felicity?"

"This has nothing to do with her. I love her, but she hasn't let me touch her in months. I'm aching for it. Consider this a medical procedure, like a sperm donation. And if you don't have a boyfriend like you say, then you must be as hard up as me. We can help each other out. How 'bout I throw in a full body massage when we're done. Tempting, right? I'll work the kinks right out of your disposition." He laced his fingers and cracked his knuckles. "You got a rubber around here?"

To end this slow torture, Joy blurted out the first lie to pop in her mind, wishing she thought of it sooner. "Can't you take a hint? I have my period."

"Ugh...gross." Victor released his grip as if she were a leper to soap his hands, scrubbing them under steaming hot water. "You could've just kicked me in the balls harder a second time. Thanks a lot for ruining the mood."

"Sor-ree," Joy sang, feigning remorse. She lifted a

careless shoulder, secretly smiling, glad her menstrual monkey wrench still worked like a charm. "I know how much you hate blood."

"Well, then…" Victor softened his tone to almost an angelic plea, eyes wide with pathetic hope. "How 'bout a little oral action instead?" His sausage-fingers popped the button of his pants.

Tsk. Is this what her life has come to? Deflecting her ex? Bad enough his overt passes made her skin crawl. Now she had to give explanations to stupid questions. "You know how they say '*it isn't what you say, but how you say it*'? This time it actually *is* what you say."

Confused, he held the waistband closed, unsure if he should tug the zipper all the way up or the rest of the way down. "So, is that a yes?"

Clueless dipshit. What did she ever see in this turd-muffin? "I'd like to help you out. Really." Joy aimed the tip of her pinky to her upper lip and let another lie loose. "But have a cold sore coming on. See?" She angled her head to show off the non-existent blister.

"Ugh, get away from me." Victor stepped back, squeezing into the tight corner of the toilet. "Keep your afflictions to yourself. Geez. No wonder you don't have a boyfriend."

Laughing on the inside, Joy left her ex hanging in the bathroom to dry out while she found her pocketbook in the living room to retrieve her cellphone charger, anxious to check the message from Tristan and get a word to him that she's all right.

****

Propped on the couch with the cellphone in hand, Tristan grew restless for information on Joy's situation.

"What is she doing?" he muttered as he alternated positions, sitting then pacing, his gaze bouncing between the clock over the fireplace and out the living room window.

He expected her to call back already after she'd disconnected so abruptly. Worse, she didn't respond to any of his texts or answer his calls, and now when he dialed her number it went straight to voicemail.

A million excuses to swing by Lorraine's house to check on Joy crossed his anxious mind, but one big, fat, stupid reason kept him in place—what she'd said today: *It's for the best.* She wanted to do this on her own terms, without his involvement; an agonizing executive decision she'd made without consulting him. She was a grown woman and probably thought she knew what she was doing, although he had an entirely different opinion, which apparently didn't count for much. Until she realized what a mistake she made, he'd give her the benefit of the doubt along with some breathing room.

Tristan dropped onto the couch, rested his elbows on his knees, and touched his forehead to the cellphone sandwiched between prayer-hands. *Her kids just arrived. She was probably getting them settled. This was something she wanted to do alone. No reason to be concerned. Please, Lord, let me be right. Don't let anything go wrong.*

When the newspaper boy slammed the morning edition against the screen door, jolting Tristan from his conversation with God, the worry he'd been holding back hit him full force. He phoned his best friend for back up and within minutes Nick came over with Lily to keep an eye on Nicole.

Tristan clipped the helmet under his chin, revved

the engine, put up the kickstand, then sped down Hollyhock Hill, keeping up with the worst case scenarios racing through his brain. For no good reason except his peace of mind, he needed to see Joy, to know she was okay.

During the ten torturous minutes following the dusty blue sky toward the other side of town, Joy's hard words infiltrated his thoughts, taunting his better judgment, making him second-guess this wary trip. Maybe he ought to turn around. If she wanted his involvement, no doubt, she would ask for it.

But what if something was wrong? She might never forgive him for being the concerned interloper but he'd never forgive himself for not listening to his gut.

Tristan could understand her concern—wanting to keep him and Victor from running into each other. The last thing this middle-aged man needed at this point of his life was getting into fisticuffs like some schoolyard punk. But putting their hearts on the back-burner for her boys seemed more severe than he could stand.

Just in case something was wrong, he'd jammed his off-duty revolver in his holster and stuffed the cuffs in his back pocket. He rode by Lorraine's house and noticed the bedroom window was dark, but the white lace curtains in the living room glowed like a blank movie screen.

Too early for Joy to be awake unless she hadn't gone to sleep yet. Was it too soon to worry?

Playing it cool, he cruised up and down the block a few times, hoping the rumbling tailpipes would pique her attention enough to open the front door. When that didn't work, he parked behind the Green Machine and quickly cut the engine, debating while dismounting

272

whether or not this was an asinine move for a grown man.

Maybe I'll just sneak a peek through the window. He hung the helmet on the sissy bar before creeping up the driveway. He'd only been inside this bungalow one other time—when he first arrived in town, tagging along for the day while Nick was the Scenic View Fire Marshal, inspecting fireplaces and smoke detectors.

Resorting to a peeping Tom had him itching for a smoke for the first time in weeks. He inched along the porch, hugging the shingles to glimpse between the eyelet drapery, wishing he could un-see what he saw— Joy in the arms of some dude. Not just any dude, he presumed by the guy's lack of height and hair, but her dreaded ex.

What the hell? Like watching a train wreck in slow motion, he couldn't rip his eyes from the damaging scene: Victor grabbing Joy, pawing at her blouse, while she struggled to get free.

Tristan's blood pressure soared. *There goes the last ounce of self-control.* No way was he leaving now. He rubbed a clammy hand down his face, deciding which bad move to make. The choices were limited to kicking down the door, which would probably yield the quickest results, or knocking casually like making an after-party pit-stop. Either one was bound to mess up the plan to keep her worlds from colliding.

Too bad.

Tristan held his breath as he jiggled the handle on the screen door, relieved to find it unlocked. Then with a gentle hand he twisted the knob of the entry door, exhaling when it turned like he cracked Fort Knox. "Hey," he shouted, one hand on the pistol at the small of his back.

"What the—" Victor let go of Joy, and she fell to the floor.

"Can't you tell when a woman doesn't want you?"

"What are you?" Victor scoffed. "The neighborhood watch?"

"Something like that." Tristan sized up Joy's ex as he stared down the short man. "No means no, buddy. I heard it from outside. Don't tell me you didn't hear her."

"Joy, who is this clown?" Victor hooked a thumb in Tristan's direction.

Joy sat on the floor stunned, covering what the torn blouse exposed.

"Don't worry 'bout who I am, Victor. You got bigger problems."

"Oh, I get it. You set me up." He shoved Joy with the tip of his shoe. "Bitch. I should've known."

"Don't blame her. You set yourself up, pushing yourself on her."

"Take it easy, man." Victor chuckled. His tight lips bent into a forced smile and his posture softened, palms up like a cornered perp, switching from offensive to defensive mode. Fight or flight, Tristan was ready for it. "Everything's cool. It's not what it looks like."

"Oh, yeah?" The scumbag's hollow words didn't sway Tristan. They only fed the fury, bringing out the bad-cop beast. "What do *you* think it looks like?"

"We're just working things out. Marital issues, you know. Thinking about giving it another try. For the boys' sake." Victor lifted Joy off the floor by her biceps. "We don't wanna deal with any more lawyers, child psychologists, and custody nonsense. Right, babe?"

Victor's story stank like a dead body. "Yeah, right." Tristan snorted. "That's exactly what it looks like."

"Geez, Tristan. Are you drunk or something?" Joy interjected with a disgusted twang. "I've asked you before, not to drop by on your way home from the bar just 'cause you see the lights on." She spat erroneous allegations in his direction while her eyes floated guiltily toward the floor. "Victor and I are working things out. Is it so hard to comprehend?" The story she spun made his head dizzy.

Tristan squinted in disbelief, speechless, struggling to make sense of the confounded situation. He'd witnessed enough domestic disputes to pick up on a lie when someone was in a threatening position. "Seriously, Joy? Everything's okay? Tell me the truth." No doubt she was strong enough to break Victor's nose so why did she let her ex treat her so bad? Unless she had something, or someone, to lose. Victor's words came back like a boomerang—*for the boys' sake*.

"Mind keeping it down?" Victor jutted his chin toward the bedroom. "Our kids are asleep."

"Look at me, Joy," Tristan insisted, but she refused. Meanwhile her ex-husband, glued to her side, hadn't taken his eyes off him.

"Trust me. We're just fine," Victor answered in Joy's place. "Right, babe? Tell your friend everything's good," he said cryptically to Joy.

"Please, just…go." Joy locked eyes with Tristan as she uttered the painful words. When Tristan failed to move at her command, she rolled her eyes. "Geez, are you deaf or something? Get out."

"I'd listen to her if I were you before I'm forced to call the cops," Victor said, with smug victory, his arm possessively around Joy's waist as she stood there letting him touch her.

Sickened by the sight of them, Tristan backed out the way he came. "No problem, man. Sorry to bother you. Bye, Joy."

He let the screen door slam then hurried down the driveway and started the Harley with an explosion that woke the neighborhood. Racing the sunrise, he swore all the way home to never listen to his gut again.

****

Kicking out Tristan was one of the most painful things Joy'd ever done, in the ranks of leaving her boys behind to set up this new life on Long Island. The distraught look in his disappointed eyes made her feel even worse. But she couldn't risk calling Victor's bluff, unsure if her ex had the power to make his threat come true.

"Sorry about that." Joy separated herself from Victor's clutches with a subtle spin as she began prepping Lorraine's couch for the uninvited overnight guest. "I can't imagine what sparked that surprise visit."

"He your boyfriend?" Victor closed the entry door and turned the lock.

"Tsk. Don't be ridiculous."

He ran his fingers over his bald head as if the hair was still there. "This is gonna sound crazy, but I think I'm kinda jealous."

Joy shot him a crooked look. "What are you talking about? He's the gay guy from work. Just a harmless friend of Lorraine's. He's probably checking up on the place more than checking in on me."

She prayed Tristan got home safe. Once she found the chance to explain the scenario to him, he was bound to understand her bizarre overreaction.

As she leaned over to spread open the afghan, Victor hovered beside her hip like a conjoined twin. "So you're really not seeing anyone?" His softening persistence was vaguely reminiscent of the hopeful college boy who sought her attention eons ago, however the odd attraction was long gone. For her anyway.

"I have too much going on. There's no time for dating." *Give it up already.*

"So you must be nice and horny then." He fondled the armrest with anxious fingers.

Joy swallowed the rising bile and straightened to her full height. "Does it matter? I already told you, it's that time of the month. Plus I've got a cold sore coming on."

Victor's tongue darted out like a reptile, wetting his lips while he stared at Joy's mouth, jogging every nauseating memory she managed to suppress. "Your lip looks fine to me. And I think I can get past the Red Sea at high tide."

Was he just calling her bluff? She hoped so. "I don't want you to do something that you'll regret. After all, you promised Felicity nothing like that would happen."

"If you keep our little booty call a secret, I won't have anything to worry about. You *can* keep a secret, right? Because maybe I can throw the psychologist's report in the shredder."

Joy locked her lips and tossed the invisible key over her shoulder.

"Good." Victor pressed his mouth hard against hers.

She clenched her teeth to keep out his penetrating tongue. It was like kissing a toad, and not the Prince Charming kind.

He pulled back and smirked. "Hold that thought. I gotta take a piss."

Thank God for small miracles. With seconds to spare, Joy grabbed her cellphone tethered to the electrical outlet, relieved it had enough juice to turn on. She found the voice recording app, pressed the Record button, set it screen-down on the end table, and covered it with a magazine just to be safe. This would only work against Victor as long as he kept talking so she needed to encourage the conversation while letting him get around the bases.

Victor returned with his pants around his waist but the button undone. "Where were we?"

She forced an attentive smile and sat gingerly on the edge of the couch cushion with her back against the armrest as he snuggled beside her with one hand around her shoulder and the other on her knee, diving in for another kiss. She turned her head to deflect his gesture, giving him the side of her neck instead, ensuring the recorder got a clear shot of her voice. "If I do this, you promise not to take my boys away from me?"

His lizard-tongue lapped the side of her face, inside her ear, everywhere but her mouth. "We'll see. I'm not making promises yet."

"Just threats."

"Threats work. You give me what I want, maybe I'll give you what you want," he rasped against her skin and she hoped the recorder picked up the sound. "I forgot how sexy you are. Take your pants off."

Joy crossed her legs tight, locking her foot behind her calf. "What's the hurry?"

"Come on." He pulled away, cupped her chin, and stared into her eyes. "This has been a long, crappy day. I'm not in the mood for games or foreplay or nonsense. Do what I say and don't make me get rough. And most of all, don't make me call the lawyer. I really don't want to take the boys away from you, trust me when I say it. Felicity can't handle them now, never mind when the new baby comes."

Joy stood, stripping off her pants and shirt without a show, more like a quick change in the dressing room at Walmart. The more dirt she collected on Victor the better she could build a case against him.

"That's it," Victor crooned. "Take it off, babe."

"Don't you feel the least bit guilty being with me while your pregnant fiancée is home alone, thinking you're just dropping off the boys?" Joy spoke louder than necessary and intentionally clear.

"She already thinks I'm screwing around on her. Accuses me all the time." Victor bit his bottom lip as his sleazy gaze trailed her cleavage to her crotch, making Joy's skin crawl. "Enough talking. Let's get down to business."

"Whaddaya wanna do?" Joy kept her distance, standing in the middle of the dim room, prepared for Victor to lunge at her.

Instead he sat back and lifted his hips as he shimmied his pants down to his shoes. "You know what I want you to do—bend over so I can bury myself to the hilt inside you. You got a rubber?"

"Why would I? I'm not dating anyone. Besides,

I've got my period, so it should be safe." Joy winced, realizing the fib could only go so far.

"No way. I ain't taking a chance doing this without one. I've got a baby on the way any day now. I'm not gonna risk knocking up my ex too."

"Let me check Lorraine's nightstand."

Victor cocked a doubtful brow. "Seriously? You mean to tell me the woman who owns this granny pad keeps a stash handy?"

"Oh, yeah. She's a total slut," Joy lied.

She tiptoed into the bedroom and shook Mason and Owen's shoulders until they groaned, fighting to keep sleeping. She opened the curtain, letting the early morning sunlight spill over their little chubby faces. "Boys," she whispered, planting the seed of an idea in their dreams, "Want cookies and milk? Come on. Wake up time." She prayed the tempting words registered as she crept out, shutting the door.

"Well?" Victor asked hopeful, his teeny peeny in his fist.

She showed him her empty hands like a magician. "I didn't find them. She must be all out. Sor-ree."

"Daddy?" Mason cried, followed by a thump on the hardwood floor then a jiggle of the doorknob. "I wanna go home." The boy emerged, rubbing his eyes.

Owen trailed behind. "Daddy? Where am I?"

Victor hiked up his drawers and jeans. "Hey, boys. Everything all right?" He shot a laser look at Joy as she slipped on the buttonless blouse then stepped into her pants.

All she had to do was invite her mother into the mix. And Bruno. And her father. Everyone. Anyone to ruin Victor's plan. Anyone except Tristan.

"Can I have cookies?" Owen asked.

Mason nodded. "And milk?"

"No, boys. Go back to bed." Victor pushed them toward the bedroom.

"But the sun is out," Owen said.

"I'm not tired," Mason added.

"Since we're all up, why don't we go to the diner for pancakes?" Joy clapped, hoping her idea was a hit.

The boys studied Lorraine's extensive tchotchke collection like some unearthed treasure fit for a fairy tale museum without glancing in their mother's direction as if she were invisible. "Where's Felicity?" they asked in unison.

While Victor fielded the question, Joy dug out a sleeve of Digestive Biscuits from Lorraine's pantry. They didn't compare to Chips-A-Hoy but were good enough in a pinch. There was no milk in the refrigerator but she located a container of cocoa powder and quickly mixed it with tap water.

"We already went over this, boys. She's home, waiting for the new baby to come."

"I miss her. I wanna go home," Owen whined.

"When are we going home, Daddy?" Mason asked, sadly.

"You're getting a new home soon, here on Long Island near Gramma Sophia and Grampa Bob."

"With you?" Mason asked his father.

"Sorry, champ." Victor rubbed the boy's mop-top. "You'll be living with Mommy."

"But I don't want to live with *her*," Owen whined.

"Me, neither." Mason glared at Joy from the corner of his eye.

"Enough," Victor shouted, rubbing his temples.

Joy sat at the kitchen table, observing the exchange. He created this war; it was his problem to fix now.

While the men hashed it out, slinging insults about Joy's mothering skills as if she weren't in the room, she sneaked away to snatch her cellphone and backed up the incriminating recordings to *The Cloud* for safekeeping.

"She's mean. I don't like her. You don't like her either, Daddy. You said so. Why would you make us live with her?" Owen wailed.

Unable to avoid the hateful words from the mouth of her babe, Joy huddled in the furthest corner of the living room to fend off the bite of oncoming tears, denying Victor the pleasure of seeing her break.

She squelched her gut instinct to phone Tristan for moral support and texted Lily instead, attaching a link to the recordings. Then she messaged Bruno to tell him Victor was in town harassing her and asked if he would come over to make sure things didn't get further out of hand.

"I thought Felicity was gonna be our mommy," Mason squealed. "That's what you said, Daddy."

"The discussion is over." Victor stepped out of the kitchen. "I've had it." Deep lines etched his exhausted face.

With smug satisfaction, Joy enjoyed watching her ex suffer. *Good.*

"I'm gonna crash on the couch for a while." He plopped down, stretched out, and flung a forearm over his eyes to block the sunshine. "You're in charge," he grumbled.

Showtime. Joy's heart pounded. Anything she said

in this moment would be used against her until the end of time. She'd better make it good.

Rather than force her God-given title as loving mother down the throats of her brainwashed babies, she'd treat them like two strange little guests, using the standoffish method that worked well with Tristan's daughter.

After a cleansing breath, she walked into the kitchen. "How're the cookies?"

Mason frowned. "Not so good."

"Yeah, well…they're my friend Lorraine's cookies. If your dad told me you'd be here today I would have gone to the store yesterday. What kind do you like? Let me guess…" She studied their faces as they turned to each other, making sense of this forgotten woman. "You're a chocolate chip guy." She pointed knowingly at Owen. To Mason, she said, "Oreos for you, right?"

They nodded, and Joy was relieved they let her win that much.

"Is this where we're gonna live from now on?" Owen's voice trembled.

"No, buddy. It's not. Our home's not ready yet. Soon, though." She hoped. "Hey, wanna take a ride with me to the supermarket? You can pick out whatever you'd like to eat."

"Like corndogs?" Mason asked. "Daddy and Felicity let us eat them all the time."

Joy fought a smile, satisfied her eldest son seemed to warm up enough to have a conversation. "Sure, you can get corndogs. Why not? They sound delish."

"And ice cream?" Owen suggested with childish enthusiasm. "Sprinkles, and whipped cream, and cherries, too?"

"We're gonna need peanut butter. Jelly. Bread. And Fluff." Mason listed the items, counting off on his fingers.

"Oh, yeah, can't forget the Fluff." Joy jotted a quick list on the refrigerator notepad as the pressure in her chest eased a smidge once she realized she'd struck the right chord.

"What about Daddy?" Mason looked concerned. "He's coming with us, right?"

"Well, he's kinda tired from being up all night." Joy could've gone for a nap too, but rekindling the relationship with her boys gave her an adrenalin high she never wanted to come down from; a rush so potent she'd forgotten about Victor's sexual harassment. "He said it was totally fine if we go shopping without him." She waved at the unconscious lump on the couch.

Owen eyed his mother with caution. "I dunno…"

"Come on, O." Mason nudged his little brother.

"Owen can stay here if he wants and watch TV while your dad sleeps. I forgot to mention…" A bright idea to sweeten the bait sparked in Joy's brain. "I thought we'd stop by Grandpa Bob and Grandma Sophia's first 'cause I know they're super-excited to see you."

"Grandma and Grandpa." Owen perked up. He ran to find his sneakers in the bedroom, put them on the wrong feet, and stood by the door. Not wanting to be the last in line, Mason followed.

So far, so good. Joy grabbed her purse, hoping this was the first turn in the right direction.

****

Tristan sat at the kitchen counter staring into a

black cup of coffee, still reeling from the shellshock of walking in on Joy and Victor.

"She just threw you out?" Nick asked.

"Yep." Tristan replayed the unforeseen conversation, trying to digest the noxious exchange. Instead of being her hero, he was nothing but a big zero. A parallel universe would have made more sense.

"I've known Joy forever. I doubt she wants anything to do with that lowlife creep. She's gotta be doing it for the boys' sake." Lily's cellphone vibrated and she pulled it from her sweater pocket. "Hold up, fellas. Speak of the devil. Joy just texted me." She showed the message on the screen to Tristan.

—*Know a good custody lawyer? I'm gonna need one*—Joy wrote.

"There's a link attached." Tristan pressed it and was directed to a Cloud account where audio files were stored.

"Maybe it's not for you to hear otherwise she would have sent it to you." Lily tried snatching the phone, but Nick caught her.

"Lily. Let Tristan listen."

Reluctantly, she sat back.

"He's nobody," Joy said, "Just someone from work. I don't even have a boyfriend."

Hearing her speak as though their budding relationship meant nothing didn't faze Tristan beyond a little gurgle in his sour stomach. She was playing Victor's malicious game, what else was she supposed to say? Still it took all his willpower to listen to the sexual exchange. Joy never said yes to her ex, but she didn't say no either.

After enduring more than enough of the illicit

conversation, Tristan forwarded the link to his cellphone.

"If her ex is threating custody of the kids in exchange for sex, she must've recorded this to use against him. Smart girl," Nick said. "I'll call my lawyer to see what he can do with this info. Victor sounds deranged. I'm sure there's enough here for Joy not to worry about losing her boys."

"Victor's pregnant fiancée won't be too happy," Lily added.

Nick and Lily left, taking Nicole along for the ride, leaving Tristan time to gather his wits and figure out his next move. He might not have the leverage to help Joy and her boys while Victor was lurking around, but there was one thing he could do…

Pushing through the back door, he marched across the side yard to finish the house so she could move in, where he could keep a close eye on her.

Chapter Seventeen

Fed up with Victor's lingering presence and tired of hearing his claim that the boys *needed* him around during their adjustment period, Joy hated herself for letting her ex win again. She wanted him gone more than she craved a decent night's rest after four long nights of sleeping on Lorraine's hardwood bedroom floor.

Why were the boys so attached to the creep anyway? Sure, the guy got mega bonus points for being *the dad*, but he wasn't that good at it. He wasn't dedicated like her father had been when she was their age, or Tristan for that matter. Victor was as self-centered as a cranky infant, with patience thinner than ice in August. Still the kids adored their dad and didn't let him out of their sight longer than a cartoon episode, so what choice did she have other than to let him hang around until Felicity demanded he come home?

Since it rained nonstop for days, the disconnected family spent most of their time cooped up in the tiny bungalow with big Bruno who came over to act as a buffer. To entertain the boys, the five-some went bowling, to the movies, and the arcade.

Thankfully her ex never laid another lousy finger on her but just being around him was awkward and uncomfortable. Apparently attempted rape and harassment was as far as he was willing to go with

Joy's oversized cousin tagging along, camping out in the living room with Victor until the jerk agreed to move into a hotel for the remainder of his unwelcome visit.

"When are you planning on leaving, Victor?" Joy asked straight out more than once. "Don't you have to get home to Felicity?"

Victor continued to avoid answering the question, which worried Joy. Not so much at first, but as the days dragged on. The man didn't seem concerned one iota his fiancée could give birth any moment. He eventually promised to depart on Monday morning, which brought Joy some relief but there was no sense getting her hopes up until he was thirty-five thousand feet in the air. He might be okay with ignoring his obligations, however Joy couldn't neglect the Christmas Shoppe much longer.

If she didn't reopen the store for the busy weekend, she risked losing Lorraine's trust and worried leaving the boys with their father may undo all the progress she made so far. Thankfully Sophia offered to entertain the children for the day as part of her grandmotherly tour of duty.

One thing that might improve Joy's mood and settle her rattled nerves was seeing Tristan, if only to apologize in person for disrespecting him in front of her ex. She hadn't the nerve to call him after all these days, not because she didn't want to, but because if she did no doubt she'd break down and she needed to keep her guard up with Victor around. However they exchanged a few brief texts.

—*How's it going?*—Tristan wrote.

—*So far, so good.*—Joy responded—*Doing the*

mom thing. I'll speak to you soon when things settle down. Miss you.—

—Me too xo—

Joy left the electronic conversation on a high note, figuring anything more would only make things worse.

After ringing and wrapping up dozens of souvenir Scenic View snowflake ornaments for day trippers en route to the vineyards for Friday night fireworks, Joy saw a break in the action around lunchtime. She finally had a chance to breathe when Tristan strolled into the shop carrying two Styrofoam cups. She couldn't speak let alone fight the smile stretching wider than the Long Island Sound. Throwing herself into his arms crossed her mind, but she kept her cool knowing if she got too emotional she'd turn into a puddle. "Hi there."

"Hi, yourself." Tristan ambled over, set down the coffee cups, and leaned his elbow on the countertop. "What's the story, Joy? Your ex is in town, so you're gonna pretend I don't exist?"

There was no sense acting like he wasn't right, so she buried her nose in some paperwork to hide her long-lost lust starving for his affection. "I'm sorry. Don't take it personally. I just have a lot going on."

"What about your dog? I'm a man—I can handle being ignored. But Rex misses you like crazy."

His words were a jagged knife in her heart making her feel even worse for neglecting her beloved pet on top of everything else but the pup was in the best possible hands. "How is he?"

"Alive. And a little depressed. He's not the only one. Nicole misses you too." Tristan glanced around the place avoiding eye contact as if the closeness was too much to bear. "But I don't think anyone misses you as much as me."

"It's just things are really complicated right now."

"You don't have to tell me, sunshine. I can figure it out by the way you threw me outta Lorraine's house."

"About that…"

Tristan put up his palm. "No need to explain. I listened to the audio file."

"That was private," Joy shrieked. "Lily shouldn't have shared it with you."

"Don't blame her. She was at my place with Nick watching Nicole so I could go look for you. I was next to her when she got the message. She didn't volunteer it. I snatched it from her hand." Tristan whipped out his cellphone, pressed a few buttons, and replayed it, fast-forwarding through selected parts.

Joy didn't recall saying the words, but the voice was undeniably hers: *"Come on, Victor. The last thing I want is to lose my boys. I'll do anything you want. It's not like we've never done this before."* Tears streamed down her cheeks and landed on the glass countertop.

"Don't cry. I didn't play it to upset you. I haven't stopped listening to it since that night. I just gotta know…did you?"

"Sleep with him?" She swiped her nose, shook her head, rolled her eyes. "Of course not. But I would've if I had to. Luckily Bruno's been sticking by my side whenever Victor's around."

"Are you *all* staying at Lorraine's?"

"Victor's been sleeping on the couch, but he finally went over to the Scenic View Inn this morning. Bruno's been sleeping in a chair. I put the boys in Lorraine's bed. And I've been sleeping on the floor."

"Well, I hope you're ready to quit roughin' it." His

gazillion-watt smile was brighter than the sun. "I came to tell you the house is ready for you. I still have a few final touches I was hoping to get done before you moved in. But it'll give me peace of mind having you next door. I can work around you and the boys." He winked.

Joy shook her head. "I'm not bringing the boys over until Victor is gone. I don't want him around when we get settled in. I don't want him knowing my business. Besides he's bound to recognize you a side-yard away. I'd rather wait until he leaves."

"When's that gonna be?"

"He says Monday, maybe Tuesday, but I'll believe it when I see it." Joy shrugged.

The jingle bell on the shop door indicated a customer, but it wasn't.

It was Victor.

"Well, well, well. He really does work here, huh?"

Joy's eyes darted from Victor to Tristan back to Victor. "He's just picking up his paycheck," she lied. She fingered the stack of paperwork and pulled out an empty envelope and handed it to Tristan. "Here ya go."

"Uhh, thanks, boss."

Victor slid a dirty look toward Tristan as he whispered to Joy, "I gotta talk to you."

"Bye, Tristan. Have a nice weekend." Joy widened her eyes and nodded toward the front door.

"I almost forgot..." Tristan smacked his palm on the counter. "I left my keys in the stockroom. Lemme grab 'em, then I'll just slip out the back, Jack. Thank God it's Friday. I'm gonna blow this baby down at Mr. Lucky's Pub tonight." Tristan waved his imaginary paycheck as he swerved around Victor to get behind the counter. "Why don't you lovebirds meet me for wings and beers? I'm buying."

Victor stared beyond Joy at the swinging doors of the stockroom, pointing his finger in Tristan's direction with confusion twisting his face. "Is that guy for real?"

"He's just being nice after what happened the other night."

The back doorbell jingled twice before slamming shut, and Joy's heart sank.

Victor grabbed Joy by the forearm so hard the edge of the countertop dug into her belly. "Where are the boys?"

"I texted you this morning—they're with my mother."

"I went by your parents' place, and no one's there."

"She probably took them out for the day. What's the matter? Don't you trust her?"

"It's not that. I'm just wondering where the boys are. Is that a crime?"

Joy lifted a careless shoulder, amused at the sight of Victor lacking total control of the situation for a change. "Did you call her cellphone?"

"No, Joy, I didn't," he snapped. "I'm looking for my kids, not a conversation."

"Why? Afraid she'll read you the riot act?"

"Yeah, kinda." He rubbed his eye sockets like this whole ordeal pained him more than Joy.

"Victor, don't take this the wrong way," she said, although deep down she didn't care how he took things anymore, "but when are you going home?"

"I don't know yet. I might stay another week. What's the difference anyway? I'm staying in the hotel."

"Isn't the baby due, like, any minute?"

He shook his head, looking wearier than she'd ever seen in all the years of knowing him.

Her curiosity piqued, she asked pointedly, "Is everything all right?"

He sighed and shook his head again.

Joy swore he seemed on the edge of tears but that would require him having a heart and somewhat of a soul. A sudden wave of kindness washed over her as she pulled a stool around to the front of the counter and offered him a sip from her bottle of spring water. "What's the matter?"

Victor closed his eyes and tightened his lips. "The baby…"

Human nature made her reach out to rub his shoulder for moral support but luckily her self-control kicked in and she shoved her hands into the front pockets of her capris instead. "Something wrong?"

He shrugged, nodded, and bobbed his head in an awkward yes-no-maybe-so motion. "It-it's not mine."

"How do you know?"

"Felicity told me last night."

"Maybe she's messing with you. Just saying it to upset you."

"No. The math adds up. She was staying with her sister during the time it would have had to happen, so it can't be mine."

"And you're figuring this out now?"

"Unfortunately my head calculated it a while ago, but my heart hadn't. I've been living happily in denial…until today."

Joy sat speechless, digesting the distressing words falling from Victor's mouth like a hokey soap opera script. She had a helluva enough experience with this bullshit artist not to fall into his narcissist, sympathy-sucking deathtrap.

"The rotten way I feel in this moment makes me realize what hell I must've put you through. Where do I begin to apologize?" Victor swiped a non-existent tear for dramatic effect. "I can't expect you to forgive me for the amount of trouble I've caused you, but I'm praying you'll put hard feelings aside until I find a way to make things right 'cause I can really use a friend right now. Whaddaya say?" He reached for her hands as if his sentimental charm was too overwhelming to resist, however she maintained her stoic stance, unaffected by his presumptuous gesture, and jammed her fists deeper into her pockets. "Just 'cause we're divorced doesn't mean I stopped caring about you. Maybe Felicity and I were never meant to be, and you've really been the one for me all this time. Maybe we weren't meant to have a life in Florida. Maybe we're meant to start one here in Scenic View. It's never too late to give it another try, babe."

Victor's string of relentless maybes drove Joy *definitely* crazy. "Let's get something squared away; you may be my boys' father, but I am not your *babe*. It's not my responsibility to put you back together again, Humpty Dumpty. Get your ass down to Florida with Felicity where you belong. Let's not forget—you *left* me for *her*. So you can go home and work it out with her."

"You're selfish, you know that?" Victor spat in disgust, his erratic mood shifting direction like a tornado, reminding her of the bully she was so used to dealing with. "Think how happy the boys'll be if we get back together."

"Don't take this the wrong way, but no frickin' way in hell. No, thank you. It'll never, ever happen, so don't mention it again."

"Seriously? You're not even willing to consider it?"

"Are you demented? Is something wrong with your brain? What part of *No* don't you understand? We've been divorced for two years. I lied to my whole family just to marry you, and I lied again when you left me because I was scared they'd realize what kind of failure I am. Now I'm finally getting my life on track, getting back into my parents' good graces, finally able to look at myself in the mirror and not want to punch the person looking back. *Now*, after all this time, you expect me to just fall at your feet?"

"Maybe I am." A slow smile slithered across his smug face. "I just thought you'd do it for the greater good of your family."

"You turned my boys against me."

"I'll fix it."

"Don't bother. You've done quite enough." Joy snorted, exhausted from restraining her tongue for so long out of fear from Victor's imaginary power, she couldn't hold back any longer. "Look, I'm sorry your life is a pile of shit, but think of all the cash you'll save once you call off the wedding. Plus if the baby's really not yours, you won't have to pay child support. Seems like a win-win to me."

"You think this is a joke, don't you? You think this is fun for me? That I really wanted to beg *you* for another chance? Forget I mentioned it."

"No problem. It's forgotten." Joy waved the words

away.

Holding her breath, waiting for Victor to leave, she picked up a cardboard box of crystal snowflake ornaments and headed down the aisle of trees toward an empty faux spruce in the center of the shop.

His slow footsteps shuffled away, but the jingle bell on the front door didn't ring. Instead the faintest snick of the turn-lock filled the void between the low-playing Christmas tunes.

Oh, holy night. Joy shut her eyes and braced for the worst, evoking the self-defense skills she'd learned in kickboxing class, digging deep to harness the power of the resilient fighter.

Bending to pick up two more fragile snowflakes, she spotted the tips of his shoes a foot behind her and ignored his lurking presence. His angry energy radiated through the back of her thin blouse as she hung the ornaments on the nearest boughs. Then with clenched fists raised to her chin, Joy spun so fast Victor jumped back, toppling one fully adorned tree into the next like dominoes, shattering Lorraine's merchandise.

Huffing and puffing like he would explode on impact, he bellowed, "All I wanted was a little kindness, but you couldn't do that for me. Could you? For the father of your children. You couldn't give me a break for once. You love to kick me when I'm down, don't you?"

"I kneed you in the groin once, but I never kicked you." She held her on-guard stance ready to clock him.

"I'm not talking physically." He shoved her shoulder, forcing her off-balance, but she bounced back into position. "I mean with your words."

Joy retreated, tiptoeing backward over shattered

ornaments crackling underfoot, plotting her next move because she had to make it count. "Did you really think I'd get back with you so easily?"

Victor shrugged and smirked as he inched forward. "I can't see why not. You fell for me once."

"You're a narcissistic son of a bitch, you know that? That was before you tore out my heart. Before you turned my boys against me. Before I knew what kind of loser you really are."

"Stop with the drama, Joy. I'll make it up to you."

"Get away from me." She kept her distance, wishing Tristan hadn't left. Stealing a glimpse over her shoulder through the wide plate-glass window, she hoped someone outside recognized the state of emergency and called the police.

Victor's open hand sprang forward and clutched her ponytail, yanking hard enough to snap her neck if he wanted. Dizzy from him rattling her skull to make his point, she clasped two hands on the spot where the ponytail connected to her scalp while he dragged her away from the window.

"All you had to do was cooperate, and I would've gladly given you your old life back."

"I don't want my old life. I don't want you." Joy screamed as he slammed her facedown on the countertop. His knees forced her thighs apart, and he rubbed the barely-there erection in his pants against her bottom.

"I know you want it," Victor snapped. "Let me hear you say it." The cold hard tip of something sharp pricked the back of her neck.

"Want what? That mushroom cap you try passing off as a penis? I didn't want that puny thing when we were married. What makes you think I want it now?"

"Drop the knife," the familiar voice rumbled from the stockroom door.

Thank God. Joy swallowed the metallic taste inside her cheek as she stole a blurry peek between her lashes at Tristan with his revolver aimed above her head.

Thankfully Victor obeyed, and Tristan holstered his weapon to cuff him.

Joy stuttered her words to the 911 dispatcher. A patrol car arrived and within seconds the officers led Victor out the door.

After Tristan spoke to the police, he locked the front door and flipped the sign to Closed. He slid to the floor beside Joy, stretched out his long denim-clad legs, and hooked an arm around her neck to pull her close.

Instinctively she crawled onto his lap seeking the sanctuary of the soft spot where she could bury her face in the crook of his neck. Oh, how she missed this. Missed him. The earthy scent of his clean skin mingled with leathery cologne and fabric softener. The safety of his tender touch. The roughness of his five o'clock shadow as he dropped little kisses across her forehead.

"You okay?" He caught her chin and tilted it upward to view her face.

She shrugged, forcing a smile. "I'll be fine." Just when she had a handle over her emotions, there came a flashflood of new tears. "I'm sorry to get you involved in this mess."

"Shhh. It's okay." He smoothed his palm over her head that Victor nearly scalped. "It's over. He won't give you any more trouble, I promise. You have nothing to worry about. No one's ever gonna take your boys."

"I know. But what am I gonna tell them?"

Tristan shrugged. "Say he went back to Florida. I'm sure you'll find the right words to make it work."

"Speaking of work...did I hear you right when you told those police officers you're *retired*?"

"The more I thought about going back on the job, the more I realized I was happier here in Scenic View swinging a hammer for Nick's company. Plus I didn't think it was fair to expect you and the boys to move to Star Harbor while your heart's set on living in the house where you grew up—but that point is probably moot since it turns out you don't plan on me meeting them, not for a while anyway," Tristan said in a single breath, followed by a downhearted sigh.

"You were gonna ask us to go with you?"

"Of course. I don't wanna live without you, Joy. When are you gonna believe me?"

"I do believe you." Her voice cracked as she tried not to cry. "I really do. I didn't think I could concentrate on us while everything else in my life is a mess. But now that I have the boys, and Victor's out of the way, I can. I love you, Tristan. I really, really do."

"That's all I need to know." He pressed a tender kiss to her lips.

Chapter Eighteen

Tristan's Father's Day started with the perfect combination of warm cuddles and a scrumptious breakfast in bed courtesy of Nicole, along with her two hairy accomplices, Cookie and Rex. The gourmet meal consisted of a bruised apple, a piece of plain whole wheat bread, and a warm bottle of spring water, served on the child's tea party tray.

"Thank you, Niblet. It's delicious. You're such a good cook," he gushed, savoring every morsel. While Nicole sat high on the stack of pillows against his back in order to style Tristan's hair with her dolly's brush, the pups curled up on the end of the bed, warming their master's feet.

Life is good.

Seemed like yesterday when this angel was small enough to fit in his two big hands with some room to spare. The bittersweet time would come one day when she'll be fixing him more advanced dishes, like pancakes and bacon, which'd mean she's growing up and he'd miss the little things, like this.

Stay little, he wished, sipping the water like fine wine.

Yes, life is certainly good. Better than he ever imagined it could be when he first arrived in this little speck of a town.

Who would've thought so much could change in

the course of a season? No sense questioning his blessings—just count them and let all the affection bestowed upon him seep into every cell.

Although he tried putting the thought out of his mind, he couldn't help but wonder what Joy was doing this morning with her boys. The triple-cherry on top of this sprinkle-loaded, heavily frosted layer cake of love would've been if they were here to share this magical morning. *Maybe next year*, if everything went according to Tristan's grand slam plan.

The cell phone rang, breaking the sentimental spell, and Nicole grabbed it off the nightstand. "Here ya go, Daddy."

It was Joy calling to say she and the boys just left Lorraine's place and would be over in a few minutes to pick him and Nicole up in the Green Machine, en route to the Scenic View Fire Department for another family-friendly barbecue.

With Victor out of the picture and the unexpected encouragement from Sophia, Joy's commitment to keep her boys and Tristan apart dwindled into the ether, never to be mentioned again.

When the van pulled up, the side door slid open for Nicole to climb inside and take her usual booster seat. Having only seen his house during Joy's drive-bys, the boys peeked out with unbridled curiosity and begged for a tour behind the new picket fence Tristan installed to separate his yard from the one next door.

Even though he gave Joy the okay to move in asap, she preferred to preserve the surprise for the boys' sake after all the trouble Tristan went through to make it perfect, which included the final touches still in progress. The four-wall murals he sketched in each of the boys' rooms—a superhero city for Mason and a jungle-theme for Owen—took longer than he'd planned. And the furniture wasn't scheduled to arrive until the first week of July.

Tristan shooed the boys into the back of the van and slammed the door before hopping into the passenger seat.

"Happy Father's Day," Joy whispered under the overpowering giggles roiling in the backseat. She slipped a sealed envelope into his lap and stepped on the gas. "Read it later."

This was one envelope Tristan looked forward to opening. He tapped it anxiously against his knee then stuck it in the sun visor for safekeeping.

With the fire department parking lot roped off, Joy found an empty spot next door behind the post office, which was empty on Sunday.

As they piled out of the van, Tristan noticed Joy didn't come with the usual lunchbox for her pescetarian meal plan. "Traveling light today?"

She shrugged. "I feel like going with the flow for a change." Going with the flow included rubbing down three kids with a thick layer of zinc sunblock from head to toe then dousing them with organic bug spray.

"Don't worry. Nick's gotcha covered. He told me he added veggie burgers to the menu."

"He didn't have to do that just for me." Joy glanced in the driver's side mirror as she applied sunblock to her face, then signaled for Tristan to lean down so she could slather him too.

"Apparently you're not the only one in Scenic View interested in a meat-alternative." He closed his eyes and let her coat his cheeks, nose, and forehead with thick white goop, enjoying her TLC. Even though they spoke every day and went on a date Friday night, he missed the daily routine of being with her. "I could kiss you right now," he whispered between his teeth.

Pink blossomed in her white-tinted cheeks as she smiled. "Me too. But not in front of the kids."

Instead of reaching for her hand as he was inclined to do, they walked hand-in-hand like a human train—Mason, Joy, Owen, Tristan, and Nicole.

From a spacious table in the shade furthest from the bandstand, Sophia waved to their little gang. "Over here," she shouted above the music.

Joy's boys broke free from their mother and raced with lightning-speed to their grandfather, tackling the man's thighs. Little Nicole tagged along, showing up last yet stealing their thunder by jumping into Bob's open arms being the lightest one for him to lift.

Seeing three kids who just met less than two weeks ago get along like they'd known each other their whole lives made Tristan's heart swell. Growing soft in his old age wasn't part of the plan but if it meant living happily then sign him up.

To boost his testosterone level, he needed to find some men-folk; someone to talk Mets baseball, NASCAR, fishing, anything to help shake this sentimental streak he was on today. But all the guys were teamed up with their kids, and rightly so. So he orbited the buffet with an empty paper plate, foraging for edible items Joy could pick on.

"Gotcha a veggie burger." Tristan placed the offering in front of her proudly, awaiting her praise.

Joy took one bite and pushed it aside.

"What's the matter?" He cocked his head. "No

good?"

"It's fine. It's just…" She slid him a sideways guilt-laden glance. "I know this sounds crazy, but I'm craving red meat. I can go for a *real* burger right now. With bacon."

"I've got a craving too." Lily skooched onto the edge of the bench patting her flat belly.

"What's that supposed to mean?" Nick aimed a troublesome glance at the fully loaded hamburger on his wife's plate.

Lily shrugged. "I could go for guacamole, watermelon, wasabi peas, and root beer."

"Where'm I gonna get wasabi peas?" Nick frowned, confused.

"Oh, Lily…" Joy's face brightened. "You're pregnant, aren't you?"

Lily glanced at her blank-faced husband, standing there like a clueless lug even after Joy blurted out the news. "Nick'll be celebrating Father's Day next year with the rest of these clowns." She nodded to a group of dads huddled with their broods, prepping for an afternoon of Father and Offspring Relay Races, known as the F-Off for short by the moms who got a chance to kick back for some R&R in the shade for a change.

"Hell, I'm celebrating this year," Nick whooped with a smile so big his face might crack. "Why didn't you tell me, sugar?"

Lily giggled. "I just did."

Their mini-ruckus drew the attention of the rest of the partiers, traveling the grapevine in nanoseconds all the way to Chief Maresca who pulled out the bullhorn and congratulated Nick and Lily on the spot. Then the band kicked into a rendition of Ob-La-Di, Ob-La-Da that would make the Beatles proud.

Nick tugged Lily by the elbow and escorted his reluctant bride to the flattened grass designated as the dance floor. Nicole hopped off the bench and ran toward her uncle and aunt where the overjoyed couple swept the child into the circle of their loving arms, leaving no doubt in Tristan's mind they'd be perfect for parenthood.

"Keep an eye on Nicole for me, will ya, fellas?" Tristan said to Joy's boys as he nodded toward the dance floor.

Although the initial meeting with Mason and Owen was standoffish, it wasn't dramatic or traumatic as their over-protective mother anticipated. After a few hours at the batting cage, plus a couple of ice cream cones, they seemed to like their mom's new *friend* as much as Joy. Still for her sake, Tristan dialed down the public displays of affection around the kids and focused on being a buddy rather than a boyfriend.

"Sure, T," the boys sang in unison, adopting the nickname Uncle Nick dubbed Tristan, then chased after the little girl.

Nick and Lily joined hands with the three tykes, making a ring that grew as more bodies made their way to the dance floor.

When no one was looking, Joy wrapped her arms around Tristan's neck and tugged him nose-to-nose, planting a kiss on his lips, nothing to sloppy with her folks sitting right next to them. "Happy Father's Day."

After tons of fun in the broiling sun, and a few reapplications of sunblock, Tristan drove the Green Machine back to his place, with Joy and three exhausted kids.

****

Tristan parked in his driveway and cut the engine. "You're not leaving yet, are ya?"

"It's still early enough. I think we can stay for a cup of coffee." Joy smiled with eyes glimmering in the orange glow of the sinking sun. "They've been begging to see the inside of your house. Especially whatever you've got hidden back there." She nodded toward the new six-foot tall stockade fence.

Relieved and thrilled by her response, Tristan snatched the envelope Joy'd given him as he slid out of the driver's seat. "Come on guys," he sang, waking the kids, rattling their knees. "Lemme show you around."

The boys grunted, rubbing their tired eyes, but once they realized the invitation they burst to life. They leaped out and raced to the fenced in yard. Tristan lifted his sleepy girl, carrying her until she got a second wind and wriggled from his arms. He lifted the latch so the gate swung open, revealing the massive jungle-gym he'd put up last week.

"Wow." Joy blinked. "That's impressive."

"I know, right? I bet you wanna climb it."

A mischievous smile tugged her lips and she wrapped an arm around his waist. "I'd rather climb something else."

While the kids played, running in and out through the back door between the yard and Nicole's bedroom, Joy followed Tristan to the garage where they chatted about the little things in life as he poked under the hood of the Camaro.

"Finally got the part you needed?"

"Yep." Tristan aimed the flashlight at the engine. "But I'm thinking I oughta trade it in for a family car."

"Too bad. It's a hot set of wheels. Way hotter than the Green Machine. Before you get rid of it, maybe we can make out in the backseat."

"I like the way you think. But I've got a big bed that's a helluva lot comfier." He waggled his eyebrows. "Are you feeling frisky?"

"Maybe." Joy drained her glass of wine in lieu of coffee, revealing a contagious smile.

"Let's find out for sure." He slammed the hood then grabbed her hips, pushing her against the fender. Ever since Victor was out of the picture, and her boys were finally in it, Joy was a re-energized, confident version of herself, like when he first brought her home. He liked her like this. And he didn't want to let her go.

Bowing her body into him, she pressed soft breasts against him in the most tempting way.

Tristan would've made love to her on the spot if not for the rumpus coming from the other side of the wall. "Let's check on the kids. And get you a refill."

He led her by the hand, following the noise where the boys pushed racing cars on the hardwood kitchen floor and Nicole rolled her favorite teddy bear in a doll stroller around the controlled chaos.

"Mason. Owen. You're gonna wreck Tristan's house," Joy squealed with panic in her voice.

"Don't worry about it. The boys're fine. It's that sneaky little troublemaker we have to keep an eye on." Tristan singled out his daughter, eating pellets of dog food from Rex's blue bowl then pretending to feed it to her stuffed animal when she got caught being naughty.

With her fists clenching the sides of her head like it might explode, Joy groaned. "I don't want to wear out our welcome after one visit."

"Stop already, will ya? Don't be so uptight." Tristan massaged the back of her neck, nudging her toward the living room to escape the racket and find a little privacy. He plopped on the couch, pulling her with him. "Move in with me, Joy. I know you wanna. I want it too. The kids get along great. Our little families are perfect together."

"Now you stop." She sat sideways with her back against the armrest, looking him square in the eyes. "Living together isn't the answer. Once we move in next door we'll see each other all the time. For the kids' sake, let's just do this the traditional way. Okay?"

"Come on…do the kids really know the difference if we were married or not?"

"I'd know."

"If it bothers you so much, I know an easy way we can fix that." He grabbed her left hand and kissed her knuckles, rubbing her finger for a guesstimate, hoping the ring he picked out would fit. Once Nick's jeweler found the perfect stone, he'd be ready to propose right.

"Do we really want to jump into something we may regret?"

"Here we go again. I love you, Joy. I'm gonna marry you one of these days," Tristan said, sounding oddly threatening to his own ears.

Thank God she smiled when she said, "Whether I like it not?"

He stroked the stubble on his chin in a mental timeout, long enough to tone down his attitude ten notches. "I'm hoping you'd be willing to marry me 'cause you can't live without me and wanna be with me forever."

"I'm not saying I don't." Joy's gaze roved the

ceiling as if it held cue cards with the right words. "I get the romanticism of love-at-first-sight and all. And maybe if I hadn't already been there, done that, with kids, I might rush to the altar with you. But I don't want to make the same mistake twice."

Boiling blood drained from his head. "Sooo, you're saying marrying me would be a mistake?" After all they've been through in a short amount of time, Tristan was sure Joy was ready to say Yes. How could he have been so wrong?

"No. That's not what I mean."

"But that's what you just said. Trust me, I know. I'm sitting right here. In fact, my brain has it on replay. You 'don't want to make the same mistake twice.'"

Joy cupped his cheeks with two warms hands. "Oh, Tristan." With an empathic shake of her head, she sighed as if mentally preparing to unleash a well-rehearsed lecture.

He braced himself for the "Dear John" speech, or worse.

"Let's just get past this summer, okay?" Like her gentle tone, her small smile was a hopeful sign. "I know you said you're ready to settle down in Scenic View, but what if you change your mind about everything once Nicole goes back to live with her mother in Star Harbor."

"I doubt that'll happen."

"But it could. I knew it when I got involved with you, still I couldn't keep away from you. Lord knows I tried." She rolled her eyes in humility and shrugged. "What can I say? You're completely irresistible." Crimson filled her chest and crept into her cheeks.

Clamor from the other room stole their attention

for a moment as the kids burst into the living room en route to Nicole's bedroom.

"But," Joy continued, "you never came to Scenic View to stay. And I don't want to be the one to stop you from what you set out to do. I'd hate to be the reason you changed your mind, and somewhere down the line you wind up regretting the decision and blame it on me. I could never blame you for moving back to Star Harbor to be near Nicole while she's with her mother. I understand what you're going through. I need you to understand I'm not saying yes because I don't want to be with you. I'm saying no 'cause you need to make an enormous decision about your future, for your daughter's sake. You need an open heart and a clear mind and I think getting married now would just cloud your good judgment."

She sat back looking sadder than he'd ever seen, deflated, like she'd released all the things cluttering her brain but was too afraid to say until now.

Restraining the urge to argue with her after she just shot down his spontaneous proposal, he said, "I think you're right. You'll only be next door. I'll wave to you over the fence." *And that'll give me time to get the ring and do things the way I planned—making you an offer you can't refuse.*

Joy exhaled like she'd won the battle but this love-war wasn't over yet as far as Tristan was concerned.

The children appeared, standing in a neat line side-by-side with conspiring grins. "We're hungry," they sang in unison.

"Aren't you tired yet?" It was nine o'clock and Niblet, who passed out by this time on a normal night, was revved up.

"Actually, I'm kinda hungry, too." Joy stood, stretching, with fingers pressed into the small of her back like the passionate conversation was as physically exhausting as it was emotionally.

While she poked holes in juice pouches, heated frozen fish sticks, and cut watermelon into bite size chunks for the children, Tristan drained the bottle of wine into the adults' glasses then arranged a platter of cheese with crackers and grapes for their grown-up palates.

Once the kids were fed and happy, they scurried off for another round of fun and games, which didn't last very long. By ten-thirty Nicole was sleeping in his bed, as she had since moving in with him, and Joy's boys conked out on the full-sized bed in the spare room while playing the video game system Tristan had installed as bait. Even Cookie and Rex were asleep on the big round cushion in the corner of the living room floor.

With the house quiet and the wine gone, Tristan grabbed two beer bottles from the refrigerator and nudged Joy toward the back porch where the moon illuminated puffs of silver clouds in the black-blue sky and neighboring lilac's fragranced the moist air.

"You try'na get me drunk so I can't drive home, Mr. Ca-sin-ooo-va?" she slurred, accepting the open beer.

"Tryin'?" Tristan chuckled as he assisted her unstable body into the low Adirondack chair. Who was he to poke fun of anyone when he wasn't so steady either, making a hard landing into the deep seat beside her. "Oh, sunshine, it's too late for that. You're already drunk. There ain't no way I'm letting you drive home."

"I'll just sleep it off out here for a while. Think how nice it'll be when I'm living next door." Joy reached out her hand and Tristan took the hint, intertwining his fingers with hers.

"It'd be nicer if you'd change your mind and stay with me now." Damn alcohol loosened his lips a little too much.

"Please, Tristan…" Her fingers slipped from his to the beer bottle standing between her thighs. She took a long gulp then started peeling off the paper label with her fingernail. "My boys are finally getting used to being with me. I can't handle any extra pressure from you right now."

"I know…I know. I'm just happier when you're near me. I miss you like crazy when you're gone."

"I miss you too. But we're adults. We're supposed make sacrifices for our kids because it's the right thing to do."

Tristan ran a hand through his hair, frustrated and numb enough to pull it from the root. "You just don't get it."

"I do get it. You're the one not getting it through your head."

Despite the armrest digging into his side, he leaned toward her to make sure she heard him right. "Marry me, Joy. I'm serious."

"We just had this conversation. I thought we were done. When I said I can't say yes, I meant it. Not yet. Maybe one day. Just not today."

Partially out of spite to get a rise out of her, to see her reaction, but mostly because the booze had him feeling invincible, he opened his fat trap and let stupidity spew out before he could put a cork in it.

"Don't expect me to beg, Joy."

She snapped her head in his direction and blinked hard like owl-eyes bringing him into focus. "I don't."

Rather than blurt out an immediate apology for saying something he didn't mean, he let his injuring words keep rolling. "Good. 'Cause I won't," he spat, sounding childish inside his hollow head.

"Fine," Joy retorted in a tone equally as immature. "Then quit asking."

"I will."

"Terrific." She shot to her unsteady feet. "If we're done here, maybe you can take us home now."

"You'll have to wait until I sober up." He pushed himself upright, swaying, anxious to hit the mattress before he hit the wood under his feet. "Let's go inside and lay down for a while." He put out a hand but Joy ignored him.

"No, thanks." She flopped back into the chair.

"You're really gonna stay out here all night?"

A defiant flame glimmered in her tired eyes. "Yep."

"You're gonna get eaten alive by the mosquitoes."

"Perfect." She gripped the armrests, securing her position as if Tristan might haul her over his shoulder like a bag of sugar.

"Look. I didn't mean what I said about—"

"Begging me to marry you?" Joy unleashed a cynical tone and scornful smile he'd only seen when dealing with her ex-husband.

"I just wanted to see your reaction."

She cut her eyes from him to the opalescent moon. "Is that supposed to make me feel better?"

"Can we just have a do-over? This has been the

best Father's Day. I don't want it to end like this."

Joy snorted, then mumbled under her breath, "Too late."

Since nothing he said was the right thing, Tristan shut up and sat back down. The pigheaded contest to see who would go inside first lasted until he couldn't keep his eyes open any longer.

Jolted by the rattle of his own snoring, Tristan awoke to a denim blue sky, chirping birds, and his T-shirt damp from the morning dew. He reached out to touch Joy beside him but the chair was empty. He rubbed his eyes to be sure. Then shot to his feet and ran into the house. She wasn't in the kitchen or on the living room couch. She wasn't in his bedroom. And her boys weren't in the spare room. The van was gone too.

"Joy," he growled, mad at himself for not knowing when to quit last night. He grabbed his cellphone off the entrance table next to the unopened card she'd given him. Before he dialed her number, he noticed her text message:

—I'm home. talk soon—
That's it?

Tristan started to text her back, not sure what to say to make things right, so he deleted everything and just typed: *xo* and pressed Send.

A moment later his cellphone vibrated with an incoming message: *xo.*

He sighed in relief; at least her response was a good sign.

He swapped the phone for the envelope and ran his finger beneath the sealed flap. It was a Father's Day card like he suspected. Nothing sappy or snarky, just a simple wish for a good man to have a good day per the preprinted sentiment. And in Joy's neat script, she added a curious poem: *Happy Father's Day to a great guy. (Don't forget—Christmas in July.)*

She couldn't let go of that harebrained idea of hers, could she?

Inspired by her creative gentle reminder, Tristan smacked the card against his forehead on his way to bed with his wheels turning as he figured out how to make this a Christmas in July none of them would ever forget.

****

Joy hated dragging the boys home half asleep at three o'clock in the morning. But once she sobered up she wanted to go home—not that Lorraine's place was home, but it was far enough from Tristan.

She loved that man without a shadow of a doubt. Why couldn't he stop pressuring her?

Just a little patience was all she needed right now. Not a proposal. The boys were just getting accustomed to being here. She didn't have the mindset for marriage, wedding plans, living arrangements, and everything to go along with blending two families when she barely got one family straightened out.

Lying on the couch, drifting in and out of sleep, she heard one of the boys crying in the bedroom so she jumped to her feet.

"Daddy." It was Owen.

Joy staggered in the dark toward his side of the bed. "Baby. Mommy's here. Shhh…"

"Mommy?" he whined with a pang of uncertainty in his tiny voice.

"It's me." She turned on the bedside lamp.

"Mommy. Why did you go away?"

Shocked by the question, she wasn't sure if the boy was talking in his sleep or if she was still drunk and dreaming. "What do you mean?"

"You left us. You moved away. Daddy said you didn't love us anymore, and that's why you didn't take us with you."

"That's not true, O. That's not true at all. You and Mason said you didn't want to live with me. You'd rather live with Daddy and Felicity."

"Well…" He sat up with the blanket rumpled at his waist. "That's because Daddy loves us more," he said matter-of-factly.

"Is that what he told you?"

Owen nodded. "He said you didn't want to be with us. That's why you left without us."

It made no sense rehashing her painful side of the story about living with Victor's mini-mes, reminding the boy if he'd forgotten. She wanted to put the past behind them all and build new memories to cherish. "I love you more than anything and anyone in the whole entire universe. I only moved to Scenic View without bringing you boys so I could have a house all ready for when you got here, but it's taking longer than I expected. Daddy and I thought it would be best if you finished the school year with your friends. As soon as school ended you came here, right?"

"And I didn't have to miss Field Day."

"See. It worked out perfectly. You just didn't know the whole plan, that's all. Now that you're here with me, we can start a brand new life."

"What about Daddy?"

"Hmmm?" Joy hadn't told the boys about the day their father attacked her in the Christmas Shoppe, and she had no intention of mentioning it, ever. All she said was Daddy went home to Felicity because the baby was coming; let Victor be the one to sort out the specifics of that terrorizing tale. "Daddy and Felicity have their new life. And we have our new life."

"When you say we, ya mean, you, and me, and Owen, *and* Nicole and Tristan?"

The brilliant boy's perception of the two families' dynamic relationship stunned Joy. "Do you like Nicole and Tristan?" she asked, hopeful.

"Do *you* like Nicole and Tristan?" he repeated, matching the upturned inflection of her tone.

"Yes, I do. Very much." She tried not to sound mushy-gushy.

"I like them too. Tristan's fun. And for a girl, Nicole's hardly a pain." Owen's soft brown eyes gazed at Joy as he asked with all seriousness, "Did you marry him yet?"

Surprised by the pointed question, Joy shook her head. "No, baby. I'm not married to anyone."

"I told Mason you weren't, but he says you and Tristan are."

"What made him say that?" Joy could only imagine how their young minds interpreted the grownup friendship.

"Well...He thinks you *act* like you're married. Like the way you're always doing stuff together with us. We're always going out to eat together. We went to the carnival together. And spent Father's Day together. He says Daddy and Felicity never do that stuff with us because they're not married yet."

"Are you sure you only graduated from kindergarten and not college? Because that's quite an interesting observation." Joy's full heart could've burst on the spot seeing the world though a child's insightful eye. "Trust me, if I get married you'll be the very first person I tell."

"Will I be invited to the wedding?"

She chuckled. "Absolutely."

Owen smiled. "The other reason Mason thought you were married was 'cause Tristan has a room for us with an Xbox and everything."

"A room for you? Really?" Joy envisioned Tristan planting the seed of a good idea in the boys' heads.

"Yep. That's what he said. We can stay over anytime, all the time, if we wanted to."

"Yeah, well… Tristan's a good host like that. Always makes a guest feel welcome. Like family."

"Ya know, if you marry him I'll be okay with that. And between you and me, if Daddy doesn't marry Felicity, I wouldn't mind a bit."

Joy concealed a smirk and didn't bother to probe the Victor and Felicity scenario. "Don't you want to get used to living with me before you get used to living with a new…dad?" This whole conversation felt somewhat wrong yet at the same time completely right. The best part was Joy didn't have to all the talking.

Owen shrugged. "I know lots of kids with new moms and dads. It's not really a big deal. Like getting a new car. Or a new dog. It's a lotta fun at first but then it's like regular stuff. No big deal. I'm not a baby anymore, ya know. I can handle a new dad and a little sister."

Joy didn't know whether to cry or laugh so she just squeezed her son so tight he yelped.

"I can't breathe, Ma."

"Sorry."

"Why ya crushing me so hard for?"

She loosened her grip, and rubbed the tip of her nose to her son's in an Eskimo kiss. "Because I love you too much, that's why. And I missed you too much. I'm trying to catch up on all the hugs."

"I love you too. But I don't wanna squash ya 'til your guts come out."

"You better go to sleep now. Tomorrow's a busy day. We're gonna tour your new school and meet your first grade teacher. Then we're meeting Lily for ice cream at Yummy-Cone's Palace. We have to pick up your baseball gear, so you're ready for your first practice next week. And I thought, if there's time, we could take a trip to the comic book store."

"I can't wait for morning." Owen squealed in delight, then slid to the edge of the bed, leaving a big gap in the middle, patting the place between him and his big brother. "Why don't you sleep here. There's plenty of room."

A hard lump filled Joy's throat. "You sure? I don't want to take up too much space."

Owen gave his mother a stern look. "Don't be silly, Mommy. Just lie down and go to sleep."

It was a sweet offer and one she couldn't refuse. "Okay."

She flicked off the light, then crawled between their little bodies, slipped under the covers, and fell asleep between her two little boys, happier than she'd ever been.

Chapter Nineteen

Joy sat on the highest row of the bleachers with Lily, wearing matching wide brimmed sunhats, and Niblet in between, dressed in a pale pink leotard and tutu. Three lovely ladies waved with wild arms like they were sending out an S.O.S. to Tristan across the field in the dugout. As the assistant coach of the Little League, his job was to praise and evenly distribute a generous amount of high-fives while Chief Maresca, the head coach, did the hard work.

After announcing the lineup of players on the Fire Balls' roster, including two additional members— Mason and Owen—Tristan checked the first batter's helmet ensuring it was on correctly before sending him to the plate. Even though Joy's boys seemed to adapt quickly to their new life, making friends in a team environment during the summer vacation would help ease the transition into an unfamiliar school in September.

For two hours of fun in the sun on the last day of June, the Fire Balls played a good game against the Crushers. The youth level was a No-Score division but Tristan still tallied the runs and errors in his head, impressed by the skillsets of all these young players, especially his two little buddies. If it weren't for Mason and Owen, he wouldn't be coaching. He'd probably be a dancing school dad, which wouldn't be bad, but Joy seemed more excited than Nicole when they signed up the toddler for her first ballet class.

When the game ended, the ice cream truck pulled up on cue, blasting the happy jingle that made the kids come running in a beeline.

"I hope you brought your wallet," Chief Maresca said to Tristan.

His wallet was in the Green Machine about a quarter mile away in the lot somewhere so it was a good thing Nick whipped out a wad of cash from his front pocket. "I've got it covered." Since he'd come into money, Nick was the Pied Piper at the park and the neighborhood referred to him as "The Fireman Who Bought Everyone Ice Cream."

"Get a load of this guy." The chief nodded toward Nick. "Are you running for mayor or something? 'Cause if you are, these kids can't vote."

"Can't vote *yet*," Tristan added.

Nick cut a dirty look at the chief and Tristan as he handed each child a napkin to go with their treat, exchanging thank-yous and you're-welcomes. "Just tell the ice cream man what flavor you want and don't start any rumors."

Once the children and parents finished their ice creams, the crowd thinned fast as the full moon competed with the setting sun for space in the clear blue sky.

Three remaining tykes—Nicole, Owen, and Mason—burnt off the last of their energy on the jungle gym under Joy and Lily's watchful eyes, while Tristan and Nick loaded the equipment into the Green Machine.

"That's everything." Tristan slammed the doors of the van before heading back to claim his *framily*—his new favorite word Mason cleverly dubbed their little circle of inseparable family and friends.

The only way this perfect Monday evening at the baseball park could get better was if his cell phone rang with the important call he'd been expecting all day about Joy's furniture. It was supposed to be delivered between nine a.m. and five p.m., which was quite a big window of time considering it was already seven thirty and there was still no call from Sophia, who agreed to wait for it at his place. Once the house was furnished, he would unveil the great surprise he'd been suffering to keep.

Since the night Joy skipped out on Father's Day neither of them mentioned a word about his untimely marriage proposal, or their spat—as if it never happened. Maybe they both overreacted but Tristan still took ownership of the error. He never should have pressed her, especially when he didn't have the diamond ring to back up his offer.

But now that he had it, and spoke to her parents, and took the trip to Star Harbor to turn in his shield, service pistol, and sign all the necessary retirement paperwork, there was no reason for Joy to refuse unless she really didn't want to get married. He wasn't even setting the wedding date unless she wanted to, only making a promise for a future together.

For the past two weeks, they tweaked their new *framily*-time routine, splitting the days between Tristan's house and Joy's temporary set-up at Lorraine's. When they went to work during the day, Joy's mother watched the boys and Lily watched Nicole, but more often than not Sophia and Lily teamed up so the kids were always together. It was a crazy schedule to juggle and well worth it. Almost too good to be true but Tristan wasn't about to question it.

Lily sucked down the last of her milk shake and chucked the paper cup in the trashcan. "That was *goood*." She covered a tiny girlie burp with the tips of her fingers. "Excuse me. At this rate I'll double my weight by the time I give birth."

"Oh, pleeease." Joy waved the words away. "I doubt it with all that power walking you do each day. You've barely gained a pound."

"I like my woman with curves." Nick wrapped his arms around his wife from behind, cradling her still-flat belly in his hands.

"One day your tummy's really gonna pop. But after you have the baby we'll get you back in shape." Joy flexed her biceps.

"I hope so." Lily frowned. "How'd you do it?"

"Oh, a little bit of this, a little bit of that, and a helluva lotta stress and semi-starvation. And when that didn't work I went the good old-fashioned route of eating whole foods and cranking up the exercise. Cut back on carbs and doubled up on veggies instead. Mind over matter." Joy tapped her finger to her temple. "It wasn't easy, but it's worth it."

"I don't think I can be a vegetarian." Lily shook her head. "I like meat too much."

"You don't have to be a vegan," Joy said, "or vegetarian, or a pescetarian. Just eat smart. Good fats. Lean meats. Food is fuel."

"Maybe you should write a book," Lily suggested.

"Hmmm… Maybe I could." Joy rambled on about her years of experience in all the facets of life Lily was just catching up to.

With the kids in tow, Tristan followed behind listening to the two women chat it up, glad his best friend's wife and Joy were already so close. It made spending time with Nick that much better. The only way to complete this picture was if Joy said yes.

"So…?" Nick dropped back in line with Tristan. "Ya gonna do it or what?" The men slowed their pace, while the kids sped up to walk with the women.

"Do what?" Tristan played dumb.

"Come on, guy." Nick smirked. "I know what you're thinking."

"Then you'd know I was waiting for a special occasion."

"Her birthday?"

"You're kidding, right?" Tristan knitted his brows. "There ain't no way I can wait 'til August to propose again."

"Whoa." Nick's head snapped. "How soon are we talkin'?"

"I'm gonna see how she reacts to the house. If it goes well I'll pop the question the right way this time, down on one knee with a ring."

"Where ya planning to live after the wedding? Your place or hers?"

"Hers most likely since she's emotionally attached to it. But for all I know she could hate the renovations."

Nick slugged Tristan in the biceps. "I doubt it, man." He smacked the muscle again for added measure and chuckled. "Hey—have you been working out?"

"Get off me, will ya?" Tristan yanked his arm from Nick's big-handed gorilla grip. "Yeah, I've been hitting the home gym thanks to Joy."

"I'm glad you two calamities straightened up your

act. She got you back in shape and you fixed up the shape of her old house—sounds like a perfect match if you ask me."

Tristan sighed. "She hasn't seen the inside, so I'm praying she likes it."

"You put your whole heart and soul into that place. I can't imagine her not loving it."

Tristan couldn't contain his secret smile. "I can't imagine it either but ya never know. And just 'cause she loves the house doesn't mean she'll be willing to marry me."

"And you're gonna ask again anyway, you sappy sonofabitch. You're a glutton for punishment, aren't ya? If she still doesn't say yes, what then?"

The painful probability made Tristan snicker. "In a couple of months, after I recuperate, I'll give her another try. It's not like I'm skipping town now that we're business partners."

"That's right. You signed a contract. Death do us part." Nick balled his hand into a fist and pumped it in the air like this was a rock concert rather than a heart-to-heart talk. "If Joy says no to you this time around, she must be crazy. Then again, if she says yes after knowing you for a season she must be even crazier."

"What are you talking about?" Tristan shoved Nick's shoulder. "Lily married you after just a few months of dating. She's the crazy one if you ask me."

"I must be crazy too, going down this road again with another woman after being married to your psycho sister."

"Leave Claudine out of it—she's a whole different breed of crazy."

"Yeah, well, I guess we're all a little crazy here."

Nick slapped Tristan between the shoulder blades. "Happy and crazy."

****

Before they piled into the Green Machine, Nicole tugged Joy's hand. "I gotta make."

"Come to think of it, I have to go too." Lily detoured, following the restroom sign. "Did you find you had to pee a lot when you were pregnant?"

"Always." Joy took the risk and lifted Nicole to speed up the process. "Hold it, Niblet. Hold it." Even though the toddler was potty-trained in the house, she still wore a diaper at night and on the road, except for today's dance class because the child begged to wear panties like the bigger girls in class.

While Joy peeled off the child's leotard, Lily draped the toilet seat with strips of paper.

"Do you have to go number one? Or do you have to go number two?" Joy held up her fingers for clarification.

"If you ladies would excuse me, I have to go number one." Lily slipped out of the family-sized stall for some privacy next door.

"I think I have to go one, two, three, four, five, six, seven." Silly Niblet showed off her counting skills.

"Then I guess we're gonna be here a while." Joy folded a nice wad of toilet tissue for the final moment. "Let me know when you're done."

"Can I call you Mommy?" The girl's question came out of nowhere.

Stumped, Joy continued to wind paper endlessly around her hand. "Umm…You have a mommy, Niblet."

"I know. But she's not here."

326

"Just because she's not here doesn't mean she's not thinking of you. I think this is a question for your daddy."

"Daddy already asked me."

Lily pulled the door open and poked her nose in. "Asked you what?"

"Asked me if I'd like Joy to be a stair mommy."

"You mean a step mommy?" Lily elbowed Joy. "When did daddy say this?"

"He probably said it a couple of weeks ago. Not recently, right?" *Not after I turned him down, twice in one day.*

Nicole shrugged, hanging onto the toilet. "He says it all da time when we say our puh'wayers at bedtime. God bless mommy and daddy and da whole *framily*. And eggspecially Joy and her boys, and that maybe, someday, if daddy is a lucky sonofabeekeeper, she'll marry him so she can be my stair mommy."

"The guy's consistent if not persistent. You better say yes next time he asks or I'll never let you live it down," Lily mumbled to Joy, wagging a scolding finger at her friend,

"Gee, thanks." Although Lily's support was appreciated, if Joy didn't say yes to Tristan's next offer, there might never be another one, and then what? How could she live with herself if she let him go?

"Daddy says if Joy doesn't say yes this time, he's gonna get his head checked," Niblet blurted out as if she knew what she was talking about. "'Cause he must have loose screws for asking again. Whatever dat means."

"Little girl, you sure you're only three and not going on thirty?" Joy shook her head in disbelief of this young mind at work, wondering what secrets she may have spit out in front of the child that could have been translated to Tristan.

"I'm one, two, three, four, five, six, seven. All done!"

Chapter Twenty

"Just because the whole town spends every holiday at the fire department doesn't mean we have to." Joy climbed into the passenger seat of the Green Machine while Tristan checked the children's seatbelts were secure in the back before he slipped behind the steering wheel.

"What would you rather do today?" He put the van in reverse and backed out of Lorraine's driveway.

Joy shrugged. "If the house is ready I could be setting up. But I know, I know...you're waiting for the *final touches* to be complete. I don't want to ruin the big surprise you've planned."

"Forget the house."

"Impossible. It's all I can think about."

"Would you rather skip the barbecue and spend Fourth of July on the beach?"

"I would, but I didn't pack for a day at the beach. I packed for a day at the firehouse."

"Wanna see a movie?"

"We've seen everything PG and under."

"Wanna go bowling?"

"I just had my nails done."

"Wanna go to the park."

"We might as well go to the barbecue then."

"Are you sure?"

Joy sighed. "Sure. What the hell. Everyone'll be

there. My folks enjoy seeing the kids."

"Ya think they'll offer to babysit?" Tristan sounded hopeful.

"So we can make out in the van?" she joked.

He waggled his brows. "Sounds good to me."

With three kids in their life, date night had become more of a pipe dream. Romance was reduced to sneaking kisses in the laundry room or wherever they could steal a moment. When Tristan visited Joy at the Christmas Shoppe on his lunch breaks, she'd flip over the Closed sign, and they'd get busy in the backroom, but it wasn't as comfortable as his big bed.

Between working all day and catering to the children, they were both beat. Sleeping together was literally sleeping together like they'd been married for forty years. And in addition to their set schedule of bouncing between his place and Lorraine's house, they spent every holiday at the firehouse. Joy worried they were falling into a rut.

"We don't have to stay all day. Just a little while." Tristan affirmed with a kiss on the back of her hand.

It wasn't that Joy minded spending time at these festive community events, she just wanted a little excitement to spice up the usual routine.

After burgers, beers, and banana splits, the band rocked until dark as the crowd waited for the fireworks. This was how she spent every July Fourth of her childhood, and now, thanks to Tristan's persistence, she could share the moment with her boys.

"We'll watch the kids tonight." Sophia sat on the folding lawn chair next to Joy.

She gave her mother a curious glance. "Why?"

"Because…" The woman never said no whenever

Joy needed a sitter but rarely did she suggest it on her own. "We miss them."

Huh? Joy leaned away from the body snatcher that stole her mother. "You see them all the time, you don't have to—"

"Don't argue with your mother, Joy," her father chimed in. "We'll keep them at our place overnight if that's all right?"

Tristan massaged the back of Joy's neck with a strong hand. "You sure?" he asked her parents.

The whole situation seemed sketchy to Joy, like the three of them were in cahoots. *Where was Lily when she needed a brain to pick?*

"Yeah. You two go have some fun." Bob waved them away.

"Daddy? For real? You wanna take three kids tonight? They're hopped up on ice cream and lollipops." Joy gave her father a doubtful eye, wondering the motive behind this generous offer.

"Don't you trust us? We raised three kids or did you forget? We can handle yours." He leaned over to kiss Joy's forehead then shook Tristan's hand and exchanged whispers.

"I'll run home to pack their PJs and toothbrushes and drop it off to you."

"Don't worry about it. We have everything they need," her father insisted.

"Where are the kids so we can say goodnight?" Joy stood, looking around, spotting them with Nick and Lily dancing by the bandstand.

"Just go or you'll never get out of here." Bob nudged her in the other direction. "They'll be fine. Now scram before we change our minds."

Tristan grabbed her hand and they weaved through the mob to get to the van.

Once they were cruising down Main Street, Joy asked, "What did he say?"

"Who?" Tristan shrugged. The man played dumb like a world champion.

"Never mind." Not in the mood to start another war, she shut up. As they wound through the narrow streets toward his house, she exhaled an enormous yawn as if her fatigued body knew his big, comfy bed was near.

"Tired?" Tristan squeezed her hand.

"A little."

"Me too."

When they got home, the dogs were bouncing around the house, freaking out after someone set off a bunch of bottle rockets in the street.

Joy kicked off her flip-flops and curled on the couch with the pups while Tristan turned up the stereo to some classical music to block out the noise.

"Don't get too comfy," he said.

"Why?"

He disappeared into the bedroom and returned with handcuffs and scarves. "I have something to show you."

"I'm so pooped I won't fight it so no need to go through the trouble. I don't remember parenting being this exhausting?"

"Trust me, it's no trouble." A cunning smile crossed the luscious lips she craved to kiss if she had the energy.

"Oh, fine…Should I take off my shorts?"

"Nope. And leave the tank top on too." He pulled her to her feet, cuffed her hands behind her back, covered her eyes, and nudged her forward.

"Where are we going?"

"Shhh…" He guided her with a gentle hand between her shoulder blades. "Pretend you're sleepwalking."

She stepped one bare foot in front of the other. By the space and distance, she figured they were headed to the kitchen. "This is a strange kind of foreplay."

"Keep going, keep going. Less talking, more walking."

The back door opened with a recognizable creak, and the muggy night air wrapped around her like a moist towel. "Don't I need shoes?"

"I think you'll be all right. We aren't going that far. Don't worry."

He marched her onto the wooden deck, down the three steps to the damp lawn, then spun her a few times like playing Pin the Tail On the Donkey. "Having fun yet?" He chuckled, seeming amused with this game.

"Oh, loads. You're making me dizzy."

"Good." He led her in a circle, then a straight line, then zigzagged until they stopped.

"Are we there yet?"

"Just about."

Joy waited for the mask to come off but instead he prodded her from the soft grass, up three wooden stairs. "All that work to go back inside?"

"Yep."

"Swell. Now that I'm all sweaty, I need a shower. Thank you."

"You're welcome."

The door didn't squeak when it whooshed open. And the flooring wasn't sticky hardwood, but cool like ceramic tile. The smell was unfamiliar, like lavender and fresh paint. "Where are we?"

"Home." Tristan pulled down the fabric from her eyes.

Standing at the center of a new kitchen, she spun slow, taking in all the sights like a kid in Disney World for the first time. Something about this place was familiar. The layout was similar to Tristan's kitchen. But rather than cabinets and counters of glossy black and shades of brown, the space was ivory and burgundy—the colors of her mother's old kitchen, with high-end stainless steel modern appliances. "Is this…? It can't be, can it?"

"It can and it is." Tristan waved his hands like a magician, presenting her with a single key between his fingers. "Is the décor okay? You seemed to like my place, so I worked with that. Plus your folks showed me old photos from when you lived here. I stuck with their scheme the best I could. Waiting for the furniture to be delivered took longer than I expected. But it's all ready for you. You can move in right now if you want."

"I want, I want," Joy shrieked, nodding, shaking off the shock. "Thank you." She would've hugged him but her hands were bound behind her back so Tristan gathered her in his arms.

"You like it?"

"I do. I really do. What's not to like?"

"I'm not sure if you'll like the living room so much."

"Tsk. Don't be silly." Joy skimmed around him, but he stopped her and pulled up the scarf over her eyes again. "Seriously?"

"Do me a favor and just play along, will ya?"

"Fine," she conceded, letting him guide her by the elbow. Then he pushed down on her shoulders until she landed on something firm yet bouncy. "New couch? Very comfortable. I wish I could see it."

"New everything." He pulled the blindfold over her head and smacked it against his palm as he let out a shaky breath. "Whaddaya think? Be honest. I can change it if you don't like it."

Joy set her eyes on the most beautiful winter wonderland she'd ever seen, more breathtaking than anything Everyday's Christmas has on display. The whole room was decorated like a Thomas Kinkade painting. From the tiny white lights in the window and fake snow kissing the glass. To the multi-colored twinkle lights on the evergreen and the soft golden glow of the big tree-topping star grazing the ceiling. Most of the ornaments were recognizable from the shop, and the special ones on the upper branches were straight from her childhood.

"Your mother helped with the decorations."

"Christmas is her favorite. I can't believe you went through all this trouble for me. The idea was to do it for your daughter."

"And it was a great idea. I hope she's as surprised as you are."

Beneath the tree were presents labeled with all of their names: Joy, Nicole, Mason, Owen, Rex, Cookie. "I don't see any presents for you."

"You're my present, Joy. And I'm going to unwrap you right now. But first…" Tristan plucked an ornament from the tree in the shape of a Fabergé egg and flipped the lid.

Inside was the biggest diamond Joy ever saw in

real life.

"I know I've asked you twice already. I'm praying three times is a charm. But if you still feel like you can't say yes, I'll ask you again someday, I can't promise when. I only hope you're so overwhelmed you won't say no this time." He chuckled as a rosy flush crept up his cheeks. "All I want for Christmas, and every day, is for you to be by my side as my wife. I love you, Joy. I can't remember life before you. I don't want to imagine living without you. Please say yes."

Too stunned to speak, she couldn't stop the silent stream of tears rolling down her cheek. "Yes, yes, yes. I'm sorry I couldn't say it before. It wasn't because I didn't want to…" Her pounding heart drowned out any doubt her conscience tried clinging too. All she wanted, all she needed, was this man, here and now, forever. "I just had to be sure you were the right one. And you are. You're the only one. Always."

****

Tristan forgot his key ring at his place, so slipping the engagement ring on Joy's finger behind her back was awkward, making it impossible for her to admire the two-karat round stone set high in the platinum band. "Lemme run next door—"

"Oooh, forget about it," Joy purred. Her breasts strained gloriously in the red cotton tank top and she rubbed them against his T-shirt, sending electric pulses straight to his pants. "I need you now."

"I know what you mean." He knelt to tear open the button fly of her snug shorts and dragged the denim down to her ankles where she kicked her way out of them. Then he nibbled and gnawed the smooth skin along the inside of her thigh, working his way toward the apex where he teased her sensitive spot with his tongue, before trailing down the other leg.

Standing with her wrists locked behind her back, Joy leaned on the wall for support, spreading her legs wider. "More…" she pleaded in a husky voice Tristan loved to hear because it meant he was doing something right.

To avoid crushing her hands, he bent her over the armrest of the couch as he thrust his hips against her bottom. "I hope you don't mind this position."

She threw a smile over her shoulder. "You know it's my favorite, silly boy."

Yes, he knew, all too well how perfectly they fit together in this pose as much as the rest. He shed his jeans and, wielding his super-sensitive sword like her knight in shining armor… Thinking of armor… "Dammit, I forgot the condoms. Lemme run home to get some protection. I'll be quick."

"No way are you leaving me hanging like this. Just go for it without one. We're getting married, we can handle the outcome."

Goosebumps rose on his arms at the thought of making a baby on their first real try. As content as he was with the three they had, having one between them was a cool concept in the heat of the moment. With no pressure to perform or reproduce, he eased inside. It always felt great before but this…God, this was what makes life worth living. Pure heaven between her thighs.

It didn't take long before they were rocking in sync. Tristan quickening the pace, driving harder and faster toward the sensational climax, then, when he couldn't hang on another nanosecond, he melted into a puddle of lust, his body limp against hers.

"Wow," Joy mumbled, muffled by the couch cushion.

He helped her stand upright and led her toward the master bedroom where she flopped onto her side to recuperate.

Then he hiked up his jeans and ran to his place to grab the handcuff key. While he was there he slipped the pups a dose of the mild sedative prescribed by the veterinarian specifically for tonight's expected racket before jogging back to Joy's.

Once he removed the cuffs she spent a long moment admiring the sparkling rock on her finger then threw her arms around his neck. "I must've been out of my mind turning you down twice. Thank you for not giving up on me."

"I'll never give up on you, sunshine." He couldn't stop the smile stretching his face at the sight of her gazing at the ring like she expected it to do something magical other than gleam.

When the first big boom vibrated the walls at ten on the dot, they stepped out on the front porch to view the show. Streaks of red, white, and blue light sizzled and popped high in the night sky but they were nothing compared to the fireworks behind his eyelids when Joy slid onto his lap, nuzzling her face against his neck and suckled his ear lobe, whispering, "I love you, Tristan Casanova."

The next morning while Joy dried her hair in her brand new bathroom, Tristan sat back on the couch with a cup of coffee and the pups, able to relax for the first time in weeks since meeting the woman who turned his world right-side up.

Bruno showed up at ten a.m. as instructed with a bag of fresh baked bagels and all the fixings, before Sophia and Bob brought the kids over to see their new home.

"What is all this, Mom?" Mason asked cautiously, scanning the new surroundings, but mostly honing in on the brightly lit tree.

"What do ya think?" Owen elbowed his brother. "It's Christmas. And look." He pointed to the wrapped packages. "Santa was here."

"I thought you didn't believe in Santa." Joy's suspicious eyes bounced between her boys' faces.

"Just 'cause Daddy said there was no Santa Claus doesn't make it true," Mason said, sounding smarter than a soon-to-be second grader.

"Don't believe everything you hear, Mommy," Owen chimed in.

As the boys knelt beside the tree divvying out presents, Lily showed up alone with an unexpected housewarming gift.

"A kitten?" Joy pulled the white fur-ball out of the cardboard box. "You shouldn't have. Really, Lily."

"Don't blame me. The boys asked for it." Lily pushed past Joy to get a front row view of the decorations. "Nice tree, guys."

"No one's excited to see the rest of the house?" Joy frowned.

"Whaddaya talking about? Excited? It used to be *my* house. I know what it looks like." Bob grabbed a bagel and coffee and sat at the end of the dining room table behind his newspaper, away from the madness but within view of the action.

"Lily and I saw it already," Sophia admitted.

Debra Druzy

"Yeah," Lily added. "We've been as busy as Santa's little helpers doing the dirty work in the background."

A few minutes later there was another knock on cue.

"Speaking of Santa…" Lily announced.

The door swung open and a fat man dressed in a plush red suit burst into the room. "Ho, ho, ho."

Nick made a believable Santa Claus however the true test would be fooling Nicole and the boys. Three little faces with big O's for mouths and wide eyes stared speechless.

"Sonofabitch pulled it off," Tristan whispered in Lily's ear. "Way to go, Nick."

Lily smirked knowingly. "Told ya so. Never doubt the power of The Suit."

"I hope you don't mind," Santa bellowed, "I thought Christmas in July would be a nice change of pace. But Santa's sweating his *cojones* off. Could someone crank up the AC in this place?"

Tristan laughed on his way to the thermostat and dropped the temperature to sixty-five degrees.

"Are you kids surprised to see Santa?" Nick skewed his deep voice, bellowing in third-person.

Three heads nodded in sync.

"I bet no one's more surprised than Santa, making this long trip for this special family on the hottest day of summer. Can Santa get something cold to drink before he passes out?" Nick swiped the sweat beading above his fake white eyebrows.

Flustered by the rush of excitement, Sophia wobbled to the kitchen to fetch a beverage for the unexpected guest from the North Pole and returned with a glass of ice water. "He looks so real," she mumbled to the grownups.

While controlled chaos shook the house, Tristan kept an eye on Mr. Barbieri watching his kin regroup under the family's old roof for the first time in over a decade. The older man nodded proudly at his future son-in-law and winked in approval, then went back to checking his lottery tickets against the numbers in the newspaper.

"Geez..." Bob choked on a prayer then shouted, "My numbers. Finally they hit. Sophia, Sophia—" He jumped off the chair and grabbed his wife's face, kissing her hard on the cheek. "I can finally retire. Key West, here we come."

"Seriously, Dad?" Joy cut her eyes at him, shoving her engagement ring between her parents to show off the glittery stone. "You had to steal my thunder? And you can't move out of Scenic View. I'm just getting settled."

"Ummm, don't get too excited over here." Lily squeezed her face between Sophia and Bob's, getting in on the expanding hug. "This pregnant woman doesn't wanna be giving CPR this morning, thank you very much."

"Pack your bags. I'm taking the whole family to Disney World," Bob announced, adding to the frenzy.

Every time Joy caught Tristan staring at her, she giggled. He couldn't help himself; she was something special, and best of all, she was all his. Better than hitting the lottery.

"Did you kids take a look outside yet?" Santa led the screaming stampede through the kitchen and out the door where Tristan had installed a jungle gym, complete with a double-decker fort, rock climbing wall, three slides, and six swings, bigger than the one in his own backyard.

"I'll race ya," Owen shouted, leading the way as Mason and Nicole followed. Lily, Bruno, Sophia, and Bob trailed them, heading for the picnic table beneath the shady tree beside the playset.

Joy slipped her arms around Tristan's waist. "Nice job, *Santa*," she said.

Tristan glanced over his shoulder to see if anyone else might be in the room. "Who me?"

"Yes, you."

"You got the wrong one. Santa's the fat guy in the red suit with the white beard." He pointed to Nick under the blazing sun. "I owe him one. I actually owe him a lot more." If it weren't for Nick, Joy wouldn't have gotten this house.

"Well, as far as I'm concerned, you're *my* Santa." She stretched on tiptoes to kiss his lips.

Squinting an eye like aiming at a target, he hoped his good intentions didn't miss the mark. "Really?"

"Really." Joy laced her fingers between his. "Who would've imagined in a gazillion years I'd fall for the first Casanova to cross my path?"

As they watched their framily enjoy the fruits of his labor, Tristan was never more content making everyone he loved happy.

Epilogue

July—One year later

It was hard to believe twelve months flew by so fast. Last year she was just Joy, wishing she had no last name, and today she was the new Mrs. Casanova after a quick civil ceremony in the Scenic View town hall.

Together with their blended family, she and Tristan were the proud parents to two boys, a girl, two pups, and a cat. It was crazy to think of fitting them all under her roof, but if the Cape Cod had fit her parents with three kids, the Casanovas would manage just fine.

As soon as Sophia and Bob took the children for ice cream after the groom kissed the bride, Tristan handed Joy a large manila envelope in the hallway.

It was too quick to be the official marriage certificate. She brushed aside the strands of hair that escaped her chignon. "You've given me so much already; I can't imagine what it could be." She hugged the big envelope against her white gypsy sundress.

"It's not from me. It's from Nick and Lily."

"What is it? A big card?"

"You'll see." Tristan jutted his chin. "Just open it."

She slid her finger under the flap then pulled out the document. "I don't understand."

"What does it say?" Tristan said with a devilish gleam in his eyes.

Flipping through the pages, she deciphered the verbiage. "It's a deed."

As if waiting for her to make the connection, he rocked on his heels with his hands in the pants pockets of his dark blue suit. "And?"

"It's got our names on it."

"And? Have you figured it out yet?"

"And…Nick and Lily gave us the house?" It was a generous gesture and almost hard to believe, but it said so in black and white.

"Nick'll be working me hard to keep up my end of the business. But yeah, the house is ours."

"I don't know what to say." Tears filled her eyes.

"I already thanked them when I signed the papers, but you can thank them again tonight at dinner."

"This is kinda perfect because…" Joy pressed her hand to her belly. "We're going to need some extra room soon, and I didn't want to have to move. Now we can just build on what we have."

"What kind of extra room are you talking about? Like a guest room?"

"Not exactly." Joy's face got hot. "More like a permanent resident. Would you mind building a nursery?"

"We're having a baby!" he whooped in the hallway, drawing attention from everyone in the office building. "And you kept it a secret?" he whispered. "I didn't know you could be so sneaky."

"I found out last week and thought it would make a nice surprise wedding gift. Do you know how hard it was not to tell you?"

"Yeah, I can imagine." Tristan chuckled as he swept her off her feet and carried her away.

A word about the author...

Debra Druzy writes Contemporary Romance. She is the author of *SLEEPING WITH SANTA* and *DARE ME* (A Candy Hearts Romance).

If you've enjoyed her stories, please leave a review wherever you found the book. Visit her online at http://www.debradruzy.com.

Thank you for purchasing
this publication of The Wild Rose Press, Inc.

If you enjoyed the story, we would appreciate your
letting others know by leaving a review.

For other wonderful stories,
please visit our on-line bookstore at
www.thewildrosepress.com.

For questions or more information
contact us at
info@thewildrosepress.com.

The Wild Rose Press, Inc.
www.thewildrosepress.com

Stay current with The Wild Rose Press, Inc.

Like us on Facebook

https://www.facebook.com/TheWildRosePress

And Follow us on Twitter
https://twitter.com/WildRosePress